THE YANKEE WIDOW

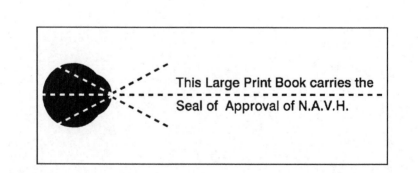

This Large Print Book carries the
Seal of Approval of N.A.V.H.

THE YANKEE WIDOW

LINDA LAEL MILLER

WHEELER PUBLISHING
A part of Gale, a Cengage Company

Farmington Hills, Mich • San Francisco • New York • Waterville, Maine
Meriden, Conn • Mason, Ohio • Chicago

Copyright © 2019 by Hometown Girl Makes Good, Inc.
Wheeler Publishing, a part of Gale, a Cengage Company.

LIBRARY OF CONGRESS CIP DATA ON FILE.
CATALOGUING IN PUBLICATION FOR THIS BOOK
IS AVAILABLE FROM THE LIBRARY OF CONGRESS

ISBN-13: 978-1-4328-5125-5 (hardcover alk. paper)

Published in 2019 by arrangement with Harlequin Books S.A.

Printed in Mexico
1 2 3 4 5 6 7 23 22 21 20 19

In loving memory of
Mary Ann Bleecker Readman,
my cousin, my conscience
and my cherished friend.
I miss you every moment of every day.

Godspeed, Bleeck. I'll see you
down the trail a ways.

1

JACOB

The first minié ball ripped into Corporal Jacob Hammond's left hand, the second, his right knee, each strike leaving a ragged gash in its wake; another slashed through his right thigh an instant later, and then he lost count.

A coppery crimson mist rained down on Jacob as he bent double, then plunged, with what felt like a strange, protracted grace, toward the broken ground. On the way down, he noted the bent and broken grass, shimmering with fresh blood, the deep gouges left by cannon balls and boot heels and the lunging hooves of panicked horses.

A peculiar clarity overtook Jacob in those moments between life as he'd always known it and another way of being, already inevitable. The boundaries of his mind seemed to expand beyond skull and skin, rushing outward at a dizzying speed, hurtling in all directions, rising past the treetops, past the sky, past the far borders of the cosmos itself.

For an instant, he understood everything, every mystery, every false thing, every truth.

He felt no emotion, no joy or sorrow.

There was peace, though, and the sweet promise of oblivion.

Then, with a wrench so swift and so violent that it sickened his very soul, Jacob was back inside himself, a prisoner behind fractured bars of bone. The flash of extraordinary knowledge was gone, a fact that saddened Jacob more deeply than the likelihood of death, but some small portion of the experience remained, an ability to think without obstruction, to see his past as vividly as his present, to envision all that was around him, as if from a great height.

Blessedly, there was no pain, though he knew that would surely come, provided he remained alive long enough to receive it.

Something resembling bitter amusement overtook Jacob then; he realized that, unaccountably, he hadn't expected to be struck down on this savage battlefield or any other. Never mind the unspeakable carnage he'd witnessed since his enlistment in Mr. Lincoln's grand army; with the hubris of youth, he had believed himself invincible.

He had assumed that the men in blue fought on the side of righteousness, committed to the task of mending a sundered nation, restoring it to its former whole. For all its faults, the United States of America was the most promising nation ever to arise from the old order of kings and despots; even now, Jacob was convinced that, whatever the cost, it must not be allowed to fail.

He had been willing to pay that price, was willing still.

Why then was he shocked, nay *affronted*, to find that the bill had come due, in full, and that his own blood and breath, his very substance, was the currency required?

Because, he thought, shame washing over him, he had been willing to die only in *theory*. Out of vanity or ignorance or pure naivety, he had somehow, without being aware of it, declared himself exempt.

Well, there it was. Jacob Hammond, husband of Caroline, father of Rachel, son and grandson and great-grandson of sturdy, high-minded folk, present owner of a modest but fertile farm a few miles south of the small but industrious township of Gettysburg, Pennsylvania, was no more vital to the noble pursuit of lasting justice for all than any other man was. In any larger scheme, neither his life nor his death would truly matter.

He knew his wounds were grievous, that a quick death was the most merciful fate he could hope for, and still he wanted so much to live, to return to his beloved wife, to his child, to the modest but thriving farm that shone in his memory, fairer than heaven itself.

The sacrifice was terrible, unspeakably so.

Was it worthwhile?

Jacob pondered that question, decided that, for him, it was.

The country had splintered, bone and blood, perhaps never to be mended. It was far from the ideal set forth by those bold intellects who had gathered in Philadelphia back in '76, in a blaze of fractious brilliance.

Somehow, in the sweltering heat of a Pennsylvania summer, and yet no doubt cooler than their collective temperaments — out of dissent, out of greed and ill humor and stubbornness and all manner of other mortal failings — these remarkable men had forged a philosophy, a glorious vision of what a nation, a people, could become.

To Jacob, bleeding into the ground, in the midst of an endless war, that goal seemed more distant than ever, hopeless, even impossible.

And still, had he been able, he would have fought on, died not just once but a thousand times, not for the country as it was, but for the noble, sacred objective upon which it had been founded — liberty and justice for all.

Whatever the cost, the Union must hold together.

So much hung in the balance, so very much. Not only the hope and valor of those who had gone before, but the freedom, perhaps the very existence, of those yet to be born.

In solidarity, the *United* States could be a force for good in a hungry, desperate world. Torn asunder, it would be ineffectual, two bickering factions, bound to divide into still smaller and weaker fragments over time, too busy posturing and rattling sabers to meet the demands of a fragile future or to stand in the way of new tyrannies, certain to arise.

We hold these truths to be self-evident, that all men are created equal . . .

That belief, inspiring as it was, had chafed the consciences of thinking people since it flowed from the nib of Thomas Jefferson's pen, as well it should have.

Like many of his contemporaries, the great man himself had kept slaves.

The inherent contradiction could not have escaped a mind as luminous as Jefferson's, nor could the subtle difference in phrasing as he wrote those momentous words. He had not written that *some* men were created equal, but that *all* men were.

Strenuous opposition to the indefensible institution of slavery had been raised, of course, but in the end, expediency prevailed. Representatives of the Southern colonies, with their vast fields of cotton and other valuable crops, would face certain ruin without their millions of unpaid laborers. They had refused to join in the rebellion against Great Britain if slavery was outlawed.

Since the effort would surely fail without them, the concession had been made.

But what was the value of freedom if it remained the province of white men while excluding all others?

Alas, the question was too big for a man in the process of dying, alone and far from home.

There was nothing to be done, save letting go. In the deepest recesses of his heart, in that calm place beyond fear and pain and fury, Jacob prayed that the will of God be done, in this matter of countries and wars.

Then, with that petition made, he raised

another, more selfish one. *Watch over my beloved wife, our little daughter, and Enoch, our trusted friend. Keep them all safe and well.*

The request was simple, one of millions like it, no doubt, rising to the ears of the Creator on wings of desperation and sorrow, and there was no Road-to-Damascus moment for Jacob, just the ground-shaking roar of battle all around. But even in the midst of thundering cannon, the sharp reports of carbines and the fiery blast of muskets, the clanking of swords and the shrill shrieks of men and horses, he found a certain consolation.

A whisper of hope. Perhaps he'd been heard.

He began to drift then, back and forth between darkness and light, fear and oblivion. When he surfaced, the pain was waiting, like a specter hovering over him, ready to descend, settle upon him, crush him beneath its weight.

Consequently, Jacob again took refuge deep inside, where it could not yet reach.

Hours passed, perhaps days; he had no way of knowing.

Eventually, because life is persistent even in the face of hopelessness and unrelenting agony, the hiding place within became less accessible. During those intervals, pain played with him, like a cat with a mouse. Smoke burned his eyes, which he couldn't close; it climbed, stinging, into his nostrils, chafed his throat raw. He was thirsty, so thirsty. He felt as dry as last year's corn husks, imagining his life's blood seeping, however slowly, into the ravaged earth.

In order to bear his suffering, Jacob thought about home, conjured up vivid images of Caroline, quietly pretty, more prone to laughter than to tears, courageous as any man he'd ever known. She loved him, he knew that, and his heart rested safely with her. She had always accepted his attentions in the marriage bed with good-humored acquiescence, though perhaps not with a passion to equal his own, and while he told himself this was the way of a good woman, he sometimes wondered if, to Caroline, lovemaking was simply another wifely chore. Yet another duty to perform, after a day of washing and ironing, cooking and sewing, tending the vegetable garden behind the kitchen house and picking apples and pears, apricots and peaches in the orchards when the fruit ripened.

Jacob was not the sort of husband who took his wife's efforts for granted. Whenever possible, he had lent her a willing hand, little concerned with what constituted "women's work"; he hadn't been above changing a diaper, gathering eggs or hanging out the wash.

No, work was work, whether it fell to a man or a woman to do it. As a farmer, though, he'd had fields to plow and harvest, livestock to tend, tools and wagons to maintain, and even with Enoch's help, getting all that done took every scrap of daylight and, often, part of the night.

Oh, but Caroline. Caroline.

She was a pure wonder to Jacob. Her price, if one could've been set, was indeed far above rubies; she might have been the model for the woman described in the thirty-first chapter of Proverbs. She was certainly virtuous, and she looked "well to the ways of her household, and ate not of the bread of idleness." Moreover, she stretched "out her hand to the poor" and reached "out forth her hands to the needy."

Caroline not only met the many demands of marriage and motherhood, she was an active member of the local Ladies' Aid Society. These women were among her closest friends, all of them determined to serve the Union cause and to sustain and encourage the soldiers who fought for it.

She had written to him about how they gathered regularly in each other's homes, these warriors on the home front, to make quilts and shirts, mend blankets and knit stockings, bottle fruits and vegetables and other foodstuffs, write letters to lonesome souls in faraway army camps, and to plan campaigns and strategies for the future.

They ventured out into the community, too, cajoling friends, neighbors and strangers alike, willing to beg and borrow, if not steal, whatever items a soldier might find useful — headache powders and other expedient remedies from the druggists, soap and coffee beans and homemade balm for chapped lips and blistered heels from anyone who had them to give.

Gettysburg was a thriving market town, with many prosperous residents and, in the early days of the war, the donations were generous. Merchants gave goods by the crateful, flour and dried beans by the barrel. Farmers brought their bumper crops of potatoes, squash, carrots, onions and turnips to the ladies by the wagonload, often with great slabs of salt pork and crocks brimming with fresh eggs, preserved in waterglass.

He has seen for himself when he was back home on brief leave how all this bounty was carefully sorted and cataloged by the ladies of Gettysburg before being sent on, mostly via the railroads, to a distribution center in Baltimore, from which it would be dispersed to battlefronts and hospitals all over the North.

Of course, as the war dragged on, and the inevitable shortages arose, the flood of goodwill had dwindled considerably, but Jacob knew from Caroline's letters that scarcity only redoubled the determination of petticoat generals such as his wife. In her words, they simply "pushed up their sleeves and worked a little harder."

Caroline was no stranger to hardship, and neither were most of her friends.

She was accustomed to enduring trouble, disappointment and heartache, having had more than her fair portion of all those things, and she bore up with remarkable stoicism, the current state of the nation notwithstanding.

The work of farming was fraught with perils; crops could be destroyed by hail or drought or a freak frost, wildfires and plagues of grasshoppers, or made worthless by a drop in prices.

He and Caroline had grappled with several disasters and come through, although not without struggle.

Still, life had been harder on Caroline than

it was on many folks, right from the first.

She'd been only four or five years old when a fever struck, sudden and vicious, carrying off her mother, father and younger sister in the space of a single day. Caroline, too, had fallen ill, but somehow she'd pulled through.

Her paternal grandparents, Doc Prescott and his wife, Geneva, had taken her in and looked after her with all tenderness, but she'd been sickly for some time, and grieved sorely for her mama and papa and beloved little sister.

More losses followed; her grandfather had died recently, and she'd mourned at the gravesides of two of her dearest friends in as many months, both of whom had died in childbirth, along with their infants.

And then, before their precious Rachel, there had been the lost babies, his and Caroline's, the first midway through her pregnancy, a wizened little creature, bloody and blue, carried away in a basin to be buried, the second, a boy, carried to term but stillborn.

It had been Enoch, God bless him, who had seen to those impossibly small bodies, laid both little ones to rest in the small family cemetery, said words over them, and wept as if they'd been of his own flesh.

Later, he'd carved markers for them, sturdy wooden crosses, less than a foot high, with no names or dates.

Now, with his own death so close, Jacob wished Caroline hadn't tried to be so strong or worked so hard to hide her grief from him, from everyone, holding it close and guarding it like the darkest of secrets. If only he'd sought her out and taken her into his arms and held her fast, held her until they could both let go and weep out their sorrows together.

Alas, Jacob's own grief had been a sharp and frozen thing, locked inside him.

There was no going back now, and regret would only sap what little strength that remained to him.

He took sanctuary in the remembrance of happier things, finding brief shelter from the gathering storm of fresh pain. In his mind's eye, he saw little Rachel running to meet him when he came in from the fields at the end of the day, dirty and sweat-soaked and exhausted himself, while his daughter was as fresh as the wildflowers flourishing alongside the creek in summer. Clad in one of her tiny calico dresses, face and hands scrubbed, she raced toward him, laughing, her arms open wide, her fair pigtails flying, her bright blue eyes shining with delighted welcome.

Dear God, Jacob thought, what he wouldn't give to be back there, sweeping that precious child up into his arms, setting her on his shoulder or swinging her around and around until they were both dizzy.

It was then that the longing for his wife and daughter grew too great, and Jacob turned his memory to sun-splashed fields, flourishing and green, to sparkling streams thick with fish. In his imagination, he stood beside his steadfast friend Enoch, once more, both of them as close as brothers gratified by the sight of a heavy crop, by the knowledge that, this year anyway, their hard work would bring a reward.

"God has blessed our efforts," Jacob would say, quietly and with awe, for he had believed the world to be an essentially good place then. War and all its brutalities were merely tales told in books, or passed down the generations by old men.

He saw Enoch as clearly as if he'd been right there on the battlefield with him, instead of miles and miles away. He stood vivid in Jacob's recollection, the black man his father had bought, freed, then hired in his own right to work on the family farm years back, grinning as he replied, "Well, I don't see how the Good Lord ought to get *all* the credit. He might send the sunshine and the rain, but far as I can reckon, He ain't much for plowing."

Jacob invariably laughed, no matter how threadbare the joke, would have laughed now, too, if he'd had the breath for it.

He barely noticed that the terrible din of battle had faded to the feeble moans and low cries of other men, Rebels and Union men alike, fallen and left behind in the acrid urgency of combat.

He dreamed — or at least, he *thought* he was dreaming — of the heaven he'd heard about all his life, for he came from a long line of churchgoing folk. He saw the towering gates, studded with pearls and precious gems, standing open before him.

He caught a glimpse of the fabled streets of gold, too, and although he saw no angels and no long-departed loved ones waiting to welcome him into whatever celestial realm they now occupied, he heard music, almost too beautiful to be endured. He looked up, saw a dazzling sky, not merely blue, but somehow *woven,* a shimmering tapestry of innumerable colors, each one brilliant, some familiar and some beyond his powers of description.

He hesitated, not from fear, for surely there could be no danger here, but because he knew that once he passed through this particular gateway, there would be no turning back.

Perhaps it was blasphemy, but Jacob's heart swelled with a poignant longing for a lesser heaven, another, humbler paradise, where the gates and fences were made of hand-hewn wood or plain stones gathered in fields, and the roads were winding trails of dust and dirt, rutted by wagon wheels, deep, glittering snows and heavy rain.

Had it been in his power, and he knew it wasn't, he would have traded eternity in that place of ineffable peace and beauty for a single, blessedly ordinary day at home, waking up beside Caroline in their feather bed, teasing her until she blushed, or watching, stricken by the love of her, as she made breakfast in the kitchen house on an ordinary morning.

Suddenly, the sweet visions were gone.

Jacob heard sounds, muffled but distinct. Men, horses, a few wagons.

Then nothing.

Perhaps he was imagining things. Suffering hallucinations.

He waited, listening, his eyes unblinking, dry and rigid in their sockets, stinging with sweat and grit and congealed blood.

Fear burned in his veins as those first

minutes after he was wounded came back. He recalled the shock of his flesh tearing, as though it were happening all over again, a waking nightmare of friend and foe alike streaming past, shouting, shooting, bleeding, stepping over him and on him. He recalled the hooves of horses, churning up patches on the ground within inches of where he lay.

Jacob forced himself to concentrate. Although he couldn't see the sky, he knew by the light that the day was waning.

Was he alone?

The noises came again, but they were more distant now. Perhaps the party of men and horses had passed him by.

The prospect was a bleak one, filling Jacob with quiet despair. Even a band of Rebs would've been preferable to lying helplessly in his own gore, wondering when the rats and crows would come to feast on him.

An enemy bullet or the swift mercy of a bayonet would be infinitely better.

Hope stirred briefly when a Federal soldier appeared in his line of vision, as though emerging from a void. At first, Jacob wasn't sure the other man was real.

He tried to speak, or make the slightest move, indicating that he was alive and in need of help, but he could do neither.

The soldier approached, crouching beside him, and one glimpse of his filthy, beard-stubbled face, hard with cruelty, put an end to Jacob's illusions. The man rolled him roughly onto his back, with no effort to search for a pulse or any other sign of life. Instead, he began rifling through Jacob's pockets, muttering under his breath, helping himself to his watch and what little money he carried, since most of his pay went to Caroline.

Jacob felt outrage, but he was still helpless. All he could do was watch as the other man grabbed his rucksack, fumbled to lift the canvas flap and reach inside.

Finally, the bummer, as thieves and stragglers and deserters were called, gave in to frustration and dumped Jacob's belongings onto the ground, pawing through them.

Look at me, Jacob thought. *I am alive. I wear the same uniform as you do.*

The scavenger did not respond, of course. Did not allow his gaze to rest upon Jacob's face, where he might have seen awareness.

The voices, the trampling hooves, the springless wagons drew closer.

The man cursed, frantic now. He found Jacob's battered Bible and flung it aside in disgusted haste, its thin pages fluttering as it fell, like a bird with a broken wing. The standard-issue tin cup, plate and utensils soon followed, but the thieving bastard stilled when he found the packet of letters, all from Caroline. Perhaps believing he might find something of value in one or more of them, he shoved them into his own rucksack.

Jacob grieved for those letters, but there was nothing he could do.

Except listen.

Yes, he decided. Someone was coming, a small company of riders.

The thief grew more agitated, looked over one shoulder, and then turned back to his plundering, feverish now, but too greedy to flee.

At last he settled on the one object Jacob cherished as much as Caroline's letters — a small leather case with tarnished brass hinges and a delicate clasp.

He saw wicked interest flash in the man's eyes, as he fumbled open the case and saw the tintypes inside, one of Caroline and Jacob, taken on their wedding day, looking traditionally somber in their finest garb, the other of Caroline, with an infant Rachel in her arms, the child resplendent in a tiny, lace-trimmed christening gown and matching bonnet.

No, Jacob cried inwardly, hating his helplessness.

"Well, now," the man murmured. "Ain't this a pretty little family? Maybe I'll just look them up sometime, offer my condolences."

Had he been able, Jacob would have killed the bummer in that moment, throttled the life out of him with his bare hands, and never regretted the act. Although he struggled with all his might, trying to gather the last shreds of his strength, the effort proved useless.

It was the worst kind of agony, imagining this man reading the letters, noting the return address on each and every envelope, seeking Caroline and Rachel out, offering a pretense of sympathy.

Taking advantage.

And Jacob could do nothing to stop him, nothing to protect his wife and daughter from this monster or others like him, the renegades, the enemies of decency and innocence in all their forms.

The bummer snapped the case closed, put it and the letters inside the rucksack and grabbed it, ready to flee.

It was then that a figure loomed behind him, a gray shadow of a man, who planted the sole of one boot squarely in the center of the thief's back, and sent him sprawling across Jacob's inert frame.

The pain was instant, throbbing in every bone and muscle of Jacob's body.

"Stealing from a dead man," the shadow said, standing tall, his buttery-smooth drawl laced with contempt. "That's low, even for a Yank."

The bummer scrambled to his feet, groped for something, probably his rifle, and paled when he came up empty. Most likely, he'd dropped the weapon in his eagerness to rob one of his own men.

"I ought to run you through with this fine steel sword of mine, Billy," the other man mused idly. He must have ridden ahead of his detachment, dismounted nearby and moved silently through the scattered bodies. "After all, this is a *war,* now, isn't it? And you are my foe, as surely as I'm yours."

Jacob's vision, unclear to begin with, blurred further, and there was a pounding in his ears, but he could make out the contours of the two men, now standing on either side of him, and he caught the faint murmur of their words.

"You don't want to kill me, Johnny," the thief reasoned, with a note of anxious congeniality in his voice, raising both palms as if in surrender. "It wouldn't be honorable, with us Union boys at a plain disad-

27

vantage." He drew in a strange, swift whistle of a breath. "Anyhow, I wasn't hurtin' nobody. Just makin' good use of things this poor fella has no need of, bein' dead and all."

By now, Jacob was aware of men and horses all around, although there was no cannon fire, no shouting, no sharp report of rifles.

"You want these men to see you murder an unarmed man?" wheedled the man addressed as Billy. "Where I come from, you'd be hanged for that. It's a war crime, ain't it?"

"We're not 'where you come from,' " answered Johnny coolly. The bayonet affixed to the barrel of his carbine glinted in the lingering smoke and the dust raised by the horses. "This is Virginia," he went on, with a note of fierce reverence. "And you are an intruder here, sir."

Billy — the universal name for all Union soldiers, as Johnny was for their Confederate counterparts — spat, foolhardy in his fear. "I reckon the rules are about the same, though, whether North or South," he ventured. Even Jacob, from his limited vantage point, saw the terror behind all that bluster. "Fancy man like you — an officer, at that — must know how it is. Even if you don't hang for killin' with no cause, you'll be court-martialed for sure, once your superiors catch wind of what you done. And that's bound to leave a stain on your high and mighty reputation as a Southern gentleman, ain't it? Just you think, *sir,* of the shame all those well-mannered folks back home on the old plantation will have to contend with, and it'll be on *your* account."

A slow, untroubled grin took shape on the Confederate captain's soot-smudged face. His gray uniform was torn and soiled, the brass of his buttons and insignia dull, and his boots were scuffed, but even Jacob, with his sight impaired, could see that his dignity was inborn, as much a part of him as the color of his eyes.

"It might be worth hanging for," he replied, almost cordially, like a man debating some minor point of military ethics at an elegant dinner party far removed from the sound and fury of war. "The pleasure of killing a latrine rat such as yourself, that is. As for these men, most of them are under my command, as it happens. Well, they've seen their friends and cousins and brothers skewered by Yankee bayonets and blown to fragments by their cannon. Just yesterday, in fact, they saw General Jackson . . . relieved of an arm." At this, the captain

29

paused, swallowed once. "Most likely, they'd raise a cheer as *you* fell."

Dimly, Jacob sensed Billy Yank's nervous bravado. Under any other circumstances, he might have been amused by the fellow's demeanor, but he could feel himself retreating further and further into the darkness of approaching death, and there was no room in him for frivolous emotions.

"Now, that just ain't Christian," protested Billy, conveniently overlooking his own moral lapse.

The captain gave a raspy laugh, painful to hear, and shook his head. "A fine sentiment, coming from the likes of you." In the next moment, his face hardened, aristocratic even beneath its layers of dried sweat and dirt. He turned slightly, keeping one eye on his prisoner, and shouted a summons into the rapidly narrowing nothingness surrounding the three of them.

Several men hurried over, although they were invisible to Jacob, and the sounds they made were faint.

"Get this piece of dung out of my sight before I pierce his worthless flesh with my sword for the pure pleasure of watching him bleed," the officer ordered. "He is a disgrace, even to *that* uniform."

There were words of reply, though Jacob

30

couldn't make them out, and Jacob sensed a scuffle as the thief resisted capture, a modern-day Judas, bleating a traitor's promises, willing to betray men who'd fought alongside him.

Jacob waited, expecting the gentleman officer to follow his men, go on about his business of overseeing the capture of wounded bluecoats, the recovery of his own troops, alive and dead.

Instead, the captain crouched, as the thief had done earlier. He took up Jacob's rucksack that Billy had been forced to leave behind, rummaged within it, produced the packet of letters and the leather case containing the likenesses of Jacob's beloved wife and daughter. He opened it, examined the images inside, smiled sadly.

Then he tucked the items inside Jacob's bloody coat, paused as though startled, and looked directly into his eyes.

"My God," he said, under his breath. "You're alive."

Jacob could not acknowledge the remark verbally, but he felt a tear trickle over his left temple, into his hair, and that, apparently, was confirmation enough for the Confederate captain.

Now, Jacob thought, he would be shot, put out of his misery like an injured horse.

And he would welcome the release.

Instead, very quietly, the captain said. "Hold on, Yank. You'll be found soon." He paused, looking serious. "And if you should happen to encounter a certain Union quartermaster by the name of Rogan McBride, somewhere along your journey, I would be obliged if you'd tell him Bridger Winslow sends his best regards."

Jacob doubted he'd live long enough to get the chance to do as Winslow asked, but he marked the names carefully in his mind, just the same.

Another voice spoke then. "This somebody you know, Captain?" a soldier asked, with concern and a measure of sympathy. It wasn't uncommon on either side, after all, to find a friend or a relative among enemy casualties, since the battle lines often cut across towns, churches and supper tables.

"No," the captain replied gruffly. "Just another dead Federal." A pause. "Get on with your business, Simms. We might have the bluecoats under our heel for the moment, but you can be sure they'll be back to bury what remains they can't gather up and haul away now. Better if we don't risk a skirmish after a day of hard fighting."

"Yes, sir," Simms replied sadly. "The men are low in spirit, now that General Jackson has been struck down."

"Yes," the captain answered. Angry sorrow flashed in his eyes. "By his own troops," he added bitterly, speaking so quietly that Jacob wondered if Simms had even heard.

Jacob sensed the other man's departure. The captain lingered, taking his canteen from his belt, loosening the cap a little with a deft motion of one hand, leaving the container within Jacob's reach. The gesture was most likely a futile one, since Jacob couldn't use his hands, but it was an act of kindness, all the same. An affirmation of the possibility, however remote, that Jacob might somehow survive.

Winslow rose to his full height, regarded Jacob solemnly, then slowly walked away.

Jacob soon lost consciousness again, waking briefly now and then, surprised to find himself not only still among the living, but unmolested by vermin. When alert, he lay looking up at the night sky, steeped in the profound silence of the dead, one more body among dozens, if not hundreds, scattered across the blood-soaked grass.

Sometime the next morning, or perhaps the morning after that, wagons came again, and grim-faced Union soldiers stacked the bodies like cordwood, one on top of another. They were fretful, these battle-weary men, anxious to complete their dismal mission and get back behind the Union lines, where there was at least a semblance of safety.

Jacob, mute and motionless, was among the last to be taken up, grasped roughly by two men in dusty blue coats.

The pain was so sudden, so excruciating that finally, *finally,* he managed a low, guttural cry.

The soldier supporting his legs, little more than a boy, with blemished skin and not even the prospect of a beard, gasped. "This fella's still with us," he said, and he looked so startled, so horrified and pale that Jacob feared the kid would swoon, letting his burden drop.

"Well," said the other man, gruffly cheerful, "I'll be a son of a bitch if Johnny didn't leave a few breathin' this time around."

The boy recovered enough to turn his head and spit. To Jacob's relief, the boy remained upright, his grasp firm. "A few," he agreed grudgingly. "And every one of them better off dead."

The darkness returned then, enfolding Jacob like the embrace of a sea siren, pulling him under.

2

CAROLINE

Nothing Caroline Hammond had heard or read about the nation's capital could have prepared her for the reality of the place — the soot and smoke, the jostling crowds of soldiers and civilians, the clatter of wagon wheels, the neighing of horses and the braying of mules, the rough merriment streaming through the open doorways of plentiful saloons and pleasure houses.

She kept her gaze firmly averted as she passed one after another of these establishments, appalled by the seediness of it all, by the crude shouts, the jangle of badly tuned pianos and rollicking songs sung lustily and off-key, and, here and there, fisticuffs accompanied by the breaking of glass and even a few gunshots.

More than once, Caroline was forced to cross the road, to avoid rows of ox carts and ambulance wagons and mounted men who took no evident notice of hapless pedestrians.

A farm wife, Caroline was not a person of delicate constitution. She had dispatched, cleaned and plucked many a chicken for Sunday supper, helped her husband, Jacob, and Enoch Flynn, the hired man, butcher hogs come autumn and worked ankle-deep in barn muck on a daily basis.

Here, in this city of poor manners, ceaseless din and sickening stenches, the effects were, of course, magnified, surrounding her on every side, pummeling her senses without mercy.

Runnels of foaming animal urine flowed among the broken cobblestones, and dung steamed in piles, adding to the cloying miasma. On the far edge of her vision, she saw a soldier vomit copiously into a gutter and felt her own gorge rise, scalding, to the back of her throat. The man's companions seemed amused by the spectacle, slapping their retching friend on the back and chiding him with loud, jocular admonitions of an unsavory nature.

Seeing the disreputable state of these men's uniforms, intended as symbols of a proud and noble cause, thoroughly be-smirched not only by all manner of filth, but by the indecent comportment of the men who wore them, sent furious color surging into her cheeks. Only her native prudence and the urgency of her mission — locating her wounded husband, possibly lying near death in one of Washington City's numerous makeshift hospitals or, if she'd arrived too late, in a pine box — kept her from striding right up to the scoundrels and taking them sternly to task for bringing such shame upon their more honorable fellows.

How dared they behave like reprobates, safe in the shadow of President Lincoln's White House, while their great-hearted comrades fought bravely on blood-drenched battlefields all over the land?

She was mortified, as well as aggrieved, but her anger sustained her and kept her moving toward the rows of hospital tents just visible in the distance.

Toward Jacob.

She thought of the newspaper clipping listing the dead and wounded tucked away in her reticule. She'd read the list over and over again from the moment the newspaper had been placed in her hands, read it during the day-long train ride from Gettysburg, the small, quiet town in the green Pennsylvania countryside she had lived in, or near, all her life.

By now, the clipping was tattered and creased, an evil talisman, despised and yet somehow necessary, the only link she had to her husband.

The information it contained was maddeningly scant, listing only that, among others, a Corporal Jacob Hammond had fallen in battle on May 3, almost six weeks ago, at Chancellorsville, Virginia. She had learned from others that any casualties from his regiment had since been transported to the capital to receive medical attention.

As the granddaughter of a country doctor and sometime undertaker, Caroline knew what her husband, Jacob, and others like him would have to endure if they survived at all — crowding, filth, poor food and tainted water, too few trained surgeons and attendants, shortages of even the most basic supplies, such as clean bandages, laudanum and ether. Sanitation, the most effective enemy of sepsis, according to her late grandfather, was still virtually nonexistent.

The stench of open latrines, private and public privies and towering heaps of manure standing on empty lots finally forced Caroline to set down her bag long enough to pull her best Sunday handkerchief from the pocket of her cloak and press the soft cloth to her nose and mouth. The scent of rosewater, generously applied before she left home, had faded with time and distance, and thus provided little relief, but it was better than nothing.

Caroline picked up her bag and walked purposely onward, not because she knew where she would find her husband, but because she didn't dare stand still too long, lest her knees give way beneath her. She tried to locate a central office of some kind, where a clerk might be able to look up Jacob's name in a volume of records and direct her to him, but the effort had been in vain. Frustrated and anxious, she had let herself be swept into the general chaos and disorganization of a wartime city.

Propelled by a rising sense of desperation, she hurried on, through the mayhem of a city under constant threat of siege, doing her best to convey a confidence she didn't feel. Beneath the stalwart countenance, fear gnawed at her empty, roiling stomach, throbbed in her head, sought and found the secret regions of her heart to do its worst.

She had no choice but to carry on, no matter what might be required of her, and she did not attempt to ignore the relentless dread. That would be impossible.

Instead, she walked, weaving her way through the crowds, crossing to the opposite side of the street in a mostly useless effort to avoid staggering drunkards and street brawls and men who watched her too boldly. Having long since learned the futility of burying her fears, she made up her mind to face them, with calm fortitude — as best she could, anyway.

As she'd often heard her beloved grandfather Doc Prescott remark that turning a blind eye to a problem or a troublesome situation served only to make matters worse in the long run. "Face things head on, Caroline," he'd always advised her. "Stand up to whatever comes your way and, if you are in the right, Providence will come to your aid."

Lately, she hadn't seen a great deal of evidence to support the latter part of that statement, but, then again, Providence was under no discernible obligation to explain itself or its ways to questioning mortals, particularly in light of the stupidity, greed and cruelty so far displayed by the human race.

One by one, Caroline confronted the haunting possibilities, the pictures standing vivid in her thoughts. In the most immediate scenario, she couldn't find Jacob, even after the most arduous search imaginable.

There had been a mistake, and he'd been taken to some other place entirely, or died in transit, and been buried in an anonymous grave, one she'd never be able to locate.

In the next, she *did* find her husband, but she had not arrived quickly enough to hold his hand, stroke his forehead, bid him a tender farewell. He'd already succumbed, and all that was left of him was a corpse lying in a ramshackle coffin.

But there was one more tableau to face and in many ways, it was the most terrible of all. Here, Jacob was alive, horribly maimed, helpless, forced to bear the unbearable until death delivered him from his sufferings in days, weeks, months — or years.

If only she knew what to expect, Caroline thought, she might be better able to prepare somehow.

But then, how *could* one prepare for the shock of seeing a beloved husband broken and torn? Suppose Jacob was so disfigured that she didn't recognize him or, worse yet, allowed shock or dismay to show in her face, her manner, her bearing?

She swayed, not daring to draw the deep breath her body craved, lest the dreadful smells of disease and suffering and death finally overwhelm her, render her useless to

Jacob just when he needed her most.

And that would not do.

For what remained of the day and into the evening, Caroline searched one hospital tent after another, pausing at the foot of every cot, forcing herself to look directly into the face of each man. Some slept, gray with the pallor of approaching death, some moaned or wept in silence, staring up at the drooping canvas roof as though they could see right through it to the sky. A few lifted an imploring hand to her, beckoning weakly, another woman's name on their lips.

Others had no hand to raise, and called to her with their eyes.

A touch to a hand, a brow. A kind word. A simple blessing. Perhaps a prayer.

So little to ask.

And so much.

Caroline made an effort to skirt the crumbling precipices of their individual sorrows, lest she lose her footing and pitch headlong into such hopelessness that she might never find her way back to air and light and solid ground.

Back to Jacob.

Because of Jacob, because he was her husband and she was his wife, she pressed on, pausing only long enough to look carefully at each face, if indeed one was visible, and not swathed in bandages, as so many were. In these instances, she studied the forms instead, the shapes and the contours, measuring lines, like a cartographer mapping the terrain.

Most bodies were clearly defined beneath thin blankets or sheets, a fact that was helpful, but sobering, too. Caroline saw too many flat surfaces where there should have been arms or legs, and had to steel herself against a compassion so overwhelming that it threatened to consume her. All the while, out of necessity rather than virtue, she trusted her most private instincts; she would, she *must* recognize the landscape, the hills and hollows, of the one body she knew intimately. Jacob's.

Somewhere, in one of these cots, one of these tents or beyond, in the overflow, he was waiting for her, hoping she would come to him, perhaps calling her name.

She must not fail him.

Time soon became irrelevant; only a driving urgency remained.

As twilight fell, lanterns were lit, their dull glow fading into the ever-thickening gloom gathering in corners and pooling upon the sawdust and dirt floors, like intangible floodwaters, silent and slowly rising.

43

There were too few helpers, mostly soldiers recovering from wounds of their own, and Caroline had no opportunity to ask if any knew where Jacob was; they were too immersed in the task of tending to the wounded and she *couldn't* interrupt them. Bandaged and gaunt and scarred, but ambulatory, moved among the cots, carrying buckets of water, holding ladles to parched lips, whispering hoarse words of awkward consolation to this one and that. In each tent, a small female contingent served as well, some apparently volunteers, others hired. All wore plain, sturdy dresses and aprons, dutifully laundered but still bearing evidence, however faint, of old stains, along with fresh ones.

These fading spills, Caroline thought, were the marks of their service, macabre medals of their valor.

She watched these women, in passing, as they carried bowls of broth or cornmeal mush to those patients who were able to feed themselves, patiently spooned the food into the mouths of the ones who were not. They seemed tireless in their dedication, and she knew they did far more than serve meals and bring water; they cleaned wounds, changed bandages, removed stitches, administered medicines, took down

44

letters dictated in halting voices and made sure they were posted. Some were sitting by bedsides and she could hear as they read aloud — messages from home, lines of poetry, favorite Bible passages. The women listened to last words and sang familiar refrains, from the most sacred of hymns to funny little ditties known to every school-child. She knew they did what they could, understanding, as they surely must, that for all they gave, it would never be enough.

And still they were here, among these men, diligently doing their best while leaving other parts of their lives unlived. Many, she assumed, were widows, while others were the wives or sweethearts, mothers or sisters, of soldiers.

Caroline, although dazed, and feeling somehow separate from herself, marveled at the courage and selfless devotion of all these women, felt the pull of it.

But she kept moving.

Until, finally, she couldn't anymore. Weariness pulsed through her like the beat of a second, much greater heart than her own. And although the smells and the surrounding horrors still sickened her, she knew she herself would have to eat soon, then find a place to rest before she resumed her search for Jacob.

She felt defeated by her own limits, emotional and physical alike.

In those first moments of realization, home seemed even farther away than it was, more dream than recent memory, a place she'd merely imagined.

Rachel. Grandmother. The farm. Jacob, on his last visit home before Chancellorsville.

She yearned for her loved ones now, and for the person she was in their presence, for the peace of the land, so green and open in contrast to this sea of suffering humanity.

Her mind drifted to the beginning of her journey. She had left in a hurry, asking her grandmother to let her friends know what happened.

The railway car had been crowded, the hard, sooty seats filled.

Bolt upright, Caroline had sweltered in her travel cloak the whole way, her bag resting on her lap, her arms tightly around it, careful not to meet anyone's eyes, scooting closer to the window when a corpulent man in a dusty Union uniform dropped into the seat next to hers. He'd smelled of sweat and stale whiskey and rotting teeth, and his bulk pressed against Caroline, trapping her.

At first, the portly soldier had attempted to engage her in conversation, but besides an initial nod, she hadn't acknowledged him. Instead, she'd stared through the murky glass at the passing countryside.

Though persistent, the stranger eventually gave up, heaving a gusty sigh and shifting about. Her relief was short-lived; she heard the strike of a match, smelled sulfur, then tobacco.

Cigar smoke had bloomed around her in a bluish cloud, stinging her eyes, scouring the back of her throat.

Miraculously, her breakfast had stayed put.

In retrospect, the incident seemed trivial now, many hours later, as dusk approached and she stood in the center of yet another tent, with human misery on every side.

A hand tugged lightly at the fabric of her cloak just then, causing Caroline to start so that she nearly dropped her travel case.

"I hope I didn't frighten you." The voice was feminine and kindly and conveyed a fatigue that no amount of sleep or leisure could cure.

Caroline turned, gripping the handle of her bag more firmly now, and with both hands, not from fear it would be stolen from her, but because neither arm could manage the weight of it without the other.

A slight woman stood beside her, plain as

a mud-hen in her brown dress. Her hair was gray and billowing around her wrinkled face, and her sad eyes gazed up into Caroline's face. "Are you looking for someone?"

A cluster of sobs rose suddenly from somewhere deep inside Caroline, and she barely managed to choke them back. "My husband," she said, with difficulty. "Corporal Jacob Hammond. He was wounded at Chancellorsville — I've looked and looked for hours, but I can't seem to find him anywhere —"

The woman patted Caroline's arm, and interrupted gently, "Do you know the name of your husband's regiment, Mrs. Hammond?" she asked.

"Yes," Caroline replied, summoning the last of her dignity. "Jacob serves with the Eleventh Pennsylvania." *The Bloody Eleventh,* he'd called it.

"Ah," the woman said with a little sigh. She brightened, no small feat at such a time and in such a place, and then added, "When possible, we try to keep the sick and wounded with their regiments, for purposes of order, of course, but mainly because they seem to do better if there's someone they might know nearby."

Caroline bent to put down her case. "Can you tell me where the members of my husband's regiment have been taken?"

The woman sighed again. "I can ask," she said softly, her face full of compassion, "but not tonight, I'm afraid. No pen pushers on duty at this hour." She patted Caroline's arm once more. "Come back first thing in the morning, and I'll help if I can."

Everything within Caroline clamored to find Jacob *now,* but she recognized that she had reached the end of her personal resources. "Thank you," she said.

The woman nodded and put out a hand to Caroline, who reciprocated. Strong, calloused fingers, gnarled and thick at the knuckles, closed around hers. "I'm Bessie Engle," she began. "And this tent is number ten. Remember that, or you might not find it again. Be sure you ask for Bessie when you get here, in case I'm out on some errand or off resting my feet."

"I'm obliged, Mrs. Engle," Caroline said, fearing her voice would break.

"Just Bessie," came the reply. Bessie was smiling, but then a frown furrowed her brow. "You have a place to stay, Mrs. Hammond? Some people here to look after you?"

Caroline hesitated, thinking how odd it was that this kindness could bring her so close to losing what remained of her composure.

"No," she said. "I plan to look for a rooming house or, failing that, seek lodging in a modest hotel. Perhaps you could recommend a respectable place — not too expensive?"

Bessie shook her head. "Have you no people at all, here in Washington City?" she persisted.

"Only my Jacob," Caroline replied.

"There probably isn't an empty room to be had in the whole city," Bessie continued. "Not one you'd want to stay in, anyhow. No, it won't do, your wandering around at night all by yourself."

"Oh," Caroline said, deflated. In her hurry to get to the capital and find Jacob, it hadn't occurred to her that there might be no lodgings available when she arrived. After all, the city was so large.

In the next moment, however, she thought of a possible solution. "I'll just walk back to the train depot, and pass the night there," she said. The depot, modest as it was, had walls and a roof. Surely people came and went, and not all of them could be hoodlums and scoundrels. She'd sit up through the night, remain vigilant. She still had a heel of bread, some cheese and an apple tucked away in her travel case, so she wouldn't go hungry.

"Nonsense," Bessie said right away. "Come and stay the night with me and the other nurses. We have a tent, and while it sure isn't much, you'll have a cot to sleep on and people around you."

Caroline, feeling thoroughly grateful, thanked Bessie again.

"You look all done in," Bessie said, clearly gratified that the matter had been decided, and to her satisfaction. "There'll be folks along to relieve me and the others in a little while, and then we'll go on and get you settled. Meantime, come sit inside for a bit, and I'll rustle up some of that mush the men had for supper."

Too tired to argue, Caroline followed Bessie along the wide aisle between still more cots, where men snored or murmured or cursed, quietly or otherwise, to a smaller tent set apart by several blankets suspended from poles, forming a partition. Here were a few chairs, a small stove and two cots covered in crumpled blankets.

Caroline dropped her bag, sat and immediately regretted it, not at all sure she'd have the strength to stand up again.

"I'll fetch that mush," Bessie told her. "You just rest."

"Please don't trouble yourself, Bessie. I have food. Cheese and bread and an apple. I'd be happy to share it with you."

Bessie paused. "I'm obliged for the offer," she said, almost whispering, "but I eat the same as these men do. Wouldn't seem right to do otherwise."

Caroline felt a touch of shame. Her humble meal, packed in the kitchen house at home before dawn that morning, would seem like a banquet to men subsisting on cornmeal mush, hard tack, thin soup and boiled beans. She knew from Jacob's letters that such foods were standard army fare, in camp as well as in hospitals.

Her chagrin must have shown in her face, because Bessie smiled and wagged a finger at her. "You go right on ahead and enjoy your meal," she ordered good-naturedly. "No reason you ought to feel bad about it." A pause. "Just don't go letting any of these poor fellas know what you've had, that's all. Hard on their spirits."

With that, she was gone, off to answer a chorus of calls from beyond the cloth partition.

Caroline sat for a while, then ate part of the cheese and all of the bread, but every bite tasted not of home, but of unwarranted privilege.

■ ■ ■ ■

Caroline spent the next morning waiting to hear from Bessie and helping out in whatever small way she could — folding bandages, addressing envelopes to soldiers' families, whatever any of the staff asked her to do. As she worked, she spent time in conversation with another young woman who told her that "a famous writer" known for his kindness and commitment to the soldiers was working as a wound dresser at some of the hospitals. When she heard the name, Caroline immediately recognized it — her grandfather had at least one of Walt Whitman's books in his library, a volume of poetry, she recalled. That brief memory of Doc Prescott brought her both comfort and sadness.

Later, in the moist, weighted heat of midafternoon, she stood at the foot of Jacob's cot, grateful and stricken, wondering if she would have recognized him at all if she hadn't eventually been escorted to this particular spot by a Union officer Bessie knew. Rogan McBride, an acting quartermaster, had searched various records, asked a great many questions, and finally encountered an ambulance worker who remembered picking up a man from the Eleventh during the battle at Chancellorsville. The boy recalled Jacob for two reasons: the soldier had appeared to be dead at first, and scared him and his partner half out of their hides when he moaned, and because of the letters tucked inside his coat, addressed to a corporal named Hammer or Harmon or Hamilton, or some such. If he recollected rightly, they'd taken the fellow to tent sixty-eight.

Now, with Captain McBride as her escort, Caroline regarded her husband.

She might well have passed Jacob by, he looked so very different, with his gaunt face; wild, matted hair; and shaggy beard, and his blank eyes that did not seem to see. There were shadows beneath them, purple as new bruises, and his skin glistened with perspiration. His skull bone protruded, and his chest, bound in grimy bandages, was sunken. It was as though he lacked substance, lacked life.

She thanked Captain McBride without meeting his gaze; he nodded and said he'd come back if and when he could. Soon a patient in uniform slipped into the tent, his left arm supported by a sling.

"We can't give him much water," he said. "Food, neither. He can't swallow much."

Caroline stared down into her husband's face, once handsome and browned by a lifetime of working under summer suns, now gray and so thin.

Jacob had just turned twenty-four on his last birthday, far from home, in a lull between skirmishes and battles, his life barely begun.

"You can sit with him a while if you like," the soldier said. "He might hear you. Hard to tell, but —"

Caroline stood frozen.

For a moment, she imagined hearing herself say, "No, I never found him," to all the people awaiting her return.

"But his eyes are open —" she whispered. But only their color, sky blue, was the same. They used to be expressive, full of mischief; now they might as well have been made of glass.

"Been that way since he got here," the soldier responded sympathetically. "He never closes them. And —" There followed a moment of hesitation that raised Caroline's apprehension a notch or two. "Well, he cannot speak. Caught himself a neck full of shrapnel, and then there's his ribcage —"

Caroline put up a single hand, a bid for silence.

All around them, men were calling out

desperately for water, or morphine or ether or death itself. The soldier cleared his throat once more, then went on his way, as the captain had done.

Caroline knelt between Jacob's cot and the one next to it, where a man slept, tossing and turning in the grip of some nightmare, destined to awaken to another, very possibly worse. Beneath the dingy sheet, his form was clearly defined, an abbreviated shape, one leg ending at the knee, the other at midthigh.

Caroline did not want to learn the poor man's name, or what had happened to him, or who, if anyone, was waiting for him at home. She couldn't bear to know.

She yearned to shut everything out, except for Jacob, until there were only the two of them, alone in the midst of a gray, shifting void. She took her husband's left hand in both of her own and whispered his name.

She saw a tear form in his eye, and knew then that he recognized her presence. She felt her heart shatter. She leaned over and gently kissed his cheek, then his paper-thin lips. His neck and chest were bandaged.

"It's Caroline, my love," she said, when she could trust herself to form the words. "I'm right here, and I will stay with you always."

She thought she saw Jacob's lips quiver, but he made no sound.

Another tear trickled down his face.

Jacob still made no sound, but Caroline knew what he was trying to tell her. He had held on somehow, through all his suffering, waiting for her.

Now, finally, she was here. He could begin the process of letting go.

Caroline's throat constricted, and it was a long while before she found her voice again. When she did, she spoke softly to Jacob, telling him how their Rachel was thriving, how she could recite the alphabet and count to fifty, how she adored her papa and always would. Caroline would see to that, see that he was never forgotten.

She told him she loved him, and that she knew he loved her in return.

She told him that Geneva, her grandmother, sent her love and Enoch sent his best wishes. Then she filled him in on the state of the crops. Finally she recited the comforting words of his favorite Psalm, the twenty-third, her eyes scalding as she finished with " 'And I shall dwell in the house of the Lord forever.' "

After that, she simply held his hand, stroked his forehead and smoothed his hair. She did not attempt to wipe away his tears, for they were his own, somehow sacred, and he had a right to shed them as he would.

For hours, it seemed she didn't move, disregarding the ache in her knees, paying no mind to the other complaints her body raised.

She could tell by the tempo of Jacob's breathing when he slept, then felt his awakening in her own flesh, a soft, jolting sensation of alertness.

Eventually, a doctor stopped by, although Caroline was only peripherally aware of him, willing him to withdraw from a space meant just for her and her husband. She was guarding that space and wanted to hold on to it without intrusion.

The doctor's words seemed muffled, as though spoken from a great distance.

Jacob's wounds were critical, the doctor told her, but no particular one had been severe enough to cause death. However, her husband could not take proper nourishment because of the injuries to his neck and throat; water and broth had to be administered drop by drop, since even a spoonful caused him to choke. He was slowly succumbing, as he could no longer stay properly hydrated.

Caroline did not look at the doctor, nor

did she speak. She simply waited for him to leave.

Still, he continued. It would not be long now, he explained. "The patient's trials —" did he even know Jacob's name? "—would soon be over."

She wanted to scream, "Jacob! His name is Jacob!"

But she didn't.

Then came the questions. Did she plan to claim her husband's body personally? Or would she prefer that it be shipped home for burial?

"It."

"The body."

As though Jacob had become something other than a person. How was he sure Jacob could no longer hear?

Was she aware that she was entitled to a death benefit? Had she brought burial clothes, or did she prefer that "the remains," be laid to rest in uniform?

Dear God, the man was offensive. Surely, it was premature to make such decisions. Indecent, even.

If it hadn't meant letting go of Jacob's hand, Caroline would have clamped her own hands over her ears, shutting out the torrent of words.

When the doctor finally left, she continued

her vigil in silence. She didn't think about tomorrow, about the answers to the doctor's inquiries, the preparations, the trip home; none of those things seemed important. Instead, she thought of Jacob, only Jacob.

She knelt beside him and held his hand, quietly bearing witness to their love, having said all she needed to say. The war had changed him. How could it not, after Antietam and all the battles preceding it? After Chancellorsville?

She'd been seventeen when they married. She'd been completely innocent, despite stolen glimpses at some of the etchings in some of Grandfather's medical books and a head full of storybook fancies.

Jacob had always been tender with her. Didn't they deserve more time together?

Her Jacob was dying. Everything else was insignificant in the light of that reality.

It was almost midnight, when Jacob gave an almost imperceptible shudder, and then rallied briefly in a way that seemed miraculous, given the hours of silence.

"Caroline," Jacob said, in a painful croak.

Startled, she gasped, cupping his face in her hands, turning his head ever so slightly toward her, gazing into the depths of his eyes.

She saw helplessness there, and a plea.

"Jacob?" she whispered, afraid he hadn't spoken at all, that she'd imagined the sound of his voice, had somehow conjured up the illusion out of her own longing and despair.

"Come — closer. So weak . . ."

Eyes stinging, Caroline leaned her head down, her right ear so close to Jacob's mouth that she felt his flagging breath against her hair and her cheek.

Jacob's next words were so labored that it hurt to hear them. "They're — coming. The Rebels. Take Rachel — get away . . ." He paused then, paused so long that Caroline lifted her head again to search his eyes.

Had he meant they were coming to Gettysburg, to Adams County, and wanted her to leave the farm, strike out for some safer place? That was the one promise she couldn't make; Gettysburg was the only home she'd ever known, and the land Jacob's ancestors had settled was their daughter's only legacy.

But neither could she lie.

Caroline bit her lower lip and said nothing. One of her own tears dropped into Jacob's scruffy beard and glittered there.

She watched, heartbroken, as her young husband, once so strong and vibrant, carried out his last struggle. Still holding his face between her palms, she waited.

Finally, Jacob summoned enough of his rapidly waning life to speak again. "I — have . . . loved you — dearly . . ."

Caroline nodded, weeping in earnest now. "I know that, Husband," she said. "And I have loved you as well." As soon as the words were out, she dropped her forehead to his, unable to bear the probing intensity of his regard.

She felt so raw, so broken, as though her flesh had been stripped away, baring every nerve, every private emotion, every secret — even those she kept from herself.

Yes, she thought fiercely, she *had* loved Jacob. She had *loved* him.

His breath moved softly in her hair, like a caress. A low, strangled sound escaped him, though whether it was a laugh or a sob, she could not tell.

"You are — so . . . beautiful," Jacob said.

She sobbed, clinging to him. "Oh, Jacob, I —"

"Hush, now," he ground out. "Be strong. Promise — me —"

Caroline raised her head, her face wet, and nodded vigorously. "I promise," she said, but even as she spoke, she saw that Jacob was gone, leaving only absolute stillness behind, like a silent echo.

She dried her tears with the back of one

hand. Jacob had always valued dignity, and she would not dishonor him by creating a spectacle in the presence of strangers.

She remained at Jacob's bedside for a long time, and presently someone came for her, murmuring condolences that could not begin to salve her sorrow. Caroline's fingers had to be pried loose from Jacob's hand, though it was gently done, and she was lifted to her feet, supported until she could stand on her own.

She looked back at her husband, saw that someone was covering his face. She knew he would be carried away soon.

And another soldier, sick or wounded or both, would lie in Jacob's place.

Bessie had been summoned, roused from her weary sleep, for she appeared at Caroline's side in her nightgown and a tattered wrapper, her gray hair twisted into a plait and dangling over her shoulder. The effect was oddly girlish.

"Come, now," she whispered, wrapping an arm around Caroline's waist. "You'll see your man in the morning, you have my word. Make your decisions then, child. Not tonight."

Caroline allowed Bessie to lead her away, as though she were a blind person, wandering a maze.

■ ■ ■ ■

Only now two days later, in the baggage car, with its slatted sides letting in speckled slices of sunlight, seated on Jacob's pine-wood coffin, over which she'd spread her cloak, did Caroline let herself remember the details of what came next. After entering the shadowy confines of the nurses' tent, once Jacob had been carried off, she recalled a cup being placed in her hands and hearing Bessie's quiet urging to drink its contents. She had obeyed mutely. Her shoes were loosened, button after button, and then removed. The drink was syrupy, sweet but slightly bitter, too.

Laudanum, she'd thought.

She had handed back the cup, empty, stretched out on her narrow cot still fully clothed, and given herself up to darkness.

Remembering, Caroline gripped the edges of Jacob's coffin now to steady herself as the train lurched into motion, whistle shrieking a shrill farewell to Washington City, with its living and its many, many dead.

Yesterday, with so much to do, she'd had no time to think beyond immediate requirements. She had refused the modest breakfast

Bessie had brought, unable to imagine a time she'd ever be hungry again. She dressed and performed what ablutions she could.

She had feared Jacob would be lost to her, necessitating another exhaustive search, but that wasn't the case. With unusual efficiency, the army had set aside a ramshackle building as a morgue, and he was there.

Caroline had seen Jacob's body, examined every wound. Given a basin of tepid water, a cloth and a scrap of soap after much insistence on her part, she bathed her husband and did what she could with his unkempt hair. At home, she would have washed those light brown locks clean, trimmed away the excess with her sewing shears. She would have shaved off his beard, for Jacob had never worn one, and then asked Enoch to dress him in his Sunday suit.

Alas, she hadn't been at home, but in the capital, on the outskirts of hell itself.

She'd agreed to have Jacob embalmed, considering the journey back to Gettysburg, the viewing and the funeral.

So calm. So practical.

Inside, she'd been screaming.

The embalming process took time but would be done that day, she'd been informed, and there was a small charge.

Caroline had not questioned the fee, but simply paid it, kissed Jacob's icy forehead, and gone to find the paymaster, who would issue her something called a widow's benefit. The sum was nominal, but she couldn't afford to leave it unclaimed, so she found the appropriate tent and, after much waiting and signing of documents, she'd been presented with a draft.

From there, she had proceeded to a nearby bank, and waited again, in a long line of civilians and soldiers, and when her turn at the teller's cage finally came, she had exchanged the draft for currency.

With so much to do, it had been relatively easy to forget the reason behind her errands. After stashing the bills in her reticule and pulling the strings tight, she'd walked to the train station and found someone traveling to Gettysburg who agreed for a small fee to deliver an urgent note to her grandmother, Geneva, who lived in town. She relayed the news of Jacob's death, asked that Enoch be told, although not Rachel, since she wanted to do that herself. Unless there was a delay, she would stop for her child at Geneva's house before going home to the farm.

In closing, she requested that Enoch be asked to meet the afternoon train from Washington City the next evening with a wagon and someone to help him load Jacob's coffin.

Having dispatched the message, Caroline had found a modest eating establishment, washed her hands and face in the cramped room set aside for the use of ladies, and seated herself at a table next to a smudged window overlooking the street. She had ordered a bowl of stew and a basket of bread and forced herself to eat, overruling the protests of her stomach. She would need all the stamina she could muster.

From there, Caroline's recollections were blurred. She knew she had returned to the morgue and waited on a bench outside the room where Jacob had lain, with dozens of others, but she couldn't have said what she thought about, beyond the comforting fact that Rachel was safe at Geneva's house.

Eventually, the grim process had been completed, and she'd been escorted to another part of the building, where Jacob rested inside a coffin still smelling of pine pitch. He'd looked better, even handsome, in a clean uniform, his skin a little rosier, though still waxen.

She'd sat with him until a soldier came and made her leave.

Another blank space opened after that; Caroline had a vague memory of finding

Bessie, offering to help with the patients.

At some point, she'd returned to the nurses' tent, accepted a light supper served on a tin plate, swallowed another dose of laudanum.

And now, here she was, the following afternoon, aboard the train, perched on Jacob's pine box and surrounded by others like it, some stacked, some resting on the floor, all splintery and marked with hastily scrawled names. Frederickson, Williams, McCullough, Johnston, Beckham.

She thought about their various home-comings, these dead men, so different from what they and their loved ones must have hoped for. Presently, the conductor, an elderly man of small stature sporting a heavy white mustache, opened the door to the baggage car and peered in at Caroline. "You changed your mind yet, Missus?" he asked hopefully. He'd made it quite clear when she boarded that he didn't approve of her riding with the trunks and crates and coffins, especially when there were perfectly good seats up front, in the passenger section. "Train's hardly crowded," he added when she didn't answer. "Seems like there are more folks headed *to* Washington City than away from it."

"I'm fine here, thank you," Caroline said

politely. She was aware of the picture she must present, a widow unhinged by sorrow, in need of a wash, a good night's sleep, a change of clothing, brazenly ignoring the proprieties. Before the war, it would have been unthinkable for a decent woman to make a journey of any distance without an escort. Since the Southern Rebellion, the rules had changed out of necessity, but even now, ladies did not ride in baggage cars with their departed husbands.

"Might be spooky in here," the conductor persisted, his mustache twitching a little. "Besides, there aren't any —" he paused, cleared his throat "— facilities."

Caroline did not move. She could make her way to the "facilities" if the need arose, though she hoped it wouldn't, because the cubicles were small and smelly and anything but sanitary.

"Are you afraid of ghosts?" she asked.

The old man reddened, took off his conductor's cap, then put it on again in a show of agitation. "No, ma'am," he said, plainly offended. "There's no such thing, far as I know."

She spread her hands. "I quite agree."

The conductor had no answer for that. He blustered a little, reminded her that she would have half an hour to stretch her legs at the next stop. Maybe buy herself a bite to eat.

She thanked him.

Caroline did not get off the train at the next stop, or the one after that, where two of the coffins were unloaded. The boys sent to fetch them stole curious glances at her, but said nothing.

The conductor brought water, along with two hard-boiled eggs and a slice of bread. Caroline was touched, suspecting he'd meant to eat the food himself.

She accepted with thanks and, when she was alone again, she ate.

There were more stops. Another coffin was unloaded, along with several crates and travel trunks.

"Still plenty of seats up front," the conductor announced, when he returned sometime in the late afternoon to refill her cup with water and offer her a much-read copy of *The Philadelphia Inquirer.*

"I'll stay here," Caroline told him.

When he left shaking his head, she stretched out on top of Jacob's coffin, covered herself with part of the travel cloak, and slept.

3

Hammond Farm, on the Emmitsburg Road
Near Gettysburg, Pennsylvania
June 18, 1863

ENOCH

The sun had begun its slow slant westward
when a neighbor boy of Caroline's grandmother Geneva, a boy named Harvey Bellows, came rustling through the cornfield
toward Enoch, waving an envelope.

Harvey was painfully skinny and so white
his face resembled a waning moon. His
britches were too big, held up by frayed
braces and the grace of God, and his shirt,
worn thin by three older brothers long
before it came down to Harvey, had faded
to no particular color and had come un-
tucked on one side.

"Mr. Enoch," Harvey blurted, out of
breath, shambling to a stop. Had he run the
whole way from town? Enoch hadn't heard

a horse or a wagon coming, but then, he'd been hard at it with the hoe, trying to work off the fear that had been souring in his belly like spoiled milk ever since the Missus lit out for Washington City a few days before. "Miz Prescott sent me out here. I brung you this note."

The envelope rattled in Harvey's hand as he held it out to Enoch, as if the bad news it carried was burning his fingers.

Enoch let his hoe drop to the ground, there between the rows of whispering green. He took the envelope from the boy, opened it and read the note inside, even though he already knew what it said. Had known since the Missus first saw Jacob's name listed in the paper as fallen at Chancellorsville.

Yes, he'd known all along, though he'd dared hope his practiced instinct for trouble might be wrong, just this one time. Hoped the constant burn in his stomach owed itself to the threat of warfare, drawing closer by the day, and by his worries about the dangers the Missus might run into, traveling alone like she was.

Now, the worst had happened; he held the proof in his hands.

Jacob, one of the few white men who'd ever treated Enoch as a true equal, like a brother almost, was dead and gone. The news came as no surprise and yet, in those moments, it rolled over him like a boulder headed downhill, crushing some essential part of him beneath its weight.

He wanted to howl with the pain of this loss, but that would have scared young Harvey Bellows, who was already nervous.

He took a five cent–piece from the pocket of his work-worn trousers and handed it to the boy.

Harvey nodded, pocketing the coin. "Miz Prescott told me to make sure you're gonna meet the train tonight, with a wagon. My pa and my brother Jonathan will be there to help you load up Mr. — the casket."

Enoch knew that the two older brothers had recently left for war, although he'd never heard which regiment they'd joined.

He managed to answer Harvey, his voice a hoarse rasp. "I'll be there," he said. *Go,* he thought, when the boy lingered, fidgeting, shifting his negligible weight first to one side, then the other.

"Mr. Enoch?"

Go. Now. "Yes?"

"You gonna be all right? Here all by yourself, I mean? It'll be hours yet before the train gets to town."

Enoch nodded brusquely.

At last, Harvey turned to leave, his scuffed

shoes kicking up dust as he dragged his feet. He looked back over his shoulder once, shook his head and finally walked away.

Through a humming fog of sorrow, Enoch heard the boy whistle, caught the answering snort of a mule somewhere nearby. Watched numbly as Harvey stepped off the strip of dirt and disappeared into the stalks.

Enoch waited, unmoving. Listening for the sound of the animal's hooves thumping over hard ground, growing fainter and then fainter still.

When he knew Harvey and the mule had reached the road, he dropped to his knees, right there in the cornfield, covered his face with both hands and wept.

The howl rumbled within him, and when his will finally gave way, the sound erupted from him, a force as elemental as nature itself. It wasn't a roar, as he'd expected, but a long, low wail of pure despair, reminiscent of the lonesome whistle of a faraway train winding through the night.

Presently, when that first flood of sorrowing rage had spent itself, Enoch rallied enough to get to his feet. He picked up the hoe he'd discarded earlier, carried it back through the rows and into the open.

He didn't look toward the big stone house; if he did, he figured he would see the memories it held, hovering at the windows like ghosts. Waiting in vain for the return of a young husband and father, dead long before his time.

Enoch made straight for the barn, where he put the hoe away, alongside other tools. A few minutes later, he fetched his favorite fishing pole from his cabin on the far side of the orchard, along with a rusted tin and a hand shovel reserved for digging worms.

Long acquainted with trouble, Enoch had his own methods of dealing with it, and catching a mess of fish for dinner was one of them. Because the warning signs were familiar — a barely noticeable singing in the shaft of his bones, a quiver in his middle, a twitch in the smallest of muscles — he did what he could to prepare himself.

Raised on a cotton plantation outside Charleston, South Carolina and sent to the fields as soon as he could pick bolls and drag sacks between the rows, Enoch had soon developed a quiet but powerful sense of bad things on the way. The skill had proven valuable, with practice, allowing him to sidestep more than one disaster. Sometimes, of course, there was little he could do besides dig in his heels and endure, but he was seldom caught off guard.

And Jacob's death was no exception; he'd

known it was coming. The pain was not lessened by this knowing, and the grief still cut a deep path, carving out canyons within him, leveling mountains, forever altering the terrain of his soul.

For all the shock of confirmation, Enoch had been holding his breath for a long while now, figuratively speaking. The nightmares, always the first sign of coming calamity, had commenced months before those of the Missus — dark and sweat-drenched dreams, pierced by unearthly shrieks, the boom of cannon, the sharp crack of carbines, vivid scenes of violence veiled in crimson and shifting smoke, gore so ludicrous it beggared belief.

Even Enoch, a freed slave well acquainted with brutality, had never imagined such tales of carnage. He'd heard them from Jacob when he was home on leave, read about them in the *Gettysburg Compiler*. No, trouble seldom took him by surprise, though there *had* been that one time, when he sure as hell should've known what was bound to happen, and he hadn't. He understood, now that he was older and, he hoped, wiser, that love could turn a seeing man stone-blind and a smart one plain stupid.

Which was how he'd found himself, on a hot Savannah afternoon in his sixteenth year, standing bewildered and scared on the auction block, about to be sold away from everything and everyone he knew.

Even after hours jostling over Georgia roads in the back of an ox cart, then spending a long night in an iron-barred cage, shoulder to shoulder with more than a dozen other men, he'd been startled to find himself for sale to the highest bidder.

A slave, livestock, not a man.

Never mind that he'd worked in the fields from sunrise to supper, and then seen his mama Sophie skulking toward the big house in the twilight, summoned by the master. He'd hear her crying on her pallet hours later when she returned.

Never mind that she'd always been subdued the next morning, this good woman, waking Enoch with hurried whispers so he wouldn't miss his breakfast, wouldn't be late getting to the fields.

He'd wanted to tell her the master ought to be the one to feel ashamed, not her, but he hadn't, knowing his mama needed to believe that her son, her only child, hadn't noticed that she disappeared on nights when the mistress was away from home.

So, for her sake, for the sake of what little pride she'd managed to hold on to, he pretended.

Inside, he knew, always, that he was as good as any other man, and better than some. He knew he was smart, for one thing, and he'd never once wished to be anyone but who he was, never wanted to exchange the deep ebony of his flesh for a lighter shade.

No matter what the world saw when it looked at him, or how it treated him, Enoch knew the truth. In his mind, in his soul, he was a free man, with choices he alone was entitled to make.

But mounting the block that afternoon in coarse trousers and nothing else, Enoch finally faced the possibility that he'd been foolish, believing himself to be the equal of any white man.

Maybe it was all true; he was just somebody else's property. Fit for work, but *owned,* nonetheless.

The gravity of all this came home to him as he stood there on that block, his skin sizzling beneath a cold sweat. He was free only in his mind; the reality was, he would probably never see his mother again, nor his beloved Tillie Mae, either.

Enoch refused to let his fear show. He set his jaw, stood up straight and held his head up high. He did not let his gaze fall upon the gathering of white men murmuring below the platform, in their tall hats and their tailored suits. Instead, he fixed his eyes on a faraway nowhere, a place that existed only in his imagination.

The auctioneer had referred to him as a fine worker and said he was fit for any kind of field work.

Enoch had let the words roll right on past him; they weren't anything he hadn't heard before.

No, it was the master's *reason* for selling him away from the only place he'd ever called home, from his mama and his friends and, worst of all, from Tillie Mae, that threatened to buckle his knees. Enoch had loved that sweet gal since he and Tillie Mae were both too little to be of much use to anybody, and that was a good while ago.

Way back, Jethro, Tillie Mae's pa, had given his word, promised that soon as his little girl turned sixteen, she and Enoch could jump the broom, hand in hand, and commence to live as man and wife.

Just a week before that long-awaited birthday, the master's eldest son, Cyprian, had come home from boarding school for a visit, taken a liking to Tillie Mae, and cornered her out behind the springhouse one afternoon, meaning to have his way with her.

Enoch, returning from the field with some errand to carry out, had heard his Tillie Mae crying, begging that white devil to please, *please* let her be, because she was promised, fixing to be married.

Blinded by a fury stronger than any he could remember, Enoch had rounded that shack, hauled Cyprian Wilcox off Tillie Mae and told him to git.

Wilcox had laughed, straightening his fine and fashionable clothes. There would be another time, he'd said. He could do what he liked with Tillie Mae, because his father owned her, and one day soon, she'd belong to him, right along with the plantation house, the fields and every other slave on the place.

"Enoch," Tillie Mae had pleaded, taking backward steps, weeping so hard her face glistened with her tears. "Don't. Don't do nothin' to young massuh —"

"I told you to *git,*" Enoch had growled, his back teeth clamped down so hard his whole skull throbbed from the pressure.

"It seems your man here," Wilcox had told Tillie Mae smoothly, his placid gaze locked with Enoch's blazing one, tugging idly at the cuffs of his shirt as he spoke, "is out to get himself whipped, good and proper."

"Enoch," Tillie Mae said. "I'll do what he

say to do, and then maybe everythin' can be all right again, and we can still git married, and you won't have no whippin' at all." She dashed at her face with the back of one small, pretty hand.

Every word she said had lodged in Enoch like a poisoned arrow shot from a bow. He'd looked into Cyprian Wilcox's smirking face and seen every white man who had ever mistreated a slave, heard his mama weeping in the darkness of their cabin after another nighttime visit to the big house — and something red and wicked and all consuming had burst open in Enoch's mind, like a fiery explosion.

He'd lunged at the master's son, closed his big hands around the man's throat and squeezed. Tillie Mae had screamed, again and again, although the sound barely penetrated Enoch's brain. There were shouts, pounding footsteps, but he barely heard them.

Finally, Wilcox's eyes had rolled back in his head, and he'd gone limp as a kitchen house rag, and Enoch kept right on squeezing.

Strong hands, as black as his own, seized Enoch then, took hold of him from all sides, dragged him off the other man, though it took some powerful doing, it surely did.

He'd struggled in their grasp, because even though Wilcox was lying on the ground, Enoch wasn't through with him. No, sir, not by a far sight.

Even years later, Enoch didn't recall much about the following hours, for it took that red storm inside him a while to burn off. Next thing he knew, he was locked up in a shack out by the slave quarters, ostensibly for his own good, and Cyprian Wilcox's father was there, looming over him.

Enoch lay on the shed's dirt floor at the master's feet.

"You'll look at me when I speak to you," the old man had said. The shed's door crashed shut behind him.

"Get up," Wilcox had spit out, his voice dangerously quiet.

Enoch had stood towering over the master. Saying nothing.

"You very nearly killed my son," Wilcox had reminded him, pacing in that way rich men did, with their hands together behind their back. "Do you realize that?"

Enoch hadn't answered, figuring nothing he said would matter anyhow. Maybe just get him into deeper trouble, if that was possible.

"You are fortunate," Wilcox went on, still seething, still unnaturally calm, "that I am so fond of your mother."

Enoch fought down a fresh surge of anger. He didn't acknowledge the remark, but he didn't look away from Wilcox's long, narrow face, either.

The planter's discourse continued. "If not for Sophie's pleas on your behalf, I would have you not just whipped, but flayed to bloody ribbons." He'd paused then, sucked in a breath, blown it out, as if resigning himself to an injustice that must be tolerated. "Alas, I owe Sophie a debt, and I will honor it by granting her this one favor. You are to be taken to town the day after tomorrow, and there you will be sold. Until then, you are confined to this shed."

By Enoch's reckoning, Wilcox owed his mama a lot more than a favor, but there was a limit to his foolishness, and talking back to a man who could do so much harm to his mother and to Tillie Mae was a risk he couldn't take.

"Have you nothing to say?" Wilcox had demanded, as his exasperation finally got the better of his good breeding.

At last, Enoch had spoken. "I'd rather take a whippin', any kind of whippin', than get myself sold away from the only folks that matter to me."

"Perhaps," Wilcox had said, with a vicious

mildness, "you should have considered that before you turned on young Cyprian and tried to strangle the life out of him. My *son*, and the heir to all my holdings. Do you realize that you nearly crushed his windpipe? The doctor informs us that he will survive, but he may never recover completely."

Enoch hadn't replied, hadn't dared to tell the truth — that he wasn't sorry for what he'd done. Wished, in fact, that he'd killed Cyprian Wilcox outright.

The master had heaved another great, long-suffering sigh and made his way to the door. "I realize, of course," he'd said in parting, "that you could tear down the walls of this shack and attempt an escape. I assure you, solemnly, that if you do that, you will be caught. Then Tillie Mae will get the whipping you so well deserve, and you will witness the punishment. Do you understand, Enoch?"

"Yes," Enoch had responded, beaten down. Holding back the "Massuh" that normally followed was the only act of defiance he could afford.

Two days later, forbidden to see Tillie Mae or his mama to say goodbye, Enoch had been bound again and hauled away like freight.

He'd had plenty of time to think along

the way.

Tillie Mae was lost to him forever and, worse, with Enoch gone, she was at Cyprian Wilcox's mercy once he recovered. He reckoned she'd be turned over to the master's son, like a plaything presented to an ailing child in an effort to speed his recovery. Cyprian would be sure to exact revenge soon as he was able.

As for Mama, well, she was still a fine-looking woman, straight-backed and proud as she dared to be, but she'd be eaten alive from the inside, broken by the loss of her only child.

By the time he'd reached that platform, with its splintered planks puncturing his bare feet, even through many layers of callouses, Enoch had given up all hope. He'd made up his mind that he would simply endure, keep his mouth shut and his eyes down. He was determined to survive.

And yet for all his imaginings back then, Enoch had never once considered that his life could be better than it had been, instead of worse.

That day, however, he'd learned otherwise.

The man who bought him turned out to be a Pennsylvania farmer passing through Charleston on the way home from a visit to a friend. Elliott Hammond had merely stopped when he saw a slave auction about to begin. When the first man went up on the block, Mr. Hammond had found himself compelled to bid.

Elliott Hammond paid the price with money he'd earmarked for other things. After that, he and Enoch had made the long journey back to his small farm outside a town called Gettysburg, where, Mr. Hammond told him, he could work off the price of his purchase, milking cows and tilling fields and with the help of Hammond's Missus, could learn to read and write. Soon as he could sign his name to the proper documents, the farmer said, he would truly be a free man.

At that point, he could stay or go. His choice.

Enoch had been puzzled, not to mention suspicious, but when they finally reached their destination, after many days of difficult travel, Mr. Hammond in a passenger car and Enoch riding with the train's baggage, he'd been struck to the heart by the green rolling hills of Pennsylvania, the sturdy stone farmhouse, the bountiful food, the quiet kindness of the Hammonds and their one son, Jacob, only ten years old at the time.

Enoch had worked hard, been flummoxed

when he was given a room off the parlor for sleeping in, instead of a corner of the barn. The Missus had made him up two sets of new clothes, and he could have all the eggs and milk and meat he wanted. She'd taught him to read and write and figure out sums, too, over the course of many months.

Then one day, Mr. Hammond had told him his debt was paid in full, and he'd be receiving wages from now on. *Wages.* Money of his own, to spend or save as he saw fit. Enoch had hardly been able to credit such a thing.

When he could sign a fine signature — the Missus wouldn't settle for an *X* — Enoch was truly free. He could leave if he wanted, but he didn't.

With the Hammonds, he had every material thing a man could reasonably ask for. People who treated him fairly and who, in fact, treated him like family. And he had books to read, coins in his pocket, plenty to eat. He'd put by most of the money he earned. His plan was to buy Mama's freedom, and Tillie Mae's, too.

Then a runaway slave showed up one dark night, to be hidden in the narrow room beneath the parlor floorboards until it was safe to move on. Enoch had of course heard about the Underground Railroad, but learned from the Hammonds how there were many "stations" in and around Gettysburg, in houses and other buildings in which local families hid runaways. The Hammonds' house was one such station. Local abolitionists worked together to help escaped slaves reach freedom in the North and in Canada.

Enoch had been startled when he recognized the man the next day. His name was Jonas, and he'd grown up on a neighboring plantation, just a few miles from the Wilcox place.

He'd been half-starved and grateful for the breakfast Enoch brought him, all but shoveling the food into his mouth. Enoch had crouched there in the secret room, facing the man, full of questions.

Jonas told Enoch that Sophie, his mama, was dead a full year by then, that she'd taken a fever and slipped away a few days later. Enoch had no blood kin at all now — his father had been a slave on another plantation, a man who'd apparently disappeared soon after Enoch's birth. And Sophie had never been able to have another baby. But at least, Enoch had often thought, she'd never had a child fathered by the master.

Jonas then reported that Tillie Mae had

been sold after the young master tired of her. Nobody knew for sure where she'd wound up, but rumors were that she'd taken the pneumonia and never recovered.

Enoch had listened, stone-faced, and done his mourning in private. But he'd gone right on saving his money as a hedge against an uncertain future. He spent little, buying penny sweets or a book once in a while, but mostly he kept the silver dollars Mr. Hammond gave him when wages were due, hiding them away in old fruit jars he kept in the cellar of the kitchen house. He seldom thought about it.

Now, these fourteen years later, he remained on the Hammond farm, a hired man, there of his own free will. The Hammonds eventually gave him a cabin to live in, which had been the original homestead. Mr. Hammond and his Missus were now dead, six years or more, having died of a fever, but the place was still home. But Mr. Jacob called him a friend and treated him like a brother and Caroline, his Missus, treated him like family. She served him his meals at the table in the kitchen house, right along with her husband and their young daughter Rachel.

Looking back over the long and difficult

road that had brought him here, Enoch knew he would miss Jacob sorely. As he held his fishing pole steady, waiting for a bite, he hoped Missus Hammond would be strong enough to bear the burdens of a young widowed mother. He also hoped that her grandmother, daughter and friends — among them the women living on nearby farms and other members of the town's Ladies' Aid Society — would bring her some consolation.

Enoch had been against Caroline going off to Washington City, all on her own, after they discovered Jacob's fate, but he'd understood her single-minded determination, too. When she wouldn't be dissuaded, Enoch had brought her twenty silver dollars, wrapped in an old handkerchief with the corners tied tight.

At first, she'd said she couldn't take the money.

Enoch had told her how much he cared for Jacob, how good the Hammond family had been to him, treating him almost as kin, and how he had to do whatever he could to help get that dear man back home, where he belonged. Where he could be looked after properly.

She'd given in, finally, and accepted his offer with thanks.

She'd sat herself down and stitched those shining dollars into the hem of her travel cloak, and he knew she was bent on bringing them back and returning them to him.

Come dawn the next morning, Enoch had driven her to town in the wagon, then waited while Caroline carried the child, Rachel, to the front door of Geneva Prescott's house.

Rachel had made a little fuss, wanting to go along with her mother, to help find her papa. The Missus had refused these entreaties firmly but gently, and left the child in the care of her great-grandmother.

After that, Enoch had driven the Missus to the train station, carried her one small bag to the platform, waited while she purchased her ticket. She'd been so brave, standing there in her best clothes.

There'd been more than enough work to keep Enoch occupied once he returned to the farm, his heart heavy, his mind troubled. The place was mighty lonely with just him there, but the cows had to be milked and fed, along with the other livestock, and there were fruit trees to prune, fields to tend, a vegetable garden to water and weed.

He'd missed the dim glow of Missus Hammond's lantern at night, missed the child, too. Most of all, though, he'd missed

Jacob, his true friend. As the war continued to rage, he wondered what future sacrifices it might demand of them all.

All these things and more ran through Enoch's stressed mind that summer afternoon, as he stood on the bank of the creek, pole in hand, hook baited, fishing for an early supper.

Jacob was dead, and that was that. He would grieve as long and as hard as he needed to, but he knew tragedy was the beginning of sorrow, not the end. There was more, much more, to fear.

For one thing, the war, a distant threat before — a thing he and the Missus read about in the newspapers and heard about from Jacob as well as Caroline's friends and neighboring farm families — was closing in on them, drawing nearer to this peaceful farm country with every passing day.

It kept Enoch awake nights, that knowledge. He was strong, there was no doubting that, but how was he, one man, going to keep the Missus and that little girl safe, as he'd promised Mr. Jacob he would? Two great armies were on the march, and when they collided, as they frequently and inevitably did, the destruction would be beyond reckoning.

Enoch knew about various battles. The

Battle of Antietam, with its massive losses, had occurred less than a year before, the previous September. And the Battle of Chancellorsville, in which Jacob had fallen, had cost a similarly overwhelming number of lives. Antietam had been a Union victory, Chancellorsville a Confederate one. And yet, with so many dead on both sides, "victory" somehow seemed a misguided word.

Something else was coming, and soon. He could feel it, lurking nearby, fixing to strike, like a snake coiled in the woodpile.

But this particular threat, whatever it might be, was immediate. Enoch's sense of its approach was an urgency that temporarily displaced even Jacob's passing, even the fear of battles to come.

He rubbed the back of his neck, where the small hairs bristled, scanned the countryside. A shiver slid down his spine, and his stomach lining burned around the meal he'd taken at midday.

Then, from the other side of a copse of leafy trees, oak and ash and walnut, came the piercing trill of a woman's scream. A sudden splashing followed, too loud to be caused by anything but a sizable horse or a mule, made worse by a burst of male laughter.

Enoch threw down his fishing pole and

ran toward the ruckus, his heart pounding hard in his throat, his mind full of old and terrible memories that shoved all present worries aside.

Enoch burst out of the trees, saw a young black woman scrambling down the middle of the creek, stumbling, weighted down by her sodden skirts and the bulge of her pregnant belly. Behind her, on horseback, a man gave chase, whooping with delight at her desperate and obviously hopeless efforts to get away. He was white, this man, but in that moment, Enoch didn't think about the color of his skin.

He thought about evil. About injustice.

Suddenly, Enoch was back on that Georgia plantation, behind the springhouse, watching Cyprian Wilcox trying to force himself on Tillie Mae. With no more caution than he'd shown on that long-ago day, Enoch descended the creek bank, waded into the fast-moving water and stopped the rider by grasping his horse's bridle in one hand.

The girl, sobbing, out of her mind with terror, had reached the creek bank.

The man on the horse looked down at Jacob and laughed.

"You best go on about your own business," he said, blithely adjusting his dirty top hat, a stubby thing with a feather tucked into the band. "And let me tend to mine. This here's between me and her and the fine lady who sent me to fetch her."

The chase and attempt to run the girl down destroyed the last shreds of Enoch's restraint.

Enoch didn't think.

He took hold of the rider's ragged clothes, jerked him down off the horse, then shifted his grip to the lapels of his thin coat. The stranger went under the swift-moving water, came up sputtering, grabbing for his hat as it floated out of reach.

"Release me right now," the man bit out, his greasy hair in dripping tendrils. "That girl is a runaway, and there's a bounty on her head, a good one. She gets away because of you, well, you might find *yourself* on the block."

The threat wasn't an idle one; Enoch knew that. Even in the North, free blacks were snatched from their homes and farms, from the streets of cities and towns, often brutalized in the process and ultimately sold into slavery. If they lived long enough . . .

Enoch held on to the man's lapels and glared into his face. "I reckon this is one bounty you ain't gonna collect, friend," he said.

Water rushed by them, icy cold and thigh-deep. From the corner of his eye, Enoch saw the horse struggle to shore and up the low slope, where it snorted and blew and shook itself off the way a wet hound would after retrieving a hunter's duck. He couldn't see the girl, or hear her, and had no idea if she'd fared as well as the horse, or collapsed from exhaustion or even slipped back down the grassy bank and drowned.

"You think you're white once you get this far North," the man spat, his skin crimson beneath a scruffy beard and weeks of accumulated dirt. "Think you can do as you please!"

"I could drown you right here and now," Enoch said, through his teeth. "And that would please me plenty." He gave the man a hard shake, to make his point. "You get on your horse and ride out of here and our business is done, yours and mine. You come after her again, and I swear by every angel in heaven and every demon in hell, *I will kill you.*"

The slave catcher spat, but he didn't say anything right away. Maybe he'd finally come to the realization that Enoch was twice his size.

Enoch turned, planning to leave him there, then saw the young woman crouched on the bank, shuddering violently, her clothes clinging to her skinny body and the roundness of her belly.

Her brown eyes were enormous in her thin face as she watched Enoch wading toward her. Then her glance shifted slightly, and she screamed, "Look out behind you! He's got a knife!"

Enoch spun around, saw the blade arching toward him, barely deflected it by manacling the other man's wrist in one hand, forcing him to let it drop.

The slave catcher fought hard and was stronger than he looked. The two men struggled, both going under, coming up again, their faces drenched with creek water and an ancient hatred.

Time blurred in Enoch's mind, no longer a sequence of hours and days, weeks and months and years, but a single, eternal moment. There was no past, no future, but only the present — only *now*.

Enoch stood firm, the muscles rigid in his arms, as his hands clutched the front of the slave catcher's coat and pushed his head into the creek, heedless of the rush of water and the bubbles that rose to the surface and then burst.

At some point, the man ceased to struggle, but Enoch didn't realize that until the young woman appeared at his side, clutching his upper arm with both hands and crying out, "Mister, you've got to leave off before you kill that man!"

Enoch's reason returned in that instant, and he hauled the stranger upward, out of the creek, sensing even before he completed the motion that it was too late.

The man's head lolled to one side, and his eyes, though open, were empty of whatever it was that made a body think and move and feel.

The young woman hung tight to Enoch's arm, shifting as she scrabbled to plant her feet on the slippery bed of the creek. Slight as she was, he barely felt her there; her voice was shrill with panic. "He's *dead*!" she said.

Enoch turned his head, looked down into her thin face. "Hush, sister," he said.

She stared at him, her brown eyes huge, the lashes spiked with creek water.

Enoch hoisted the drowned man up and over his right shoulder, his eyes still on the young woman. He saw she was trembling, her breathing too quick and too shallow. She had gumption, that was plain, but she'd all but used herself up.

"Girl," he said, "you take hold of my belt and don't let go till we're out of this water, hear?"

She gulped, nodded and did as she was told.

Together, they slogged to the creek bank, slowed by the strong current and the weight of their wet clothing.

Once they were on solid ground, the girl released her hold on Enoch and crumpled to the grass, winded and, from the looks of her, fixing to go into shock.

Enoch threw his head back and gazed up at the sky for a long moment, gathering himself. He could *feel* those armies coming, almost hear the steady march of boots on the hard-packed dirt of country roads as soldiers in blue and gray alike marched relentlessly onward. Even now, he knew, they were trampling fields, fording streams and rivers, crowding the once-peaceful streets of small towns as they passed through. They were harbingers of chaos, whether friend or foe, with their cannons and their rifles, their wagons and horses and mules, two vast and unstoppable forces, equally fierce in their differing convictions.

Collision was inevitable, and the scale would be catastrophic; the ground would splinter, the sky would rain fire, and the rivers would run red with blood.

And, in a few short hours, the evening train would pull into town, carrying a new widow and a coffin containing the body of a man Enoch had loved like a younger brother. He would be there to collect both.

In the meantime, however, there was the girl to see to, and the slave catcher's remains to bury in some out-of-the-way place. Whatever the provocation might have been, a black man had killed a white man, and even in a free state, there would be hell to pay.

Enoch scanned his surroundings, saw no one; although he knew that didn't mean they were safe, he and the young woman. The body still slung over his shoulder, he moved quickly into the shelter of the trees, dropped his burden into a brushy thicket of undergrowth and covered it with leaves and sticks.

Then he went back for the girl. "Can you walk?" he asked.

She nodded. "I think so," she replied shakily, but she sat with both hands on her distended belly.

Enoch extended a hand, helped her to her feet.

"My name's Enoch Flynn," he said. He was already leading her toward the copse of trees where he'd just hidden the dead slave catcher's body.

"Mine is Jubilee. Folks call me Jubie."

"Pleased to meet you," Enoch answered, once they were out of plain sight. The words seemed inadequate, but there was no time for anything more complicated just then.

Jubie looked up at him, her face dappled by the shadows of dancing leaves. He paused, thoughtful. "That dead man," he said. "You know his name?"

Jubie glanced nervously in the direction of the mound of leaves and twigs, and Enoch noticed a bluish-gray hand protruding from the pile.

A shiver ran down his spine, which he put down to his wet clothing, although he moved quickly to cover the evidence.

"Said he was called McKilvoy," Jubie murmured. She was hugging herself now, and her teeth chattered. Enoch was becoming aware of the time. He still had to hitch up the wagon, drive to town to meet the train, bring young Jacob home to be buried with his kinfolk — and who knew what kind of state Missus Caroline might be in. Not only that, he couldn't leave Jubie here on her own.

"McKilvoy — was he riding alone or with a gang?"

"When he caught me yesterday morning, he said I better not give him no more grief or he'd let all his friends have a turn at me,"

Jubie said. "I never seen any of them, though." She shivered again, hugged herself even harder than before. "You reckon they'll come looking for him."

It wasn't a question.

"Seems likely," Enoch said, eyeing McKilvoy's mount, grazing at the edge of the copse. The gelding was no beauty, bowlegged, mud-brown in color, ribs standing out beneath his dirty hide, but that didn't mean he would go unnoticed. In farm country, most folks knew everyone else's livestock by sight, same as their own. He was thinking aloud when he added, "We'd better hide the horse, too."

Enoch was already leading the horse into the shelter of the trees, taking down the coiled lasso hooked to a strap on the saddle, forming a loop on one end, then slipping it over the gelding's head and knotting the rope so it couldn't be pulled taut.

"Mr . . . Mr. Flynn. I — I don't know what to say. Don't know what happens next. I need to get North, have my baby in a safe place, maybe Canada, and I've heard that there's people who can help me . . ."

"You're a runaway, with a price on your head. McKilvoy's friends will be hunting for you soon, if they're not on your trail already. You come on back and stay in my cabin for the time being. I have a sorry errand to do in town. When I get back, we can figure out a way to keep you safe. That's the main thing. You can tell me your whole story later or whenever you are ready — or not at all. I don't need to know anything more than you are a young woman in need of protection."

With that, Enoch patted the horse on the neck and walked away without looking back. He followed the path of the creek with Jubie beside him and bent to retrieve his fishing pole when he came across it.

4

Gettysburg and Hammond Farm
June 18, 1863

CAROLINE

Feeling exhausted to the point of incoherence, Caroline was relived — and grateful — to see Enoch waiting for her at the train station on Carlisle Street, flanked by Edward Bellows and his son Jonathan.

She and Enoch exchanged a tearful glance, and that was enough. Nothing needed to be said, not here and not now.

The three men bowed respectfully and, just as respectfully, removed the coffin and transferred it to the farm's wagon.

All of them stood there in silence for a moment. Then Bellows and his son gave their condolences to Caroline, backed away, bowing again, and left to return home.

Enoch, still not speaking, placed Caroline's bag in the front of the wagon, then helped her into the seat. She arranged her cloak around her, despite the evening's warmth. Darkness was gradually overtaking the sun's setting light and the gas lamps had been lit.

Caroline finally looked at him, smiling faintly. "Thank you, Enoch."

He nodded. "Whatever you need, Missus Caroline . . . Now let's retrieve the young miss from your grandmother's."

"Thank you," she whispered again.

They drove to Geneva's house on Baltimore Street to collect Rachel, who was waiting impatiently by the front door, her great-grandmother beside her. Rachel threw herself into her mother's arms, alternately yawning and chattering. Once her small bag had been put next to her mother's, they both hugged Geneva goodbye and Rachel scrambled into the wagon front with a boost from Enoch. Caroline followed behind her. Rachel gave a brief glance back at her father's coffin, then hugged her mother tightly. Caroline had decided Enoch would come for Geneva the following day, an hour before the funeral her grandmother had quickly arranged at Caroline's request.

Then the wagon went back to the farm, along Baltimore Street and then the Emmitsburg Road — Enoch, Caroline, Rachel . . . and Jacob.

The following morning, the little Methodist church at one of the other crossroads seemed to sag in the heat, as though its clapboard walls might actually melt away and leave Jacob's poor, rough pine coffin and the group of mourners in the open. After taking the exhausted Caroline and Rachel home the night before, it was so late that Enoch had transported the coffin to the church with the help of the current minister, who brought keys to lock the building. Once the funeral and formal condolences were over, Enoch would bring Jacob back to the farm for one final night.

Reverend Thurgood, long past the days of his eloquence, had returned to the pulpit only because his latest successor was serving as chaplain in some distant Union encampment. That morning, he labored through a lengthy sermon that made little sense to Caroline.

Flies buzzed in through the gaping doors of the church, and bees hovered about the unadorned windows, seeking their way out.

The congregation had dwindled steadily since the beginning of the war. That day, the mourners consisted of a few dozen wives and widows, including her Ladies' Aid Society friends, several restless children, coerced into attendance, as well as a number of local farmers. And one Albert Dunsworthy, a white-bearded old man with an unnerving tendency to shout out the occasional "Amen!" or "Hallelujah!" seemingly at random.

A small cadre of uniformed men occupied a rear pew, every one of them missing an arm or a leg or an eye or in some other way maimed. They had all grown up in or near Gettysburg and knew Jacob and liked him. They, too, had answered the call to volunteer.

Once, they'd all been laughing boys together, full of mischief and bright, vital plans for a future. Now those dreams would never come to fruition. Blissfully unaware that they were of a generation marked for the cruel realities of a conflict they couldn't possibly have imagined, even as rumors stirred in faraway places, they had worked and studied, played rowdy games and fished or swam.

Their fathers had fretted over what they read in the newspapers. Certainly their mothers had worried, sensing the slow but inexorable waking of a great and ravenous monster of war, however remote it might have seemed, here in the peaceful Pennsylvania countryside.

As young men, however, they had begun to hear, with their minds and hearts if not their ears, the summons and thrill of beating drums, faint at first, but always thrumming, thrumming. Intrigued, knowing nothing of cannon fire and cavalries, bloodshed and bayonets — for how *could* they know of such things, these sons of farmers and shopkeepers, blacksmiths and schoolmasters — they had fancied themselves soldiers. They had believed, along with virtually everyone else in this place, that the Southern rebellion would be put down with quick and glorious ease.

Caroline had once believed that, too.

Four-year-old Rachel huddled between her mother and her great-grandmother on the hard pew. Overwhelmed by her grief, Caroline was keenly aware of the need to show a quiet strength in front of her daughter.

From the pews behind theirs, Caroline heard shuffling, whispers, the clearing of throats.

The reverend droned on, never once mentioning Jacob's name. Caroline could only assume he'd forgotten, as he'd forgotten so much else.

Just when Caroline was about to stand up and call a merciful halt to the proceedings, Mr. Dunsworthy intervened.

"For God's sake, Thurgood," he boomed, at a volume that belied his tiny, withered frame, "show some Christian mercy and stop your infernal ramblings before we all die of the heatstroke!"

Caroline did not turn around.

"Hear, hear!" someone else interjected.

"My heavens," her grandmother murmured.

Caroline faced forward again, saw the reverend blinking as though he'd just awakened from an afternoon nap.

"All right, then," he said agreeably. "May our beloved deceased soldier find everlasting peace. Amen."

Enoch stood up and strode purposefully up the aisle, his broad face drawn with grief. The two Bellows boys and their father joined him, looking neither to the right nor the left.

The men in uniform got up, hobbled to the aisle, and stood at attention, three on either side. Those who could salute did so, while the others held their heads high and stared straight ahead.

Enoch took his place at one end of Jacob's coffin, the Bellows boys at the other, their father trailing slightly behind.

Caroline and the rest of the congregation rose as well.

She and Rachel and Geneva were the first to follow as Jacob was carried down the aisle and outside, into the dazzling sunshine.

As she passed the soldiers, honoring their boyhood friend and fallen comrade in the only way they could, she laid back her veil and looked each man in the face, silently thanking him for this tribute.

Outside, another soldier waited, bugle in hand. He'd lost both legs at Bull Run, and been confined to an invalid's chair ever since. Now, in full uniform, trouser legs pinned at midthigh, he raised the horn to his mouth and played taps.

Enoch and his helpers hoisted the coffin into the rear of a wagon.

Caroline, surrounded by women friends, embraced her grandmother as another of the Bellows brood stepped forward to help Rachel onto the high seat.

"You and Rachel must come and stay with me for a few days when the burial is over," Geneva fussed, her plump and kindly face wet with tears. "Let Enoch manage the farm."

Caroline shook her head. "Jacob would want me to carry on as usual," she said.

"But thank you, Grandmother. Thank you for everything."

"Jacob would want you and Rachel to be *safe*," Geneva objected, in an anxious whisper. "You must know we're all in grave peril. Some say the Confederates are moving toward us, even now . . ."

Caroline stepped back, clasping her grandmother's hands in her own. She knew the rumors were probably true; some of her friends and neighbors had already packed what goods their wagons would carry and fled, and others were preparing to do the same.

As sensible as escape seemed, she couldn't bring herself to abandon the farm to marauding armies and scavengers; she had to defend it. That fertile ground, those lush trees, bearing their sweet fruit in late summer, the sturdy house, the sparkling stream, brimming with fish — all of those things added up to more than a home. More than a refuge.

The land had become part of Caroline, in ways she couldn't have explained, even to herself. When she stood very still, she could feel the living force of it rising through the soles of her bare feet, sharing its strength with her. Someday, it would receive her, as it would receive Jacob.

To leave it would be a betrayal.

Again, Caroline shook her head. "Whatever happens," she told her grandmother, "I will not leave the farm." *I will* not *leave the place Jacob loved to the exclusion of all others. The place that is his legacy — and Rachel's.*

"Think of Rachel!" her grandmother pressed.

"I *am* thinking of Rachel," Caroline said quietly. "If I have to send her away, I will, but I hope it doesn't come to that."

"You are as stubborn as your father was, Caroline Prescott Hammond, and your grandfather, too," Geneva said.

Caroline managed a fragile smile. "I know," she said softly.

"Then I shall come to you," her grandmother said.

"I think that's a very good idea," Caroline replied. If the Confederate army was indeed on its way, and if their regiments arrived before the Union forces, who were bound to confront them at some point, it seemed to her that they would occupy the town proper before they began foraging in the surrounding area.

"Very well," her grandmother said. "Send Enoch for me tomorrow, whenever you can spare him. Perhaps sometime during the evening? I will gather my things and will be ready by then. I'm sure the reverend will take me home in his buggy."

Caroline nodded, grateful. She loved her grandmother and looked forward to her company in the trying time ahead.

The other mourners, those who'd offered their condolences earlier, were dispersing, no doubt relieved to return to their own homes.

The remainder of the service was to be private and would take place the next morning; Jacob would be laid to rest in the family plot on the Hammond farm, not in the cemetery adjoining the churchyard. Only Caroline, Rachel and Enoch would be present for the burial, although Ed and Jonathan Bellows who lived close by had agreed to come back to the farm now, to help unload the coffin into the house, then return once more in the morning to load and unload it one final time before it was lowered into the waiting earth.

Enoch set about digging the grave himself after briefly checking on Jubie who stayed hidden in his cabin, exhausted from her ordeal. Mr. Bellows and his son had offered to help, but Enoch had been adamant; this was his job, and he would do it alone.

Now Caroline sat in the rocking chair in the front parlor, Rachel on her lap, and watched numbly as Hannah and Patience and her other friends from the Gettysburg Ladies' Aid Society, along with neighbors, moved past Jacob's open casket, paying their respects through the afternoon and into the evening. Each one brought a gift — a jar of preserves, a pie or a cake, a ham, and Caroline had received these offerings graciously.

Rachel stared steadily at her papa's coffin, which rested on three sturdy wooden sawhorses brought in from one of the sheds for that purpose. She gazed at her father's unmoving face, her own expression never changing, and Caroline waited for the questions that were sure to come. Lanterns and candles burned, lending the scene a soft eerie glow.

When Rachel could no longer keep her eyes open, Caroline carried the child upstairs to her bed, undressed her, then helped her into a nightgown and tucked her in.

"I have questions," Rachel said sleepily.

Caroline, seated on the edge of the bed, bent to kiss Rachel's forehead. "I will answer them," she promised. "Every one."

"Tomorrow?"

Caroline had smiled. "Tomorrow," she replied. "And the day after, too."

Rachel considered the question before giving her answer. "I suppose," she said, with a huge yawn.

"Good," Caroline responded.

"Don't forget." Rachel's voice was small and sleepy.

Rising, Caroline asked, "Shall I leave the door open a little way?"

At Rachel's barely audible "yes, please," she crept out.

Downstairs, Caroline had taken up her post in the parlor again, determined to keep her Jacob company one last night.

When the final guests had gone, only Caroline and Enoch remained, and the silence between them, though thick with sorrow, was soothing.

Hours later, Caroline woke to a pinkish-gold sunrise, still seated in the rocking chair. The lanterns and candles had long since been extinguished, and she was alone with Jacob.

She rose stiffly, went to stand beside him. She smoothed his hair, stroked his bristly beard, and said her final goodbye.

Then she gently lowered the hinged lid and left the room.

"Will Papa go into the ground?" Rachel asked, gripping Caroline's hand very tightly as they stood together in the small grassy cemetery well beyond the orchards, watching as Enoch and the two Bellows boys assisting him carried Jacob's coffin from the wagon bed.

Caroline crouched so she could look directly into her daughter's face instead of looming above her. "Yes, sweetheart," she replied softly.

"Won't he be scared?" Rachel fretted. The poor child was exhausted.

Caroline tried to smile. "No," she said. "You see, the part of him that was your papa, his spirit and soul, is gone."

Rachel brightened a little, although she was still pale, much in need of a long nap. "Is he in heaven?"

"I think so," Caroline said, her eyes scalding. Then, with more certainty, she added, "Yes."

"Will Papa come back and visit us sometime?"

Caroline's throat closed for a moment, making it impossible to speak. She shook her head and said, "No, honey. I'm afraid not."

"Oh," Rachel said, with the resigned disappointment of a child. She was pensive, watching as Enoch, assisted by Harvey and Jonathan Bellows, placed ropes beneath the coffin and lowered it slowly into the loamy earth.

Caroline stood very still, holding her daughter close against her side.

Rachel looked solemnly up at her. "I still have questions," she said sagely.

Caroline could only nod.

They were silent after that. The Bellows boys said their farewells, mounted their mules, tethered nearby, and took their leave.

Enoch took up his shovel and plunged it hard into the heap of dirt beside the grave. The sound of that first rocky clump striking the lid of Jacob's coffin made Caroline squeeze her eyes shut. When she opened them, she saw that Enoch, the most stoic of men, wept as he worked to fill in the grave.

There were prayers, hers and Enoch's.

When she could bear no more of standing still, Caroline clasped Rachel's small hand and led her back toward the house, a quarter of a mile distant.

Enoch stayed behind.

Once she and Rachel were home again,

and Rachel was playing quietly in her room with her favorite doll, Caroline proceeded to the bedroom that was now hers alone and exchanged her heavy black funeral dress for a serviceable calico. She filled the basin with water from its matching pitcher and splashed her face, then took down her hair, brushed it thoroughly, and pinned it up again, in the loose chignon she usually wore.

"Mama?"

Caroline turned to see Rachel standing in the doorway, her beloved doll, a gift from her papa, dangling from one small hand, resembling a figure clinging to the edge of a high cliff.

"What is it, sweetheart?"

The little face was solemn. "I heard a noise."

Caroline crossed to the child, lifted her into her arms. "What kind of noise?" she asked. As her grandparents had done, raising her, Caroline avoided any note of condescension when she addressed her daughter, and she made a practice of listening as closely as she would to an adult.

Now she heard the noise, too, a shuffling at the back door. Then it opened — and Enoch appeared, a woman-child in a ragged dress standing beside him. They came inside, with Enoch supporting her, then decisively shutting the door.

For a moment Caroline was speechless.

"Who are you?" she asked, but she looked at Enoch. The girl's presence, of course, was Enoch's doing.

Enoch quickly explained that Jubie was a runaway whom he had rescued by the river right before he met Caroline at the station. He had not wanted to trouble Caroline in her grief, so he had let the girl stay in his cabin to keep her safe from any slave catchers on her trail.

"My name is Jubie," the girl said politely. She squirmed uncomfortably. "I'm sorry, Missus, but may I use the privy," she said.

"I'll show you the way," Rachel volunteered, cheerful. She was staring at the girl, fascinated.

Caroline said to her daughter, "You will do nothing of the sort." Then to Jubie, she said, "Follow me, please, Jubie."

"Yes, Missus," Jubie replied.

Reluctant to let the girl venture outside in broad daylight, Caroline nonetheless led her along the narrow hallway at the back of the house and through the door, toward the distant privy. It was some comfort that they could not be seen from the road, but they were surrounded by open fields, broken only by the expanse of the fruit orchard.

Rachel, true to form, had not stayed inside the house, as she'd been told. "Mama," she whispered loudly, "who is that young lady?"

"Never you mind who she is," Caroline said. "We'll discuss this later." A pause. "You must not mention her to anyone. Do you understand?"

Rachel nodded, her little face bright with innocent curiosity.

"Mama, you promised I could ask questions."

"*Tomorrow.* That was our agreement."

"There's a baby inside that lady's tummy," Rachel remarked. "When it gets born, can I hold it?"

"*May* I hold it," Caroline corrected automatically.

Rachel waited.

"We'll see," she answered belatedly. "Jubie may not be here when her baby comes."

"But if —"

"Rachel Louise Hammond."

This time, it was Rachel who sighed.

Jubie emerged from the privy.

"There's a place to wash up," Caroline told her, indicating the hand pump near the rear entrance to the house. "Then I'll bring you something to eat."

Rachel ran ahead to the pump, although she was still too small to work the handle.

She was delighted by Jubie, with all her mystery, and eager to be helpful.

Caroline filled the enamel basin kept on hand for the purpose. She smiled, remembering the patience Jacob had shown when she'd first come to the farm, a new bride, used to living in comparative luxury in her grandparents' brick house. Since the task of drawing water, both for the household and the vegetable garden, would fall mainly to her, he'd taken pains with his instructions for how to use the pump. "You'll want to alternate between your right arm and your left. That way, one will be as strong as the other," he'd told her.

She blinked, looked away for a few moments. It was bittersweet, this remembering, and she knew it would be with her always, although she hoped the pain would lessen with time.

Jubie broke into her thoughts with a quiet, "I'm real sorry 'bout your man, Missus. It's a mighty burden to bear."

Caroline swallowed, nodded. "Thank you," she said softly. "Now, let's get you back into the house."

For the next hour, Rachel tagging after her, fairly pulsing with unasked questions, Caroline busied herself seeing to Jubie's needs. She brought a plate of cold ham and boiled greens from the kitchen house, along with a glass of milk, and gave them to the girl, who ate and drank with touching eagerness.

After that, she selected a plain cotton dress, underthings and a pair of shoes from her own wardrobe, and offered them to Jubie. Although Caroline was slight herself, standing only five feet one inch tall, the garments would hang on the girl's scrawny frame, even with her obvious and fairly advanced pregnancy.

"Thank you for your kindness, Miss Caroline," Jubie murmured, wide-eyed, when Caroline brought them to her. She arranged for the girl to sleep in the back room where Enoch had slept before moving into the old cabin beyond the orchard. "I . . . I can't take these."

"Of course you can," Caroline replied kindly. "Besides, they're nothing fancy."

When Enoch returned to the house, he was wearing clean clothes, and his coarse, close-cropped hair was still damp from washing.

Rachel was upstairs by then, taking a much-needed nap, and Jubie was resting on the narrow bed in the back room, having taken a sponge bath and slipped into one of Caroline's nightgowns.

"Sorry I didn't get a chance to tell you about Jubie before, Missus, what with seein' to Jacob." Enoch said, finding Caroline seated in the parlor, reading.

"I understand, Enoch."

"As you know, many a slave has been hidden on this farm. It's been the Hammond way, right along," Enoch said.

Caroline nodded, thinking about several such fugitives whom they had sheltered on their way North since she and Jacob were married. She'd never mentioned the secret room, even to her grandparents, even though both of whom had been abolitionists, and had most likely harbored escaped slaves themselves.

A long charged silence fell, reverberating through the room like a series of silent echoes, before Enoch went on. "I killed a man, Missus," he said. "I didn't intend to, but there was nothing else I could've done, under the circumstances."

Caroline's entire body hummed with alarm, but she didn't speak. Enoch was an educated man, taught by Jacob's mother. She trusted his words.

Slowly, he relayed the entire story, finishing with, "I buried him at the far end of that field we left fallow this year, with his belongings. Problem is, his horse won't stay gone, no matter how many times I run the critter off. He's out there in the barn right now, and I reckon there are some might recognize him."

"Dear Lord," Caroline murmured.

"It's a serious thing, killing a man," Enoch allowed miserably. " 'Especially when a black man killed somebody white. I don't want to bring any trouble to this household. You tell me to move on, and I'll do it, Missus."

Caroline rocked for a while, thinking, saying nothing. She would never blame Enoch for what he'd done; she was sure he'd saved Jubie's life.

Finally, she said, "We will just have to take things as they come." She kept her voice down, in case Rachel had awakened from her nap and crept down the stairs to listen. "Without your help, I couldn't possibly keep this farm going, and Rachel and I rely on your protection, now that Jacob is gone."

Caroline continued, "We are in a most dire situation, you and I. For all that, however, we are also in the midst of a war, one we may very well be caught up in all too soon, if the rumors can be believed."

Enoch absorbed her words, then asked, "What about the horse. The one the slave catcher was riding. The man I drowned yonder, in the creek."

"Well, with luck, the first army to reach us will confiscate him. In that event, of course, the horse will be a minor concern, at best."

Enoch shook his head, as though marveling. "Aren't you afraid, Missus Caroline?"

"Naturally, I'm afraid," Caroline said calmly. "In fact, I'm concerned for all of us."

"Then why don't you take Rachel and high-tail it for safer territory?"

"This land is all I have, Enoch, all any of us has. Generations of Jacob's people — *Rachel's* people — have lived and worked and died here. They have endured every kind of hardship in order to preserve these acres for their children and their children's children. How can I do anything less?"

"Beg pardon, Missus," Enoch said, "but with two armies on the move, it's a fair bet they're going to collide sometime soon. If they happen to meet up anywhere close to here, there's bound to be a fight bigger than anything your husband's ancestors ever had to deal with. Bigger than you and I can even imagine."

Sounding far braver than she was, Caroline said, "Something else might happen — one or both armies might change direction and miss Gettysburg entirely."

"Forgive me for saying so, Missus, but you are one obstinate woman. I can't say I agree with your logic." Enoch straightened. "That little girl of yours? What's to become of her if Lee's army turns up at our doorstep?"

Caroline looked away, then looked back at Enoch, rising slowly from her chair. She had given the matter a great deal of thought, gone back and forth between one option and another, for months. "My daughter is, and will always be, my first consideration," she said. "I will do whatever I must to keep Rachel safe and well."

"Except take her far from this farm until the danger is past?" Enoch ventured, very quietly. He knew he was overstepping his bounds, but he pressed on anyway. "Lots of folks have already packed up and left," he reminded her, "and there are more taking to the roads every day. I heard from Ed Bellows that one of his neighbors, a carriage maker, is planning to leave with his family tomorrow. If you won't take Miss Rachel away yourself, then send her with someone else."

"You know as well as I do, my daughter is only *four years old,* Enoch," she said. "And who is to say she would be safer anywhere else? Suppose she's lost, or falls ill, or winds up in an orphans' home somewhere? We might never see each other again. And she's all I have left of Jacob."

Enoch sighed. "Then why not place her in your grandmother's care, send them both to relatives in Philadelphia or even Baltimore?"

"You know my grandmother would never leave here," Caroline replied, having already considered the possibility.

At last, Enoch recognized the truth of Caroline's words. His suggestion that Caroline take Rachel and go North to safety were futile.

Caroline also knew his concern was genuine. He was, with Jacob and her grandfather both gone, her only protector. She liked and respected Enoch, and she trusted his judgment, too, but she was Rachel's mother, her only living parent, and the responsibility for her child's well-being was hers and hers alone. Now, having weighed one set of dangers against another, repeatedly and in all possible depth, mentally debating the question from every conceivable side, and getting nowhere with the endeavor, she had no choice but to listen to the always-reliable voice inside her: her intuition.

"My grandmother has agreed to join us here on the farm. Will you please hitch up the wagon and drive into town to fetch her and her belongings? She promised to be ready by nightfall."

"I'll do that," Enoch said.

5

Hammond Farm
June 20, 1863

JUBIE

"Can I stay in my bedroom?" Jubie asked plaintively, when Enoch informed her of Mrs. Prescott's imminent arrival. They were at supper in the kitchen house, eating by the dim glow of a single lantern. "Or will Missus Prescott be needing that?"

Caroline didn't tell her about the secret room under the floor — and why Jubie might eventually need to hide there. Geneva had her own room here at the farm, but Caroline wasn't planning to discuss household arrangements just now.

"Yes, you may," she said vaguely.

The rest of the meal passed in silence. Jubie ate her cornbread and beans with undisguised eagerness, followed by the peach preserves intended for dessert.

When they'd finished, Enoch left the kitchen house to harness the mules to the wagon again, while Caroline filled two washbasins from the kettle of hot water steaming on the cookstove. Jubie simultaneously cleared the table and cajoled Rachel to eat just one more bite, then another.

"I can help you around the house, Missus," Jubie said earnestly. "I know I can't go outside in the daylight, but I can clean and look after Miss Rachel when you're busy with other things. That's what I did before — took care of the mistress's house and the children."

"Thank you for the offer, Jubie," Caroline said, "but the most important thing is that you stay safe. You don't have to keep to your room all the time, as long as it's just the family here. But as much as possible it would be wise not to leave the main house."

"You go on and see to Miss Rachel now," Jubie urged. "This day was a sad one, all right."

"Yes, it was." Caroline studied the young woman beside her. Jubie was practically swallowed by her borrowed dress, and she seemed ready to give up on the too-big shoes Caroline had lent her.

Caroline had a great many questions she wanted to ask about the life Jubie was fleeing, not the least of which concerned her pregnancy and when she might give birth, but now did not seem to be the time.

Perhaps, like the previous runaway slaves the Hammonds had sheltered over the years, Jubie would be spirited away soon by another member of the secret network of antislavery volunteers who served as single links in a long chain of rescuers, careful to remain strangers even to each other.

On the other hand, given the increasing likelihood that the fighting was coming closer, it was entirely possible that Jubie would be with them when she went into labor, and that required preparation.

She touched Jubie's arm briefly. "Get some rest yourself now, Jubie." Then, gathering a yawning Rachel into her arms, she carried her back to the main house and upstairs to her room, with Jubie not far behind.

A single lamp burned in the parlor beside Caroline when she heard the team and wagon and went out to welcome her grandmother. In the light of the moon and the millions of stars spangling an indigo sky, she saw Enoch help the elderly woman down, somehow managing to tip his battered hat to her in the process.

Spotting Caroline, her grandmother bustled toward her. "Oh, my darling, thank you for waiting up on this long day. I've brought the last of your grandfather's medical supplies in case we need them in the future. Or perhaps the Ladies' Aid Society could use them in an emergency," she said, with a gesture toward the wagon. The back was piled high with indiscernible goods. "Mr. Flynn has agreed to unload them right away." Caroline smiled a little, weary and heart-sore though she was. Had it truly been just that morning that she'd seen her husband buried?

Her grandmother had always referred to Enoch formally as Mr. Flynn, which was not surprising, considering that Caroline had never heard her speak of her own husband in any way other than Dr. Prescott, the doctor, or simply, your grandfather.

"That was wise of you," Caroline said. "We may need supplies if the fighting comes our way."

"Oh, it will, my dear," Grandmother said in confidential tones. "It's all the talk of the town."

Ominous words, Caroline thought, grateful for the distraction of simple duties. It seemed like weeks now since she'd sat with her friends as they sewed uniforms and

132

made bandages to be shipped to the troops. They always shared the latest news they had heard in town or garnered from letters sent home by their husbands and sons.

Enoch had unloaded a sizable trunk, presumably containing clothing and other personal necessities, and he paused on his way to the house to ask where he should put it.

Caroline directed him to the empty bedroom upstairs, just down the hall from Rachel's.

"Don't forget about the bandages and sutures, Mr. Flynn," Grandmother said. "There's laudanum, too, along with morphine and ether, so be sure you don't leave them where my great-granddaughter might find them."

Enoch gave a chuckle. "Yes, ma'am," he said, moving on. "Reckon the whole lot ought to be put away in the cellar under the kitchen house for the time being."

A while later, after they'd each had a cup of tea in the parlor, Caroline helped her grandmother up the stairs and then settled her in the room that was Geneva's whenever she visited. She lit the oil lamp on the table next to the bed.

Earlier, Caroline had filled the water

pitcher on the bureau and set out a towel and washcloth, along with a small bar of soap.

"Do you need anything else, Grandmother?" she asked. She'd planned on telling her about Jubie, who was happily shut away in Enoch's old room downstairs, but she didn't have the strength for a long discussion tonight.

Her grandmother lifted the edge of the spread and attempted to peer beneath the bed. "If there is a chamber pot," she whispered, "I will be quite comfortable. At my age, I have no desire to go traipsing out to that privy of yours in the dead of night."

"You won't have to do that," Caroline said, amused. Then, imagining the old woman on her knees, attempting to retrieve it, she backtracked, knelt and pulled it within easy reach of the bedside.

Grandmother was used to an indoor commode, complete with flushable water, but she seemed undaunted by the humbler facilities of the farmhouse.

Just as Caroline was about to leave the room, her grandmother hurried over to embrace her.

"I am so sorry about Jacob, my dear," she said, with tears in her voice. "It is a dreadful thing to lose a husband, especially so young."

For a long moment, Caroline allowed herself to cling to her grandmother, the way she had when she was a child, lonely for her own parents and sister who had perished in a fast-moving epidemic. Her grandfather had died of a sudden infection only a year before, so she knew her grandmother's grief was still palpable. Caroline's throat was thick with emotion, rendering speech nearly impossible. Their embrace said it all.

Grandmother patted the back of her head tenderly. "Perhaps it is too soon to say so and I know it is hard to imagine," she said soothingly. "Grieving takes time. But one day you *will* meet another good man, maybe even remarry. You will be happy again."

Caroline drew back, sniffling a little, shaking her head. "I doubt I'll ever meet someone who will love me as much as Jacob did. Besides, how can anyone be happy, ever, with this dreadful war devouring every good thing, like some insatiable beast? What will be left — to any of us — when — if — all this killing finally ends?"

Her grandmother smiled gently, but said nothing.

"Before I went to Washington City, I *thought* I knew so much about war, what a travesty it is, what an evil — I was even a little smug, I think. What else was there to know? After all, my own husband was a soldier. I read the newspapers and rolled bandages and collected food and blankets for the cause. I'd seen men and boys come home on crutches or in invalid's chairs, some of them missing arms and legs, others blind or mute or deaf, and still others, like Jacob, in coffins. All that evidence, and yet I never truly credited the true cost."

Caroline paused, overwhelmed by weariness and sorrow and pure dread of all the horrors yet to unfold. "But now I feel the cruelty and loss, so painfully. I miss my Jacob." She put one hand over her mouth, lest she howl like an animal caught in the cruel teeth of a trap. "What I saw in Washington City — the horrors and carnage. Nothing could have prepared me." Long moments passed before she dared to go on. "Dear God, Grandmother, how can we live with what we are? With what we do? How does one go about raising a child in a world like this one?"

Geneva Prescott's expression was tender, patient. "We do whatever is before us, Caroline, the next right and sensible thing. That is the challenge and the sacrifice needed to preserve this great country."

Despair sharpened Caroline's response. "Only because we have no choice," she whispered fiercely.

"But we *do* have other choices, my dear. We can turn our backs on all that we know is right, sit ourselves down, fold our hands and allow wickedness to go unchallenged and therefore to prevail. We can run away and hide. *Or* we can stand our ground and fight inequality to our last heartbeat, knowing that if we perish, we have done all that we could, and others will carry on, just as those who came before us have done."

"It's just that kind of talk that has brought us all to this mayhem," Caroline objected, barely able to keep her voice down. "With all due respect, Grandmother, you might not speak so if you'd seen and heard —"

Geneva took both of Caroline's hands in hers and squeezed them with surprising strength for a woman of her years. "I am a doctor's wife," she reminded her, "and, war or no war, I have seen things so unspeakably terrible that I would not dream of planting the images in another person's mind, knowing the burden they are upon my own. *But,* Caroline, I have also witnessed miracles. I have looked on in wonder as shattered minds became whole, and bodies knit themselves back together, bone by bone, tissue by tissue. I have marveled at the sacredness and mystery of death, and I know it to be no less a part of life than green and flourishing youth. I do understand."

Her grandmother had always been practical by nature, and quite forthright in her opinions, though unfailingly kind. But, like many women of her privileged background, she had also been pampered and protected, first by her parents, and then by her husband. She didn't cook or clean; in her circles, those tasks were the lot of servants. Even in small, modest Gettysburg, she'd had household help for as long as Caroline could remember, employing a series of hired girls, some the daughters of local farmers, though a number of them, mostly Irish, had been imported from places like Baltimore or New York. And, although she was well-read, having made good use of Grandfather's vast collection of books, Geneva's education had consisted of the delicate female arts, such as proper etiquette, at table and elsewhere, letter writing, painting dreamy landscapes in watercolors, stitching intricate samplers, learning to speak both French and Italian and, finally, achieving reasonable competence at the harp and the organ.

"Are you saying," Caroline ventured, having weighed these facts and found herself no less startled than before, "that Grandfather subjected you to the suffering of his patients?"

"Your grandfather 'subjected' me to nothing. If he'd had his way, I would never have set foot in his surgery or accompanied him on calls. But there were times — so *many* times, particularly in the early years — when he clearly required my assistance, whatever his objections might have been. I wasn't *about* to sit before the parlor fire, read poetry or stitch some silly motto onto a piece of cloth while he attended the sick and the injured. I learned to suture wounds, set broken bones and deliver babies, and I dare say I acquired a great many other useful skills, too."

Caroline's admiration for this woman, always considerable, expanded greatly. "I never knew," she said, astonished and, somehow, comforted. Grandmother's absences, especially when Caroline was at school, hadn't particularly registered with her. She supposed now that she'd assumed Geneva had been at social functions . . . And, of course, her grandparents had always protected her.

"Suppose you die, too?" Caroline asked, her voice small and tremulous. She had lost so many loved ones: her mother and father, her cherished sister, Grandfather and now, of course, Jacob.

"Oh," Geneva said, "I assure you, I will . . . eventually. So will you, and all the rest of us. In the meantime, obviously, we must do our part, trusting that our best efforts will suffice."

Caroline could not speak for the tightness of her throat.

"Now try and get some sleep. You have had a long and sorrowful day," Geneva said.

The two women embraced once again, and parted for the night, to try and find what rest they might, in preparation for yet another uncertain tomorrow.

There had been no real opportunity for Caroline to explain to Geneva the reason for Jubie's presence since her grandmother arrived the evening before. Jubie stayed in the back bedroom the next morning and Enoch brought her meals. At Jubie's own request, Caroline had given her some mending to do to keep her busy.

Caroline was surprised by Rachel's silence.

She had planned on telling Geneva about Jubie that day. But first both she and Enoch knew they had to make Jubie familiar with the Hammond Farm's hidden room — a "station" on the Underground Railroad, like the better-known McArthur's Mill and the Dobbin House. "We all need to be prepared," Caroline told Jubie. "We can't be sure who might come here or why."

First they led her into the parlor. Then Enoch bent to remove a small rug from beneath the old harpsichord and opened the trap door. He instructed Jubie to take the steps down, a steep and treacherous flight. And once she saw the hidden room itself — dark, dusty, with no shortage of spiders — she had to make an effort, not entirely successful, to disguise her reaction. Jubie was not impressed with the space.

But, as Caroline and Enoch let her know when she'd carefully climbed out, this dreadful little place could save her life, as it had saved the lives of others. Ideally, she wouldn't need to spend any time there at all, but if there *was* some sort of risk . . .

Showing Jubie the secret room was prophetic, as it turned out . . .

Barely two days later, in the middle of the afternoon, Jubie was sitting with Rachel in the back bedroom, carefully staying away from the windows, just as she'd been instructed.

Caroline heard at least two horses in the farmyard — the stomping of hooves, the slap of reins — and heard them approach the back door. Peering outside, hidden by the curtain, she saw two unfamiliar men, not uniformed or distinguishable in any particular way. She decided to wait for Enoch to address them, confident that he would've heard them, too, and make his way to the house as quickly as he could. He did, and they dismounted; from his gestures, she saw that he'd invited them to tie their horses to the porch rail. He raised one hand, signaling that he'd be back, then hurried to the door, which she opened a scant few inches. "Slave catchers," he whispered. "Looking for McKilvoy. And Jubie. I'll stall them while you get her downstairs."

Caroline gasped, the kind of weak-heroine reaction she hated in books and plays, but she couldn't stop herself. "Yes," she whispered back, then shut the door and ran for the bedroom.

"Jubie!" she muttered in the girl's ear. "Down to the hiding place! Quick!"

Jubie didn't ask questions but immediately ran to the parlor and, throwing back the small rug under the harpsichord, she made her way down to the secret room in less than a minute.

Caroline replaced the rug, then went to collect Rachel, who was sitting on the bed, paging through an illustrated book. "Sweetie," she said, "you stay with me. There are two men here, and if they come to the door, you say *nothing,* you understand?"

"But Mama, where's —"

"Not a word," Caroline emphasized. "I'll tell you later." Not that she had any idea *how* to explain this to her young daughter, but . . .

There was an impatient pounding at the side door. Caroline took her time getting there.

With one arm around Rachel, Caroline pulled open the door and stared at the two scowling, disheveled men standing there, while Enoch, wearing an expression of indifference, stood a foot or so behind them.

"Missus Caroline," he said. "These here are Mister, uh, Smith and Mister Jones."

Smith and Jones? It was all she could do not to roll her eyes.

"What can I do for you gentlemen?" she asked.

The one introduced as Smith bowed in a manner she could only describe as mocking and said, "We're looking for a friend, ma'am. Named McKilvoy. Last we heard, he was in this vicinity. Near your farm. On business."

"Oh? What kind of business?" she asked despite Enoch's frown.

"Looking for some . . . personal property his client lost."

"You mean a *slave*?" Once again she couldn't resist, and Enoch frowned even more heavily.

"Uh, that could be," Mr. "Smith" replied.

Caroline shook her head. "I'm sorry, sir. We know nothing about this. If you'll give Mr. Flynn an address where we can reach you, we'll be in touch if we learn anything."

Then so-called Smith turned to look at Enoch and back to her. "He can read?"

"Yes, dammit!" Caroline rarely if ever swore. "Mr. Flynn runs this farm. Now, if you'll leave, we can return to our tasks."

More exaggerated bows, then they collected their horses and rode off.

Ten or so minutes later, Enoch was back at the house "Oh, Missus," he said ruefully. "Best not to provoke them."

She sighed. "I know. I hope I didn't create any further problems." She paused. "I think Jubie should remain in hiding for the rest of the day."

Enoch agreed. "I'll keep an eye and an ear out, in case they return."

Rachel stepped out from behind Caroline then. "Are those *bad* men?" she asked in a hushed voice. "Bad enough," Enoch replied.

Later that day, Geneva was telling Caroline about some of the recent Ladies' Aid activities in town. Caroline decided it was time Geneva learned about the secret room. And about Jubie . . .

Early evening, once Rachel was in bed and while Enoch brought Jubie her meal, Caroline told Geneva she was harboring a fugitive slave who had arrived the day she brought Jacob home from Washington City. She took Geneva to the hidden trap door. "Careful," she warned. "These steps can be dangerous."

She helped her grandmother down the steps, walking behind her, holding her around the waist.

There was a faint light below, coming from the lantern on the small table. Jubie was lying on the mattress beside it.

"Grandmother, I'd like you to meet Jubilee, known as Jubie. And Jubie, this is Geneva Prescott."

Jubie struggled to a sitting position. "How'd you do, ma'am?"

"I'm doing very well, Jubie." Geneva

looked at her sharply. "How far along are you?"

"Seven months or so." She paused. "Maybe eight."

Geneva nodded. "Do let me know if you need any advice. My husband was a doctor, and I've helped birth more than a few babies. And make sure you get as much rest as you can."

Caroline smiled, a bit grimly. "We're asking Jubie to stay down here for a short time until a certain . . . risk is gone. So she doesn't have much choice other than to rest."

"Please, Missus Caroline, is there something else I can do to help? I'm finished with the mending you gave me."

"Do you know how to knit, Jubie?" Geneva asked.

"Yes, ma'am. Simple things."

"Then I'll bring you some yarn and you can start on a baby blanket tomorrow."

6

Hammond Farm
June 30, 1863

CAROLINE

At first they straggled past the farm gate, half a dozen at a time, seemingly worn-out young men in dusty blue, riding weary horses. A few doffed their campaign hats to Caroline, who stood on the front veranda, Jacob's old squirrel gun out of sight but at the ready, in case there were looters among them.

Enoch waited beside the road, buckets at his feet, and several soldiers paused to water their thirsty mounts, while others drank deeply from the ladle offered, or filled their canteens. When the pails were empty, Enoch trudged back to the well for more.

It seemed a poor brand of hospitality to Caroline, for these were, after all, Union troops, and presumably friendly. She had

147

no idea what regiment they were in or where they were from, but Jacob might have fought alongside any one of them. Surely, in her place, he would have offered the wayfarers sustenance, invited these comrades to rest themselves and their horses in the shade of the trees lining the creek.

But her Jacob was dead, now buried in the peaceful plot on the low hill beyond the orchards. She would never see him again, never touch him, or laugh with him, or watch him swing a delighted Rachel onto his shoulders.

She was raw with this knowledge, wanted only to wander like some despondent biblical figure, covered in ash, wailing and tearing at her clothes. She wanted to rage at the heavens, shake her fist at God, weep and, finally, come to terms with the realization that deep down perhaps she had not loved Jacob well enough. Not, at least, in the ways a wife should love her husband.

Not in the way Jacob had loved her.

Alas, there was no time for such scouring of the soul; the soldiers passing by on the road in front of her were proof of that. The war had, at last, come to this quiet place in the Pennsylvania countryside, and though she prayed there would be no confrontation on these grounds, her deepest instincts warned her to prepare and, certainly, to be on her guard.

It seemed odd, perhaps even shameful, this wariness, because these men clad in Union blue were protectors and certainly not the enemy. They served a cause Caroline revered, and yet they were strangers to her. Sadly, the color of their uniforms did not guarantee their individual integrity and honor; men of low character might well be among them.

She had heard stories from her friends and neighbors of perfidy on the part of common soldiers on both sides — chicken coops raided, milk cows led away or even slaughtered for meat, crops ravaged or ridden down, orchards stripped of their fruit, rail fences used as firewood, houses and barns burned, evidently for sport. Such offenders were punished if caught, the perpetrators marked as "bummers," to be despised and scorned, but, all too often, they escaped the notice of their superior officers, if not entirely, then at least until after the damage had been done.

In the more notorious instances, compensation was promised by Mr. Lincoln's government. However, with Union resources constantly dwindling under the enormous cost of putting down the rebellion, payment was slow in coming, if it came at all, and was never enough to fully restore what had been lost.

Worse than the unruly rank and file were the stragglers, the renegades and deserters, drifters with no allegiance to either side, and certainly none to God or their fellow human beings. Though the majority of these were simply petty thieves, stealing chickens and eggs when hungry, shirts and trousers from the wash line in someone's backyard when their own garments grew too ragged to wear, others were more like wild animals than people. She had heard from friends in town and from neighbors that, apparently without conscience, they did unspeakable things, and Caroline feared them. Why, only two days ago, Cecelia McPhee, a farmer's wife from half a mile down the road, had told her about a man who'd broken their windows and rummaged through their house. He'd made off with money hidden in a bureau — and left them a threatening note, scrawled on a kitchen wall.

These were dangerous times. For Rachel's sake, for that of her grandmother and Enoch and Jubie, and, of course, for her own, she must be vigilant in all circumstances, including the ordinary kind, when one might logically expect to be safe.

Today, for instance.

The weather was hot, and the slanted roof of the veranda afforded little relief, capturing the thick humid air of that final day of June. The heat pressed in on Caroline from every side, and she longed to wade barefoot in the stream, or sit beneath a shade tree, reading or stitching., At the moment, she couldn't help wondering if such simple pleasures would ever be hers again.

Just that morning she'd met in town with her friends Hannah and Patience; Enoch had taken her in the wagon, since he had supplies to pick up. During that hour's visit, the three women had shared the latest news about General Lee and his troops' movements; they'd heard that the Confederates were on their way, in fact might already be in Cashtown, a few miles to the west. They'd discussed their own hopes — and more significantly, their fears.

As the war continued, life was bound to grow more difficult, and in its aftermath there would surely be little time for indulging ordinary whims. Whatever the outcome of this dreadful conflict, there would inevitably be hardships to face, losses to mourn, suffering to be endured.

As Caroline stood on the porch, the creak of the door alerted her to the presence of another person.

"Caroline," her grandmother said quietly. "You've been out here in this awful heat long enough. Come with me to the kitchen house, and we'll have tea."

Caroline turned to face the older woman. "Tea? On a scorching day like this?"

Geneva Prescott, clad in a plain black skirt and a white shirtwaist, her cherished cameo brooch pinned at her throat, seemed completely at ease. "Yes," she said, firmly but with a note of compassion in her voice. "Tea has medicinal properties, you know. It's soothing in any kind of weather." She paused, drew a soft breath, and exhaled. "Besides, Rachel may be frightened by the passing troops, and she needs her mother. I've tried to distract her, but she can't seem to settle down."

Caroline glanced at the squirrel gun resting against the porch railing and sighed. The weapon would be of little use against a single marauder, let alone an army, but it had given her the illusion of taking some definite action to protect her home and family.

She followed her grandmother into the kitchen house, where the air was marginally cooler. Rachel stood waiting for her, wide-eyed and worried.

"Mama," she said, in a small voice, "I hear more soldiers coming. I hear their boots on the road."

Caroline held out her arms to her child, and Rachel ran to her, flung herself into her mother's embrace. "I think you've been peeking out the window," she told the little girl gently. "You saw those men stopping to water their horses out by the gate, didn't you?"

Rachel nodded rapidly. "There are more of them coming, Mama. I think Jubie hears them, too. From her . . . new room."

At the periphery of her vision, Caroline saw her grandmother stiffen slightly and then nod.

Caroline gave the child a reassuring squeeze. "You mustn't be afraid," she said softly. "Those soldiers you've seen are part of the same army as Papa was. They are our friends." *Dear God, may that be true.*

"Jubie told me there's *another* army, though," Rachel insisted, still worried. "A different one from Papa's. An enemy army."

"Grandmother has suggested we go to the kitchen house and have tea," Caroline said, hugging her daughter once more before setting her on her feet. "I think that's a very good idea."

Rachel's trepidation gave way to excitement. "May I have tea, too, Mama? Like you and Grandmother?"

"You may," Caroline said. Together, Caroline and Geneva followed Rachel. By then, she was dashing across the yard, paying no attention whatsoever as the first band of men rode on, only to be replaced by another, larger group.

"Rachel seems to be taking her father's death in stride," Geneva remarked, as they walked through the lush grass toward the kitchen house.

Caroline's eyes smarted, and she swallowed before answering. "I'm not sure she understands. She's so young, and she's used to her papa being away."

Geneva's gaze strayed to the road, where Enoch was gathering the buckets as they were emptied by the thirsty soldiers and horses, and gave a shudder. "I fear we shall all see more death than we can credit, and soon. We must prepare ourselves, and Rachel, too."

"I know," Caroline said.

Geneva forced a bright smile and squeezed Caroline's shoulders. "Let us drink our tea and think of happier things, while we can."

It was nearly sunset when the wagons drew up at the gate, one after another, in a long line. Supper was through, and the dishes had been washed and dried and put away. A tired Rachel had already gone to bed.

Enoch stood in the yard, just beyond the path of lantern light falling through the open door of the kitchen house, and Caroline and her grandmother soon joined him.

A rider bent to lift the gate latch, then rode through, leaving the rest of the party behind. Another mounted man closed the gate after him.

"Now, you ladies have to stay calm," Enoch said. "These here are Yankee soldiers, not Confederates. They mean us no harm."

Caroline watched as the rider came nearer, showing no signs of urgency. She hoped Enoch was right and they had nothing to fear, but the stories were there in her mind, just the same.

The man sat tall in his saddle, his blue uniform dusty but still impressive, with its brass buttons, gold trim and epaulets. It struck Caroline that there was something faintly familiar about him, although she quickly discarded the idea as wishful thinking.

He wore a campaign hat, rather than the kepi cap, common to regular soldiers and, as he drew nearer, he removed it respectfully, revealing a head of thick hair, dark as ebony.

Caroline felt a second jolt of recognition in that moment; this was the man who had helped her find Jacob, back in Washington City.

His smile flashed white in his sun-browned face as he spotted Caroline. "Well, Mrs. Hammond," he said. "It is a fine surprise to see you again."

"You know this man?" Geneva whispered.

"Yes," Caroline said, searching her mind for his name. Their acquaintance had been a brief one and she had been understandably distracted, having searched for her wounded husband for so many hours, without success.

It came to her as he dismounted. Captain Rogan McBride.

He was a captain, and he was kind. That much she knew. An acquaintance of the nurse Bessie who had befriended Caroline, given her food and a place to sleep, helped her arrange for the delivery of her letter.

"Captain McBride," she said, with a brief nod of acknowledgment.

He walked toward them, his hat still in his hand, but stopped a short distance away. "How does your husband fare?" he asked.

It was Enoch who answered. "Corporal

Hammond is dead." he said. His voice was flat and a little hard. He had been glad to provide water for the passing men all that day, as long as they stayed on the other side of the gate, but now he sounded cautious.

"I'm sorry to hear that," the captain replied, still keeping his distance. "I'm sure he was a good man and a fine soldier."

"He was," Caroline said. She wasn't afraid of this man, but his presence was cause for concern. "Do you have business here, Captain McBride?"

"I do," McBride said, glancing back over one shoulder at the line of wagons. "Indications are, there's going to be fighting close by. My men and I will be moving out right away, but we need a place to leave these provisions. Frankly, I was hoping whoever lived here wouldn't mind keeping an eye on them for a day or two."

"*How* close by?" Geneva asked. "This fighting you mentioned, I mean?"

Captain McBride gave a weary sigh. "Our men are in Gettysburg now, and camped all around it as well. The Rebs are holding back for the moment, but they're here, with more following."

The news was not unexpected — she'd heard it from her Ladies' Aid Society friends — but a chill coiled in the pit of Caroline's stomach just the same. She felt a short, violent urge to race into the house, gather Rachel in her arms, and flee North.

It was a foolish thought, and it shamed her a little.

Weeks ago Enoch had tried to persuade her again. When it was rumored that Robert E. Lee and the Army of Northern Virginia meant to invade the North, an exodus had begun. Terrified, people abandoned their homes and businesses, farms included, piled their families and belongings into whatever conveyance they could procure, and had gone.

Caroline had adamantly refused to leave back then. Settled and defended by Jacob's ancestors, the farm rightly belonged to him and, eventually, to Rachel. She had worked hard on this land since her marriage, and she'd had no intention of leaving it to be picked over, inside and out, occupied by soldiers, and finally left to fall into ruin.

She felt no differently now, though she sometimes wished, in her darkest moments, that she'd held firm when her dear friend, Susannah Kronecker, left for New York where she had family. Susannah planned to stay with them until the war was over and her husband, an army surgeon, came home.

Before her departure, Susannah, who had

no children of her own, had begged Caroline to let her take Rachel along. At first, Caroline had steadfastly refused, but Susannah was persistent, and thoroughly trustworthy. Rachel would be safe in that great and distant city, with Susannah and her kin, and she would lack for nothing.

Except, of course, her mother.

Caroline reconsidered, but then Rachel's pleas to be allowed to stay had been heartbreaking, and Caroline had given in to her daughter.

"What's in them wagons?" Enoch asked, bringing her mind back into focus.

"Food, mostly," Captain McBride answered mildly. "Some blankets, medicine, a few tents."

"No guns?" Enoch pressed. "Or ammunition?"

The officer shook his head. "Nothing like that."

"What if the Rebs get here before you come back for these goods? What are we supposed to do then?" Enoch asked.

McBride looked tired, although his voice had lost none of its strength. "No," he said. "If the Confederates get past us somehow, and come here, they will indeed take the wagons and everything they contain, along with whatever else they can scavenge from the place." His gaze moved to Caroline for a moment, then back to Enoch. "If that happens, don't try to stop them. Hide if you can, and don't come out until you're absolutely certain they've gone."

Enoch blinked, drained of bluster, and looked at Caroline with a question in his eyes.

"I have no objection," Caroline said, "as long as the wagons aren't visible from the road."

"Thank you, Mrs. Hammond," McBride said, with a slight inclination of his head. "You're behind Union lines here, and we'll do our best to see that you remain so."

Caroline nodded in circumspect agreement.

Enoch remained cautious. "This farm," he said evenly, "is all the Missus has. She's a recent widow, with a child to provide for and keep safe, and she's loyal to the Union . . ."

"I understand, Mr., er —"

"Flynn," Enoch practically barked. "Enoch Flynn."

At that moment, the captain surprised everyone present. He put out a hand to Enoch, and said, "You have my word, Mr. Flynn."

Minutes later, the gate was open and the

wagons rolled in, passing between the house and the barn, bound for the field hidden behind the blossoming orchard.

wavers rolled in, passing between the barn
and the barn, exiting ... the field fenced
behind by the summer wind.

7

North of Gettysburg
June 30, 1863

BRIDGER

Bridger Winslow of the 6th Georgia Regiment raised his field glasses, peered through their scratched lenses, and gave a low whistle as the long thread of blue sprang into bold relief, widening into a river of men, thousands of them, marching in formation, rifles and muskets at their shoulders. And that was just the infantry.

"You ever seen so many blue-bellies in one place, Cap'n Winslow?" asked Lieutenant Reed, who'd been hovering at Bridger's side for the past several minutes.

Bridger took in the trail of heavy artillery, the cavalry, the supply wagons, ambulances, mules and spare horses. As the first of the Federals filed into the small Pennsylvania market town and began to break ranks, others dispersed to make camp in the surrounding countryside.

By nightfall, he thought, there'd be as many supper fires burning outside Gettysburg as there were stars in the sky. Or, at least, it would seem that way.

"No," he answered, after a moment had passed. "I haven't."

He knew Reed had been hoping for a different reply; a few comforting words, perhaps a jocular reassurance that their own Army of Northern Virginia truly was invincible, as General Lee believed, even in the face of a horde like the one flooding the rich valley below.

But Bridger was a seasoned soldier, and he knew better than to underestimate the foe, for all that he'd seen Union forces make monumental mistakes, especially under the cautious leadership of George McClellan. Beloved of his troops, if not Lincoln, Mc-Clellan's Commander in Chief, "Little Mac" had missed chance after chance to run Lee to ground, corner him and crush any possibility of Southern independence for years, if not decades, to come.

McClellan had since been relieved of his duties, recently and very briefly replaced by Joe Hooker. Now, according to the latest intelligence, the Union army was headed by

Major General George Meade. The Yankees clogging the streets of Gettysburg and spilling into the surrounding countryside were under his command.

These Yanks were an industrious lot, pitching tents and tearing down rail fences to be sawn into firewood, digging latrines, unloading wagons. When viewed with the naked eye, they resembled a massive hill of blue ants.

Seen through the field glasses, those near enough for Bridger to make out clearly were individual soldiers — some solemn, some distracted, some pale with fear. Others, though, were laughing and joking with each other as they worked, like guests at a lawn party, the newest recruits, then, with little or no experience of actual warfare.

Bridger felt a pang of sympathy for them, enemies though they were, as much as he felt for his own men. A lot of them were mere boys who could have no way of knowing, outside of the stories they must have heard, what it was to undergo that first hellish baptism of fire and blood. To come to that initial, utterly horrific realization that war was no schoolyard game of king-of-the-hill, as they had probably imagined.

There would be no going home to supper at day's end, to chores and lamplight and kinfolk, no falling into a familiar bed to dream the innocent dreams of boyhood.

"Sir?" Reed said, interrupting Bridger's glum reflections.

Bridger lowered the field glasses again and turned to the other man. "What is it, Lieutenant?"

Reed reached into his dusty tunic, with its sweat-stained underarms, pulled out a thick packet, extended it with a hand that trembled slightly. "With the Yanks putting on a show like they are," he said, with a barely perceptible quaver, "I near forgot about this here letter. A few mail bags came through on a supply wagon a little while ago, and I was around for the sorting out. Saw your name and said I'd bring this to you personally."

"Thanks." Bridger accepted the battered envelope, examined it briefly, distractedly. He noted the familiar Winslow crest embossed in the upper left corner, the smudged but elegant sweep of his younger sister's handwriting.

Amalie. Always the diligent but sometimes deceptive correspondent.

Bridger loved his sister, and looked forward to her letters, although reading them was often an emotional expenditure he could not afford. She usually included uplifting quotes, mostly from her favorite poets, humorous anecdotes about people they knew, the best and worst aspects of a recent sermon and accounts of increasingly rare social events.

The reality of his sister's life, he knew, was usually hidden somewhere between the lines, and he sensed that she didn't want to distract him with worries. But she also found a careful way to keep him abreast of what was happening at home and in the fighting close by.

She filled him in on the state of the house, how their father and the few slaves still at Fairhaven were managing. How the water supply was holding up and whether it had been contaminated. Which friends and cousins were listed as missing, captured or dead in the local newspaper or on the bills posted regularly at the railroad station.

Amalie wasn't his only source of information, of course. He knew that because of the Northern blockades, most necessities and nearly all once-common luxuries, such as coffee, books, fine writing paper and sweets, were sold at black-market prices, when they could be found at all.

Amalie, just shy of eighteen, pretty and unspoiled and primed since infancy for a spectacular social debut, with all the requisite beaus, ball gowns, cotillions, garden picnics and house parties, had to be profoundly disappointed. The world she'd known all her short life had vanished, leaving her unprepared for hardship.

Although Bridger privately considered the tradition of dressing young women up in silks and satins and herding them into the marriage market to be worse than backward, he ached for Amalie. He could do nothing about her circumstances, but he did send her money whenever he was paid — since the plantation's income had declined. And he reminded her often that this war, with all its devastation and privations, would end at some point.

At least, it would end for some. Bridger wasn't counting on a future of his own, not with all those Yankees in plain view, any one of whom would be happy to put a bullet in his head or a bayonet through his heart. He watched, grimly fascinated, as Meade's advance forces made themselves at home in the distance.

"I sure would like me a pair of them good Yankee boots," Reed observed, reminding Bridger of his presence — and the thwarted but not entirely abandoned plans of a good many Confederate soldiers to scavenge Gettysburg for badly needed shoes before the battle commenced, which would likely be the next morning.

Bridger indulged in a brief, bitter smile, thinking that if there was one thing he wanted from those Yanks, it was a halfway decent cup of coffee, hot and rich and laced with sugar. Maybe it was his imagination, since the smells of wood and tobacco smoke, human sweat and horse manure were all-pervasive, but he thought he caught the pleasant aroma of the stuff, just the same, already brewing over the freshly laid campfires below.

On the Confederate side, even the most basic rations were in short supply, if there were rations at all. He knew the rank and file foraged for much of what they ate, and what the army called coffee tasted more like last night's dishwater than the rich, chicory-tinged cup the more prosperous Southerners had come to favor.

"You reckon General Lee will want to engage?" Reed asked. "Some of the men say Longstreet will be against the idea. And Longstreet ain't the only one with objections, the way I hear it."

Because of his family's elevated social position, Bridger was acquainted with both Lee and Longstreet, and numerous other high-ranking officers. Longstreet was anything but a coward. Like General Lee, he was a prudent man and a master strategist. The difference was that Lee hated to pass up an opportunity, *any* opportunity, however risky it might be, and he seldom did, even when counseled to do otherwise.

Already a legend, grudgingly admired even by some in the North, all but worshipped by his troops and the folks back home, Robert E. Lee was a man of dignity, intelligence, honor and restraint. If there was, in Bridger's mind, a trace of arrogance in him, he hid it well. He lacked the eccentricities of some of his best officers, such as the late Thomas Jackson, whom he had addressed fondly as "Tom" in relative private and "General Jackson" in public. He might spare a wistful smile when he heard the man referred to as "Stonewall," but he never used the moniker himself.

Lee was the classic Southern gentleman, well-spoken and erudite. He was married to one of George Washington's stepchildren, and was the son of the legendary Light-Horse Harry Lee, later disgraced but still revered as one of the greatest soldiers America had ever produced. Along with the graces of his mother's illustrious family, Lee had inherited a considerable portion of old Harry's fearless audacity. When there was the slightest chance of furthering his military agenda, Lee could be utterly ruthless, driving his men, half-starved, barefoot and battle weary, far beyond the limits of their considerable endurance.

Nine times out of ten, he got results.

"Yes," Bridger said, replying to Reed's question at long last, "I believe General Lee will choose to fight."

Reed seemed to deflate a little at this, but he recovered quickly enough. He was a good soldier, with plenty of courage, and Bridger liked him, although he knew little of the man's history, and that was fine, because it was plenty difficult to see a comrade struck down in battle. Seeing a friend killed was far worse.

Even if that friend happened to be a Yankee, like his old military prep school friend, the now Captain Rogan McBride.

Bridger didn't believe he could end McBride's life, should they find themselves confronting each other on the field; the bond between them, formed in their teens at boarding school and during visits back South at his family home, ran deep.

Then again, it was easy to make such an assumption at a distance, not yet embroiled in the fierce atmosphere of combat. He hadn't seen Rogan in several years, but wondered before each battle if this would be the one where they'd be forced to fight each other. Perhaps his friend had changed and become embittered by the inevitable losses and sorrows of war.

Was Rogan down there someplace, thinking similar thoughts?

Remembering better times?

Bridger and Rogan, sharing a room at St. Luke's, the military prep school on the outskirts of Boston, had formed an uneasy alliance in the early days of their acquaintance, coming from markedly different backgrounds as they had. Both had been forced to attend the school, and both had felt aggrieved about being sent away.

Bridger had essentially been exiled to his mother's people, Northerners all, a few months after her death from pneumonia, when his natural wild streak had, in his father's opinion, rendered him incorrigible.

Rogan, too, had been banished from New York City, where he'd been born to an Irish housemaid, out of wedlock, and raised to stay out of everyone's sight, including his mother's. He'd never met or seen his father, a stable hand — or so he'd been told — at another wealthy home. When Rogan was seven, Rosie McBride had apparently exhausted whatever maternal instinct she'd possessed in the first place, marched him to the nearest Catholic church and left him there, seated in a back pew, with a heel of bread and three copper pennies to sustain him.

By his own account, shared only after six months or so, when he and Bridger had finally put their initial wariness behind them, the young Rogan had sat for hours, waiting for his mother to come back for him, the way she always had before. Rosie would be in a temper for a while, he'd reasoned, but when she calmed down, she would show up, tearful and apologetic. She'd wrap him tightly in her arms, call him her darling boy, and then take him home to their attic room in her employer's enormous brick house. There, she would fuss over him, offering him sweets, no doubt purloined from the pantry, making promises and pleading for his forgiveness.

This time, however, she did not return.

The next morning, Father Hennessey, who looked too young to be a priest, in Rogan's opinion, had found the boy asleep on a pew and promptly delivered him to the nuns, who had surrounded him like a flock of peevish crows, pecking at him with their questions. What was his name? How old was he? Who were his parents? Where did he live? How long had he been left alone?

Bewildered, he'd accepted a hot meal and then been placed in a room full of other children, some older and some younger, where he was handed a slate and a piece of chalk. In the meantime, Father Hennessey had gone in search of Rogan's mother, only to return the following day, shoulders stooped, face glum. Miss McBride, he'd told the nuns, while Rogan listened outside his office door, had relinquished all claim to her son. She'd finally found a husband, she'd explained, and her betrothed was not inclined to take on another man's brat. This, Rosie had told the priest, was her chance at a fresh start, and she wasn't about to let past mistakes stand in her way.

And that was that.

Rogan stayed on with the nuns and Father Hennessey and the other children, mostly orphans, a few crippled in body or mind, others simply unwanted, as he was. At first, he'd missed his mother and continued to hope for her return, but that soon passed. At the master's house, he'd had to stay in the attic most of the time, hidden away like the shameful secret he was, but at St. Swithin's Home for Children, his view of the world expanded considerably. He'd learned to read and write and cipher and, after class and on Saturdays, he spent hours outdoors, running and climbing and playing games with the others. He'd had enough to eat for the first time in his life, slept in a bed all his own, and even though his clothes were secondhand, they fit him. He had shoes that didn't pinch and a warm coat and mittens for winter.

He was happy enough, insofar as he knew what happiness entailed.

He'd excelled in his studies at St. Swithin's and behaved himself — until he turned ten and, suddenly restless, ran away for the first time.

That was the beginning of a cycle. Periodically, the cops rounded him up, along with the other street rats, slapped him around a little and hauled him back to St. Swithin's, where the nuns renewed their efforts to put the fear of God into him and Father Hennessey shook his head sadly and told him he must learn to resist temptation in all its forms.

Finally, when Rogan was fourteen, and neither boy nor man, he'd reached the far borders of even Father Hennessey's remarkable patience. By then an accomplished thief, Rogan had been arrested after smashing a shop window and helping himself to items within.

This time, he received more than a boxing of his ears and a series of lectures on the wages of sin and the horrors of Purgatory. He was brought before a judge and given a choice between jail and military school. Luckily the good Father had somehow finagled a place at St. Luke's Military Preparation Institute in Boston and a scholarship for him.

He chose St. Luke's, albeit reluctantly, for the school, as he'd suspected, was strict, a repository for the unmanageable and recalcitrant sons of wealthy families. While he didn't have a family, wealthy or otherwise, Rogan certainly met and exceeded the other two criteria.

There was something comforting to Bridger in remembering his friend Rogan. It was a way, he reckoned, of verifying that even if death came for him, in an hour or a day, *he had lived something of a life.*

And Rogan McBride had been part of it. On some school vacations, Rogan had even come home with him to Savannah and visited with Bridger's father and sister. Then, after four years at the Preparatory Institute, they had gone their separate ways, Rogan back to New York to study law, Bridger home to Savannah, to the Winslow plantation, where he raced horses, engaged in drunken brawls, fought duels, chased women and rapidly earned himself a just reputation as a wastrel and general no-account.

He was the despair of his father, the classic second son, the born rebel bent on scandal and ultimate destruction.

As such, Bridger was well suited for war, if not exactly for the Southern cause. When the conflict finally erupted in April of 1861, he had been among the first to enlist in the ragtag Army of Northern Virginia — after he'd seriously considered taking up with the North, instead.

Growing up with slaves, he had come to hate slavery, euphemistically referred to as "the peculiar institution" by most Southerners, and he hated it still. He was not fighting to uphold the practice, he was fighting to defend the ground in which his mother and elder brother and all his Winslow ancestors were buried.

Now, here he was, about to join a battle he sensed would be pivotal, fiercer and bloodier than any he'd fought in before. A certain amount of introspection seemed in order.

He might never marry, or sire children. Never again raise hell in a brothel, play chess with a skilled opponent, enjoy a rich meal or ride one of his fast horses for the sheer joy of it.

Whatever his destiny, he would meet it bravely, and with honor, at Gettysburg.

If he perished in Pennsylvania farm country, so be it. He was, after all, a soldier.

Should he survive the encounter he knew was coming, he would be grateful for the sweet privilege of drawing breath beneath the bright blue arch of the sky, sleeping under a blanket of stars and awakening to the first light of morning.

Time would tell.

In the meanwhile, Lee was on his way, with Longstreet and others, dogged in his intention to press his hard-won advantage and drive deep into Northern territory, determined to take Philadelphia and Baltimore and, ultimately, the capital. In Lee's view, once they fell, Lincoln would be compelled to recognize the Confederate States of America as a free and sovereign nation.

Bridger, who had seen something of the North, with its great, densely populated cities, its sprawling farms and busy factories, its vast networks of railroads and telegraph lines, was not as optimistic as his fabled commander.

Lee had firsthand knowledge of Northern

resources himself, having studied and eventually taught at West Point, with a great many other accomplishments following. Lee's military record was, in fact, so impressive that Abraham Lincoln had originally offered him full command of the Union army.

He had refused that honor, with dignity and probably a degree of regret, explaining to the President that he could not raise his hand against his home state of Virginia. Subsequently, at the request of Jefferson Davis, Lee had taken charge of Confederate forces and, despite smaller numbers, untrained troops, scarce and crumbling railroads, inadequate bridges and poor supply lines, resulting in an almost constant lack of food, medicine, weaponry and ammunition, he'd claimed victory after victory.

The general was undeniably a brilliant strategist; his training as an engineer, as well as a military leader, served him well. Lee was fiercely intelligent, but it was his boldness Bridger admired most, his mastery of the surprise attack. When he struck, he did so with the deadly stealth and swiftness of a copperhead.

For all that, Lee had been extraordinarily lucky, too.

And Bridger Winslow, an experienced

gambler, knew just how fickle fortune could be. Every winning streak came to an end, sooner or later.

Before turning away to attend to his responsibilities — seeing to the care, comfort and instruction of his company — he took one last look at the ominous pageantry playing out in and around Gettysburg.

Was his friend there somewhere in the midst of the blue-coated horde, preparing for battle? There was no way of knowing, of course, and even if Rogan was present, the odds against their meeting in the chaos of combat were minimal, given the size of both armies.

And what of the sudden prickle at Bridger's nape, the rise of the small hairs on his forearms?

No believer in signs and portents, he dismissed the sensations as fear, a sensible emotion in the circumstances and, less admirably, a certain sense of anticipation.

After all, he'd always relished a good fight.

8

*Seminary Ridge, near Gettysburg,
June 30, 1863, 9:00 p.m.*

ROGAN

Campfires flickered in the night like fallen stars as Captain Rogan McBride and his small Yankee detachment reached the outskirts of Gettysburg. They were bone-tired to a man, their bellies so empty they ached, their tongues dry with dust, their horses faring no better.

For the last several months, Rogan had served as a regimental quartermaster, though the post was meant to be temporary. He'd been assigned the duty after the previous job holder had fallen at Antietam the previous September, mainly because he had a strong organizational ability and an aversion to the pilfering of rations.

It was a relatively safe occupation, his unlucky predecessor's fate notwithstanding, but Rogan disliked jockeying bags of beans, crates of hardtack, barrels of flour and such, like some transient storekeeper. He knew the task filled a vital purpose but, at heart, he was a soldier, and he longed to return to cavalry duty.

Growing up in an orphanage in New York City, he'd never ridden a horse, though he'd seen plenty of nags pulling carriages, street cars and peddler's carts, pitiful plodders, the lot of them, tormented by flies, their ribs jutting under their quivering hides, their heads lowered. He'd wanted to set them all free, turn them loose to graze in some peaceful pasture, far from the noise and the whip and the long days spent pulling, pulling.

It was later, at St. Luke's, when he was fourteen, that Rogan finally learned to ride, as part of his academic program. His sympathy for the poor beasts he'd seen hauling their heavy loads along city streets grew into a quiet passion for horses, and this affinity rapidly blossomed into skill.

When the war began, he'd left his two-man law practice in New York City and enlisted in the United States Army as a second lieutenant, cavalry, and thereafter advanced steadily to his present rank of captain. He had fought with all his might, somehow living through every skirmish and battle, though he'd lost several horses, and mourned them still, at times even wishing he'd died in their stead.

Rogan took no pleasure in bloodshed, in the severing of limbs, the shattering of skulls and spines and kneecaps. He did not love war, with its incipient horrors.

He did, however, enjoy the outdoor life. And inactivity didn't suit him. If he wasn't thinking, he was *doing.* Of course he abhorred the inevitable killing and maiming of battle, but there were parts of military service that appealed to him — secretly, he reveled in the challenges of close combat, when everything was at stake. Liked the way his mind seemed to rise above itself at those times, entering a state of concentration so keen that it was as if his brain took over the whole of his body in an instant, overriding conscious thought and guiding every motion, every maneuver of horse and rifle and sword arm.

Tonight, however, his thoughts weren't solely on the approaching melee, or the strange, deadly grace he'd experienced on other battlefields — and nowhere else.

Instead he was oddly preoccupied with the young widow whose farm he'd left a few hours before.

Mrs. Hammond. Caroline.

When he'd first met her in Washington City, a short while back, he'd noticed that she was unusually striking, with sandy hair and hazel eyes, but these details had slipped his mind soon enough, for she'd been worried and anxious at the time, desperate to find and console her wounded husband. He was one among thousands of sick and injured soldiers billeted all over the capital. They lay suffering in army tents, on the pews and floors of churches and in private homes, as well, and though some placement records were kept, they were haphazard at best. There were simply too many casualties pouring into the city, day and night, to allow for total accuracy.

Many of these unfortunates had to be shuffled from one place to another, as cots and floor space became available, usually courtesy of the recently expired. Those with lesser wounds or milder illnesses were either patched up and sent back to their regiments or handed a blanket and directed to a vacant lot or someone's lawn, with hasty assurances that they would be attended to "presently."

All of which obviously meant that Corporal Hammond might have been just about anywhere. Hammond's lovely wife had remained determined, despite the odds she faced. He had examined records, asked exhaustive questions of clerk after harried clerk, and finally tracked Corporal Jacob Hammond, 11th Pennsylvania, to a certain cot in a certain hospital tent.

Subsequently, he'd led Mrs. Hammond to her husband's bedside. She'd offered distracted thanks, and Rogan had left her there and gone back to counting bullets and beans.

She'd lingered in his thoughts for a long time afterward. And that was a peculiar thing; he'd seen so many wives and mothers, sisters and sweethearts come and go, in the capital and on far-flung battlefields, where conditions were even worse. He'd been of whatever assistance he could, yet he couldn't recall a single one of their names or faces.

Then, this very evening, in the course of his duties, he'd encountered her again.

A strange coincidence — one he might follow up on, should he successfully guide his men to victory in the fighting to come.

He sighed. Tomorrow or the next day, or perhaps the day after that, there would be more men killed or crippled, more coffins built and stacked and, eventually, shipped home.

Fools, Rogan reflected, as he swung down from the saddle and set about attending to his current mount, a sorrel gelding he had come to love, even though the animal, dubbed Little Willie somewhere along the way, belonged to the US Army, not to him. *We're all fools, the lot of us, Yanks and Rebs alike.*

Thoughts of Rebels inevitably led to thoughts of his best friend from military school, Bridger Winslow, the one man he truly trusted, other than Father Hennessey.

He wondered, as he always did on the eve of battle, if he and Bridger would finally meet again, this time on horseback, in the thick of the fighting, swords drawn.

Much as he'd like to see Bridger, he prayed it wouldn't happen before this damnable war ended, or at least moved to neutral ground, if there was such a thing. He had no intention of raising his hand against a friend, and he was all but certain Bridger would feel the same way.

Still he was troubled by the possibility, not because he was afraid of Winslow, but because, in all that chaos and confusion, even a moment's hesitation on his part could easily cost other men their lives.

After settling his horse for the night, Rogan joined his men at the campfire nearby.

Coffee was brewing, and someone had set a kettle of leftover beans in the embers to warm up.

Army food, Rogan thought, with wry disparagement. A man had to be hungry as a bear just out of hibernation to eat it.

If he managed to get through the fighting tomorrow, let alone the rest of the war, he vowed he'd never eat another boiled bean or bite into another piece of hardtack. No, sir. He'd live on fried chicken and juicy beefsteaks to the end of his days.

In the meantime, though, his choices were definitely limited, and it had been a long time since breakfast.

Seated away from the fire, lest they roast themselves before the beans were ready, the other men talked in hushed voices and looked over their shoulders at regular intervals, as if they thought Johnny Reb might take a notion to creep out of the evening darkness to cut their throats or skewer them on a bayonet.

Rogan's companions greeted him with nods as he joined them. One or two murmured "Cap'n" in deference to his rank.

The youngest among them, a lad named Hastings, had drawn supper duty, hastening forward to stir the beans with a wooden spoon at intervals, and backing off quickly.

Hastings claimed he was nineteen years old, but Rogan gauged him closer to sixteen, probably a generous estimate.

Alderman, a butcher from New Jersey, cooked when there was meat, which wasn't all that often. Tonight, the older man bent over a letter he'd received months before, reading it for what must have been the hundredth time.

As far as Rogan knew, no one had ever asked Alderman about the letter, who it was from or what it said, or why Alderman read it over and over, until it was practically transparent, almost luminous in the glow of the firelight. Oh, they wondered over all the whys and wherefores, all right, but each and every one of them held his peace. A man's mail was his own business, his to share or keep to himself, as he wanted.

Another fellow, Josiah Pickering, who hailed from the state of Maine and spoke with the corresponding New England accent, brought out his mouth harp and blew a tune so slow and somber that it sounded like a lament.

And it probably was.

Pickering, a lobsterman by trade, with a wife and a passel of children, was stalwart in the light of day, but he tended toward homesickness when dusk fell and supper rations were doled out. Unlike Alderman, Pickering got plenty of letters; when the mail caught up with the intended recipients — always an uncertain process — his portion was always generous.

By now, the fisherman had so many thick envelopes from home, faithfully penned by his clearly devoted wife and children, that he had to store them under the seat of the supply wagon he drove, or he'd have had no room in his rucksack for his kit. As most soldiers did, he saved every last letter, and he'd once told Rogan that he liked to grab them up in bunches because it felt like holding home itself in his hands.

Rogan rarely received mail — an occasional missive from Father Hennessey and, now and then, from some loyal female supporter of the Union. Usually, the women were strangers to him, having secured his name through the offices of some ladies' service organization; they used good stationery and undiluted ink, and the paper was always perfumed.

Finally, there was his law partner, Mr. J. T. Archer, who was diligently keeping the doors of their practice open in Rogan's absence, or so he claimed. He wrote accounts of cases won and lost, described clients, agreeable and otherwise, with a slight emphasis on the latter, and kept Rogan up-to-date on the latest public and private scandals, especially those involving judges he disliked.

Rogan read the letters without much interest. Although he had worked with the man for nearly three years, he'd soured on him when Archer put up three hundred dollars in gold to avoid conscription.

Rogan might have been able to overlook even that, much as it galled him, if Archer hadn't made off hand remarks such as, "Let the micks and all those other babbling foreigners go marching off to war. It'll get them off the streets into the bargain."

Remembering, too late, that Rogan was himself a "mick," albeit an educated one, Archer had reddened slightly, but he hadn't retracted the observation.

Rogan had refrained from breaking the smug bastard's nose, though just barely.

He'd suspected the letters were Archer's way of making sure Rogan came back to the law practice at war's end.

Rogan had worked hard to earn his degree, and harder still to establish himself as a respectable man of law, but army life had changed him in ways that went far beyond the obvious tribulations of watching other soldiers die. Of nearly meeting his own demise more times than it might be prudent to reckon up.

It wasn't that he enjoyed sleeping on the ground, not under *these* circumstances, anyway, sweltering in summer and half freezing to death in winter, or wearing the same uniform for weeks, even months, at a time. He was fed up with lice and flies and the disgusting stink of open trenches roiling with the shit and piss of whole regiments, and he doubted he'd ever sleep through a single night for the rest of whatever life remained to him, without waking up at least once.

Rogan reined in his thoughts, accepting a mug of the sludge the army presented as coffee from Pickering, who sat at a manly distance, watching him with an expression of mild concern.

"Something particular on your mind tonight, sir?" Pickering asked.

Rogan liked Pickering, and he wasn't about to burden the man with disturbing analogies or, for that matter, fatuously confide his fears and worries about the future. He wasn't sure he wanted to return to his previous lawyerly profession and all that went with it — spending his days shut up in cluttered offices and stuffy court-rooms, pandering to people he could barely tolerate. Like Archer.

Instead, he hedged, a skill that had served him well since childhood, when he'd often had to talk his way out of trouble. "Do you ever wish you'd lived a different life, Pickering?" he asked.

Pickering smiled wearily, shrugged one beefy shoulder. "You know what they say about wishin', Cap'n," he said. " 'Wish in one hand and shit in the other and see which hand gets full faster'?"

Rogan gave a raw chortle and shook his head. "What I meant was —"

The words fell away. What *had* he meant?

"I wouldn't be a soldier if I could choose again," Pickering said thoughtfully, and his smile was gone, replaced by a wistful expression, fraught with yearning. "But that's all I'd be willing to change. I work hard, and it seems as if that old boat of mine needs patching up every time I turn around. But running my line, hauling in my traps, emptying the catch and then setting them again, well, that's a fine way to make a living. Come nightfall, the lamps are lit, shining so bright in the windows of our little house that I can make them out from clear down at the harbor. My Sarah is there waiting for me when I come through the door, smiling sweetly as any angel in heaven, and our youngsters press in on me from every side, all of them talking at once." Pickering paused then, drew in a long breath and released it. "The whole place smells of supper."

Rogan listened, taking in the lobsterman's words, letting them weave pictures in his mind. He saw it all there, and it made him ache for Pickering, for the loved ones awaiting his safe return and, briefly, for himself, too.

"I don't reckon I'd want to change anything either, if I were you," he finally said.

After that, there was little conversation. Just thoughts about the battle that awaited them. Rogan ate along with the other men, then left to check his horse once more before washing up as best he could and dropping, fully clothed, onto his bedroll.

Hours crawled by before Rogan slept, his mind full of the impending battle. To distract himself, he focused on the widow Hammond, hiding all those supply wagons on her modest farm, alone except for the hired man and an old woman. If things went wrong, and the Rebs took the victory, if he fell to bullet or blade, what would become of her and the others?

The images — of Pickering's contented

home, of Caroline Hammond on her farm — followed him into his dreams. For a little while, there was no war, no battle looming just the other side of sunrise.

Then the nightmares came, as they always did, like swarming things with tentacles and claws, and Rogan jolted bolt upright on his bedroll, soaked in sweat, fighting for breath.

Pickering and the others snored in their beds of grass and stone, undisturbed.

Rogan got up, his breathing still ragged, and spent a quarter of an hour walking off the effects of the nightmare. When he'd calmed himself sufficiently, he sat down on his rumpled bedroll and gazed up at the vast sky, spangled with stars, waiting for morning.

9

Hammond Farm
July 1, 1863

CAROLINE

It was around four o'clock in the afternoon when the first deafening boom shook the ground beneath her feet and caused the very air to shudder around her. She'd heard from Enoch, who'd spoken to George McPhee, a nearby farmer, that the fighting was on Seminary Ridge, north and west of town, and that the Union army was gathering in force. Another volley followed, then another.

Caroline, weeding the vegetable patch, straightened her back and looked around, half expecting to see the earth split wide open at her feet.

There had been intermittent gunfire throughout the day, the crack of rifle shots, the low thunder of muskets, muffled by distance and the weight of the summer's heat, but this, she knew instinctively, was no random skirmish, as the others must have been.

No, this was heavy artillery. Even Rachel, who had been playing nearby, chasing a ball between rows of carrots and parsnips, seemed to sense the far greater import of this onslaught of noise, for she shrieked and covered her ears.

Enoch suddenly came racing over, bursting from the cornfield at a dead run, skin glistening with sweat, eyes round with fright, shouting, "Get in the house! All of you, *get inside,* now!" Still some distance away, Enoch hollered more frantic instructions, but Caroline couldn't make them out, because just then another eruption of cannon fire broke the reverberating silence of the initial blasts, drowning out his words.

Caroline stood motionless, as if frozen, unable to move, when Rachel suddenly started to scream.

Go to her, Caroline commanded herself. *Go to your child!*

Jubie shot to the side door from the bedroom of the house where she was now staying, to see where everyone was.

Geneva, who'd been seated in the shade of the giant oak tree, leaped to her feet in alarm, dropped her mending on the grass, and headed toward the house.

Caroline finally recovered enough to scramble toward Rachel, and when she reached her child, took her hand and together they ran inside.

Rachel trembled as she clung to Caroline. "Hush, now," Caroline whispered. "Mama's here. You're all right, sweetheart. I promise, you're all right."

As the cannon blazed only a few miles away, Caroline prayed silently for her little girl's protection. She felt every blast jolt up from the ground, rising through her knees and thighs to her torso, causing her heart to quake within her.

Then the cannons had gone blessedly silent, but the pulse of their blasts could still be felt, a vast, silent echo of deadly power.

The three women and Rachel stood still in the parlor as more volleys rolled across the fields to assail their hearing. Each new explosion became part of the those that had come before, until it seemed to Caroline that every thunderstorm in the history of the earth had ventured forth from its own time to coalesce in Adams County, Pennsylvania.

Then came another lull.

Enoch had finally reached the yard, and

he waited in the doorway, chest heaving, fighting for enough breath to speak.

Minutes later, he'd recovered his equanimity.

"You all stay inside the house," he said. "I'll go see to the animals and be right back."

No one questioned the order. Caroline sank into her rocking chair. Rachel lowered her arms from around her mother's neck, but stayed settled wearily in her lap.

The firing resumed, as Caroline had known it would, and went on for some time, rattling the glass in the windows and causing the few ornaments on the mantel and side tables to wobble, though the sturdy stone walls of the farmhouse buffered the noise a little.

Caroline waited, gently rocking Rachel, although each time the child drifted off, the cannon started up again, waking her.

Geneva had seated herself in the chair that had been Jacob's, her face pale, her fingers entwined in her lap, her gaze fixed on something only she could see.

Jubie paced, fretful, holding her distended belly in both hands. She stayed well away from the windows, a caution that had been emphasized by all.

No one spoke.

It was Enoch, returning from the barn during one of the intermittent periods when the guns weren't firing, who broke the silence.

"That poor ol' milk cow is plenty riled," he said. "We'll be lucky if she doesn't dry up on us."

Out on the road, horses thundered by. "Cavalry," Enoch said, in a low rumble. "In a big hurry to get to the fighting, it looks like."

"Union or Confederate?" Caroline asked very quietly. She thought Rachel had fallen asleep, but saw no point in carrying the little girl upstairs to bed; the next round of cannon fire would only wake her again, and she'd be more terrified than ever, finding herself alone.

"Confederate," Enoch replied, remaining at the window. "Good thing they're in such an all-fired rush to get themselves blown to bits on the battleground. Doesn't look as if they're of a mind to stop by and pester us any."

Not now, anyway, Caroline reflected, too numb to be afraid. "Thank God for that," she said aloud.

A moment later, Jubie vanished to her room in the back.

Enoch remained standing on the cold

hearth, his back to the mantelpiece, and took in the room. "Why don't I get you some water, Missus Geneva," he offered.

Geneva smiled wanly and fluttered one hand. "I'm quite all right," she said, determinedly cheerful. She turned bright eyes to Rachel, who was awake now. "You come over here and sit with me, darling," she added. "I'll tell you a story."

Rachel sprang from Caroline's lap and hurried to squeeze in beside her great-grandmother.

"It might be better if you both try to rest," Caroline said, sighing a little as she rose from the rocking chair.

Neither of them paid her any mind.

"This used to be my papa's chair," Rachel told her great-grandmother earnestly. "Before that, it belonged to *his* papa."

"I see," Geneva replied, her tone so gentle that sudden tears stung the backs of Caroline's eyes.

"He got killed in the war," Rachel confided, in a near whisper.

Geneva patted the child's hand. "I know. I'm so sorry that happened."

"I hope he wasn't scared," Rachel went on, solemn now. "It must have been *real* loud, where he was. Like today."

Caroline did not hear her grandmother's

reply; she hurried from the room, pressing one hand to her mouth as soon as she was out of sight.

The artillery roared almost continuously until nightfall, then ceased.

When the silence fell, everyone walked carefully and quietly to the kitchen house. Caroline and Geneva, with help from Enoch, created a simple meal, and an hour later they assembled around the table, except for Jubie, who stayed back in the main house for safety. They were tense, as if preparing themselves for yet another blast. Only Enoch made a move to take up fork or spoon and partake of the nourishing meal of stew, salad greens and freshly baked biscuits, even after grace had been said.

The day had been a long and difficult one, and Caroline understood the timeworn expression, "dead on her feet" as never before. If her stomach hadn't felt so hollow that it might have been scraped bare on the inside, she would have put Rachel to bed, spent an hour or so reading, and turned in herself.

Tired as she was, however, she knew she wouldn't sleep until she'd had something to eat. Besides, she needed to keep up her strength; they all did.

She smoothed her checkered cotton napkin on her lap and surveyed the other diners, starting with her grandmother. Geneva was clearly preoccupied but, thankfully, not in the near-comatose state she'd fallen into earlier, during the barrage. She seemed to be pondering the stew pot in the middle of the table, as though it were an oracle or a crystal ball, about to reveal the future.

Rachel sat, as usual, on Caroline's right, perched atop a thick musty volume containing the entire history of the Roman Empire. Jacob had always intended to build a dining chair for the child, a special one with a high back, raised seat and arms to keep her from toppling to the floor.

At the mere thought of Jacob, Caroline felt a piercing stab of loss. She closed her eyes briefly, and when she opened them, her gaze connected with Enoch's.

He did not look away, but when he spoke, it was obvious that he wasn't addressing Caroline alone. "Reckon there won't be more shooting tonight. Too dark to take aim."

The words were quiet ones, and it was doubtful that they came as a revelation to any of them, yet the effect they had on the group was powerful. There'd been no opportunity as yet for them to learn which side had won today's battle on Seminary Ridge; still they all seemed to feel a palpable sense of *relief.* It was over — for now. And tomorrow . . .

Suddenly, Geneva, Caroline and Rachel all started talking at once, Geneva about tents and medicine. Rachel chiming in with earnest comments about wanting to help, Caroline laughing. Smiling to himself, Enoch refilled his empty bowl and crumbled the first of several biscuits into it, saying nothing.

Much later, when Jubie had eaten the supper Enoch had brought for her from the kitchen house, and Rachel had finally dozed off in Caroline's bed — where she'd begged to sleep, terrified of being alone all night — Caroline and her grandmother sat quietly in the parlor, a single lantern burning on the small table between their chairs.

Geneva, who could not stay idle, held the mending basket in her lap and resumed her darning. Once she'd established Jubie with knitting needles and yarn, she'd taken over whatever repairs remained to be done.

Caroline, who'd hoped to read a book she had long ago borrowed from her friend, had quickly given up, watched her grandmother as she stitched, her needle flashing silver in the dim light. The stocking Geneva was repairing so industriously had been Jacob's and, of course, he would have no need of it, although Caroline didn't mention that.

"How long?" Caroline asked, very softly, catching herself off guard, since the question had not been deliberate. "How long will it be before I can speak Jacob's name, or even think of him, without wanting to weep?"

Geneva paused. "Hard to say," she replied, after a period of consideration. "Grief is the same for everyone, in many ways, but there are differences." She paused for a moment or so. "When the fever took your folks and your baby sister, the sorrow was nearly unbearable sometimes, but your grandfather and I had you, and each other, of course, and we knew we had to go on."

Caroline nodded. "And when Grandfather died?"

Geneva sighed gently. Her gaze was still direct, but tears glimmered in her eyes. "It was the same — and it wasn't. I loved my husband dearly, and losing him felt — well — it felt like an amputation. I wasn't sure I would survive, at least in the beginning, but as the days passed, then the weeks and then these last few months, being alone has come easier."

"But you weren't alone," Caroline said

kindly. "You had me and Rachel."

"Yes, dear," Geneva agreed, with a sniffle and a tender smile. "You have been such a comfort to me, as you still are now. And that precious child of yours, well, I'm not sure there are words to describe the joy she brings me. Why, the girl warms my soul like bright sunshine on a cold winter day. And Jacob was so kind, so helpful, he might as well have been my own son.

"Still," she went on, "I couldn't allow myself to become a burden to you. You were mourning your grandfather, too, after all. When Jacob went away to fight, you were left with this farm, and a little girl to bring up." Geneva lowered her head, and resumed her mending with new vigor. "Just listen to me, a foolish old woman, nattering on, when all you wanted to know was what to expect of widowhood."

Caroline merely shook her head; her fatigue, already crushing, seemed to settle into the marrow of her bones. She found herself wandering in an inner maze, a place of shadows, full of twists and turns and dead ends — thoughts of Jacob and how he was wounded and what that must have been like for him.

"Caroline," her grandmother's voice was quiet. "It's time we retired for the night.

You need your sleep, and heaven knows, morning will be here all too soon, and with it more worry."

More soldiers, more rifle shots, more cannon fire, Caroline added silently. *And yes, a great many reasons to be afraid.*

Except that she couldn't afford to be afraid. Could not spare the energy that fear required of a person.

Rachel depended on her, as did her grandmother and Jubie and, to some extent, even Enoch.

"You're right, Grandmother," she said. "But what if this winter is hard, and the food we've put by doesn't last until Enoch and I can plant again? And don't say we could buy food, because there might not be any *to* buy, once these armies are through!"

"You can't worry about all that now, my dear," Geneva said reasonably, putting away her mending. "You have to focus on taking care of yourself first."

"But we're standing square in the path of two armies, Grandmother, both of them bent on wiping out the other, and they may very well wipe *us* out in the process!"

Geneva put a finger to her lips, shushing Caroline. "You don't want to wake Rachel and worry her, my dear, talking that way."

"You're right. Even though everything I've

said is true," she said in a whisper.

Caroline could hardly imagine worse circumstances, at least in that moment. With a final hug, she and Geneva hurried up to their rooms.

Rachel lay curled up in the center of Caroline's bed, plump-cheeked and rosy with sleep, a tiny smile resting, light as a fairy's wing, on her mouth. After all that had happened, the child was dreaming sweetly, probably of puppies, tumbling and frolicking in the grass.

Caroline's troubled heart eased as she watched her little girl dream.

She put out the lamp, pulled the curtains closed and began to undress. She was a miracle, this child of hers, a glorious gift.

And perhaps one miracle in a lifetime was enough.

10

ENOCH

That damn horse was back.

Again.

The critter showed up out of nowhere, as though formed of the night itself, and came right up to Enoch, who'd been sitting cross-legged in the shadow of the barn, Jacob's shotgun resting across his knees. The horse buried its wet nose in Enoch's neck and snuffled companionably.

He'd been keeping watch ever since Missus Caroline and her grandmother had gone upstairs to bed, but he must have nodded off, since he hadn't heard the animal coming. His intent, his goal in staying awake, had been to prevent any stray Rebel or Union soldiers from coming in to loot the farm.

"You get on out of here, horse," Enoch said, although he figured he was wasting his breath. He'd already run that gelding off three times in the past weeks, but it always came back. Somehow the animal had managed to free itself from the tree Enoch had loosely tethered it to. "Stay around these parts," he muttered, "and you might find yourself joining up with whichever army happens along."

"I've got enough troubles," Enoch went on, holding the shotgun carefully while he got to his feet, "without getting myself hanged for a horse thief." Not to mention a killer.

The animal nickered again and stood its ground.

Enoch chuckled, in spite of his predicament, and gave the horse a pat on the neck. "Reckon I'd better give you a name, if you're going to be coming around here, making a nuisance of yourself." He started toward the barn, and the horse ambled peaceably along behind him, blowing out loud gusts of breath as though trying to hold up his end of the conversation.

Inside the barn, Enoch opened the last empty stall, and the gelding went inside, just as if he belonged there. The milk cow, the two mules and Old Tom, the ancient horse Enoch hitched to the buggy when the Missus drove to town or went off to church on a Sunday, didn't pay the newcomer any mind.

"I believe I'll call you Trojan," Enoch said. "Like as not, you're plumb full of trouble." He set the shotgun aside, took up one bucket, then another. The trough was empty so he'd have to fetch enough water to fill it.

Trojan gave a low whinny.

Accustomed though he was to hard work, Enoch felt his shoulders and upper arms throb. He'd hauled up plenty of water for all those soldiers the day before, lugged bucket after bucket out to the road, then trudged back for more. He hoped some of those blue-coats would recollect the kindness if they came this way again.

"You mind your manners while I'm gone to the well," Enoch said to Trojan as he left the barn.

Thinking he heard hoof beats far down the road, he paused in a part of the yard where the moonlight didn't reach, glad of his dark clothes, and listened hard. Things had been quiet since that troop of cavalrymen rode by, except for the cannon, of course, but there could be more of them along at any minute.

The latecomers might not be in as much

of a hurry as the others had been, and thus inclined to tarry a while, help themselves to the food stored in the cellars, raid the chicken coop, strip the corn from the field and the trees in the orchard of their green fruit. Give them a bellyache for sure, that fruit, and the corn wouldn't be ripe for more than a month, but hungry men weren't choosy.

Two riders appeared in the night, riding fast toward Gettysburg, but they went right on by without slowing down. In the darkness, Enoch couldn't make out the color of their uniforms, but it didn't matter which side they were on if they took a notion to raise some hell.

He wished he had a pistol to stick under his belt; he had left his shotgun behind in the barn, since he needed both hands to carry the buckets. If a fight came his way, he'd have no weapon other than his two fists.

Renegade soldiers weren't the only threat, of course; one had to be on the lookout for deserters, drifters and thieving outlaws in times like these.

And slave catchers, like the one he'd drowned in the creek. And the ones who'd come to the house the other day, looking for their missing companion — and for Jubie.

A shudder ran through Enoch. Luckily they hadn't caught sight of Trojan. But what if they came back? If they did, they'd recognize the horse for sure. Then they'd go poking around the place some more, maybe even bring in the law.

He waited, as still as a boulder set deep in hard ground, his heart pounding fit to bust clean through his chest. He wasn't afraid of slave catchers, but he sure as glory feared the law. Even here in the North, his reasons for killing a white man wouldn't count for anything — only the black color of his skin would signify.

So he listened until the last echo of shod hooves pounding over a hard-packed road had faded away. Then he went on to the well.

He lowered the buckets, one by one, and cranked them back up again, full.

Back and forth he went, carrying water to fill Trojan's trough, thinking all the while. He thought about the pregnant runaway Jubie, and young Jacob lying six feet under, a good man, a good friend dead long before his time. He considered the slave catcher, too, in his shallow grave, and wondering if McKilvoy had folks somewhere, waiting for him to come home, possibly believing he was a soldier, fighting bravely for the Confederate cause.

With all that was going on in his mind, Enoch nearly jumped right out of himself when somebody stepped onto the path in front of him.

"What you doin' out here in the middle of the night?" he asked when he recognized Jubie.

"I need to talk. To you," she said in a near whisper.

"Lordy, woman," he croaked. "You can't go surprising a man like that! If I'd had my shotgun, I might have sent you straight to kingdom come, in a whole lot of pieces."

He shook his head. "You get on back to the main house, Jubie, where you'll be safe."

She stepped aside so he could go on toward the barn, then trailed along behind him. "I need to talk to *somebody*," she said. "Somebody who will understand." There were tears in her voice. "I might crack wide open if I don't."

The barn was dark and quiet.

Enoch heaved a sigh.

She sat down on an empty nail keg, despondent.

Enoch's heart twisted just a little. "You want to tell me about your mistress, and your baby's father and how you came to be a runaway, that's fine. But I've got to keep an eye out for trouble, and if it's coming, it'll be by way of that road out there, so I need to stand watch."

With that, he left the barn, Jubie right on his heels.

Enoch already knew that he'd listen, that he'd take in every word — and not just out of kindness or compassion.

Jubie rested her hands on her belly, where her baby kicked and turned, as if it couldn't wait to get out of her. There'd been times when she would have welcomed death, or *thought* she would, rather than see her child sold away from her into slavery if she was caught. But when that slave catcher was after her, trying to run her down with his horse in the middle of a creek, she'd wanted to live more than she'd ever wanted anything before.

It was harder in some ways, this will to survive, no matter what it took.

"Where did you come from?" Enoch asked her gently. "Before you ran away, I mean."

Jubie felt oddly shy now that she didn't have to fight to get him to listen. "Alabama," she murmured.

"Alabama," he repeated, as if he couldn't believe it. "You came all the way from Alabama to Pennsylvania on your own?"

"No, not on my own" Jubie said. "The mistress brought me. She was set on seeing her husband — he was with Stuart's cavalry — and he had been away from home a long time. We came as far north as we could on the trains, but her husband, he wasn't where he was when he wrote last. And then we heard went to Virgina . . ." Jubie said. "The mistress figured we'd meet him there, but we never found him." Closing her eyes, she added, "Stuart had moved on by then. In . . . this direction." She saw Mr. Flynn nod thoughtfully.

"Only reason she brought me," Jubie continued, "was so she could shame me in front of her husband. Tell him all about how I tempted their son and was now pregnant by him." Humiliation washed through Jubie, and she swallowed. "She said she was going to arrange for my baby to be sold . . ."

Mr. Flynn was quiet for a while. When he finally said something, it was only, "Go on."

"The mistress wasn't telling the truth. I tried to keep clear of her son, but he was having none of it. He cornered me one day, when I was out picking berries for the cook, and he — he —"

The man beside her took her hand, just long enough to give it a little squeeze. "You don't have to say what happened then," he said, and it came out so gentle that Jubie broke down and cried.

"You believe me?" she asked, incredulous, dashing at her tears with the back of one hand.

"Yes," he answered. That was all. Just "Yes."

But it was enough.

Jubie drew in a deep breath, feeling stronger. "I told the mistress what really happened, over and over. She called me a liar every time. Sometimes she slapped me, too, really hard." She paused. "When we finally got to the camp, in a place called Upperville, in Virginia, the husband was off somewhere with Stuart. We waited for a week, and the mistress got madder and madder. She rented this little room in a boarding house in a town named Hanover. She took the bed, and I slept on the floor on a nicely woven rug. I didn't mind that. But one day the landlady came in, didn't knock, and there I was. So this lady said this here is the *North,* and up here, folks don't sleep on the floor. The landlady said good riddance and we were gone, just like that, with no place to lay our heads."

Enoch took her hand. "Slow down, Jubie," he said. "We've got time."

"The mistress said it was all my fault the landlady had thrown us out. She said the master was bound to be even more furious, and he'd surely have me whipped and sell me off to a sin house down in New Orleans. I had to wait outside while she went in another place to ask after a room. So I thought about what was about to happen to me, and . . . I just ran. I hid in liveries and the like at night, and I was scared, too, but I was a lot more scared of being sold into a sin house."

"You traveled at night?"

Jubie nodded. "Yes. Folks helped me along the way. Gave me rides in their wagon, or let me stay in their barn. Shared their food, too. I also heard, from folks along the way, that there were Underground Railroad stations around here that would help me get to Canada."

"That's true. And the Hammond place is one of them, as you found out." He paused. "But then McKilvoy, the slave catcher, found you."

She nodded. "The mistress was offering a lot of money to find me, but I knew he was gonna do plenty to me before he handed me over."

"You still planning to head for Canada?" Mr. Flynn asked, after he'd spent a long time weighing the tale in his mind.

"Yes. I surely am," Jubie answered, with a lot more confidence than she felt. "Me and my child. You ought to come with me. Only way people like us can ever be really free."

She thought that Enoch might consider the idea, but she knew he wouldn't really leave this place, or the woman who held the deed to it.

She stood up. "It ain't no use, you know," she said, very quietly. "You lovin' Miss Caroline, I mean."

He didn't stand, but turned his gaze toward the empty road. She wondered how many times he'd thought about following it away from this farm, away from this war.

"I reckon you ought to tend to your own affairs," he said, when she was beginning to believe he'd turned mute. "First of all, I am a free man, you know. And the Missus was the wife of the best friend I ever had — maybe the *only* friend — and I gave him my word I'd keep her safe. The little one, too. And that's what I mean to do."

Jubie believed him, just as he'd believed her. "But don't you want a wife?" she asked. "One that's like you?"

"I loved a woman once," he said, without

217

looking at her. "Love her still, to tell the truth, and I don't expect that to change. Only thing is I don't know if she is still alive."

Jubie didn't respond — what could she say? Instead she headed silently back to the main house.

Once in bed, she turned onto her side and smiled a little, thinking of her child. He would be a mixture of two races, and there was a good chance neither would accept him. Unless things changed — and she prayed they would.

She patted her belly gently. "Never you mind," she whispered. "Your mama, she wants you plenty. And you're gonna be free as anybody. Just you wait and see."

The baby settled down a little, as though he'd heard the promise and taken it as gospel.

She'd hoped to fall asleep right away, now that she'd been able to confide in Enoch.

Instead, she was wakeful.

She thought about all the things tomorrow might bring, and about her own mama, dead so long now that Jubie couldn't bring her face to mind.

Most of all, though, she thought about Enoch Flynn, and what a fine man he seemed to be. Was there hope for more between them, for something strong and real?

Up here in the North, or across the border in Canada, she'd heard that folks like her might be able to get married legally by a preacher, all legal, instead of jumping broom handles, hand in hand.

Jubie sighed and closed her eyes. She didn't know a whole lot about Enoch, but she was sure of two things. First, he was a good man. And second . . . he'd been too long on his own.

A sad smile lit on Jubie's mouth, flew off again, quick as a hummingbird flitting from one blossom to another. She was a fool to hope for anything, but she didn't know how to stop.

11

Cemetery Ridge
July 2, 1863

ROGAN

In the unlikely event that he lived long enough to get old, Rogan thought, barely able to breathe — or see — for the smoke and fire all around him, his hearing mercifully dulled by the thunder of artillery fire, he'd be hard put to tell his grandchildren where he and his horse Little Willie were on any given day, in relation to landmarks.

Equally hard to know where the situation stood with regard to the fighting right now. They hadn't moved once they'd reached Cemetery Ridge; General Meade had arrived sometime after midnight, and Rogan expected the Union army would be ordered to advance on Little Round Top, under the command of Daniel Sickles.

He knew little more at the moment —

except for the fact that yesterday, July 1, had been a Southern victory . . . and a Northern disaster.

Other soldiers told tales of fighting on hilltops and in valleys; they described rivers running red with blood and creeks dammed with the corpses of men and horses and mules. Rogan had seen all these horrors and more, of course, but what he remembered was the heightened state of awareness in both mind and body, the sense that he had somehow separated into two distinct entities.

When he had the luxury of reflection, which today he didn't, he wondered if this phenomenon was an indication of insanity. After all, losing one's mind was common in his current line of work.

This morning he'd left his horse behind the lines so he could muster out with Pickering and the other teamsters under his immediate command, although as a cavalryman, he would've preferred to ride into battle with his regular regiment. Until he was reassigned again, these men were his responsibility.

He had young Hastings beside him when the charge hit just ahead, landing with the force of a meteor, belching fire and smoke and driving both of them to their bellies.

Otherworldly shrieks speared Rogan's brain as he lunged to the ground, grabbing Hastings's arm and hurling him down, too.

Rocks and shrapnel fell like hail, and Rogan let his rifle lay where it was, crosswise beneath his chest, and covered his head with both hands. He felt the shower of stones first, then the peppering of metal fragments, every one of them hot as a branding iron.

His nape and the backs of his hands burned like hell, but when he raised his head, he didn't examine his injuries. Instead he turned to look for Hastings.

The boy lay on his back, covered in soot from one end of his skinny frame to the other. His face was all there, and so were his limbs, but the rush of relief Rogan felt was short-lived. The kid's eyes were open, but he stared blankly up at the smoke-shrouded sky.

"Hastings!" Rogan yelled, as another blast, farther away, rocked the ground under him. "You hit?"

"Yessir," the boy managed to say. "I believe I am."

"Where?" Rogan demanded, as the bombardment went on.

"About everywhere, I reckon," Hastings said. "Feels like somebody went and lit little bitty fires all over me, and there's something broken inside, too."

"Hold on," Rogan ordered, as inhuman screams sounded from everywhere, amplified to a pitch that sickened his soul. He wanted to disappear into some hidden part of himself, where the agonized cries couldn't reach, or at least squeeze his eyes shut, but he didn't dare do either one. "You hold on, you hear me? I'll get you away from here as soon as I can."

Hastings actually tried smiling; it was a pitiful sight. He was a boy, not a man; should've been home, chopping wood and eating his mama's cooking. "Save yourself, Cap'n. Ain't no savin' me."

When yet another blast sent another rain of hot metal to falling, Rogan sheltered the kid as best he could, felt the downpour burning through his tunic and shirt to his flesh. The smell of scorched wool filled his nose, and he knew his coat was smoldering, but he waited until the fire shower let up before rolling onto his back to put the flames out.

"Best you keep moving, sir," Hastings said.

Rogan lifted his head again, squinting, to look around for a place to shelter the boy, but there was nothing — no breastworks, no trenches, not even a good-sized rock or a God-damned tree. "I'm giving the orders here, Private," he barked.

Again, that haunting smile. Rogan didn't reckon he'd ever forget it. "Yes, sir," he said, and lifted one filthy, bleeding hand in an attempt to salute.

"Tell me your Christian name," Rogan said quietly.

"It's Ethan, sir."

Why had he never asked this kid who he was, aside from a soldier?

"Well, Ethan," Rogan proceeded with deliberate calm, "where's home?"

"Right here in Pennsylvania, sir," Ethan Hastings replied, struggling to speak. "My ma and pa have a little place outside Harrisburg. It's nothing much, but I sure wish I was back there now."

Rogan's eyes stung fiercely. He figured it was the smoke. "You'll be there soon enough," he said, then had to stop and cough. "I'll see to that. Meanwhile, you've got to hang on."

With that chilling placidity Rogan had seen too many times before, the boy shook his head. A lone tear cut a channel through the grime covering his face. "I truly wish I could do that, sir," he replied, every word requiring an effort. "There's a favor you could do me, though, if you're of a mind to."

Despair hollowed out a place inside Rogan and settled in to stay. "What's that?" he asked, lowering his head so he could hear Ethan's faint reply.

"Ma will be mighty torn up when she finds out I'm gone," the boy answered, whispering now. He labored for every breath, and there were long gaps between words. "She knew this could happen, so I guess she's as prepared as she can be. Pa will be all right, once he squares things away in his mind. It's my dog, Sweet Girl, worries me the most. Pa calls her a useless critter, and I'm afraid he'll shoot her or something, first chance he gets."

The voice fell away, and the boy's effort to rally the last of his strength was a painful thing to see.

"You want me to go get your dog?" Rogan asked.

"Yes, sir," Ethan murmured. "Find her a place. Ain't nothin' I want more than to know my Sweet Girl is with kindly folks who'll look after her."

"I'll fetch her," Rogan promised, though he wasn't sure he'd live out the day, or whatever was left of this particular fight, let alone how he was going to travel all the way ιο Harrisburg, find the Hastings farm and claim the dog, but he'd do it, or die in the trying.

"I am obliged to you, Cap'n," the boy said on a wavering breath.

And then his eyes rolled back and his chest stopped rising and falling.

He was gone.

Sixteen years old at the outside, and he was *gone.*

The rage that seized Rogan in those moments was a ferocious thing. He wanted to take the boy hard by the shoulders and shake him back into the world, shout orders at him, throw back his head and bellow at the waste of a life barely lived.

Instead, he crossed Ethan Hastings's arms across his narrow chest, weighted his eyes shut with two flat pebbles, retrieved his scorched kepi, which had been sent flying when he fell. He placed the cap gently over the still, narrow face, where no trace of a beard would ever grow.

He knew the fighting had moved on for the time being, knew there were dead and could hear dying men scattered all around him, perhaps for miles. There was nothing he could do for the boy now, but it felt all wrong to leave him out there, in that grisly company and yet thoroughly alone.

So he stayed where he was, on his knees beside the dead child, oblivious to his own condition, stricken to the heart.

"He was a good kid." The voice was gruff, full of weariness and sorrow. "But he's lost to us now, Cap'n, and you're hurt. Let's get you over to the field hospital for some tending."

Rogan turned his head, recognized Josiah Pickering, the lobsterman. Pickering had seen hard fighting himself, judging by the state of his uniform, but he was all in one piece, standing on his own two feet, unlike hundreds, if not thousands, of other men.

He put a hand out to Rogan, helped him stand.

Belatedly, Rogan shook his head. "No field hospital," he said. "I'm all right." He looked down at the boy again.

The Maine man put his hand to Rogan's back again, steered him away from the body. "Come along, Cap'n," he said. "The boy's gone, and if you won't let a medic take a look at you, we'd better see to the ones that are still living. It'll be a while before the ambulance wagons get here, and they'll be in need of water and whatever help we can offer."

Rogan half walked, half stumbled along beside Pickering. Nodded his head once.

"How does it happen," he wondered aloud, "that you're not with Chamberlain and the 20th Maine? They're a fine outfit."

Pickering's stride was slower than usual. "I wanted to join up with Chamberlain and his bunch, but my wife wouldn't hear of it. Said he was naught but a glorified school-master, and barely dry behind the ears into the bargain. If I was going to march off to war at my age, she told me, I had to promise to serve as a clerk or drive a supply wagon — do something safe."

They both smiled at the word *safe.*

Mundane as the exchange was, it was calming as well. Proof that there was still a world out there, despite the war — a world full of people doing ordinary things.

"Do you ever wonder what your good wife would've done if you'd refused to follow orders?" Rogan asked, sadly wry.

"No need to ponder that question, Cap'n," Pickering answered. "She made it plain from the beginning. If she learned I was marching with the infantry or the like, she'd borrow a team and wagon from her cousin, pack up the children and everything we owned, right down to the bait in the mousetraps, and light out for her brother's place in Bangor. I'd come home at war's end to an empty house, provided I didn't get my damn fool head blown off before-hand."

"Would she do that?" Rogan asked. No matter how bad things were, it lifted his spirits a little, just hearing stories about regular families.

"Sure she would. She's a spirited woman, my Sarah. She'd have me back eventually, but it would take some doing on my part to persuade her to leave her brother's fine, big house and come on home with me."

Men ran past, carrying stretchers.

Rogan could feel the small pieces of metal lodged in his flesh, but he didn't let on that he was in pain. The wounds burned but were minor, he was sure, and casualties had been heavy all day; with wounded men pouring into the hospital tents, the surgeons were surely overwhelmed as it was.

He couldn't expect them to set aside crucial operations to pick pieces of Confederate iron out of his hide.

"You'd go after her, your wife, I mean? Court her all over again?" he asked, to keep the conversation going a little longer.

Pickering chuckled, but his eyes were solemn. "On my knees," he replied.

The battle raged until there was no light to see by, but Rogan and every other able-bodied man with two good feet to stand on worked well into the night, carrying stretchers to the hospital tents as rapidly — and as mercifully — as they could.

Past the Union picket lines, the Rebels were hard at work, too, recovering their own wounded and dead by lantern light.

The task was horrific, the casualties legion. They gathered Federals and fallen Confederates alike, leaving the dead behind for the time being, their bodies sprawled where they'd fallen.

The sights and sounds would spawn unimaginable nightmares in the minds of the survivors for years to come, decades, perhaps. Rogan was mute with exhaustion, and he was grateful for that, if only because it numbed his senses.

He didn't allow himself to think about Hastings, lying out there in the darkness, with stones on his eyes, one of the thousands of dead littering the ground.

It was after midnight when orders came down from on high; there would be more fighting the next day, and every soldier, regardless of rank, was to return to camp, take his food and get what rest he could.

For all the lifting and carrying they'd done, it seemed to Rogan that they hadn't made a dent in the job. Soldiers still cried out for help, for water, for the mercy of death.

Rogan felt both anger and a buckling of the knees when the command was relayed to the men. How could he eat and drink and fall senseless onto his bedroll, when so many people still needed help?

And yet the orders made a grim kind of sense. What use would he or any of the others be in battle, without rest and food?

Going back to camp was the hardest thing he'd had to do — yet — but Rogan was a soldier, and an order was an order.

So he returned to the spot where Hastings had brewed his vile coffee the previous night. Pickering and Alderman were there ahead of him, staring, spent and silent, into the low-burning fire.

He sought out Little Willie first, gave the gelding water and brushed him down, since that was the only way he knew to soothe a frightened horse.

After that, Rogan found a basin, poured water into it and gave himself a cursory splash. Every muscle in his body screamed for a hot bath, plenty of soap, and enough whiskey to wipe July 2, 1863 from his mind.

He joined the other men in the general area of the fire — it was too hot, even at night, to sit near it — and nobody said a word.

Alderman got up, poured coffee and handed it over.

Rogan nodded his thanks. The stuff kept some men awake, he knew, but he wasn't one of them. He accepted the mug, found its contents as foul as always, and drank it. He forced down a serving of boiled beans, on their third day and starting to sour, and took care not to notice the empty spot where Hastings had slept away the last night of his brief life.

He listened stalwartly to the piteous calls of the wounded, as the beans roiled in his stomach, threatening to come back up with a vengeance.

There were other sounds, too — the stomping and nickering of horses, sad tunes played on banjos and harmonicas around other campfires, men talking, arguing over a game of cards or the throw of the dice. Ballads were sung, and, now and then, raucous laughter broke out somewhere nearby.

Rogan didn't ask himself how a man could laugh, or make music or gamble, in such a time and such a place.

It was a way of bearing the unbearable.

He muttered a good-night to Pickering

and Alderman, and went to lay out his bedroll.

He slept little, despite his exhaustion. He hadn't yet heard about the battle's full cost — the casualties, the wounded, the missing — on either side. Nor did he have that information about yesterday's disaster.

His pain was considerably worse now that he was lying down, and as the countless campfires burned to embers and the soldiers quieted, the injured continued to call out for someone, anyone, to come to their aid.

Mostly, they called in vain.

12

Cemetery Ridge
July 3, 1863

ROGAN

Pickets swapped shots throughout the night, and at around half past four that morning, some quarter of an hour before the sun rose, the fight on Culp's Hill, about a mile from Cemetery Ridge, was on again, in earnest. The cries of the wounded were muted, but they continued, getting inside Rogan and twining around his guts like some fast-growing vine, fit to drop him to his knees.

His flesh smarted with yesterday's shrapnel wounds, but he didn't pay that much mind.

Ostensibly, there were a hundred men in his command, including two lieutenants, several sergeants and a corporal or two, but the number fluctuated considerably, depending on various factors, such as Confederate raiding parties, sudden illness and, more and more often these days, desertion. A teamster's work was hard, dangerous and generally thankless, for all that the freight they carried kept the entire army on the march.

That morning, most of Rogan's company was in transit between supply depots and field headquarters, and he was glad of that. There were more than enough men here, by his reckoning, to face the horrors to come and, alas, do their part to make them worse. Twelve of them — make that eleven, with Hastings gone — were present and accounted for.

He sent Alderman and Pickering back to stretcher-bearing duty, where their help was badly needed and they might be out of the line of fire, while the rest fell in with the nearest company of infantry, most of them eager to prove they were soldiers, not mere mule skinners, hauling hardtack and coffee beans from one camp to another.

Leaning over the pommel, the crack and boom and smoke of battle already gathering all about, Rogan patted Little Willie's neck a few times, raising dust from the animal's hide, and spoke quietly. "Stay on your feet, my friend," he said, "and we'll both get through this."

"We'll get our fill of fire and blood today," he added. "And then some."

The words were prophetic.

Under the leadership of Brigadier General George Armstrong Custer, the US cavalry fought hard that day, in what soon became known as East Cavalry Field, where the Union artillery exchanged thundering rounds with the Confederates. The objective was to hold off Jeb Stuart's Rebel horsemen, and the fighting was fierce.

If Stuart reached the lines of artillery above, the consequences to the Union forces would be dire.

Little Willie proved agile, and he didn't spook once, for all the minié balls and bullets salting the air around them. There were harrowing shrieks everywhere, as men and horses alike went down, but the Confederate war cry, a strange, piercing whoop usually called the Rebel Yell, chilled the blood.

As the roar of over two hundred cannon shook the ground and turned the air to smoke so thick it seared the eyes and scraped the throat raw, Rogan fought on.

Friend and foe fell on every side.

Then another horse bumped Little Willie on the flank, and Rogan turned, sword raised, to defend himself.

And froze.

There, grinning through a whorl of smoke, rode his old friend Bridger Winslow, a pistol in each hand. "By God, I thought that was you," he said, raising his voice to be heard over the din.

Rogan gave a strangled burst of laughter, mostly a reflex, born of surprise. "Damn!" he bellowed.

It had finally come to pass, after all these years. The meeting each had anticipated and dreaded. Friend against friend in the heat of battle.

Bridger's mount danced fitfully beneath him, ears pinned back, but he kept his pistols in hand, rather than take the reins. He wouldn't have seen the need, given that he could control any horse with a slight motion of his knees or heels. "Unless you mean to use that sword," he said, his teeth flashing white in the filthy expanse of his face, "you ought to lower it a while. Easier on your arm that way."

"Maybe," Rogan responded loudly, "we ought to do our jawing later on. And somewhere else."

Bridger threw back his head and laughed, then nodded and gestured with one hand. "Between the picket lines, soon as the smoke clears," he shouted back. "Bring as many coffee beans as you can scrape together."

During that brief exchange, the battle seemed suspended, pushed aside somehow, but it soon reasserted itself.

"Look out!" Rogan yelled, when he caught sight of another Union cavalryman riding up behind Bridger.

But it was too late.

The bayonet struck, coming clean through Bridger's right shoulder; it turned as the blade was yanked free, blood soaking his tunic and streaming down onto the horse. Before a second thrust could be made, he shot the man at close range, the blast propelling the other soldier out of his saddle, with his arms spread wide apart and a crimson stain blossoming across his chest.

Bridger faced Rogan and, incredibly, he was grinning again. "I really wanted that coffee, too," he said, just before his eyes rolled back in his head and he fell, unconscious, to the ground.

Rogan swore under his breath, looked around quickly, noting with a degree of relief that the men around them were preoccupied with fights of their own, then dismounted and crouched beside his friend.

He found a pulse at the base of Bridger's

throat, weak but steady.

After scanning his surroundings a second time, he caught hold of Bridger under the arms and dragged him into a cluster of brush nearby. Reminded of the end Hastings had met the day before, he felt sick, but he spoke the words called for, useless as they probably were.

"Hold on and stay put." His friend's eyes were shut, so there was no telling if he heard or not. "I'll be back for you first chance I get." He paused, ran a forearm across his face. "And I'll bring that coffee."

Praying Bridger wouldn't bleed to death, or be discovered and finished off on the spot, Rogan ran to his horse, swung up into the saddle, and fought on, staying as close to that brush pile as possible.

Meanwhile, the cannon fire went on, destroying anything — and anyone — in its path, lasting more than two hours.

Stuart struck again and again, but Custer, a fierce little man with a head of golden hair, held the line. Both sides paid dearly over the course of the conflict.

Rogan had no sense of time passing.

He barely noticed the slash of a Confederate sword, slicing open his right thigh, but he registered his horse's cry of pain when the same blade cut a deep nick in his withers. Rogan was never sure whether he ran that Rebel through to defend himself or to avenge his horse.

When he dropped to the ground, minutes later, two Union infantrymen dragged him into a copse of trees. He passed out before he could ask them to fetch Little Willie from the field, but when he came around, hurting everywhere it was humanly possible to hurt and yet still whole, the horse was standing over him, reins dangling, head down to nuzzle at Rogan's chest.

He sat up, but a fresh wave of pain rendered him breathless. He checked his wound. Several minutes had passed before he realized that night had fallen and the fighting had ceased. A deep silence coursed beneath the inevitable moans and cries of the wounded, the shuffle of men's feet as the stretcher bearers came and went, the pop of a gunshot as an injured animal was put out of its misery.

Rogan knew he ought to be out there, doing what he could to help, but he wasn't sure he'd be able to stand up and he wasn't ready to try. He remembered Bridger, hidden in the thicket, and wondered if he'd been found.

If dead, he'd be left where he was.

If alive, he would be taken prisoner and,

eventually, someone would see to his wounds. Naturally, he wouldn't be a priority, but he might fare a little better than a foot soldier, because of his rank.

At least half an hour had gone by before Rogan figured he was ready to see if he could stand. Even then, getting to his feet took some doing. If it hadn't been for Little Willie, he might never have managed at all, but the stirrup gave him a handhold and, from there, he pulled himself up just enough to get a grip on the saddle horn.

Little Willie stood patiently, letting Rogan lean heavily against his side until the dizziness subsided and he could catch his breath.

Finally, he felt strong enough to keep his feet without the horse to hold him up.

He took the reins in one hand and led Little Willie out of the deep shadows beneath the tree that had, somehow, sheltered them both until the battle was over.

Bodies everywhere, some dead, some wounded, but several ambulance wagons were there to receive the living and the soon-to-be-dead. Stretcher bearers came and went, but the pace was so hectic that, remarkably, Rogan and Little Willie went unnoticed.

Rogan searched, his heart pounding, and found Bridger still lying in the brush. In the dim light of the moon, Rogan saw his friend's chest rising and falling. The motion was nearly imperceptible, but it meant Bridger was alive, and for now, that was enough.

"Stand," Rogan said to Little Willie, and dropped the reins.

The horse obeyed, as always.

Rogan made no effort to go unseen; it would have been impossible, if anybody took a notion to look.

He squatted next to Bridger. "Hey, there, Reb," he said quietly. "Can you hear me?"

Bridger opened his eyes, and one corner of his mouth twitched upward, fell into line again. "Hell, yes, I can hear you," he responded, very slowly. "I'd know that Yankee twang anywhere." He paused, struggling visibly to draw his next breath. "What news? Of the battle?"

"All I can surmise is that it's over. Things are quiet now — as quiet as possible. There was a Rebel charge up Cemetery Ridge this afternoon. Far as I can tell, they withdrew." Despite the chaos, he'd heard that much from one of his teamsters. Shrugging, he said, "That's all I know. Oh, and one of the Rebs, a major general, is called Pickett. Another is Longstreet."

"Know of him." Bridger gave a slight nod,

then asked, "Where's my coffee?"

In spite of the pain and the filth and the fear of the sights and sounds he'd never be able to forget, Rogan had to smile. "We'll get around to the coffee later," he said, adding a silent *If we're lucky.* "Right now, we have other concerns."

Bridger chortled, a miserable sound, but courageous, just for the making of it. "Yes," he said, closing his eyes. He was unconscious again, or maybe asleep.

Rogan stood and took another look around. The bodies were far-flung, some so distant that they might not be found and buried for hours, perhaps days.

Far, far out in the darkness, Rogan crouched beside the corpse of a Union soldier, checked for a pulse and found none. He ducked his head and closed his eyes for a few minutes. He didn't recognize the young man but in some ways that left him feeling even greater guilt over what he was about to do. He offered a brief prayer of hope and thanks.

Then, when he could make himself do it, he rolled the body onto its side and began working the right arm free of the sleeve. Slowly, and as gently as he could, Rogan removed the dead man's blue jacket, rolled it up tight; next he took a bloodstained piece of heavy paper, with the soldier's name and regiment written on it, from the pocket and slipped it inside the white shirt he wore underneath. Then he returned to the place where Bridger lay.

This time, he tried to be quick, getting his friend out of his soiled gray tunic and replacing it with the one he'd stolen. He couldn't do much about Bridger's trousers, but they were covered in dirt and blood enough that a person would be hard pressed to make out their color in the dark.

He looked around again and, to his astonishment, spotted Alderman and Pickering, not fifty yards away.

Bridger regained consciousness just as Rogan turned his head and yelled, "Pickering, Alderman — over here!"

When he looked back at Bridger, he saw confusion in his friend's face.

"Do as I say," Rogan muttered. "Keep your mouth shut and do your damnedest to look like a Yankee."

Bridger, not surprisingly, didn't have the strength to object.

Alderman and Pickering rushed over, carrying an empty stretcher.

"Cap'n?" Alderman gasped.

Pickering's grin nearly split his grimy face in two. "We thought for sure you were

244

dead," he told Rogan.

"I came close a few times," Rogan said.

They glanced down and saw the bloody slit in his pants.

Rogan gestured toward Bridger, who lay prone in the bushes. He would have time to think about the shrapnel and the sword wound to his right thigh later. All he felt now was a distant throb. "I know you're mighty busy, but I'd appreciate if you'd load this fellow next."

The two men, although worn ragged from a day spent hauling the wounded to and from ambulance wagons, obeyed without hesitation.

Bridger's gaze locked onto Rogan, but he followed instructions and didn't say a word, obviously aware that his Southern drawl might cause confusion.

"What about you, Cap'n?" Pickering asked, when he and Alderman had Bridger on the stretcher and hoisted off the ground. "You need to tend to that wound or you might get gangrene. You'll be needing both legs when this fighting is done."

"I'll be all right for now," Rogan said.

"We'll get this fellow taken care of, then," Alderman said. After a quick look around at all the carnage, the erstwhile butcher said, as if to himself, "I might have to find another trade when all this is over."

Rogan rested a hand on the man's shoulder, just briefly. "You're doing a fine job, both of you," he said, and he meant it. He'd thought to spare them the dangers of battle by assigning them to this duty, and they were alive. But they were both exhausted, covered in gore and blood and dirt, with wounds of their own, the hidden sort that often fester for a lifetime in the mind and heart.

Both men nodded, and started off toward the line of ambulance wagons waiting in the near distance.

"Wait," Rogan said, noting that Bridger had passed out again. This was both a relief and a concern — less chance his friend would say something that would give him away.

But he'd lost a lot of blood, and there was no telling how badly he was injured.

Alderman and Pickering were at a standstill, waiting for further orders.

"Take him back to camp," Rogan went on. "That is, if it's still there."

Both men studied him closely, but neither spoke.

Rogan thrust out a sigh. "I'll ride there first, and make sure. Then I'll bring back one of the supply wagons."

Alderman remained silent.

"This man a friend of yours, Captain McBride?" Pickering asked.

Sprawled on the litter, one arm dangling, Bridger moaned.

"Yes," Rogan replied, having neither the energy nor the words to elaborate.

"There's a buckboard you can use," Alderman said. "We've been using it to haul medicine and bandages and the like from the main supply tent. We can take him there."

Pickering nodded, in apparent agreement. His expression was grim and his eyes were watchful, but if he had any suspicions, he kept them to himself.

"Good," Rogan responded. "Lead the way." After a few moments of hesitation, during which he decided that offering the horse to one of these good men while he helped carry the stretcher would meet with instant refusal, he mounted Little Willie.

The act of swinging himself up into the saddle made the ground tilt sideways, but he managed to keep his seat.

Ten minutes later, they found the buckboard hitched to a pair of army mules and partially hidden by a stand of oaks and maples. Bridger made a gasping sound when they placed him in the wagon bed, between crates of ether and morphine, but he didn't open his eyes.

Without being told, Alderman and Pickering unloaded the crates and stacked them on the ground; Rogan knew they'd retrieve them later.

He tied Little Willie to the buckboard and stripped off the heavy tack, tossing it in beside Bridger, while the other two men stood, awaiting further instructions.

With a sigh, Rogan dragged himself into the box, took up the reins, and asked, "Any further news from the front?"

Alderman smiled. "Yes, sir. General Lee's been routed, good and proper. Whole Rebel army will be headed South, moving as fast as they can. This little scrap is over."

Rogan released the brake lever with his left foot, glad he didn't have to use his wounded leg. The shrapnel stung him all over, like a swarm of wasps. "Do what you can here, gather the other men, and meet me at the widow Hammond's farm," he said, too weary to comment on the assumed victory; it was too soon to declare a winner, although the brass was always ready to raise the flag of triumph.

Lee was a wily fox, quick on his feet, and his retreats, rare as they were, tended to be strategic ones.

If General Meade ordered the army to give chase — immediately — they could strike a decisive blow while the Confederate forces were weakened, and the war might finally be over for good.

Unfortunately, Union generals, at least in his experience, seemed to prefer long and ponderous deliberation over swift action. McClellan and Joe Hooker had led them to miss a number of opportunities to corner Lee, and Rogan had no reason to think Meade would be different.

Pickering and Alderman both saluted again, then hurried back to their task.

And Rogan set out into the dark but hardly silent night, his best friend lying insensible in the back of the buckboard, his weary, faithful horse plodding along behind.

He could still hear the cries of the wounded and the shouts of the men helping them into the ambulance wagons. Where they might survive. Or not.

13

Hammond Farm
July 4, 1863

CAROLINE

They came in the small hours of the morning, before the cows were milked or the chickens fed, before Caroline had roused herself from her bed, following yet another restless night.

Enoch called quietly from the base of the stairs. "Missus? You better come on down here, right away."

There was no urgency in his tone, and Caroline wouldn't have heard him at all if she hadn't been awake, staring up at the ceiling, watching shadows dissolve slowly into light. She scrambled out of bed, careful not to disturb Rachel, who slept on, curled into a tiny ball, like a baby bird yet to hatch from its shell.

Caroline pulled on a wrapper and stepped

into the hall. "What is it, Enoch?" she asked, as softly as she could. She'd heard hoof beats, the rattle of wagon wheels and even footfalls on the hard-packed road throughout the night, holding her breath at intervals, afraid the farm would be overrun by fragments of a fleeing army.

When none had paused, she'd managed to doze for a few minutes, only to start awake when she heard mules braying, or men shouting, or any of the hundred other sounds of a large company passing by.

Now, a steady rain drummed on the roof and beaded on the windows. It was a blessing, she thought, always mindful of the crops; perhaps the downpour would offer a respite from the accursed heat, settle the dust and disperse the lingering smoke.

And cleanse the innocent earth of the blood shed over three days of furious battle.

"Take a look out front, Missus," Enoch replied.

Caroline hurried across the bedroom, clutching her wrapper closed but leaving the ties to dangle at her sides, forgotten. Below, in the dooryard, she could barely make out the shape of a single wagon, drawn by a team of two mules. The driver, somehow familiar but hard to identify in the predawn dimness and the rain, secured

251

the brake lever and looked straight up at her window, just as if he'd known she was there.

Captain Rogan McBride.

She whirled from the window, shedding her nightgown and donning fresh underthings and yesterday's calico dress as quickly and quietly as she could. Sliding her feet into house slippers, since her shoes would take too long to fasten properly, she rushed downstairs.

Enoch waited there, silent, respectful and clearly worried.

"It's Captain McBride," Caroline said, strangely anxious. "He's come back for the supply wagons." With that, she started for the door.

Enoch immediately stopped her, taking hold of her elbow and letting go the next moment. "Best you let me speak to him first, Missus Caroline," he said.

Caroline shook her head, puzzled and a little impatient. "If that's Captain McBride out there, I don't imagine we have cause to fear him."

Enoch nodded, although he still looked unconvinced. "Most likely, we don't," he agreed soberly. "Just the same, it wouldn't do for you to go rushing out there, especially in this rain. There's too much we don't know about the situation. When the captain was here before, he was on official army business, but it looks to me like his fortunes might have changed for the worse these last few days. So you let me do the talking, for now. Then we'll figure out the rest together."

Caroline nodded once in reluctant compliance. She truly didn't believe the captain meant them any harm, but Enoch had reliable instincts. If he advised caution, she would pay heed.

"Might be prudent to put on some shoes," he added, turning toward the door.

"Bring him to the kitchen house," she said, raising both her chin and her dignity.

"Yes, ma'am," Enoch said. "Friend or foe, that man is in want of a place to dry off."

Five minutes later, Caroline was dashing through the torrent, a shawl covering her head and wearing her sturdy work shoes.

By the time she got inside the kitchen house, she was drenched to the skin. The rain was warm, though, and when she'd built up the fire in the cookstove, her clothes would dry soon enough.

The room was dark, so she lit a kerosene lantern and considered the contents of the larder. Flour and salt and baking powder for biscuits, last year's potatoes in the cellar, eggs, too, suspended in a large crock of glass.

Caroline added more wood to the stove.

Moments later, Enoch and Captain McBride stood in the open doorway, supporting a third man between them. Wet and muddy, from the top of his head to the soles of his boots, the stranger was clearly unable to stand.

Captain McBride, although upright, looked every bit as bedraggled as his companion. His pale face was stubbled with the beginnings of a dark beard, and his eyes, blue as indigo ink, were full of ghosts.

"Put him there," Caroline said, arranging the kitchen chairs into a makeshift pallet.

Enoch and McBride half dragged, half carried the man across the room. He groaned aloud when they eased him onto the pallet.

"Enoch," Caroline said, "please go back to the house for Mrs. Prescott. Tell her she'll need Grandfather's medical kit."

Enoch nodded and lumbered toward the door, head turned so he could look back at her. "Yes, Missus," he agreed, with a brief glance at Captain McBride. "I'll be back in no time."

Caroline lathered her hands with strong soap, dunked them in the nearly scalding water, and dried them on a clean dishtowel. "This soldier was hurt in the battle?" she asked.

McBride stared down at the man on the pallet.

"Yes, pretty badly," he said, his voice hoarse. He did not look at her as he spoke; it was as though he believed that by watching the other man, he could somehow *will* him to rally. "He took a bayonet through his right shoulder."

"What is this officer's name?" Caroline asked.

"Bridger. Captain Bridger Winslow." McBride bowed his head. "He's . . . an old friend."

Caroline moved to the man's side, tucking her soaked skirts beneath her as she knelt. Oddly, the man's tunic, though in a dreadful state, muddy and smelling of blood, was not torn where it should have been.

Her hands trembled a little as she carefully unbuttoned the tunic and laid it open.

She gasped when she saw what was beneath; the man's shirt-front was crimson with blood, and puckered around a jagged puncture wound, already beginning to fester.

Silently, she pleaded with her grandmother to hurry, *hurry.*

Outwardly, though, she probably appeared calm. "Infection is setting in," she said very quietly.

"Can you help him?" McBride spoke so earnestly, that Caroline felt emotional.

"I will certainly try, Captain McBride."

"There will be more," McBride said, but she didn't immediately comprehend his meaning. "More wounded men," he explained.

She looked up at him, horrified yet not surprised. Enoch had gone to town the night before, once the firing had stopped, to see what he could find out. Upon his return, he'd told her there were bodies everywhere, that he'd never seen the like of it, but then he'd made a strangled sound and left the house.

"The Union lost, then?" she asked, almost in a whisper.

He shook his head. "The Union won the Gettysburg campaign — no thanks to General Meade," McBride said scornfully. "At least in the opinions of some. He appears to be in a hurry now, from what I gather. Too much of a hurry to take any further aggressive action against the Confederates."

"You should sit down, Captain McBride," Caroline said.

The captain drew a chair back from the

256

table and eased himself onto the seat. The way he rested a hand on his right thigh confirmed what Caroline had already guessed; he, too, was wounded.

A moment later, Geneva burst in, carrying her late husband's battered medical bag, Enoch directly behind her.

Geneva had reached the spot where Captain Winslow lay on the makeshift pallet, put down the medical bag and shed her wet cloak. "Mr. Flynn," she said with brisk authority, "please place this man on top of the table, and be gentle about it."

Together Enoch and Captain McBride hoisted Winslow onto the table. Watching, Caroline winced.

"Caroline," Geneva said, as she gestured for Enoch and the captain to strip Mr. Winslow of his clothing, "We shall need a great quantity of hot water, clean cloths and blankets." The old woman turned to Enoch then. "If I recall correctly, Mr. Flynn, you placed the medical supplies I brought with me in the cellar. I will need bandages, since there are few in my late husband's case, God rest his soul." Next, she addressed Captain McBride. "As for you, sir, I would advise you to sit back down before you collapse. I will tend to your injuries as soon as your comrade seems stable."

"Yes, ma'am," he replied wearily, sinking into his former chair at the table. The poor man *did* look as though he might keel over at any moment.

Caroline filled three of the large kettles she used mostly in canning season, hoping her water supply wouldn't run out, and set them to boil.

When Enoch returned from the cellar with the requested bandages, along with a couple of blankets he must have found in one of the crates brought from Geneva's house in town, he immediately saw the need for more water and set out to fill buckets at the well.

Geneva unfolded the blankets and spread them over the patient.

Caroline began preparing a breakfast, making room for her cast-iron skillet among the kettles.

She sliced bacon, peeled and chopped potatoes and mixed biscuit dough, grateful for the distraction the tasks provided. She made space on the counter to roll and cut the dough.

When Enoch returned with more water, his clothes soaked through from the continuing rain, he noticed the food and gave a wan smile of appreciation. "I looked in on Miss Rachel and Jubie," he said. "They're still asleep. I'll take in their breakfast when it's ready."

"Thank you, Enoch. Why don't you sit here by the fire for a while, dry off a little?"

But Enoch shook his head. "No time for that," he said.

Just as she was about to put the biscuits in the oven, Geneva spoke. "Caroline, is that water ready? I cannot treat this man's wounds properly until he's been bathed."

"Almost ready," she said.

The patient seemed to be coming around a little, mumbling at first.

His voice seemed to have a distinctly Southern drawl.

Caroline turned her head, startled, and her gaze collided with that of Captain McBride. He looked rueful, but stubbornly determined, too.

"McBride?" the other man asked.

"I'm here," the captain said.

"Where am I?"

"At a farm on the Emmitsburg Road. Having your wounds tended to."

"My horse?" Winslow asked.

"Probably gone for good," McBride answered.

Caroline glared. "That," she accused tersely, "was unkind."

"The truth," the captain said, "is often unkind. Nevertheless, it is still the truth."

259

"Some truths," Caroline countered, still nettled, "can be withheld until a more appropriate time."

"Not this one," McBride said, with a note of finality. "There's no good in giving a person false hope, Mrs. Hammond."

Caroline turned away again, without a word, and went on with the making of breakfast.

Enoch filled a bucket and set it on the table when the water had finished boiling. Then Geneva asked Caroline for her assistance in bathing the wounded Captain Winslow.

"Come, Caroline," she said. "We'll all be doing this and much worse in the days ahead."

"Of course, Grandmother."

Was that a twinkle she saw, dancing in Captain Rogan McBride's Union-blue eyes as she passed his chair?

He could bathe *himself,* she thought.

Over the next half hour, Caroline helped bathe Captain Winslow, even though this task brought back painful memories of bathing Jacob in Washington City, after his death.

Bridger Winslow, however sorely wounded, was very much alive. His flesh, as revealed by soap and water, was sun-browned and strongly muscled.

His hair, when washed, turned out to be the color of caramel. And, when he opened his eyes briefly, she saw they were golden brown. They appeared to hold a glint of mischief despite the pain as he regarded her.

He was, she decided, even in his present state, much too handsome for his own good.

Worse, she suspected he was almost certainly a Rebel. An enemy soldier, despite the Union jacket. She was curious about his story.

He'd spoken with an unmistakable accent, smooth as sweet custard, but that didn't necessarily mean he was a Confederate soldier, she reminded herself. There were, after all, Southern men who had opposed secession and thrown in their lot with the Union. And he was a friend and in the care of Captain McBride.

Even General Robert E. Lee himself was said to be against the idea of secession. He'd left the United States Army with reluctance, out of loyalty to his family, friends and home state of Virginia.

None of these insights, Caroline realized, made bathing a naked stranger any less disturbing.

Once Captain Winslow was fully clean,

Geneva set about treating his shoulder's deep wound. She could do little about any internal injuries, she said, not being a surgeon, but she believed the puncture was a clean cut and would heal if properly disinfected.

When she poured what seemed to be whiskey into the wound, he erupted with a howled curse. Then he fainted.

"Thank heaven for small mercies," Geneva murmured, unwinding a roll of bandages. "The pain must be excruciating." With that, she tore narrow strips of gauze, doused them in more whiskey and began packing the wound.

When the bandages had been wrapped, Enoch and Captain McBride lifted the patient and placed him carefully across the chairs again.

Geneva immediately asked for more hot water and strong soap, and scoured the table thoroughly. This strong, competent woman was the grandmother Caroline knew and loved — taking charge, giving orders, rising to the occasion. Her strength inspired Caroline.

The table had no more been scrubbed when Captain McBride succumbed; his knees gave way and he began to fold toward the floor. Enoch caught him from behind, beneath the arms, just in time to break the fall. Caroline helped Enoch get him on the table.

She wondered how many soldiers she'd have to tend to before the crisis was past, and the war moved on to ravage some other community.

Together, the two women disrobed the half-conscious man. The captain's back and arms were pocked with sharp bits of metal, some large and some small, and he had sustained a bayonet or sword wound to the right thigh. He'd shed a considerable amount of blood at the time, and as it dried, it had bonded the fabric of his trousers not only to the surface of his flesh, but deep inside it as well. Even the drenching he'd gotten, driving in the rain, had not dislodged the scorched cloth.

Geneva asked Caroline to prepare a hot compress, while she gathered instruments from the medical kit, to be boiled before use.

While they waited for the water to boil, both Caroline and her grandmother washed their hands again.

The soap was harsh and stung Caroline's skin, but it would not have occurred to her to complain. Though she had her small and private vanities, she was a country woman used to working with her hands, accustomed to thorns and stings in summer, chilblains in winter, and callouses the year around.

Tending to Captain McBride remained an awkward business; they had to prop him up so that Geneva could pull the metal shards from his back with a set of tweezers. He'd exhausted whatever strength remained in him, which meant that Enoch had to hold him in place. Caroline simultaneously applied a compress to the blade wound in his muscular thigh, soaking the embedded fabric until it could be pulled free without doing further damage.

McBride, when conscious again, endured all these processes stoically, although he gritted his teeth when Geneva, satisfied that Caroline had removed every fiber and thread of cloth, used whiskey to disinfect the wound.

With infection seemingly present, the wound could not be sutured shut, even though its location, on his leg, would advise that. Instead, they bandaged it.

Once more, Enoch braved the rain to head for the house, soon returning with more blankets and some of Jacob's clothing for the men.

The two uniforms, beyond any hope of repair, were burned in the cookstove, while a pot of strong coffee brewed.

Finally, with both men resting comfortably, Caroline finished making breakfast, which she and her grandmother ate standing up.

Then Enoch carried plates for Rachel and Jubie to the house, the food covered with cloth napkins and tucked inside a lidded basket, then he came back to take his own meal.

"How is Rachel?" Caroline asked Enoch as he ate. "And Jubie?"

"They're both doing fine, Missus," Enoch answered gently.

Using the blankets he'd brought, he made a bed on the floor for Captain McBride, next to his sleeping friend, and helped him rise from the table, then lie down again. He was in too much pain to eat.

Caroline studied the empty table numbly. No matter how thoroughly she would scrub those familiar planks, she thought, she couldn't imagine ever again sitting down to it for a meal.

Yes, the war had definitely changed their lives.

14

CAROLINE

Within an hour, two more men rode in on mules, grim-faced and soaked through, followed directly by several ambulance wagons and half a dozen mounted soldiers, all clad in Union blue. It was now past dawn.

Caroline, having left Geneva watching over the two captains in the kitchen house so she could check on Rachel, heard their approach. She stood at the window in the parlor, Rachel on tiptoe at her side, smudging the fogged glass with one small palm as she cleared a spot to peer through. Jubie took a place behind Caroline's right shoulder, careful not to be visible to the outside.

"Them soldiers aren't looking for me," the girl said, probably addressing herself rather than Caroline or Rachel.

"No, Jubie," Caroline agreed. "I think they've come for the wagons and supplies they left behind before the battle."

They watched as Enoch went out to meet the party of men. The rain was still pounding down, splashing into deep puddles on the ground, lashing the grass until it lay flat.

"Reckon they'll move on, soon as they get the wagons," Jubie said hopefully. "Maybe they'll take the captains away with 'em."

Caroline said nothing, but kept her gaze fixed on Enoch, who seemed impervious to the rain as the discussion went on.

Finally, he stepped aside, gestured for the group to proceed.

The two men on mules dismounted, striding toward the kitchen house. Three ambulance wagons bumped and jostled after them, while the soldiers on horseback rode doggedly on, in the direction of the orchard, water pouring from the brims of their caps.

"Jubie, would you take Rachel upstairs to her bedroom to play," Caroline said, turning from the window at last. She knew her brief respite was over, perhaps for a very long time.

Rachel was usually well-behaved but unwilling just now to stray from her mother's side. "But, Mama," she argued, "I don't *want* to go upstairs. I want to stay with you."

Caroline leaned down and placed her sore hands against the little girl's cheeks. "We must all do our part, darling Rachel," she said. "And your part is to be very, very good, so that Mama and Great-grandmother can look after the soldiers."

Rachel's small face crumpled. "I could help you, Mama," she said, tears welling in her eyes. "Please? I could sing songs and recite."

Caroline's heart, numbed by the day's demands, awakened only to break into pieces. "That would be very nice," she replied wistfully, determined not to cry. "But not now, sweetheart. When the soldiers are feeling better."

"The men in those wagons look like they've been shot full of holes," Jubie said. "They'll need tending to."

Caroline raised her eyes to Jubie, mutely asking her to be silent.

Jubie took the hint. She put one hand on Rachel's head, summoned up a smile and said, "How about you sing me some songs, Miss Rachel? Recite some pieces, too — from the Bible and such. Might settle this babe of mine — he's been jumping around in my belly like cold water spilled on a stove lid."

Rachel paused, looked from her mother to

Jubie and back again. "Would that be helping, Mama?" she asked, her voice small and
uncertain.

Caroline smiled. "Yes," she said. "That
would be a very great help."

Rachel regarded the bump under Jubie's
dress as though entertaining suspicions.
"Can your baby hear what I say?"

Over her head, Caroline's gaze met Jubie's, and a tacit agreement was made.

"Sure he can hear," Jubie told her. "And
like I said, your singing will help settle him
down."

"Well, all right then, as long as I'm helping *somebody.*"

Caroline bent again and placed a kiss on
the child's head. "I'll be back as soon as I
can," she said.

Rachel and Jubie were already on their
way upstairs. Caroline hurried out the door.

As she passed the ambulance wagons,
which stood near the barn, with their teams
of forlorn mules still in harness, heads down
under the continuing onslaught of rain, she
looked inside — and was stunned at what
she saw.

In one, men were stacked on top of one
another, like sticks of firewood. In another,
soldiers lay insensate on the floorboards, or
sat with their backs to the sides. Blood was

everywhere, as though splashed randomly from buckets, dripping slowly between the cracks in the wagon beds, staining the grass beneath.

There were moans and pleas, and several soldiers, surely too young to fight, appealed to Caroline with outstretched hands, murmured entreaties for help, or stared despondently.

Her heart went out to them, but she knew she needed to stand back from them, at least for now; if she held one soldier's hand, she had to hold them all, and that was impossible.

"You're safe now," she told them, repeating the promise at each wagon except the one loaded with the dead. "We will do all we can for you."

She might have stayed longer despite the rain, trying to reassure these desperate souls, if Enoch hadn't come and squired her hastily into the kitchen house.

Her eyes sought her grandmother first.

Geneva was seated in the rocking chair, her face dangerously pale, it seemed to Caroline. But when her grandmother looked up, she smiled.

"Is Rachel fine? Is she with Jubie? And did you have a rest?" she asked.

"I have," she answered, not wanting to

worry Geneva. "I'm quite restored. And Rachel and Jubie are spending time together." She resisted saying that Geneva, too, needed a rest. She knew there was no point in even suggesting it.

Geneva patted Caroline's hand.

Caroline managed a slight smile and turned toward Enoch and two more soldiers who had come inside, now warming themselves. In contrast to the wounded and dead boys in the ambulance wagons, this pair seemed almost elderly.

"Things are bad at Gettysburg," one of them was saying. "I've never seen anything like it."

The other nodded, shrouded in sorrow, stoop-shouldered and incomprehensibly weary. "Thousands of bodies. Folks from the town and some of the soldiers been burying the dead as fast as they can, but the graves are shallow, and this rain is washing them out. Bringing the bodies right to the surface."

"Going to have to burn what's left of the horses and mules," the first man put in, and Caroline saw tears standing in his eyes. "No, sir," he went on, blinking rapidly, gazing at nothing. "Never seen anything like it."

Caroline felt her legs weaken, and braced herself. "Where are the ambulance drivers?"

she asked, surprised at the steadiness of her voice. "Those boys need shelter, and the mules have been left standing."

"They've gone to bring the supply wagons down," Enoch replied quietly. "Once that's done, we'll help set up the tents and get the wounded men settled." He paused and heaved a great sigh. "Meantime, I'll see to the mules."

Caroline was nearly overwhelmed by the bleakness of the situation, but she knew she could not give in, could not fall apart.

"Tents?" she asked belatedly.

One of the mule riders turned to look at her then. "Yes, ma'am. We'll put some of these poor lads in the barn, if that's agreeable to you. Least till the tents are up."

She looked around, took in Captain McBride and Bridger Winslow, both of whom were asleep on their makeshift pallets. "But it's dryer in here," she reasoned. "And cleaner, too. Surely, they'd be more comfortable, out of the weather . . ."

The man shook his head, a sad smile lingering in his eyes for a moment, but never reaching his mouth. "There won't be room for them all, ma'am," he said. "Kind of you to offer, but it just won't do."

Caroline could not let the matter go. Those were *human beings* out there in those wretched wagons, suffering and wet and afraid. They were sons and brothers, husbands and fathers, far from their homes and the people who loved them. "There's the barn and the cabin and —"

But the man shook his head again. "No, ma'am," he said. "Like I told you, it's a kindly thought, and we appreciate your generous spirit, but these boys are just the first of hundreds, maybe thousands . . . They're lying in every church and store and house in Gettysburg as it is, and before this crisis is over, every farm for miles around will be overrun with dead and dying men."

Caroline wavered on her feet again, swamped by the magnitude of such a disaster. "Dear God," she murmured. "What are we to do?"

She felt a hand grip her own, realized that her grandmother had risen from the rocking chair and come to stand beside her. "We are to do what we can," Geneva said quietly. "And we will."

Grateful, Caroline squeezed her grandmother's hand. "Yes," she said. And she could only feel proud, that her farm — *Jacob's* farm — had become a field hospital.

At sunset, the rain was still coming down hard, pounding the earth like the vengeance of heaven.

Six large tents were erected and cots set up inside, quickly filled as Enoch and the other men carried stretchers loaded with bloody, rain-soaked boys, some out of their heads with pain and fever, others ominously still.

Geneva and Caroline covered them with blankets, served them ladle after ladle of drinking water, whispered merciful lies and administered doses of laudanum from Dr. Prescott's stores to those who would — or could — swallow.

All the while, more ambulance wagons arrived. With them came more soldiers, able-bodied but stricken by all they'd seen and heard, along with a surgeon.

Hours later Enoch persuaded Geneva and Caroline to leave the wounded long enough to eat something, then go on up to the main house. He promised to take a meal himself, and give Captain McBride and Mr. Winslow food and water as well, if they were awake.

They weren't.

Caroline managed to swallow a biscuit and a slice of cold bacon left over from breakfast; Geneva ate even less. Arm in arm, the two women headed for the house, holding Caroline's cloak over their heads like a canopy as they hurried through the rain, wending their way between tents and busy men.

Inside, Jubie was waiting for them. "Miss Rachel sang and played with her dolls until she couldn't keep her eyes open," she said. "I put her in your bed again, Miss Caroline, because that's what she wanted, and she's sleepin' sound."

"Thank you," Caroline said, almost too tired to speak.

Jubie took Geneva's arm. "I'll get the Missus to her room," she said, in a tone of authority. "Then I mean to go on out there and see what I can do by way of helping them soldiers."

Caroline blinked. "I don't think that's wise, Jubie," she told her. "It'll put you at too much risk. You never know what people are thinking, what they might do. And you have your baby to protect."

"I suppose you're right." Jubie was already leading Geneva toward the back stairway. "But I want to tend them anyway."

Caroline felt a new respect for Jubie then, and no small admiration. "Fine — but don't overdo things. And . . . be careful. You've got to think of your baby."

Glancing back over one scrawny shoulder, Jubie nodded. "Yes, Miss Caroline," she agreed. With that, she rounded the corner and started up the stairs, murmuring encouragement to Geneva as they made the slow climb together.

Caroline paused for a few minutes, drew a deep breath, then followed them upstairs. She needed to rest, too, and think, absorb all that had happened.

After looking in on her grandmother, Caroline went to her own room. She did not light a lamp, but undressed and washed in the darkness, listening to the rain and trying not to think of the hundreds of dying men still lying helpless on the battlefields, at the mercy of the weather. And she tried not to picture the shallow graves washed open, water pooling around the corpses.

Even at a remove, the images were hideously vivid in her mind.

Moreover, she wondered how her friends and the rest of the townsfolk had fared, the stubborn ones who, like Caroline and her grandmother, refused to leave. So far, there had been no direct news from or about her friends and acquaintances, people she and Jacob had known since childhood. Perhaps she could make a brief foray into town in the next day or so, stopping at some of the neighboring farms on the way . . .

Donning her nightgown without removing her camisole and pantaloons, Caroline stood beside the bed, gazing down at the small, shadowy figure of her child. Had she made a mistake, allowing Rachel to stay with her, instead of sending her on to New York with her good friend, Susannah Kronecker? Keeping the realities of war from her daughter had not been difficult in the beginning. Jacob was away, of course, and they both missed him, but there'd been those brief furloughs, and his letters, frequent and always lively, full of good cheer, funny stories and plans for the future.

How different that future will be, Caroline reflected sadly, easing into bed beside Rachel. So different from the future Jacob had envisioned for the three of them. Or possibly a bigger family, if he'd lived.

Lying on her side, Caroline touched her sleeping child's cheek. She'd upheld the illusion of safety somehow, even after journeying to Washington City and returning with Jacob's earthly remains in a pinewood box. As carefully as Caroline had explained her papa's death, and despite the fact that Rachel had seen at least glimpses of him in his coffin, she was simply too young to comprehend the full meaning and permanence of such a tragedy. No father had ever loved a daughter more than Jacob loved Rachel; he adored the child. And yet, like every other man, he'd also wanted at least one son, someone to carry the Hammond name into a new generation. Someone to help run the farm and, one day, take it over entirely.

Had she given birth to a second child, another daughter even, one who thrived, like Rachel, he would have been pleased. Overjoyed, in fact. But her dreams of more children had died with Jacob. It would be just the two of them, Caroline and Rachel, on their own now.

Undoubtedly, her daughter still believed, on some level, that Papa was merely "away," as he had been for so much of her short life, and that he would return at some point, with small gifts hidden in his coat pockets, smiling and offering piggyback rides.

Understanding would come with time, Caroline thought. She had seen no point in forcing the issue these past few weeks. It was too soon. Grief was a natural process; it was right and proper to mourn her husband, and to allow Rachel to mourn her father.

Caroline had intended to wear black for one year, as was customary, but the only black dress she owned was the fancy one she'd worn to Jacob's funeral. Given the present circumstances, she was not prepared to order the necessary yard goods, lay out patterns, pin them in place, and cut out the many pieces, much less stitch them together into day dresses, skirts and bodices. She knew her friends would help her if she asked, but so far she hadn't. She wasn't even sure she could find the fabric and notions in the first place, at a price she could afford. With the war devouring the output of virtually every mill and factory in the North, such things were scarce. Not only that, she and her friends had more important things to do in the aftermath of the battles that had taken place.

Nevertheless, if she continued to wear calico and gingham in lieu of dour bombazine and crepe for too long, certain women of her acquaintance were likely to gossip, although with the war so close to home now, they'd hardly have the time. But she could well imagine a future when scandalized whispers, the clucking of tongues and shaking of heads might prevail.

Then her thoughts turned to a more pressing reality — the two injured officers in her kitchen house, one of whom *might* be a member of the enemy army, and the crop of tents housing grievously wounded soldiers. Mere boys, most of them. The nearby battles had, by all reports, devastated the town and the countryside alike, leaving thousands of dead men, horses and mules behind.

She dreaded what tomorrow might bring.

15

Hammond Farm
July 4, 1863

BRIDGER

Bridger groped his way back to consciousness, a slow and arduous effort, with ever-greater pain as its only noticeable reward. By the time he finally managed to raise his eyelids, his shoulder wound burned as if it had just been cauterized with a red-hot poker — and simultaneously ached like a broken bone. He tried to raise himself from his pallet, but a flash of sheer agony forced him to lie down again.

"Rogan?" Bridger asked, breathless from the exertion and the pain. Had he really encountered his old school friend on the battlefield? Until now, he would have described the faint recollection as a fragment of a fever dream, if he'd thought about it at all.

"Yes, it's *Rogan,*" the voice replied, in none too friendly a fashion. Evidently, McBride's Irish was up. "Who else would be fool enough to risk hanging to save your miserable, contrary hide?"

"I'll be damned," Bridger said, exhausted. And smiling.

"A certainty if I've ever heard one," Rogan muttered. At school, and afterward, he'd been famous for his quick temper, which had been equally quick to subside. He'd loved an all-out brawl, McBride had, but when the fight was over, he'd generally put out a bloody-knuckled hand and haul his adversary to his feet.

"I smell coffee," Bridger said, quickening a little at the thought.

"Our luck it's probably cold," Rogan said. "And there's no one here to light the stove and warm it up."

A moment later, Bridger heard a stove lid clatter.

From the shuffling sounds, Bridger guessed Rogan had managed to rise off a pallet of his own and make his way to the stove.

The fact that he'd succeeded in getting to his feet was more than a little galling. Rogan lit a lantern and cranked the flame up high, and the outlines of a table and chairs, shelves and a cookstove sprang from the shadows.

Then Rogan loomed over him, oddly clad in loose trousers and something that resembled a nightshirt. He was bandaged, his face gaunt and sallow under the bristle of a new beard, dark as his hair.

"You look like hell," Bridger observed. "Guess a man has to expect to take a beating or two when he takes up with an invading army."

The breath Rogan expelled in response might have counted as laughter, if not for the bitter scraping sound it made. "For Christ's sake, Bridger, *shut up.* I'm trying to think here. Figure out what to do next."

With difficulty, Bridger raised himself onto his elbows, gritting his teeth against the pain.

"Here's what you ought to do next," Bridger told his friend. "Help me get to my damn feet. I'm at an unfair disadvantage, lying on my back like some old turtle turned wrong side up."

Rogan grinned, his teeth white as bare bone beneath that scruffy beard. But then he leaned down, a move that obviously brought him significant discomfort, and extended a hand.

Bridger took it, forcing back a moan as

Rogan hoisted him up off the floor.

He swayed slightly, breathing hard, but managed to avoid collapsing again by bracing himself against the heavy wooden table.

"Thanks," he whispered when the worst had passed.

"About time you showed a little gratitude," Rogan said. "Considering that you'd be under a foot or two of good Pennsylvania dirt by now, if I hadn't intervened."

Bridger took in his surroundings. Overhead, rain tapped at the roof like the beating of a million drums. Outside, wagons came and went, and men called to each other, and berated horses and mules. Beneath all this din, he heard the stark, muffled cries of the wounded.

"Never mind your heroism," he said grimly. "Where are we, exactly?"

In the room's poor light, Rogan's dark blue eyes were nearly black. Like Bridger, he was hurting, and not merely because of whatever injuries he'd sustained on the battlefield. The screams and moans were a constant, inescapable part of war, a reminder that, in this supposedly glorious game of kings and knights, it was the pawns who shed the most blood.

"This is the Widow Hammond's farm," Rogan said at last. "Her Christian name is

Caroline, and she is a fine woman."

Had there been a warning couched in that statement? Bridger wasn't sure and, for the moment, he wasn't inclined to pursue the idea.

Instead, he pulled out a chair and sank into it. "We're behind Union lines," he said. It wasn't a question.

"Yes," Rogan answered without triumph. He drew back a chair of his own and sat down across from Bridger.

"The battle — ?"

"Over," Rogan said. "The whole Gettysburg campaign is over and finished."

Bridger grimaced. "And?" he prompted.

The coffee was coming to a boil over there on the stove, and the smell of it was a comfort, even in the midst of spectacular misfortune.

"It was a Union victory," Rogan told him. His expression was bleak. "So-called, anyhow. Seems to me there's no way either side can call that kind of carnage 'winning.' "

The coffee pot overflowed at the spout, some of its contents sizzling, fragrant, on the stove top.

Bridger's mouth watered. He was half-starved, with no clear memory of the last time he'd eaten, but he could endure that. It was coffee he craved, hot and strong, the way a drunkard craves whiskey.

"Thank you," Bridger said as his friend handed him a cup, and he meant it. The stuff was just barely off the boil, and a gritty foam rode the surface of it, but he had to hold himself back from lapping it up like a thirsty dog on a creek bank.

Bridger was briefly stymied by the bounty of these ordinary things, once taken for granted, now prized. "Thank you," he repeated.

Rogan nodded in acknowledgment as he brought over a jug filled with cream and a small pot of sugar. He added generous portions to his coffee. Stirred industriously.

Bridger did the same, but more tentatively. He'd heard that the Yankees had to deal with short rations now and again, but they were a way of life in the Confederate army. Sugar and molasses were available when supply lines held, but coffee had long since vanished, thanks to Union blockades; it had been replaced by a variety of poor substitutes ranging from chicory leaves and ground acorns to tree bark, boiled singly or in combination.

He'd been hungry for long stretches, like most of his comrades, but he'd never been desperate enough to drink such sludge.

His left hand, being usable and the one he

favored anyhow, trembled slightly as he raised the cup to his lips. The brew scalded his tongue, but that wasn't why he sipped it so slowly. He wanted to savor every mouthful.

Rogan pushed back his chair, stood carefully and went back to the cookstove. He took the coffeepot by the handle, and carried it to the table. He refilled Bridger's cup, then his own, and sat down again. Then he carried over two plates fixed with food that had been placed on the counter. By Caroline Hammond? Her hired man? Or perhaps one of his staff? He assumed they'd been left for him and Bridger.

Each plate was piled high with sliced pork and fried potatoes, salted and peppered and crisp around the edges.

Bridger went weak at the sight. As an officer, he'd occasionally had access to more and better food than the regular soldier, but sitting down to a meal while his men went hungry was not something he could square with his conscience.

"Go easy," Rogan advised him quietly. "If I'm not mistaken, that Confederate stomach of yours won't take kindly to a whole lot of grub at one sitting."

Bridger knew his friend was right, liked him all the more for the way he'd spoken, with no condescension and no pity. Just the same, it was all he could do not to get all that good food inside himself as quickly as possible.

"Might be my last meal," he said. The pain still blazed through him, nauseating him, but at the same time, his very bones felt hollowed out with hunger.

"It will be for sure if you keep running off at the mouth about riding with Stonewall Jackson and Jeb Stuart," Rogan remarked.

He ate moderately, Bridger noticed, as though trying to set a slower pace for the sake of his starving Confederate friend, and there was something touching about that.

"I am a prisoner of war," he said, between bites of food so good it made the backs of his eyes burn and his throat tighten. "What did you expect me to say?"

"For a start," he replied pointedly, "you could stop talking like that — saying you're 'a prisonah of whah,' for instance."

Bridger raised his eyebrows with more than a little sarcasm.

Rogan shook his head. "Oh, never mind that. We've got bigger problems at the moment."

"I beg to differ," Bridger said. "*I've* got bigger problems. You, on the other hand, are a hero. Wounded in battle, you nonethe-

less managed to capture a Confederate officer on the field. If anything, you'll be
handed a medal, maybe promoted, while
I'll be hanged, or worse, left to rot in some
Yankee prison camp."

Rogan laid down his fork. "Are you
through?" he asked.

Bridger said nothing. He understood well
enough that his friend's intentions, where
he was concerned at least, were good, even
noble. Rogan had saved his life and risked
his own in the process. Brought him here,
to this farm, where some kind soul had
cleaned and dressed his wound.

He was grateful.

Still, he didn't see how he was going to
avoid capture, with God knew how many
Yankees right outside the door, not all of
them lying helpless on cots, from the sound
of it. He'd lost his horse, and even if he'd
had one, he was barely able to remain
upright, let alone ride.

"I know what you're thinking," Rogan
said, breaking the ponderous silence.

"I'm thinking," Bridger responded rhetor-
ically, between forkfuls of fried pork, "that
we both might've been better off if you'd
left me on the battlefield."

"Well," Rogan responded, picking up his
fork again, "I didn't, though, did I?"

"No," Bridger agreed. "You brought me behind Yankee lines. As favors go, my friend, this one leaves something to be desired."

"You would've been fine if you hadn't spoken with that damn drawl of yours the second you opened your eyes this morning. Damn it, Bridger!"

"Perhaps we could move on and discuss — say — how the hell I'm going to get out of here without being shot, lynched or sent to some Yankee shit-hole of a prison?"

"I'll tell you, if you'll listen," Rogan said, gesturing with his fork for emphasis. "I'm an acting quartermaster, and as such I have access to supplies. I can get you a Yankee uniform —"

"Heresy!" Bridger couldn't resist interrupting.

Rogan glared at him.

Rain drizzled at the windows and pattered on the roof, and a piece of wood snapped in the stove. Sunrise couldn't be far away, and damned if he could guess what the day might bring, although it was hard to imagine anything worse than three days of wholesale carnage in the pastoral Pennsylvania countryside.

He shuddered at the recollection.

Rogan continued to stare him down.

Bridger grinned, remembering their school

days. They'd arm wrestled, fought with their fists, fenced and raced each other on horseback, competed for the highest marks in their studies and for the prettiest girls at dances and socials off the campus grounds. In every instance, they'd finished dead even, both of them exhausted from the effort, forced to declare a draw or die butting heads.

"All right," he said, with an exaggerated sigh. "Explain your master plan, oh, great seer of the North. Not that I'm agreeing to anything, mind, because I'm damn well not."

One corner of Rogan's mouth twitched, but he managed not to smile and thus give an inch of ground. Boneheaded Irish bastard. "You should know I'm as much motivated to save your hide for your sister's sake as for your own. I promised Amalie in my last letter that I'd keep an eye out for you should I ever run into you on the battlefield — or off. And I like to keep my promises."

"Funny, I recently got a letter from Amalie myself. She made no mention of you!" That was the truth. But Bridger remembered the innocent closeness his sister and his friend had enjoyed when Rogan visited Fairhaven during their long-ago school days.

Rogan ignored his remark. "Here's the

plan. First, you pretend to be a loyal member of Mr. Lincoln's army," he said. "I'll get you a uniform, and papers, too. The cat's already out of the bag with a select few where your accent is concerned, but if anyone challenges you on those grounds, we can say you were opposed to secession and were forced by your principles to help restore the Union.

"Anyhow, it shouldn't be too difficult for you to stay out of people's way," Rogan continued. "You're a convalescent, after all, so you won't be expected to stand guard or tend the wounded. When our orders arrive, the men out there will strike the tents, load patients into ambulance wagons and move on. It'll be mayhem, and that means you can get lost in the confusion easily enough. Until then, you'll recuperate. Even after we leave, though, you'll have to lie low for a while — there will be patrols on all the main roads, and no matter what uniform you're wearing at the time, you'll be stopped and questioned as to why you're headed in the wrong direction."

Bridger weighed all that. As highly as he regarded Rogan McBride, the thought of passing himself off as a damned blue-belly galled him. Despite his intense disapproval of slavery, he couldn't help feeling a sense of disloyalty to his home and family, his state, his fellow soldiers . . .

On the other hand, though, he wanted to live. Wanted to get back to his own army, too, although the two eventualities might well be mutually exclusive.

Bridger began, "What about the widow you mentioned before? Harlan — Halland — ?"

"Hammond," Rogan clarified. "Caroline Hammond. Her husband fell at Chancellorsville, back in May."

Bridger didn't want to think about Chancellorsville. His cavalry commander, the great Stonewall Jackson, a man he'd admired, had fallen there, losing his arm and, only days later, his life.

"She's loyal to the Union, of course. Did she hear me speak? Wouldn't she resent my being on the other side, seeing as she's a recent widow?" he ventured thoughtfully.

"Of course she's loyal," Rogan confirmed. "But she also strikes me as a warm, kind woman. I met her briefly when she came to Washington City in search of her wounded husband." His tone was somewhat guarded.

"Even so, won't she be inclined to turn me in to the first Yankee officer she sees?" He grinned. "Aside from you, I mean."

Rogan was quiet for a long time. He laid

his knife and fork on his plate, crisscross fashion, pushed it away, and averted his eyes.

Some minutes later, he met Bridger's gaze again and replied, "I don't know Caroline — Mrs. Hammond — very well, but I somehow think she's more complicated than that. In any event, we'll have to chance it. From what I gathered when I was here the first time to drop off supplies, she'd just buried her husband. She and her grandmother seem knowledgeable about medicine and helped look after both of us yesterday. She might be driven more by humanitarian concerns than ideology."

Rogan seemed to be playing his cards close to his vest when it came to the lady, Bridger thought. That was unlike him, in the context of their friendship, anyway.

He decided to find out. "Sounds as if you're taken with this angel of mercy," he said.

Rogan swallowed visibly, and his eyes narrowed, but he didn't offer a reply.

Bridger sighed. "God Almighty," he muttered. "I thought you had better sense."

Rogan's hands, resting on the table, knotted into fists, relaxed again. "Caroline is a fine woman," he said, his voice grating. "A *decent* woman. If you're implying otherwise,

I might have to do some damage to that aristocratic face of yours."

"Aristocratic?" Bridger tried to laugh. He rubbed his beard-stubbled chin with one hand. He was wearing someone else's clothes, and a Yankee had carved out a tunnel that ran clear through his shoulder. He did not feel at all like gentry.

"I'm not implying a damn thing," he said presently. "Mrs. Hammond is a total stranger to me, after all. I'm sure she's everything you say she is, and more. All of which is beside the point."

"And that point is . . . ?"

"You said it yourself. She's a widow — a *recent* one. A major battle has just been fought, practically in her own backyard, and now there's a field hospital on her property. She's in no position, my friend, to receive your heart, however honorable the offer. Move too quickly, and you will leave her with no choice but to break it."

Rogan let out a long, slow breath, sitting back in his chair. Pondering. After a lengthy silence, he said, "Don't assume anything. But you're right. I have a war to fight, and she has a husband to mourn." He paused and attempted a smile, which faltered into a grimace almost before it took shape.

Bridger, who knew the pitfalls of loving a

woman he couldn't have, was fairly certain Caroline Hammond would be on Rogan's mind for a while. But before he could frame a response, the heavy door of the kitchen house swung open and a small, cloaked figure hurried in, emerging from the gray wet of predawn.

Simultaneously, Bridger and Rogan rose to their feet, an awkward scramble, oddly urgent.

This, Bridger thought, with a sense of detachment, *is Caroline Hammond.*

"Please," she said, this striking woman, seemingly woven of mist and summer heat and the scent of lilacs, "be seated."

Neither man complied.

She stepped into the circle of lantern light, bringing her face into sudden, sharp relief, pushed back the hood of her cloak and offered a tentative smile.

"Good morning, gentlemen," she said, probably surprised to find her charges alive on that drizzly early morning, let alone standing upright. "Do sit down. Please."

Bridger did not sit, nor did Rogan.

She blinked, confused by this unintentional resistance to her invitation. At least, it was unintentional on Bridger's part. He found himself inexplicably *unable* to respond in any way, a state that was foreign to his nature. And he had no explanation for it.

A brief, uncomfortable silence ensued.

Finally, Caroline spoke again. "I see you are both starting to recover," she said, slipping the damp cloak from her shoulders as she turned away, then crossed to the door again, and hung the garment from a nearby hook. "That's a relief."

Taking an apron from a drawer, she turned to face them, and as more light seeped in through the windows, Bridger got a better look at this woman his best friend seemed to fancy.

Her eyes were bright and intelligent. And her clear skin and lush crown of wheat-colored hair, uncertainly pinned and slightly askew, made Caroline Hammond instantly magnetic. She gave an impression of strength, of sturdy roots running deep into the singular essence of life itself.

God help Rogan, Bridger thought, *and God help me.*

He groped for his voice, found a fragment, dragged it upward to his tongue. "A gentleman," he heard himself say, "does not sit in the presence of a lady."

Caroline had been moving toward the stove, but she stopped when she heard Bridger speak and studied him with a mixture of consternation and surprise. "You are of Southern extraction, sir," she said. He suspected she'd noticed that before . . .

It was not an accusation, merely a statement.

Rogan, silent all this time, cleared his throat.

Bridger did not heed the warning, well-meant as it surely was. He had deceived many a woman in his time, by flattery, by omission, although never with malice; yet for some incomprehensible reason, he could not lie to this one.

"My name is Bridger Winslow," he said. "And I am a captain in the Army of Northern Virginia, currently under the command of General J. E. B. Stuart."

Caroline's eyes widened, and she stopped in the act of tying her apron strings.

Rogan groaned in obvious disgust.

Caroline glanced from Bridger's face to Rogan's, then back again. Her elbows jutted out at her sides, her hands suspended behind her.

"Did I hear you correctly, sir?" she asked.

"No," said Rogan, just as Bridger replied, "Yes."

She stiffened, finished with the apron ties and dropped her hands to her sides. "Which is it, gentlemen?" she demanded. "Yes or no?"

"Yes," Bridger repeated.

Standing a few feet away, on the other side of the table, Rogan made a sound of pure exasperation.

Bridger, conversely, felt a sense of mild, if precarious, relief. He even smiled a bit, a response that was in keeping with his generally audacious nature, and probably ill-advised.

Caroline's gaze shifted back to Rogan, and Bridger found himself begrudging the loss of her regard, however briefly. It was then that the realization came to him — Rogan might not have simply been confiding a personal interest earlier, when he'd admitted his admiration for this woman. Had he been staking some kind of claim, perhaps even drawing a figurative line Bridger was not to cross?

"And you, Captain McBride?" she asked. "Are you collaborating with the enemy, or are you loyal to the Union cause?"

Though Bridger did not look away from Caroline, he was aware of Rogan's reaction to her forthright questions. He sensed that his friend had straightened and turned to face her.

"I am loyal," Rogan said, his voice rough

and proud.

Caroline raised her eyebrows and folded both arms across her bosom. Bridger was quietly amused. He'd just placed his freedom, if not his very life, in the hands of a woman he had never met and knew next to nothing about.

"Captain Winslow and I are old friends from military school," Rogan finally told her. "I think I mentioned that before — or at least that we're longtime friends." His tone was respectful, with a note of misgiving. "And I'll be deuced if I don't wish it were otherwise, just now anyway."

"I see," Caroline said, bemused. But clearly, she *didn't* see. Her brow was furrowed, and her smooth cheeks had gone pink. She regarded Bridger again, solemnly. "You are a prisoner of war, then?"

Bridger was still puzzling out a reply when Rogan interceded. "No," he said adamantly. "He is not."

"No?" Caroline echoed, attractively confounded.

Rogan gave another sigh and drew back a chair at the head of the table. "Please sit down," he said wearily. "If you don't, I'll have to go right on standing, and my leg is about to buckle from the pain."

Caroline approached the table, sat down

in the chair Rogan had offered. She smoothed her apron again, briskly, and waited.

Bridger, still in the thrall of whatever spell this farm woman had unwittingly cast, dropped back into his own chair, and Rogan did the same.

Slowly, reluctantly, sending the occasional glare Bridger's way throughout the coming explanation, Rogan told Caroline how he and Bridger had met as boys, while at boarding school, and forged a deep and lasting friendship. How Bridger's father and family, including his younger sister, Amalie, had welcomed his orphaned self and showered him with Southern hospitality; how he'd often spent school breaks with the family and considered them his own. And how when he had discovered Bridger wounded in the field of battle, he felt compelled to bring his friend to safety.

Bridger listened as Rogan explained their relationship, his body ablaze with the pain of his wound. He was touched by Rogan's fierce commitment to the unlikely bond between the two of them, friends who'd come from such different backgrounds, and his determination to maintain that friendship, despite their differences.

He hoped his friend knew he felt the same way.

Some ties could not be broken — war or no war.

Woman or no woman.

And yet . . .

He began to understand what drew his friend to this warm, forthright and appealing woman.

16

CAROLINE

Rogan's words had given Caroline much to think about, but she simply didn't have time to sit around pondering the dilemma in which she found herself. Too many wounded soldiers were on her farm in dire need of help; there was no opportunity to think about herself — to think the matter through in her usual logical fashion. Nevertheless, as she spooned medicine or water or thin broth into mouths of the fallen, as she cleaned and bandaged wounds, washed all manner of disgusting fleshly effusions from helpless bodies, she considered the situation.

To treat a suffering Confederate soldier was an act of mercy and humanity, not of treason, surely. If she did as Rogan asked, however, and allowed Union officers to believe that Bridger Winslow was part of their own army, with the ultimate objective of helping him escape, he would most likely return to the opposing army and take up arms against Federal troops. She would then be at least partially responsible for every man he might kill in battle. Men like her own Jacob, like the sweet, naive boys from her own town, and other towns like it, all across the North.

Was one life to be preserved at the risk of so many others?

And could she expect Geneva and Enoch and Jubie — even innocent little Rachel — to share in the deception?

Clearly, she had sound reasons to refuse her complicity, but none of them were answers in themselves, not for Caroline.

Bridger Winslow, after all, was a flesh-and-blood *person,* not merely a name on some official list of wounded, missing or dead soldiers. She had helped to treat his injuries, perhaps even to save his life. The experience had affected her relationship to him, just as tending Rogan had, and as looking after the others was changing her now.

The choice between speaking up and holding her peace would have seemed an easy one, even a week before.

Now, it was full of conflict.

Throughout that morning, while she and Geneva and several young soldiers ministered to the patients, Caroline fought an inner war of her own. She was no closer to resolving the problem at noon, when Jubie came to take over her nursing duties for a while, so Caroline could spend some time with Rachel, than she'd been in the moment she'd first understood exactly what was being asked of her.

She was grateful to Jubie, who spent hours every day helping soldiers — offering food, water and comfort — and Caroline now felt that the girl's insistence on tending the wounded had been the right decision. She admired her willingness to put herself at risk of being seen. Enoch, too, spent time in the hospital tents, assisting mainly with the lifting and moving of patients.

Entering the main house now was like finding refuge after a long and difficult journey, fraught with danger. Caroline let out a sigh of relief as her child greeted her at the door, small face at once joyous and troubled.

"Mama!" Rachel cried, flinging herself into Caroline's waiting arms. "You came back!"

Caroline gathered her up, held her tightly, closed her eyes as she breathed in the scent of a healthy little girl's clean, warm skin and hair, reveled in the solid heft of her wriggly form. "Of course I came back," she murmured. "Did you think I wouldn't?"

Rachel leaned back in Caroline's arms and studied her solemnly, shook her head once. "I heard screams," she confessed in a near whisper. "I was scared."

"Did Jubie explain what's happening?"

Again, Rachel shook her head. "I sang songs to her baby in her tummy, and then we played with my dolls and she told me stories. I asked her if the people in those tents were screaming because they were having bad dreams, and she said I should wait and ask you."

Caroline smoothed Rachel's hair away from her earnest little face; she wished she could shield the child from the terrible situation in the yard where, not long ago, she'd played happy childhood games, and knew it wasn't possible. "There are soldiers in the tents," she replied carefully. "Some of them are very badly hurt and in pain. That's why they cry out."

The expression on Rachel's face shattered something inside Caroline, perhaps for good. "Because they have to do a war?"

Because they have to do a war.

"Yes," Caroline choked out, trying to

smile and failing utterly. "It's because of the war." Reluctantly, she set Rachel back on her feet, although she would have preferred to go on holding her, tightly and for a long time.

"The war that made Papa die?"

Tears burned in Caroline's eyes. "Yes, darling. The same war,"

Rachel took Caroline's hand, squeezed it with her small, strong fingers. "Are you hurt too, Mama?" she asked, clearly worried. "Is that why you're crying?"

"I'm not hurt, sweetheart," Caroline responded with a sniffle, hastily dashing at her eyes with the back of one hand.

"War makes people very sad," Rachel said wisely, still gripping Caroline's hand. "Doesn't it?"

"Yes," Caroline replied. "It does."

Rachel's little brow furrowed with confusion. "It's not nice to fight," she announced. "Grown folks ought to stop doing it."

"I completely agree," Caroline said, and this time, her smile was real. There was no rational way to explain war to a four-year-old, of course — especially when she didn't fully understand it herself — but the subject could not be swept under the rug, either. It was, unfortunately, a reality, and would leave its mark on all of them, young and old alike. They'd reached the parlor by then, and without thinking, Caroline went directly to the harpsichord, seating herself on the bench, Rachel beside her.

"Play something, Mama," the child said.

Caroline was not an accomplished musician by any standard, but she knew how to play a few simple tunes and hymns.

"I don't know," she said hesitantly, even as her feet found the pedals and her fingers flexed on the cracked, ancient keys. The instrument was an heirloom, treasured by three generations of Hammond women, and on the rare occasions when Caroline played, she felt vaguely guilty, as though she was poking through someone else's belongings.

Furthermore, there were men suffering, some of them terribly, within earshot. Too merry a tune would certainly be inappropriate, but a mournful dirge wouldn't serve, either.

"Please, Mama?" Rachel whispered, hopeful.

Caroline reminded herself that she had been the one to sit down in front of the instrument. Perhaps if she played softly, the sound wouldn't carry far enough to disturb the wounded. As a child and a very young woman, she'd learned rudimentary musical skills, including the ability to read music.

She thought for a moment, then worked the pumps and stumbled awkwardly through the first verse of a favorite hymn, "Nearer, My God, to Thee."

Rachel watched while her mother's fingers played the keys.

"More, please," the little girl pleaded when the last notes had quivered into silence.

Caroline smiled and hugged her daughter close against her side for a long moment.

Rachel's eyes were alight with a heartrending eagerness for the ordinary pleasure of music. "I like that song Mr. Enoch used to play on his fiddle," she said. "The one about turkeys kicking straw."

Caroline laughed, an awkward sound, not recently practiced. " 'Turkey in the Straw'?" she asked. "That wouldn't be at all fitting, I'm afraid."

Rachel pondered that information somberly. "Why not?"

How, Caroline wondered, was she to explain that the tune might be too cheerful? Before she was required to answer, she heard a rapping sound from the arched doorway behind her, and turned to see Rogan McBride standing in the opening, looking chagrined.

"I knocked at the side door," he said

awkwardly. "I guess you didn't hear."

Caroline did not know what to make of his presence in her parlor. It wasn't an affront, just . . . unexpected. "I'm sorry if we've disturbed anyone," she said, about to rise from the bench.

The poor man looked as though he might collapse. "No," he responded quickly. "It isn't that. It's — well — the men . . . They'd like to hear more. It's a comfort to them, the sound of an organ. Carries them homeward."

Caroline did not point out that she hadn't been playing an organ, but a harpsichord. "I'm surprised they could hear it outside," she said.

"If we could open a window or two — maybe a door?" Rogan stumbled on, his expression as touchingly hopeful as Rachel's had been earlier. "I mean, if it wouldn't be an imposition?"

"That would be all right, wouldn't it, Mama?" Rachel asked eagerly. "Opening the doors and windows so the soldiers can listen, too?"

Caroline could only nod as she felt herself, once again, overcome with emotion.

The force of Rogan's smile, wan though it was, nearly brought her to tears. "Thank you, Mrs. Hammond," he said.

"Caroline," she corrected him, mentally searching her musical repertoire, then realized she needed to make an introduction. During the few days Rogan and Bridger had been here, they hadn't met Rachel, who'd been taking her meals in the main house, often with Jubie. "Oh! Captain McBride, this is my daughter, Rachel."

Rogan smiled and bowed politely. "Honored to meet you, Miss Rachel."

She grinned widely. "Me, too, Cap'n!"

Slowly, and with some help from Rachel, Rogan opened the side windows in the parlor and, on his way out, left the door ajar.

Caroline drew a deep breath and began to play.

She closed her eyes as the strains of "Abide with Me" flowed from her fingers and through the keys, to pulse entreatingly from within the instrument. She followed with "Home, Sweet Home," which brought more tears as it coursed through the windows into the moist heat of the afternoon, and then the rousing, "Battle Hymn of the Republic," a favorite of Mr. Lincoln himself.

Caroline became lost in the music, finding sweet solace even among the saddest compositions. At some point, she began to sing, allowing her own grief to find its place in lyrics of loneliness and sorrow.

When Jubie appeared at her elbow, holding out a battered copy of a songbook, small enough to carry in a pocket or a rucksack, she started slightly. The girl's face was a study in gentle fervor and a strange resolve.

"I can hear one of them Rebel boys through the open windows," she said, "and he's begging to hear this song. He won't be with us long, from the looks of him." Awkward though it might be, Caroline knew there were Southerners, although not many, in a few of the tents. Everyone, from the surgeon to those who took care of the wounded, seemed to treat them with a kind of practical compassion.

Caroline took the song book, a volume well used.

She peered at the music, drew yet another deep breath, and began.

The strains of "Dixie" bloomed around her, filling the parlor, drifting into the yard and the tents erected there.

The music filled her with yearning for the peaceful time when the North and South were still one country, undivided.

"No more," Caroline said brokenly, when she'd finished. "No more."

With that, she rose from the bench, leaving Rachel in Jubie's care, and walked. She walked fast, weeping as she went, not knowing where she was headed until she reached the quiet place under the tree where she'd buried Jacob only a few weeks before.

She dropped to her knees beside his grave, bent double with grief. She cried for herself and cried for Jacob and cried for the loss of peace and graciousness and all civility. She sobbed, rocking back and forth, thinking of their Rachel, fatherless now, the child Jacob would never look upon again, never hug again.

Sorrow welled within her, too great to contain, and she wailed with the agony of it, the unfairness, the pure cruelty of all the years that were unfairly lost to Jacob, and to so many men like him on both sides.

She cried for mothers and fathers, sisters and brothers, sons and daughters. She cried for Mr. Lincoln and the devastating burdens they bore, day by day, night by night.

She wept for the nation she loved so dearly, forged in the fires of hardship and hope and courage in the face of impossible odds, only to lie broken and bleeding less than a century later.

Finally, she was spent.

The weight of a hand, calloused and strong, came to rest upon her shoulder. "It's all right, Missus Caroline," Enoch said hoarsely. "It's gonna be all right."

Caroline couldn't speak. She allowed Enoch to take her arm, help her to her feet.

She nodded, acknowledging his presence. Made no attempt to wipe the wetness from her face.

Enoch held her by the elbow. "You come on back to the house, now," he said, his voice both gentle and gruff. He seemed to know that, although she could not utter a word herself, she found great comfort in his quiet talk. "You been too brave, that's what. You lost a mighty good husband, and now you've got men dying right outside your door, and if ever a woman had reason to cry, you do."

Caroline listened, stumbling along beside Enoch, thankful for his friendship and the strength of his hand, holding her upright.

"And you did a fine thing, playing that music a while ago. It soothed those poor boys plenty, it did. Took them home."

Caroline nodded again, still unable to speak.

"Did my heart good, too."

She longed to ask Enoch what she should do about the soldier Bridger Winslow. She dare not mention her unexpected attraction to him. She wanted to ask how on earth she was going to raise her daughter in a world torn asunder by war. She knew that if she tried to talk about any of this, she'd just fall apart again.

The question of Bridger Winslow would have to remain unresolved for now.

She returned to the house, and to Rachel, and remained there until her grandmother came in, exhausted. As Geneva sank into a chair in the parlor, she took her great-granddaughter onto her lap. And Caroline went back out to tend the wounded.

The work seemed endless — so much need, impossible to meet. Caroline functioned by rote, like a person in a walking stupor. She smiled, stroked their hands and foreheads, brought water to their lips and took down letters to distant loved ones. Each one could have been her Jacob.

And when she could go on no more, she went on anyway.

Early the next morning, after a deep and blessedly dreamless sleep, Caroline arose, washed and dressed, and finding Jubie up and around, asked her to stay with Rachel and to do what she could to dissuade Geneva from going about her nursing duties without having breakfast first.

Jubie nodded her acquiescence, but said little. Like everyone else, she was exhausted.

But she was also pregnant and her uncharacteristic silence worried Caroline.

Caroline paused. "You'll rest when you can? Put your feet up?" she asked.

Jubie nodded again. "But we all have to do what we can for those poor men," she added. "Our needs are nothing compared to theirs."

Men were suffering and dying in her yard, Caroline thought as she was getting ready to go out. She expected Captain Winslow to be in decline, too, given the severity of his wound. Just the same, thinking about him for those few seconds touched something intangible within Caroline, leaving her feeling briefly light-headed.

For a moment, the two women gazed at each other in silence, and it seemed to Caroline that an understanding passed between them. It was then, Caroline would think much later, that she and Jubie moved beyond helper and helped, protector and protected, to become true friends.

Jubie smiled, and the expression brightened her face. "I'll go see to Miss Rachel first. And later I'll help in the tents, take over from you for a few hours. Oh, and Miss Caroline, Enoch tells me Captain Winslow got a fever in the night."

Caroline was hardly surprised. But buoyed

by this young woman's strength, as well as her quiet smile, she said, "I'll go there right away. But please, Jubie — don't call me 'Miss' anymore. I'd rather you used my given name."

The request obviously gave Jubie pause, but she recovered quickly. "I might have to get used to that . . . but thank you, Caroline."

Caroline felt a smile take shape on her own mouth, before she again remembered the wounded men in the tents outside, and Captain Winslow's fever.

They went their separate ways, Jubie heading upstairs to look in on Rachel, Caroline out the side door to go to the kitchen house and check on the men there. She felt nauseated, taking in the stench of blood and sickness, then hurried past the tents. She refused to feel sorry for herself, whatever her trials, while so many around her had to endure suffering on a scale she could not have imagined before the war.

The kitchen house door stood ajar, and as she entered, she saw Rogan standing at the stove, gaunt and still unshaven, clad in remarkably clean uniform trousers, a cotton shirt and braces. He was cooking, frying side-pork, fresh eggs and potatoes in familiar skillets, and he seemed competent at the task, even well practiced.

"Good morning, Captain McBride," Caroline said, coming to a stop several feet from him.

"I thought we agreed to use our first names," Rogan commented.

She leaned in slightly, in search of Winslow. She found him on his pallet on the far side of the room, a fitful shadow. "Enoch says Captain Winslow has developed a fever," she murmured. "Jubie told me. You've . . . met her? She's been helping soldiers in the tents out there."

Rogan paused in his cooking duties and nodded. "We've spoken a time or two. Jubie's . . . extraordinary." Then he glanced toward the restless patient. "Yes, Bridger's very ill," he said gravely, before turning his head to face her again. "His skin's hot as one of these skillets. Maybe if we bathed him in cold water — ?"

Caroline swallowed anxiously and felt her cheeks warm. Raised in the home of a physician, she knew how quickly disease could spread. Her own parents and sister had fallen gravely ill in a matter of hours, seemingly fine in the morning and dead before sunset. She did not want to expose Rachel or Geneva to such a risk.

Children and the elderly were particularly

vulnerable to the horrors of cholera, typhoid, smallpox and scarlet fever, among other maladies, though of course anyone could get sick. Some of the wounded had already succumbed to infections, while others had contracted pneumonia. However, she assumed that in all likelihood, Captain Winslow's fever was the result of an infection in his wound and therefore not contagious.

Rogan seemed to be reading her every thought, just by watching her expression and comportment. "If you'll tell me what to do," he began, his voice ragged, "I'll take care of Bridger myself. Maybe you ought to keep your distance, just in case."

Caroline braced herself. "I would think it's too late for that kind of precaution," she said, with as much good cheer as she could manage. For all her reluctance, a part of her was drawn to Bridger Winslow and, disturbingly, to Rogan as well.

What in heaven's name did *that* mean?

Drawing on every ounce of resolution she possessed, Caroline crossed the room and knelt beside Mr. Winslow, then touched his forehead with the back of her right hand.

It was like touching a glowing ember, and she flinched, withdrawing instantly. Then, shamed by her skittish reaction, she carefully raised his loose-fitting shirt and tugged aside the seeping bandage to inspect the shoulder wound beneath.

The smell seemed to intensify now. Yellowish pus filled the gash, and streaks of red radiated from it.

"I shall need plenty of very hot water," she said, and the words had a distant, echoing quality, as though they'd been uttered by someone else. "Clean bandages and carbolic acid, as well. The supplies are in the cellar. You can manage the step?" she asked. She sensed Rogan's approach, felt him standing just behind her. "Caroline," he said hoarsely, as if preparing to object or send her away.

"Please," she said, closing her eyes for a long moment while she collected herself. "I can ask someone else to help, if you aren't up to it."

He made a sound of mild exasperation. "I can do it," he said as he crossed to the cellar door, opened it and descended the stairs.

Caroline remained on her knees beside Mr. Winslow, gently smoothing his matted hair from his forehead, touching his beard-roughened cheek. He stirred, groaning a little, but did not open his eyes.

Just as Rogan returned from the cellar, bearing the items Caroline had requested, the main door swung open and Enoch entered, with Geneva close behind.

Geneva hurried over, although she didn't kneel. "Mercy," she said, "I had quite forgotten the *smell* of infection."

Caroline looked up at her grandmother, struck by the older woman's composure.

"I was about to change the dressing and disinfect the wound," Caroline told her.

Geneva turned to address Enoch. "This man must be moved into the main house," she said. "In his condition, he ought to be in a proper bed, not on a hard floor."

"But where would we put him?" Caroline asked. Geneva occupied the spare bedroom upstairs, and Jubie slept in the back room off the parlor.

"Why, in Rachel's room, of course," Geneva replied briskly. "She's been sharing your bed. We can move her playthings into your room."

"Very well," Caroline agreed. Although the idea of a strange man taking his rest in the bedroom next to her own was, while clearly necessary, still unsettling.

"I'll move to a cot in one of the tents," Rogan said.

But Geneva had other ideas. "It would be much better," she announced, "if you shared your friend's quarters. You've suffered injuries yourself and, besides, this gentleman should not be left unattended during the night."

There was only one small bed in Rachel's room, but Caroline didn't point that out, knowing her grandmother would dispense with any objection she raised. When Geneva Prescott set her mind on a specific course of action, she could not easily be dissuaded. They would just add a cot there.

"Captain McBride," Geneva continued, proving Caroline's unspoken point, "perhaps you could ask one of the guards for a stretcher and then prevail upon Mr. Alderman and Mr. Pickering to carry the patient into the house?"

"Yes, Ma'am," Rogan replied.

Enoch, meanwhile, stood in attentive silence, no doubt anticipating orders of his own.

"Captain McBride was kind enough to prepare breakfast," Caroline said, adopting some of her grandmother's brisk authority. "Why don't you sit down, Enoch, and have something to eat?"

He hesitated, though his gaze trailed in the direction of the stove, where the meal Rogan had assembled was rapidly turning cold. Then, with a slight motion of his head, indicating the tents just outside, he said, "Plenty still to do, Missus."

Caroline proceeded to disinfect Winslow's wound and rebandage it while he waited to be moved.

"You'll be no good to anyone, Enoch Flynn," she said as she worked, "if you don't take proper nourishment."

She paused, studying her friend, this good man who had come to rescue her from despair the previous day at Jacob's grave.

"Sit down, Enoch," she added quietly.

By then, Rogan was outside, accompanied by Geneva.

Caroline moved to the stove, where a small amount of hot water steamed in a kettle. She poured it into a basin, reached for the soap and lathered her hands thoroughly.

Enoch stood in the same place as before, his expression uncertain.

"Sit down," Caroline repeated. "You look as though you might fall asleep on your feet, and you must be half-starved."

Enoch frowned, folded his brawny arms across his chest. "It isn't right, Missus, you serving me my food."

Caroline rinsed her hands, dried them on a dish towel, then took a plate from one of the nearby shelves. "Nonsense," she said.

"You've been working hard, and you're tired and hungry. So, please *sit,* unless you mean to eat standing up." She brought the meal to the table, and set it down at Enoch's usual place. "I'm not going to tell you again, Enoch," she finished.

The big man lowered his hands to his sides and sighed heavily, but there was a glint of weary amusement in his eyes. "Well, in that case," he said, unbending at last, "I reckon I'd better do as I'm told."

With that, he drew back his chair and sank into it.

Rogan returned, followed by Alderman and Pickering, the two of them carrying a crude stretcher, filthy with blood and who knew what else.

Geneva, already spouting instructions, brought up the rear. "Be very careful," she said. "You mustn't jostle the poor fellow about too much."

Her gaze came to rest upon Enoch, seated at the table with a meal set before him, and narrowed when he started to rise. "Stay put," she ordered. "We'll need your assistance in a little while, and it won't do if you're too weak to lend it."

"Yes, Missus," Enoch said, though he looked mighty uncomfortable retaining his seat at the table in the presence of ladies.

He thanked Caroline, took up his fork and began to eat.

In the interim, Alderman and Pickering laid the empty stretcher alongside Bridger's pallet and, with plenty of advice from Geneva, shifted him onto the soiled canvas.

Though still unconscious, Bridger cried out once. Caroline stiffened, hearing it, and her hands trembled as she poured coffee into a mug for Enoch.

Now, Geneva took the lead ahead of the stretcher bearers and Rogan. "Have a care — don't drop him — do watch out for the doorjamb."

Once the way was cleared, Caroline moved to follow the others, then paused in the door and looked back at Enoch.

"Thank you, Enoch," she said. "For yesterday, I mean." She blushed. "And for everything else you do, of course. I truly don't know how I could manage without your help."

Enoch made to stand once again, and Caroline raised a hand, palm out, then turned and hastened out of the kitchen area, into the bright morning sunlight, hurrying after the small group crossing the yard, moving around tents and a few ambulatory soldiers toward her house.

Glancing over one shoulder, Rogan saw

her and slowed his pace until she caught up to him. After a quick look around, to make sure no one was within earshot, he met her eyes and spoke in a near whisper.

"Have you decided?" he asked, his eyes earnest and intensely watchful. "About turning Bridger in, I mean?"

Caroline felt a stab of emotion. "I don't suppose I will," she said, her tone mildly defensive. "I haven't spoken to my grandmother or Enoch, however, and I feel I must do that. But I can't promise they'll cooperate, once they understand what they are being asked to do."

"Keep a badly wounded man from wasting away in a prison camp?" Rogan retorted with a barely perceptible edge in his voice.

Caroline bristled. "Or," she countered, in a sharp whisper, "aiding and abetting the enemy and virtually assuring that he'll return to the Confederate forces at the first opportunity to take up arms again and kill *our* Union soldiers! Who happen also to be *your* fellow soldiers."

Rogan seemed taken aback, though surely he must have known to expect some sort of reaction. In fact, he came to a halt at the base of the steps leading to the side door, through which Geneva, Bridger and the other two men had just passed.

Caroline stared at him and waited stubbornly for his response.

It came soon enough. All vestiges of his former consternation had disappeared, replaced by steely determination.

"All I can say for sure," he told her, "is that I can't and *won't* let my best friend rot or be hanged in some hellhole of a camp up north, no matter what."

Caroline gestured toward the tents, where men moaned and wept and sometimes screamed in agony, around the clock. "What about *them,* Captain McBride? Do you feel any kind of loyalty toward these men, torn to pieces by Confederate cannon and minié balls — or the thousands of others like them?" *Like my Jacob?*

He did not shrink from her vitriol, but leaned in close until she could feel his breath on her face.

"Do you think, Mrs. Hammond, for *one damn moment,* that I don't know what war is like? I am military-trained, as is Captain Winslow. I enlisted in the Union army to fight for my principles and I don't regret it, but that doesn't mean I don't understand why Bridger made a similar choice for different reasons. He's a decent, honorable man, not some bloodthirsty fiend out for senseless slaughter!"

Caroline spoke carefully, furiously, quietly. "What," she demanded, "is decent and honorable about enslaving other human beings, Captain McBride? About running a young woman — an expectant mother — down like an animal?"

"A young woman — you mean Jubie? What — ?"

"*Yes,* Jubie." Caroline was shaken, and not at all sure she could keep her voice down if this discussion continued, so she climbed the steps and entered the house, with Rogan right behind her. "How can you — how can *any* sensible person — discount the injustice, the cruelty — ?"

"I'm not defending slavery," Rogan said, with conviction. "You must know that. And neither is Bridger."

She whirled on him, there in the shadowy corridor. "Of course he is," she insisted, outraged, but very aware that Rachel was in the house and might overhear their heated exchange. "Why else would he fight?"

Rogan was rimmed in sunlight, but his face was in darkness, and she could not read his expression. "He's *fighting,*" he replied, "because the South is his home. Wouldn't you do the same, Caroline? Wouldn't you fight to defend this ground? Your child, your grandmother, your friends and neighbors?

Your town and the folks who live there?"

"It isn't the same," Caroline sputtered, a mite less certain of her opinions than before, but still unprepared to back down. All her life, it seemed to her now, she had deferred to the supposed wisdom of men — her husband, her grandfather, teachers and doctors and ministers — keeping her own ideas to herself, even when righteous opposition brewed and roiled within her.

"Isn't it?" Rogan asked, closing the door behind them.

They stood in the dim, cool corridor, looking at each other. Geneva's voice trailed down the back stairway, and there were thumps and bumps as Captain Winslow, a member of the very army that had killed her husband and thousands of others, was installed in her daughter's bedroom.

"No," Caroline answered, gathering her skirts and making for the stairs, Rogan close behind her. He would be gone soon, she reminded herself, with his army and his good looks and his misguided views on the subject of loyalty. She would not suppress her beliefs. "You know it isn't the same. Captain Winslow would not have been called upon to 'defend his home' if the South hadn't left the Union in the first place."

Rogan offered no response to her remark, and she supposed that meant she had won the argument.

The small victory, if it *was* a victory, seemed strangely hollow.

What seemed most hollow of all was the fact that this very day was the anniversary of the country's founding. A day meant to be a commemoration, a celebration — but could be nothing of the kind.

Several hours later that same day, Jubie shyly approached Caroline in the kitchen house. "Miss, I was just helping in the tents, and a soldier asks if I can write a couple letters for him. I said I can't —" She shook her head sorrowfully. "Will you do it? Sooner is better. He's in the third tent closest to the barn and his name is Gregory."

"Of course!" Caroline replied.

"I'll watch the little miss here and carry on with making dinner."

Caroline thanked her and retrieved a stack of papers and a pen from the main house. She hurried over to the tent and, with a question or two, identified Gregory Lauder from upstate New York. A farmer's son, he couldn't have been more than twenty and had served with a volunteer infantry regiment. In a painfully cracked voice, he told her he'd been shot at Cemetery Ridge; he also said he knew he might not survive. Several of his ribs were broken — but worse, his lungs had been punctured. He frequently coughed up blood, and his shirt, the sheets and blanket were stained with it.

She settled on a camp stool beside Gregory's cot and prepared to write.

He coughed, weakly wiped his mouth and began by giving her his parents' names and their address, near the city of Rochester. "Please tell them I love them . . . and that I believe I made the right decision to fight for the Union."

As she began the letter, Caroline first introduced herself to his parents, then wrote down, carefully and clearly, everything Gregory said.

"I am presently in a field hospital near a town called Gettysburg in Pennsylvania. Due to my injuries, I will almost certainly not see you again. I am sorry for what grief this will cause. As you know, I had planned, eventually, to take over the farm. I hope young Daniel will understand what a privilege it is." He paused to cough again.

"I will miss all of you more than I can say."

"Your loving son and brother, Gregory."

Caroline wondered if he'd have the physical stamina and emotional strength to dictate another letter. But several minutes later, he seemed ready to begin again. He said she could send his fiancée's letter in the care of his parents.

"My dearest Eliza," he dictated. "It pains me to tell you this. I do not believe I shall survive my injuries. Therefore, I do not expect to see you again."

Once more he explained where he was and that he took pride in being a soldier on the Union side. "I love you," he went on, "as much as any man can love a woman. Please forgive me for leaving you and understand why I did what I did. I shall hope to see you and my family in a better world. All my love . . ."

Gregory's eyes were closed by now and Caroline was in tears. She placed a discreet kiss on his forehead and hurried inside to prepare the letters for posting.

17

Hammond Farm & Town of Gettysburg
July 8, 1863

CAROLINE

The young men who were physically able tended the wounded and cooked over a single bonfire some distance from the house, fueling the blaze with wood they had purchased from Caroline at a fair price. They were unfailingly polite whenever she encountered them, and stayed well clear of the house.

Except for two of them. Captain Winslow sprawled on Rachel's narrow bed upstairs, still as death for the most part, but prone to raving, flailing about and shouting curses when overtaken by delirium. And then there was Captain McBride, who took what little rest he could on a nearby army cot in the same small room.

Recovering rapidly, Rogan spent his days

helping Enoch and a small detachment of soldiers with the grim task of digging temporary graves for the dead, each plot carefully marked and recorded in a ledger, so the bodies could be recovered later, sent home to loved ones for proper funerals and reinternment or, in some cases, buried at places like Arlington.

Yesterday, the fourth day after the battle, Rogan had ridden to town, accompanied by his men, Pickering and Alderman, and Enoch, who had gone along at Geneva's request, so that he might visit her house and bring news of its condition.

When the men returned, hours later, they were grim and silent. Rogan, who had bathed, shaved and requisitioned a crisp new uniform as soon as he regained the necessary strength, had been pale as milk, the lower part of his face stubbled with the beginnings of a new beard, his clothing rumpled and dirty, his boots dull with dust.

He had looked, to Caroline, more vanquished than victorious, and the bleak expression in his eyes had stirred an ache of sorrow deep within her. She'd felt an unseemly urge to run to him, as she would once have run to Jacob.

She had not succumbed to the impulse, thank heaven, though her desire to do so had lingered far longer than she deemed proper. No, she had merely watched, stricken by the need to console a near stranger, as he dismounted, led his horse into the barn, the pair of them vanishing into the shadows.

In the kitchen house, an hour later, hunched over his untouched supper plate, Enoch had related some of what they'd seen to her and Geneva, although Caroline had known his words were but pale sketches of a devastation that fate had drawn in bold lines.

The Prescott house had been used as a field hospital, he reported; the carpets had been rolled back, and the floors were stained with blood. The beds and armchairs and settees were beyond salvaging, the draperies had been torn from the windows, probably to be used as blankets, bandages and tourniquets, along with sheets and dishtowels; and the pantry and cellar were bare.

In spite of all this, there were no signs of the vandalism or wanton destruction both armies had been known to leave behind — and of which he'd seen many signs on the streets. Broken windows, scattered belongings and worse.

Geneva had been visibly relieved, but still concerned. "What of the people?" she had asked, one hand resting at the base of her throat, as if to hide the pulse pounding there. "The other houses — the shops?"

"There was a woman killed . . . on Baltimore Street," Enoch had replied haltingly. "Your street . . . Looking after her sister, who'd just had a baby. The way I heard it, she was in the kitchen, kneading a batch of bread dough, when a stray bullet came right through the door and struck her dead."

Caroline had sagged into a chair, suddenly as breathless as if she, too, had been struck.

"What was her name?" Geneva had asked quickly.

"As I recall, it was Wade. Miss Virginia Wade."

Caroline had gasped, covered her mouth with one hand. Geneva shook her head, tears filling her eyes. Jennie, as Virginia was called, Wade had been born and raised in Gettysburg, and they'd both been especially fond of her. She'd had a sweetheart away in the war, Jennie had, and she'd lived for his letters.

Reluctantly, Enoch had gone on to deliver still more dreadful news. The fields were littered with graves and bodies, he'd said, and the remains of dead horses and mules had been dragged behind wagons and teams of borrowed oxen, left in great, rotting heaps to be burned, being too numerous to bury.

No one pressed Enoch for any further information. It would have been cruel, and quite unnecessary, since the land would bear the scars of battle far into the future, stark and plain for all to see.

The next day in her sun-splashed garden, Caroline remembered her conversation with Enoch and shuddered, running an arm across her brow to wipe away the perspiration.

She reached for her daughter, secured the bonnet, and smiled at the little girl's upturned face, already smudged with garden dirt.

"Did my nose peel off, Mama?" Rachel asked, wrinkling the feature in question.

Caroline nearly laughed, until she raised her eyes slightly, and was reminded that a fragment of the Union army was encamped squarely between the house and the barn. "It might," she replied distractedly, "if you don't keep your bonnet on."

Taking in the tents and wagons nearby, and those soldiers who were well enough to tend the wounded moving about, she yearned for peaceful days gone by. Long days, full of hard work and, yes, worries, with a war going on and her husband far from home and constantly in harm's way, but still blessedly *alive* at that time penning long letters to her whenever he had the chance. Letters of promise — *we'll have more children, Caroline, sturdy boys and girls, you wait and see — we'll save every spare cent and buy more land — keep beef cattle and raise hogs — and when our sons and daughters have all grown up and married, we'll travel. We'll see New York — maybe even sail across the Atlantic, visit places like Paris and Rome and London —*

Oh, Jacob, she thought sadly. Jacob.

He'd had such wonderful, high-flying dreams.

Her own aspirations had been so much simpler; she had wanted more children, certainly, but otherwise, she would have been content to live out her entire life on that modest farm, raising babies, growing and preserving vegetables, milking the cow, separating the cream and churning the butter. She hadn't yearned to go on long journeys, however spectacular the sights; she'd been to them all, at least in her imagination, through the pages of her grandfather's many books.

Jacob, on the other hand, had never tired of making extravagant plans, though he, too, had loved the farm and being part of a small community. But how his eyes had shone when he spoke of traveling far and wide. The loss of him constantly weighed her down, but she was determined to do anything the grim circumstances that faced her required.

Caroline once again fixed her attention on the doings before her. Soon, according to Alderman, the men assembled on her grass would be moving on, with tents and their wounded, and those who were able would fight again. She decided she'd return to town to be as useful as she could be. She'd see her friends in the Ladies' Aid Society, Hannah and Patience and the others, and help with whatever she could.

In that contrary way of human nature, she both looked forward to the soldiers' departure and dreaded it. She and the rest of the state would move ahead, perhaps tentatively at first, pushing up their sleeves, collecting the scattered pieces of the lives they'd lived before the battle and then beginning the long and arduous process of rebuilding. Most people would get through, somehow, sharing what remained to them, helping one another when the need presented itself, discreetly minding their own business the rest of the time.

Caroline would always remember that she

had been treated fairly by the Union army, although she knew the courteous forbearance the soldiers had shown her was at least partially due to the presence of Captain McBride's well-stocked supply wagons, which seemed to contain all that the visitors required, other than the mercy of others. She had indeed been fortunate; other farmers, townspeople and shopkeepers nearby had surely not fared as well, their food and supplies at times pilfered.

Her practical nature soon reasserted itself; she had a garden to tend and a child to look after, and she could not afford to waste precious daylight wallowing in the futile yearning for a gentler world than the one she now lived in.

Just as she was about to call out to Rachel that her bonnet was slipping again, she saw Rogan McBride round the corner of one of the tents and stride toward her.

He was so comely, this man, with his raven-dark hair and dark blue eyes, his straight, uncommonly white teeth, and that innate sense of competence, an ability to forge ahead, even while wounded. His build was lean and agile but muscular, and it seemed to Caroline that, for all his quiet exterior, some unique combination of inner qualities blazed inside him like a furnace, not merely sustaining him, but generating the power to overcome any obstacle placed in his way.

"Good morning, Caroline," Rogan said, as he stopped at the edge of the garden, a few feet from where she stood.

"I've been hoping to speak to you," Rogan began, lowering his voice. But watching her, he fell suddenly silent, as though something in her expression or her manner had given him pause.

Before he could pick up the dangling thread of his words and make another beginning, Rachel appeared and flung herself at him, giggling, and he bent, scooped the child into his arms and held her, just the way Jacob used to do. He laughed and tugged the wide brim of Rachel's calico bonnet down over her eyes, then grinned as she stubbornly pushed it up again with a chubby hand.

Clearly, despite her efforts to keep her child apart from the soldiers, these two had, somehow, become friendly. Or was it simply that in his blue uniform, Rogan reminded Rachel of Papa?

If it wasn't too late, Caroline decided, she would try to make sure that Rachel didn't form an attachment to Rogan, only to endure another parting when his duties called him away.

"Rachel," she said, rather more sternly than she might have in other circumstances, "please go back to the main house."

Rogan set the little girl firmly on her feet, smiling down at her, and inclining his head in the direction of the main house.

Rachel looked up at him and frowned.

"Go," Rogan told her mildly.

She went, scampering, toward the house.

Caroline cleared her throat, found her voice. "There was something you wanted to say, Captain McBride?"

He turned to look at her, no longer smiling. "There are plenty of things I'd like to say," he replied seriously. After a pensive moment, he tried again, meeting her gaze. "We received orders when I was in town to transport the wounded to the railroad terminal in Harrisburg and see that they're boarded on a troop train to Baltimore. Those who are capable of it will rejoin General Meade as quickly as possible."

This should have come as a relief to Caroline, but it didn't. Not entirely, anyway.

No more sick and dying soldiers on the farm. They and their tents would be gone, along with the wagons, horses and mules. No more cries of pain. No more temporary graves being dug. No more heartrending letters to be set down on paper and addressed to faraway mothers, wives and sweethearts. She had, at least, learned that Gregory Lauder had so far survived . . .

She would be able to resume some part of her life, such as it was. At least she'd be able to join her friends in town and help with nursing the casualties. Or cleaning up damaged homes and properties. Or repairing clothes. Or . . . Whatever was needed now that the fighting in and around Gettysburg was over.

Still she was surprised by her mixed feelings. She would miss McBride, in spite of his determination to safeguard his Confederate friend, who she assumed would be moving on, as well. She now realized how much she'd miss being constantly needed, doing her small part to further the Union cause. Moreover, as disruptive as the experience of having her property conscripted for military use had been, the presence of so many soldiers, not all of whom were incapacitated, had been comforting, too. And the practical reality was that once they moved on, the place would be far more vulnerable to stragglers, deserters and other outlaws. She'd already heard, via Enoch, that another farmer, closer to town, had some of his crops stolen and his home vandalized.

She did know that Lee's army had left; she'd learned from the *Gettysburg Compiler* that he'd set out on July Fourth with a wagon train of Confederate wounded, heading south — a convoy that had been a shocking seventeen miles long.

"Oh," Caroline said, in belated response to Rogan's announcement.

Rogan was watching her closely now, as though assessing emotions she hadn't successfully hidden. Then, grimly, he told her, "If you're worried about the Army of Northern Virginia paying a visit, you can put that out of your mind. According to our scouts, they're limping south at a snail's pace." Rogan paused, then said, "This war might have been over, once and for all, if our own General Meade had the gumption and foresight to chase the Rebels down and finish the fight before Lee could pull that ragtag, barefoot army of his back together. Instead, like McClellan, Meade seems to suffer from a case of *the slows,* as the President would say, and another opportunity is gone."

Caroline didn't tell him she knew that, didn't tell him she'd followed the course of the conflict in the newspapers, when they were available. And she'd always garnered some information from Jacob's letters, for all that he'd written almost nothing about battles or commanders, preferring to gloss over the horrors he'd witnessed and the hardships he'd endured. She knew little about most generals and their proclivities but, like most Northerners, she was well versed in the legend that was Robert E. Lee.

He'd worn a blue uniform then, not gray, Caroline thought sadly, serving under a banner of stars and stripes, rather than the flag of rebellion. Later, Lee had returned to West Point as its chief administrator, and many of his former students and colleagues were high-ranking officers now, some fighting with him, and some against.

As the head of the Army of Northern Virginia, he was a truly formidable opponent. It seemed to Caroline, especially in light of Rogan's remarks, that the North was in sore need of a general as bold and clever as the Confederate commander.

"Can he be defeated? General Lee, I mean?" she asked tentatively.

"Yes," Rogan said without hesitation. "He is a man, not a god, though you wouldn't guess it to hear the stories. He's neither young nor in the best of health. A good number of his troops are barefoot and half-starved, and his horses are dropping beneath their riders, from hunger and exhaustion."

"Why doesn't he quit and go home to his family? Allow his army to do the same?" Caroline said.

Rogan sighed, shook his head. "I don't think the man has it in him to quit," he said, with conviction and regret.

"You sound as if you know General Lee," Caroline observed. "Personally, I mean, and not simply by reputation."

"I met him once, before the war," Rogan answered, looking away, and then back. "He came to dinner at Fairhaven — that's Bridger's family plantation, outside Savannah. I used to spend some vacations there, between terms at school." He smiled somewhat wistfully at the memory. "It was a revelation, for an orphan like me."

"You were impressed by Lee?"

"Yes, partly."

"Partly?"

"The general wasn't famous then, remember. He was a mere colonel at the time, if I recall correctly, a dignified man with a gray beard and fine manners, a friend of the Winslow family. I'm afraid I was a lot more interested in the house and the land and the way Bridger's family lived — fine clothes, the best food and wines, blooded horses in the stable, and a house so big and so grand that it rendered me speechless the first time I saw it. And their kindness toward me was . . . memorable. Bridger and his father and sister could not have treated me better." He paused again, obviously remembering a more gracious time and place. "You see, my mother was a housemaid in a mansion on Park Avenue when I was young," he added presently, his voice quiet and somehow sad. "So I'd had glimpses of the way rich people lived, when I was a servant's brat and expected to stay out of sight. At Fairhaven, I was a guest, with all the attendant privileges. I wore Bridger's clothes, ate like a king and rode horses with a far better pedigree than my own. I danced with girls so pretty they might have stepped out of a book of fairy tales — and, since I was all of fifteen years old that first time, it probably won't surprise you that I was far too callow to appreciate an introduction to the colonel."

Caroline smiled, imagining Rogan as a boy of fifteen, dining in such lofty company. She imagined him as raw-boned and awkward, tall for his age, still growing into his height, probably eager to make a good impression — or simply to avoid making a fool of himself.

She would've liked to hear more, not about his summers at Fairhaven, though that was interesting, but about his *real* life, especially as a "servant's brat" and a "street urchin." Alas, this was not the time or place for such an exchange; there were other things to discuss.

"What is to be done with Mr. Winslow?" she asked. "He is, as you must know, still in no fit condition to travel." Neither, she thought but did not say, were many of the Union wounded, who were to be hauled to Harrisburg like so much freight, and shuttled onto a train bound for Baltimore. Having heard more of the history Rogan and Bridger shared, she understood Rogan's desire to protect his friend a little better.

Rogan sighed, rubbed his chin with one hand, and replied, "Frankly, I was hoping he could stay right here. As soon as he's well enough, he'll leave on his own. Perhaps in civilian clothes."

"And if he does not recover?"

The suggestion alone caused Rogan visible pain. "He *will* get better," he insisted, as though he could will it so. "He's half again too cussed to die, especially behind Yankee lines. I'll leave money for Bridger's keep, along with a uniform — Union blue, in case he needs to maintain the charade —

and a pair of boots before I go. Probably hide them somewhere in the kitchen house after dark, so there won't be any questions."

Caroline folded her arms. She'd seen Jubie and Rachel leave earlier and saw them pass by now, headed back to the house, and she half expected her daughter to reappear, wanting more of Rogan's attention.

"Suppose word gets out that I'm harboring an enemy officer? What then?"

"That would be a problem," Rogan said. "Better to make sure word *doesn't* get out."

"But if it does?"

"Then you tell the truth. Bridger couldn't be moved, and you acted out of plain human compassion."

"How simple you make it all sound, Captain McBride, with your plans and your offer to pay Mr. Winslow's board and room. It's all so easy — *for you.*"

"That's where you're wrong, *Mrs. Hammond.* This situation is anything *but* easy for me. I don't like leaving my friend behind, too sick to defend himself. I don't like burdening you with a problem that should never have been laid on your shoulders in the first place. And I sure as *hell* don't like having to load several dozen wounded men into wagons and driving them over rutted roads, under a hot sun, all the way to Harrisburg. Because I know how much they'll suffer, and then suffer *again* crowded into railroad cars like so many cattle!"

Caroline was sorry now for her harsh words, but resisted the impulse to backtrack or apologize. "Perhaps," she ventured bravely, "you will pass this way again, once Mr. Winslow has recovered, and collect him yourself."

Rogan regarded her in silence for a minute or two, as if puzzled or intrigued by the suggestion. "Perhaps I will," he said thoughtfully. Then, as though he'd resolved something in his mind, he added, "Most likely, though, Bridger will be long gone from here before I have an opportunity to return." He paused again, as if rallying internal forces, and a faint flush stained his neck. "With your permission, I'll write to you. To ask after Bridger and send along whatever provisions he might need."

Caroline pretended to consider her reply, though in truth, she very much liked the idea of receiving correspondence from Rogan McBride, and she hoped his letters would contain more than inquiries regarding Mr. Winslow's progress of recovery. Of course he could not be expected to include sensitive military information, such as planned troop movements, because of the risk that his letters could fall into enemy hands, but perhaps he would tell her a little about the things he saw and heard and thought.

Jacob, with the best of intentions, had mostly sought to shelter Caroline from the hard truths of battle, only informing her occasionally about the more mundane aspects of army life.

She loved Jacob for his efforts to shield her from the ugliness and horror of his experiences, but now that she'd seen some of the ravages of war for herself, first in the hospital tents of Washington City and more recently here on her own farm and in her own town, she had changed in unexpected ways. She knew sorrow would always be her companion, no matter what happiness life might hold in store. And while her innocent illusions were forever lost to her, she had been forced to seek and find inner resources she had never imagined she might possess.

"I should like to correspond with you," she told Rogan. "But there are terms."

He smiled wearily at that. "Of course there are," he said, without rancor.

Caroline drew a deep breath and exhaled slowly. "I will respond to your inquiries about Mr. Winslow's state of health honestly, in detail and as promptly as possible. I will keep a record of any costs I undertake on your friend's behalf and, should your contributions exceed the amount required, you may trust that I will set the excess funds aside to be returned to you at the first opportunity."

Rogan raised one eyebrow slightly. "More than fair," he replied. "Those are your . . . terms? If so, they ought to be easy to meet."

"There is one thing more," Caroline said. Why was it so difficult, she wondered, to make even a simple request? The Captain had asked — practically decreed — a far greater undertaking of *her,* hadn't he? And without noticeable hesitation, for that matter.

He waited, saying nothing, a smile dancing in his eyes. Whether his expression was a show of patient respect or of some private amusement, Caroline didn't know.

"You must give a reasonable account of your experiences and your opinions," she blurted, on a single rush of breath. Then, relieved that she'd finally gotten past her own reluctance, she added more slowly, "I want to know the true state of things, as you see them from day to day, with no concessions to my . . . being a woman."

He smiled again — at her involuntary

blush, she presumed.

"I am not fragile, though my late husband might have perceived me as such."

"No, I see that," Rogan said. He seemed strangely pleased by her demands, rather than put off, as some men would have been. "Far from fragile, Caroline Hammond, you are a remarkably strong and generous woman with a fine mind and a great many other noble attributes that I will keep to myself for the present, lest I be accused of flattery."

"Thank you," she said, averting her eyes for a moment, in the hope that he wouldn't see how flustered she was.

When Rogan gave a brief, hoarse laugh, Caroline's eyes flew back to his face. "You'll have your unvarnished description of events," he promised her, "at least as I view them. It remains to be seen how thankful you'll be after you've had to put up with Bridger for a while longer. He's fairly easy to deal with now, but once the fever breaks and he becomes his genuine self again, you'll probably want to throttle him person-ally — or have him horsewhipped."

Caroline smiled at Rogan's comments, surely made in jest. She remembered her brief exchanges with Mr. Winslow before the infection and fever had set in. The Rebel captain seemed to be primarily a gentleman, well-bred and endowed with a corresponding measure of Southern charm, a practiced quality that was easily assumed when called for, yet somehow inherent to his nature.

She would deal with Winslow as best she could, from day to day, keeping their differences constantly in mind. In due time, he would be gone — one way or the other.

"When?" she heard herself ask. "When will you and the others be leaving, I mean?"

"Tomorrow," he said. "Or perhaps the next day."

Too soon, she thought once again. Rogan and the others would be gone too soon.

And yet not soon enough. She knew she had a great many things to tend to.

There was nothing more to be said, and she acknowledged Rogan's answer with a nod. She turned back to her vegetable patch, where she crouched and began yanking stray sprouts from among the viable plants, the ones that would provide nourishment.

Like sorrows, and just as common, weeds seemed to spring back from the earth mere minutes after they'd been pulled up by the roots and thrust aside.

18

Hammond Farm
July 12, 1863

BRIDGER

He slept restlessly, half-aware of the waking world around him but unable to rise to it. His flesh burned with heat, even as hard chills wracked him, fit to splinter his very bones.

He was in a bed inside a house, he realized. A *real* bed, with a soft mattress and crisp cotton sheets that smelled faintly of fresh air. He clung to the blessed normality of that ordinary scent, followed it back and back, to the time before, when he had taken such graces as cleanliness and comfort, and so many other things like them, as his due.

Hot biscuits, for example, smothered in rich butter or Cook's thick sausage gravy, peppery and steaming on a china plate. Flourishing rose gardens and spacious, venerable houses where longcase clocks ticked off the leisurely hours. Sultry summer nights, scented with promise. Regular baths in a copper tub, long enough for his tall frame and deep enough to soak in. Heirloom bureaus and wardrobes, bulging with garments laundered in soapy water and dried in the sun; supple breeches and shirts starched and pressed to perfection; finely made, polished boots.

Stables full of handsome, spirited horses, every one of them fast and muscular and boasting a flawless bloodline —

Home.

The yearning for Fairhaven, and all it represented, fell upon him suddenly, with a weight so crushing that it forced the breath from his lungs and left almost no room to draw another.

Then as he dragged in one painful breath, he clung to what remained of his reason as a sailor might cling to the mast of a storm-tossed ship.

He thought about his sister Amalie — the only immediate family, other than his father, that he had left. The sister he loved so much. And wondered how she was managing the responsibilities that came with a place like Fairhaven.

His relationship with their father had

never been what Bridger would have desired; his older brother had always been the clear favorite. Amalie rarely mentioned their father in her letters. He pictured her sitting on the porch swing with a puppy on her lap and a book of poetry in her hands . . .

In his responses to her letters he'd told her little about his experiences of war and grief — he'd wanted to spare her, he supposed. And her letters to him had focused on their home, both the estate and the city of Savannah, that inevitably made him nostalgic. She'd written about their friends, her own work with the local Ladies' Aid Society, her concern about him . . . He had been wounded and suffered pain, suffered it still, but he hadn't, so far, experienced the unspeakable agony of severed limbs and shattered bones and organs spilling from a belly slashed open by a bayonet or a sword, or blasted to fragments of bloody gore by a minié ball.

As he lay there, in the clean bed, in a room he didn't recognize, Bridger concentrated on forcing himself to move from one breath, one heartbeat, to the next. He closed his eyes, hoping to sleep.

Instead, he found himself drifting somewhere between wakefulness and sweet oblivion. The pain was still with him, but at a remove; it had softened from a searing spike to a vague nuisance.

"Captain Winslow?" The voice came from somewhere above him — familiar, insistent, and most definitely an intrusion.

Wrenched back to the surface, Bridger opened his eyes and found himself gazing straight into a face he recognized.

Caroline Hammond's.

Everything came back to him now: the smoke and flames, the screams of rage and agony, the blinding chaos of full engagement, and the simultaneous events of coming face-to-face with Rogan just as a sword pierced his shoulder from behind. He recalled a flash of white-hot pain as the point tore through his flesh, another as it was wrenched free, followed by the long, slow fall from the saddle.

He recalled Rogan pulling him over the smoldering ground, depositing him in a thicket of brush, leaving him there. Bridger had tried to crawl from his hiding place, intending to get back into the fight by whatever means availed themselves, but the effort had not only proved futile, it had sapped the last of his strength. He had no idea how long he'd lain there on the fringes of the continuing skirmish, helpless and bleeding.

In time, Rogan had returned, cut away his gray tunic, replaced it with another. He remembered his friend speaking to him in low, urgent words that had not registered in Bridger's brain and eluded him yet.

Later, in Mrs. Hammond's kitchen house, Rogan had told him he'd been loaded into a wagon and brought to this farm to recover — and to hide.

He noticed the pervasive silence.

No voices rising on the sweltering summer heat. No wagons coming and going.

"Where," he croaked, "is Rogan?"

"He's gone," replied the Widow Hammond, pursing her mouth slightly.

"*Gone?*" Bridger tried to sit up and failed.

The widow's face softened a little, and her eyes, hazel at present but capable, he somehow knew, of shifting to pale shades of blue or green, or darkening to gray. "I didn't mean to alarm you," she said. "Captain McBride is very much alive. As far as I know, he's fine."

Bridger released a long breath and glared up at the ceiling. "But he's no longer here," he muttered bleakly.

"No," she replied, almost gently. "He was called away, with all the others. There were orders, you see." A pause, during which Bridger saw, from the corner of his eye, that she had summoned up a wobbly smile, too tentative to last. "You are on my farm in southern Pennsylvania, as you may recall. And although you're behind Union lines you are, for the time being, quite safe."

"Safe," he repeated, with a touch of bitter mockery. Still avoiding her gaze, he stared up at the ceiling, trying to guess the hour by the play of light and shadow he saw there.

"Insofar as any of us are safe, yes," the widow allowed. "Considering."

"When?" he asked.

"When did Captain McBride leave?"

"Yes."

"Three days ago," answered Mrs. Hammond. "He left instructions."

Bridger attempted a laugh, a mirthless sound. "Did he, now? Tell me, ma'am, were these instructions intended for you or for me?"

"For you," she said. "Mainly."

He smiled. "I see," Bridger said. "What, pray tell, is the gospel according to Rogan McBride? As it applies to me, I mean."

Caroline seemed to hesitate. He was reminded that they weren't allies but enemies, and that harboring him was putting her and her whole farm at risk.

"Rogan —" She stopped, regrouped, and started again. *"Captain McBride* expressed the hope that you will recover swiftly and be on your way."

"How gracious of him." Bridger was caught off guard by Caroline's use of Rogan's first name. How was it that she and his best friend had dispensed with polite formality before they parted?

Still, Bridger wasn't surprised. Rogan had been straightforward about his attraction to Caroline Hammond, despite the near impossibility that anything would come of it.

Such familiarity was uncommon between acquaintances, though, even in wartime and, while Rogan might not be concerned with the proprieties, Caroline, as a recent widow, a mother and a member of a small community, surely was.

He realized he knew very little about this woman, but Bridger couldn't imagine her challenging convention in such a blatant manner.

She was far too strong-minded.

Unless, he mused, having been left to fend for herself and her child in a world ravaged by war, she felt she had no choice but to find another husband as soon as possible. She certainly wouldn't be the first strong woman to seek shelter in marriage for reasons of expediency, especially now, when times were hard and suitable prospects were scarce.

He had to admit his friend was prime matrimonial material, educated, decent and well-spoken. A woman could do worse. He'd once fancied Rogan marrying his sister, Amalie, and becoming his brother-in-law, but that was pure speculation on his part. After all, they hadn't seen each other in years, since Bridger and Rogan's school days, and now with the war they had opposite loyalties.

And yet, Amalie had apparently written to him . . .

He remembered how much Amalie had enjoyed Rogan's company. And he knew Rogan would be a devoted husband and father — whenever he decided to take a wife. He was both honorable and trustworthy.

Then why, knowing all this about his friend, did Bridger have qualms when he heard Caroline use Rogan's first name?

The answer was difficult to admit.

He himself had been taken with Caroline Hammond since the moment she'd swept into the kitchen house days before and listened to Rogan's plan to pass Bridger off as a Yankee and hide him on her farm until he was well enough to escape.

Though he'd been half out of his head with pain, Bridger had been surprised that she hadn't flatly refused and headed straight outside to report him to the highest-ranking Union officer she could find.

Instead, she'd accepted him into her home, a stranger, a member of the very army responsible for making her a widow. She had nursed him through a fever, kept his wound clean and kept him alive. The kindness of Enoch and the young woman, Jubie, both of whom had been introduced to him, both of whom had helped him in various ways, impressed him, too. But no one had done more for him than the widow Caroline Hammond. Why would she take such a chance, particularly having just lost her husband, when she so clearly despised everything he represented?

Simple compassion had been a factor, of course; he'd encountered more than a few generous citizens during this war. They'd been womenfolk mostly, alone and vulnerable, but willing to share what little they had with hungry, footsore boys far from home, whatever their differences.

He'd seen sorrow in the eyes of those wives and sisters and mothers, and the hope that their own loved ones would meet with a similar kindness, wherever they might be.

Caroline, too, had acted out of mercy; there could be no doubt of that. She had worked tirelessly for days, tending the wounded and sick. Rogan had told him about that. Just the same, if compassion had been her only motive, the small room Bridger occupied would have been crowded with injured and ailing men.

Union men, like Rogan, not Confederates.

Patients could be recovering in other parts of the house, he supposed, but he doubted that. The place was too quiet.

Caroline had granted him, the enemy, sanctuary for one primary reason — because Rogan had asked it of her. Despite significant reservations, all of which were justified, and fully aware of the risks involved, not only for Rogan but also for herself, she had nonetheless agreed.

The implications of that would bear some consideration.

But before Bridger could form a comment or a question, let alone utter one, she was out of her chair and on the move.

Instead of leaving the room, however, as he expected her to, Caroline went to the bureau, picked up a bundle wrapped in brown paper and brought it over to him.

"This is a parcel Rogan asked me to give you," she said. "The uniform he promised you. There's a letter, too."

He nodded wearily. Letter, parcel — he'd worry about them later.

"Do you need Enoch's assistance with anything — well — *personal*?"

"No," he replied. "But thank you for all you've done for me." Bridger felt the sudden need to close his eyes.

A moment later, he heard her retreating footsteps, then heard her close the door quietly behind her.

19

CAROLINE

In the absence of tents and soldiers and army livestock, the crops and orchards and pastures of Hammond Farm seemed to quicken all around Caroline; it was as though nature itself had retreated from the strife of battle, holding its breath.

On her way to the kitchen house, Caroline stepped around deep gouges where stakes had been driven into the ground, and where horses, mules and men had tramped this way and that. Long ruts crisscrossed the wide expanse of flattened grass in strange patterns, etched by the wheels of heavy wagons as they came and went.

Much blood had been shed here, but Caroline saw no trace of it now; it had probably seeped into the rain-softened earth, helped along by Enoch, lugging buckets full of water from the well and pouring it over the stains until they faded from rusty crimson to pale pink and finally vanished entirely.

Gone, too, were the heaps of horse manure and the clouds of black flies, banished to the pile behind the barn, where waste ripened into fertilizer for the cornfield and the vegetable patch.

Sensing the mysterious processes going on all around her, just beyond the reach of her eyes and ears, Caroline felt her spirits rising.

She paused outside the kitchen house, listening with her heart as blades of grass unbent themselves, drawn upright by the sun, and the nearby stream flowed on, bubbling and splashing over stones that gleamed like jewels, cleansing itself as it had for centuries. She felt the fruit trees in the orchard and along the stream bank as they spread their branches to gather light and air, with their leaves dancing in the slightest breeze, as if celebrating their many secrets.

It was the way of the earth to endure disaster, to slowly, stubbornly restore itself and, finally, to flourish. And she, like the rest of humanity, was somehow a part of all this. The same inexplicable force that drove seeds to sprout and rivers to seek the sea and trees to stretch themselves ever-skyward was in her, in everyone.

The insight was not a discovery, exactly; it was more a remembrance of something familiar and yet too easily forgotten. Nonetheless, Caroline found comfort in the idea.

She entered the kitchen house, took a basin from its shelf and proceeded to the cellar door to collect some potatoes stored there. The scent of raw earth and stored root vegetables greeted her as she started down the steps, squinting in the faint, dust-specked stream of midmorning sunshine from the brighter world above.

Caroline waited for a few minutes, letting her eyes accommodate themselves to the receding shadows, and when they had, she saw the crates and barrels crowded in among her grandmother's dwindling supply of medicine and bandages and her own diminishing staples such as flour and corn-meal, salt and precious sugar and coffee beans.

Distracted from her original errand she approached one of the barrels and ran her fingertips carefully across the splintery wooden lid, bent to examine the block letters stenciled on the side. She felt a sense of puzzlement.

Beans, she read silently. *United States Army.*

Caroline straightened, with a little gasp of surprise, raising one hand to cover her mouth and grasping her basin in the other. She examined every container, feeling guilty alarm and pure delight in equal measure as she identified the contents — dried meat, turnips and squash, several varieties of apples, corn starch, more flour and sugar and cornmeal.

In a war-torn world, with winter still months away but drawing ever nearer, with upheaval and scarcity always threatening, even farm owners like her were not immune to hunger, however hard they worked or careful they were, wasting nothing, putting up preserves by the bushel.

Finding this unexpected bounty was, for Caroline, like stumbling on Aladdin's cave, glittering with treasure.

Even as she marveled at her good fortune, though, she felt a sharp pang of conscience. So much food — enough to sustain her own small household and several others through the bitterest of winters.

But what about the soldiers, men like her Jacob, fighting battles, marching mile after mile in the course of a day, lying in hospital cots, in need of sustenance? Clearly, the contents of these barrels and crates had been intended for them, not for civilians, whatever inconveniences they might have had to endure on behalf of passing troops.

Caroline knew her benefactor had to have been Rogan; in his capacity as a Union quartermaster, he was the only person she knew who had access to such largesse. She knew also that he had meant this gift as a kindness, a show of gratitude, perhaps as a matter of fair payment — and yet, coupled with his determination to protect Bridger Winslow, the act was disturbing.

Still more disturbing was her own collaboration, her agreement to shelter a man who had willingly taken up the Rebel cause, turning against the country she truly loved, despite its faults, the hopeful nation his own ancestors had fought and died alongside hers to establish, less than a century before.

Jubie must have been aware of these provisions, since she'd been doing much of the cooking lately, while Caroline and her grandmother took turns tending to all but the most intimate of Mr. Winslow's needs.

Enoch must have known about the extra food, too; nothing escaped him, there on the farm or anywhere near it.

Why, then, had neither he nor Jubie said a word about this to her?

Troubled, Caroline took up the basin again, filled it with the potatoes she had grown herself, adding several onions as an afterthought, and climbed back up the cellar steps.

Enoch was there, dropping an armload of wood into the box beside the stove. At the same time, she could see Jubie reaching the main house and stopping to chat with Geneva, who stood on the porch, Rachel close beside her.

Enoch turned his head, nodded a greeting, dusted his hands together. He looked a little gaunt, and uncommonly weary.

For that reason, and for others she didn't pause to identify, Caroline decided not to ask him what he knew about the stockpile of army food crowding the cellar. She'd, naturally enough, assumed the supplies had left with Rogan.

"I'll start a pot of coffee brewing if that's all right with you, Missus," Enoch said.

Caroline set the basin on the work table, wiped her dusty palms on her apron. "Why, of course it's all right with me, Enoch," she replied, a little taken aback at his request. Enoch was, after all, a valued helper, and virtually a member of the family. "You must know you don't need my permission for such things."

Enoch nodded again. "I thank you for saying that, Missus Caroline," he answered, after a period of solemn consideration. "And I know you mean it, too. All the same, I'd rather ask."

Saddened, Caroline made no reply. Here was Enoch, an intelligent, hardworking man, legally free and yet bound by a myriad of conventions, large and small. She didn't suggest he forego calling her "Missus," since that was likely to make him uncomfortable. He'd used this term of address since the moment she'd married Jacob.

She respected him, loved him in the way she might have loved an elder brother, if she'd had one. For all her independence, Caroline did not know how she'd carry on without him.

He did all the heaviest work around the farm, things she couldn't physically manage, and she depended on his help. She depended even more, however, on his quiet stoicism, his common sense, his regard for the Hammond clan, living and dead, his willingness to protect her and Rachel from all harm.

"Here," he said, with a note of tired humor, "give me those spuds and I'll carry them on out to the pump, give them a good scrubbing."

Caroline smiled, a bit wanly. She had a dozen things to do if she wanted the midday meal on the table, but she was still standing in the same place when Enoch returned.

She thanked him, took the basin and picked up a knife, then began paring away the wet peels. Later, she'd toss them to the chickens, delighting, as always, in their eager squawks, their flapping wings, their wildly pecking beaks.

And she would be especially grateful, as she looked on, that the birds had not been claimed by the army.

The army.

The abundance of food that had appeared, as if she'd conjured it up, in her cellar.

She was back where she'd started — fretting over what was right and what was wrong. No matter how hungry she might be, she knew that, come winter, every bite she took would be tainted by guilt.

Enoch lingered, which was unlike him, since there was always work to be done somewhere on the farm.

Caroline shook off her self-absorbed thoughts and looked at him.

He seemed uneasy. Restless. And before she could ask what was the matter, he spoke, his gaze fixed on something far away.

"A man can't hardly set his foot down," he said, not addressing Caroline but ruminating aloud, "without stepping on somebody's grave."

Caroline dropped her knife, along with a half-peeled potato, wiped her hands on her apron again, and turned to face him. "Captain McBride assured me that the army will send men to reclaim the — the remains," she said softly.

Enoch returned from wherever he'd gone wandering and met her gaze. Caroline thought she saw him attempt to smile, but his mouth curved into a grimace instead. "That's what I'm afraid of, Missus," he said.

Caroline winced; with all that had been happening, she had forgotten Enoch's confession, made soon after she'd returned from Washington City with Jacob's body. He'd killed the slave catcher pursuing Jubie, buried the body somewhere on the farm.

"Is it likely . . . that they'd find the dead man, I mean?" she asked, bile surging into the back of her throat. "Among so many others?"

So many others.

"There are nearly thirty men buried on this property, Missus," Enoch answered glumly, "and they're all in the far section of that field Mr. Jacob said ought to lie fallow for a few years, before he went away the first time, so the soil could rest. He told me, 'Enoch, that dirt is too tired to grow anything but weeds.' " He paused, and a look of pain crossed his face, a reminder to Caroline that he was grieving, just as she was. "I decided that was as good a place as any to hide that slave catcher's remains, out of the way, far from the house and the stream. I reburied him there the next night, soon as I had a chance."

He hadn't told Caroline that, but would she have wanted to know? She doubted it.

"Trouble is," he went on, "the United States Army scouted around a while and came to the same conclusion as I did. They figured on digging some temporary graves and laying those poor dead soldiers to rest, just until they could be retrieved and sent on home to their kinfolks."

Once more, Enoch fell silent, no doubt thinking of Jacob's last homecoming, as Caroline was. Like her, Enoch had probably envisioned her husband's return as a time of celebration, of smiles and embraces and modest feasts . . .

Instead, Jacob had made his final journey sealed inside a pinewood box, in a dark and lonely baggage car, with only Caroline and a stack of other crude coffins, destined for various other places where there'd be no joyful welcome, either.

"Go on," she said softly.

"Those soldiers came close to digging up what was left of that dead slave catcher more than once. If I hadn't been there to steer them away, they'd have found him for sure. And they might have asked plenty of questions, ones I'd have been hard put to answer."

Caroline closed her eyes briefly, trying to resist the morbid images that blossomed in her mind and, of course, failing. She forced herself to listen, and to look into Enoch's worried face without flinching.

He was guilty of murder, even if justified, and although she hadn't been there, Caroline felt she wasn't completely blameless. All her life she'd prided herself on being a person of integrity, of principle, above compromise and shady dealings.

Yet here she was, complicit, a keeper of dangerous secrets. Because war changed everything.

"What are we going to do?" she asked, picking up her knife again, and slashing away at the already discolored potato she'd been peeling before.

What Enoch did then was unprecedented. He covered Caroline's hands with one of his own, tightened his calloused fingers around them. *"You,"* he replied grimly, "are not going to do anything. Except cut yourself to shreds, if you aren't more careful."

Caroline heaved a great sigh.

Enoch released her hands.

She focused on the potato, working slowly now, keeping her eyes down. "You could move him — it —" She faltered. "Bury him again, I mean. In another place . . ."

Out of the corner of her eye, she saw Enoch step back. Shake his head. "I've thought about that," he said, "but I'm not convinced it would do any good. I reckon everything depends on how soon the army sends a detachment back to collect their dead. If it's right away, or even in a week or so, they might notice that somebody's been digging and wonder why."

Caroline went on paring. "I should think they'd be too preoccupied with their own duties to notice," she ventured. "The army men, I mean. Obviously, disinterring bodies is unpleasant work, the kind a person might be in a hurry to finish."

"Maybe," Enoch allowed, but he sounded uncertain. "Seems to me, though, if anybody's used to gathering up dead folks and hauling them someplace, it would be a soldier. They'll have a map with them when they get back here, showing which man is buried where, and they'll be expected to account for every one of them, too."

While he was speaking, Enoch fetched a cooking pot and ladled water into it from a bucket. He placed the vessel within Caroline's reach.

With a rueful smile, she put the potatoes in the kettle. "If that's the case," she remarked, "wouldn't they be satisfied that the numbers match? That every soldier's name can be crossed off their list?"

"They might be," Enoch agreed. "Or, they might not. They might notice that extra plot, and want to know where the body got to."

"I don't suppose you could plant something there — a seedling tree, perhaps, or even one of my rose bushes? People do that kind of thing to honor the departed."

"*Women* do that kind of thing," Enoch pointed out mildly. "Not soldiers. Besides, I'm not looking to draw attention to the spot, Missus."

"I guess you're right," Caroline admitted, discouraged. How had she wound up in such a moral dilemma, scheming to deceive the United States Army? *Jacob's* army?

And not just once . . .

"That blasted horse keeps coming back, too," Enoch continued, frustrated. "No matter how many times I drive that critter off, he won't stay gone."

Finally, Caroline had peeled the last potato. "What horse?" she asked.

"The one he was riding. The man who came after Jubie."

"Oh, yes," she said, "I remember." She felt even more discouraged than before as she headed for the doorway with the kettle in hand, intending to strain the potato water onto the ground and replace it with fresh. When she returned, she set the pot on the stove, added salt and reached for the ladle.

"There must be plenty of stray horses around," she said, as though there'd been no break in their conversation. "One more shouldn't be difficult to explain."

Enoch nodded, sighed. "I was hoping one of the armies would claim him. Didn't matter to me which it was, either . . ."

"The horse — is it distinctive in some way?"

"No," Enoch answered. "He's just a plain bay gelding, but that doesn't mean he wouldn't be recognized if he happened to catch the wrong person's eye. Especially if that person turned out to be searching for somebody who'd passed this way. Say the searcher's another slave catcher, like the ones we had here before. Or a whole gang of them."

Despite the heat, Caroline felt a chill. She wrapped her arms around herself, shivering. "Surely such men would have fled, with two armies around and all the fighting. They're most likely outlaws, possibly deserters. Likely to be hanged, if they get caught."

"Yes," Enoch said grimly "Trouble is, any of 'em still around might not have gone far. There's a price on Jubie's head, probably a high one, and they won't forget about that. They'll want to track down their partner, make sure he didn't cut them out of their share of the reward." He gave a bitter, mirthless laugh. "For all I know, they're right about that. I don't care one way or the other, but I don't want them turning up here."

The thought terrified Caroline, too. She would have preferred to deal with a whole division of Confederates, given the choice. They, according to the newspapers, were under stern orders from General Lee to leave all civilians, North or South, unmolested, along with their property. Women and children, especially, were to be left alone, and the penalties for disobeying the general's command were serious indeed.

Still, there were scoundrels, stragglers and deserters, the sort of dishonorable men Jacob had called " 'bummers." Union or Confederate, they cared nothing for orders; they were opportunists, and they took what they wanted without qualm, often by violent means.

Caroline found herself wishing Captain McBride had left behind an extra rifle or two, and plenty of ammunition, along with all that food.

"Well, then," she said, "we shall have to be very careful, do what we can and hope for the best."

The statement sounded naive, even to Caroline herself. Clearly she was a woman in need of a better plan.

Enoch didn't reply, and no wonder. He was too polite, and too kind, to point out Caroline's faulty reasoning.

He simply put on his hat and left the kitchen house.

"It's time for me to return to home," Geneva announced, when they all sat down for the noon meal Caroline had prepared. "It's been a while since the fighting has ended and it seems time."

The kitchen house was insufferably hot,

with the cookstove in use, and Caroline felt cranky and drained. Leaving the door open to capture a breeze — there was none — had served only to let the flies in.

"No, Great-grandmother!" Rachel said. She was fitful and ready for a nap. Tears pooled in her lashes and her lower lip protruded. "You mustn't go away. *Everybody* goes away!"

"Rachel," Caroline began somewhat ominously, but Geneva waved her to silence.

Jubie and Enoch kept their eyes on their plates.

"Darling," Geneva chided gently, smiling at the child, "I've been here a while. I have a house of my own, and from what Mr. Flynn has told me, it is in dire need of cleaning and repairs. My friends and neighbors have been through a dreadful ordeal, too, and I want to help them, if I can." She shook her head. "And," she added, "it has been far too long since my friends and I have seen each other or worked on any of our Ladies' Aid Society undertakings. I think *they'd* say they need me."

Rachel was unmoved. "*We* need you," she sobbed.

Caroline opened her mouth to scold the little girl but, once again, her grandmother stopped her with a single, eloquent glance.

She turned a warm, understanding smile on her great-granddaughter.

"You know I will visit often," Geneva said. "And once things are more — normal — you and your mama will come and see me, like before."

Enoch excused himself, pushed back his chair and stood, plate and utensils in hand. Without another word, he placed his dishes on the work table and went out.

Jubie also stood, preparing to leave the table, but Caroline stopped her by looking pointedly at her unfinished meal and saying, "Eat a little more, Jubie," she said. "For your baby's sake, as well as your own."

"I'm fine for now, Miss — I mean Caroline." Her voice was strained, the use of Caroline's name sounding rather forced.

The young woman settled back into her chair, picked up her fork and idly shunted her food from one side of her plate to the other, then back again. She kept her eyes down and said nothing.

Caroline wondered what she was thinking.

After another few minutes, Jubie glanced up. "I'm not real hungry," she said. "Reckon it's this heat."

Caroline nodded, holding Rachel close. The child continued to weep, but not as loudly as before.

"I'll carry a plate up to that Rebel, if you want me to," Jubie offered. She stood and cleared her place at the table. "And I'll do these dishes after, so you just leave them be."

"Thank you, Jubie," Caroline said.

Rachel shuddered in Caroline's arms, sagging against her.

Jubie gave them both a slight smile and headed back to the main house.

Caroline murmured to her child, rocking very slightly from side to side.

She stayed there, in her chair until long after Rachel had fallen asleep.

Geneva returned to Gettysburg late that afternoon. She'd packed her belongings and given detailed instructions concerning the medical supplies she'd brought from her husband's surgery before the battle, telling Enoch which she would leave behind and which she'd probably need when she got back to town.

Rachel was napping when Geneva, perched beside Enoch in the wagon seat, waved a handkerchief in farewell. Watching from the front porch, Caroline responded with a wave of her own, careful not to let her smile slip too soon.

Caroline knew from her brief trip into town earlier in the week, when she'd accompanied her friend Cecelia McPhee, that while the town buildings themselves still stood, the walls were pockmarked and soot-stained. Flowerbeds were trampled by boot soles and hooves, many garden plots and kitchen shelves stripped of anything remotely edible.

But the surrounding countryside told the true tale of those first three days of July, 1863.

Makeshift graves were everywhere, mostly dug by women. The charred remains of horses and mules stood in gruesome hillocks, some still smoldering, and the stench of death was all-pervasive, clinging to the hair and clothing of the living, sinking into every pore and absorbed with every breath.

Behind Caroline, the seldom-used front door creaked open. "You ought to come on in here now, Miss Caroline," Jubie said. "Your little one just woke up from her nap, and she's wanting her mama."

Caroline turned slowly.

"Jubie," she chided gently, "it's better for you not to come out the front door. You might be seen from the road. No telling who's wandering past these days."

Jubie nodded in agreement. "You're right,

385

Miss. But those soldiers saw me plenty when they were here."

"I'll wager most of them were too pre-occupied with their pain to remember. And I know that at the time they appreciated everything you did for them."

Jubie nodded again. "Only takes one. To remember, I mean."

"What will you do now?" Caroline asked when she and Jubie were both inside the house, the door firmly shut behind them.

"You want me to go, Miss?" Jubie asked.

Caroline took both of Jubie's hands in her own. "Stop," she said. "I'm not asking you to leave. I merely wondered if you have any sort of plan."

Jubie's smile was a bright flash, beautiful and brief. "Yes, Miss," she said with spirit. "I do have a plan. *Enoch* and I have a plan." She paused. "He's asked me to jump the broom. To marry him. We were waiting for the right time to tell you. We only figured it out this morning."

Caroline stared at her. "Oh, Jubie! I'm so pleased! For both of you." She smiled. "For all *three* of you. So Enoch will be the baby's father . . ."

"Yes, he wants to. And he says he cares for me. I could tell that by the way he acts with me, the way he is, but it was so *beauti-*

ful to hear him say it."

"I think this is a marriage that was meant to be."

"Thank you, Caroline. Enoch and I have been talking — about staying here if you'll allow it . . ."

"*Of course!* I would love to have you become part of the family."

"Thank you," Jubie said again. "We hope to live in his cabin, have more children." She grinned down at her burgeoning stomach.

Still thinking about Jubie's news, Caroline started toward the main stairway. She probably shouldn't have allowed Rachel to sleep so long.

She was halfway up the stairs when a peal of sweet laughter rang out, followed by a rush of words, each one like a tiny chime.

Puzzled, and then vaguely alarmed, Caroline hurried up the remaining steps and along the hallway, passing her own closed door and moving swiftly toward Rachel's, which stood open.

"That," she heard Rachel say between delighted giggles, "was a silly story. Horses can't fly, because they don't have wings!"

Caroline stopped and listened.

"Well, most of them don't," Captain

387

Winslow agreed with solemn good humor. "Pegasus was the exception."

Caroline summoned up a smile and stepped through the doorway of Rachel's room.

Bridger Winslow was sitting up in Rachel's narrow bed, decently covered to the waist by sheet and blanket and wearing a rough-spun shirt so big on him that it must have belonged to Enoch.

Rachel sat in the child-size rocking chair Jacob had built for her within days of her birth, clutching one of her dolls.

"Mr. Windlesnow told me a story, Mama," Rachel proclaimed, beaming.

"Mr. *Windlesnow* needs his rest, honey" she said. "You mustn't bother him, Rachel."

Rachel smiled up at her, eyes shining. "I only wanted to get Dolly," she said. "I was very, very quiet, too." The little girl raised an index finger to her lips, as if to demonstrate. "But I guess Mr. Windlesnow heard me anyway, because he woke up and told me a story about a horse that can *fly*. Its name was Pegglemuss."

"That's very nice, sweetheart," Caroline said. She would speak to Rachel about strangers later, when she'd had a chance to think. Her daughter was only four years old, after all, and lectures on propriety and prudence would be beyond her. "Why don't you take Dolly and go back to Mama's room? I'll be there in a minute to help you with your dress and shoes."

Rachel continued to rock in her tiny chair. She so resembled a little old lady that Caroline very nearly laughed.

At the edge of her vision, Caroline saw Captain Winslow grin.

It stirred her, that warm, guileless grin, especially after all the gloom. But Caroline was wary of being stirred . . .

Rachel suddenly stood, clutching Dolly in both arms, and toddled over to her mother. "All right, Mama," she said, so cheerfully that Caroline was taken by surprise.

Caroline stepped aside to let Rachel pass, heard her scamper along the corridor, chattering to her doll.

"Caroline," the captain said, very quietly. "I would never harm a child."

He'd called her "Caroline," without her permission, and yet it sounded so natural that she couldn't object.

"I know, but one must be cautious," she said.

Deep down, she knew this man presented no danger to her daughter or to her, must have known it from the first. She would not have allowed him into her home, wounded or not, if she hadn't.

"Absolutely," he agreed. His amber eyes had darkened to a rich brown, it seemed to Caroline, and she saw gentle amusement in them.

The stirring was there again, slowly evolving into a faint ache, one that was not entirely unpleasant. Confused, she felt heat spread along her neck and pulse in her cheeks.

"Absolutely," she repeated, awkwardly.

He smiled. "You will be fine, Caroline," he said, as if she'd asked his opinion. "And so will your daughter."

Caroline found herself lingering in the doorway.

The uniform Rogan had left for Bridger was nowhere in sight, but a letter from the same parcel lay on the bedside table, opened. She wondered who'd sent it — mother, sweetheart, *wife*?

None of her business, she reminded herself silently.

"I am glad that you seem to be feeling better," she heard herself say.

"I'm slowly getting there," he replied. "I suppose any kind of progress is better than none."

Caroline nodded. It was time to leave and go about her duties, but her feet refused to carry her away.

He'd seen her glance in the direction of the letter.

"From my sister, Amalie," he said.

Amalie had only one purpose in writing it — to tell him their father had just died of pneumonia. She'd said it had all happened very quickly, and that the funeral service would be limited to a few local landowners and "house staff." She meant the slaves, of course, like Rosebud — because of the current difficulties with travel, thanks to the Union blockade, among other problems. He'd be buried in Fairhaven's small private cemetery.

She'd urged Bridger not to even consider coming. What Amalie didn't say was that she understood his conflicted feelings toward their father — feelings he'd experienced for most of his life.

He didn't tell Caroline any of this.

"Oh," she finally said. "Well . . ."

"My name is Bridger," he said next. Another answer to a question she hadn't asked, although she already knew his given name because Rogan had told her. *Bridger*. She liked the sound of it. Besides, it was certainly less awkward than Captain Winslow.

"Unusual," she commented.

"It's been passed down through my family for generations, like a porcelain gravy boat or a Revere bowl," Bridger explained. "Always conferred upon the second son, possibly meant as a consolation."

"And you're a second son?"

"Technically, yes."

"Technically?"

"My older half brother, Tristan, was killed at First Manassas."

"Oh, I'm sorry," Caroline said.

Bridger did not respond. He settled deeper into his pillows and studied the ceiling.

It was as though he had released her from some spell; suddenly, she was able to move of her own volition.

She stepped into the corridor, pulled the door closed behind her.

Rachel immediately emerged from Caroline's room, her pinafore on backward, her shoes unlaced, but on the right feet, at least.

"Did Mr. Windlesnow fall asleep?" the little girl asked.

"I think so," Caroline said, extending one hand.

Rachel came to her, shifting Dolly to her left arm, then placing her index finger to her lips, the way she had before. "Shhh," she said.

Finally, she took her mother's hand.

Downstairs, Caroline crouched to draw Rachel's shoelaces tight and tie them in sturdy bows. After standing up again, she set the little girl's pinafore to rights as well, but in a matter-of-fact way, to show that she appreciated Rachel's earnest effort.

"There," she said. "Let's go feed the chickens, shall we?"

Rachel nodded eagerly. She'd been confined to the house most of the time soldiers were present, and that had been difficult for her, as she was an active child and loved being outdoors.

After fetching the basin of potato peelings from the kitchen house and a bucket of grain from the barn, mother and daughter strewed feed everywhere, watching with pleasure as the chickens flapped their wings and busily pecked the ground.

In those sun-washed moments, with dusk still several hours away, Caroline could almost believe there was no war, that Jacob wasn't dead and buried, but merely working in the fields with Enoch, or off on some errand in town, sure to be back in time for supper.

Almost.

They had just entered the kitchen house when the shamble and clatter of an approaching wagon put an end to the pretense of normality Caroline had so carefully constructed. She knew this wasn't Enoch back from town, because she knew the sound of the Hammond wagon, as well as those belonging to most of her neighbors. For all their commonalities, each rig had its own unique rhythm of squeaks and thumps and rasps.

"Stay here," she told Rachel, using the soiled fabric of her apron to wipe her hands.

As was usual, Rachel didn't stay, but dashed out of the kitchen house through the open door and into the yard.

Caroline hurried after her, half-frantic and every bit as curious as her child.

The vehicle wending its way up from the gate was enclosed, like a gypsy wagon, lacquered in black but dulled by layers of dust. An old man in shabby clothes sat high above the ground, holding the reins, shocks of white hair protruding from under his once-fine bowler hat.

Two scrawny mules pulled the rig, heads down, flank muscles straining.

Caroline caught up with Rachel a moment before she might have fallen beneath the hooves of those poor animals.

"Mama," Rachel cried joyfully, "is that a *circus* wagon?"

The question nearly broke Caroline's

heart. To her, the vehicle looked more like a hearse.

"No, darling," she said gently. "I'm afraid there's no circus."

"Ho, ho!" cried the jovial old man, lifting his bowler hat completely off his bedraggled head in greeting. "Mordecai Splott, purveyor of fine goods and sundries, at your service!"

A peddler, Caroline concluded. When had she last seen one?

Reluctantly, she waved. She was too frugal to purchase anything, but one did not turn away weary travelers, particularly so late in the day.

She would invite this Mr. Splott to supper, allow him to water his mules and turn them out to graze in her pasture, and permit him to spend the night in the barn, if he wished.

"Ho, ho!" Mr. Splott shouted again, leaping from the seat of the wagon, nimble for a man of his years.

"Ho-ho!" Rachel replied with such delight that Caroline smiled.

Mr. Splott strode over to them and, still holding his hat in one hand, executed a deep and remarkably graceful bow. When he straightened, somewhat less easily than he'd bent himself double moments before, he sent Caroline a conspiratorial wink and turned his crystal-blue eyes to Rachel.

"I don't suppose you would happen to be Miss Rachel Hammond, of Gettysburg, Pennsylvania?"

Rachel squealed in happy wonder. Clapped her hands. "That's *me!*" she crowed, all but jumping up and down.

Caroline was far less enthusiastic. Who *was* this man, and why did he, a total stranger, know her daughter's name?

"Well, then," Mr. Splott said expansively, "you are just the person I've been searching for, lo these many weary miles." He glanced at Caroline again, his eyes full of kindness beneath their bristly brows, then returned his attention to Rachel, who was still bouncing on the balls of her feet. "And what a magnificent thing it is to finally make your acquaintance, Miss Hammond."

Caroline cleared her throat delicately. "What is this about, Mr. — er — Splott?"

Splott's eyes twinkled with merry mystery. Instead of answering, he raised one index finger in a cheerful bid for patience, turned and strode toward his wagon, and before Caroline could stop her, Rachel ran after him.

Caroline followed, nearly stumbling over the hem of her dress in her haste.

Rachel and Mr. Splott were standing behind the wagon when she reached them.

"My instructions," Mr. Splott said ebulliently, "were to deliver my cargo to one Miss Rachel Hammond and none other."

Behind the ornate door of the filthy wagon, something scratched and whimpered.

"Is there a *tiger* in there?" Rachel wanted to know.

"Something far better than a tiger, my dear." Mr. Splott worked the latch and opened the door, and a small brown-and-white dog leaped out so suddenly that Caroline started.

"A dog!" Mr. Splott whooped theatrically.

Rachel shrieked with pleasure, dropping to her knees in the scarred grass and laughing as the little animal jumped up and repeatedly licked her face.

"A gift from Captain Rogan McBride," Mr. Splott told Caroline, with the satisfaction of a job well done. "The dog's name is Sweet Girl, I'm told, and I can vouch for her good temperament, having journeyed from Harrisburg in her singular company."

"Ho, ho," Caroline muttered.

20

BRIDGER

He had been rolling his wounded shoulder in slow, agonizing circles, knowing the muscles would continue to atrophy if he didn't use them, when he heard a single wagon lumbering up from the road.

Drenched in sweat, his stomach churning with nausea from the pain, Bridger went still, listening, his attention trained on the sounds he could hear. Previous attempts to leave the bed had gotten him no farther than the edge of the mattress, where he'd lain trembling and gasping for breath until the pain subsided and he'd found the strength to shift onto his back.

Now, here was another lesson in humility. He, the expert horseman, the cavalier, the inveterate charmer of women, girls, dogs and small children, completely helpless.

His father would have been pleased.

All he could do now was listen. And think.

One wagon, drawn by no more than two horses or mules. A jovial male voice calling out an old-fashioned greeting.

The child, Rachel, chiming a response.

The happy yip-yip-yip of a dog, most likely a small one, judging by the pitch of its bark.

He heard footsteps on the stairs and briefly hoped that Caroline was returning.

Instead, when his door opened, Jubie stood on the threshold, bearing a bowl of steaming, fragrant soup. A spoon handle jutted up at one side.

"Who is that?" Bridger asked, inclining his head slightly in the direction of the window.

"Some peddler fella brought Rachel a dog," she said.

She had reached his bedside but his letter from Amalie was in her way; she clearly didn't want to rest the bowl of soup on the nightstand while it lay there.

Using his left hand, Bridger gathered the pages and held them. The words seemed to seep into the flesh of his fingers — *Papa* — *pneumonia* — *funeral* — *come home, no, don't* — *blockade* — so he withdrew his hand, leaving the letter to spill across the blanket.

Jubie set the bowl down.

The scent of boiled beans, ham and onions repulsed him, but he was ravenously hungry.

"Thank you. I can feed myself," he said. He managed to raise himself as far as his elbows, then a little farther, so that he was almost, but not quite, sitting. Awkwardly, he picked up the bowl, centered it in his lap, and brought a spoonful of decidedly good soup to his mouth.

Such a small accomplishment, but an important one, at least to him.

"Miss Caroline don't seem too pleased about the dog," Jubie commented.

"Every farm ought to have at least one dog," Bridger said in one of the exasperatingly slow intervals of lowering his spoon to the bowl. "They make for good company."

Jubie did not look in his direction. "Do you keep slaves, Mr. Winslow?" she asked suddenly.

Shocked, Bridger wondered for a second whether they were talking about dogs or humans. "My father did," he admitted. "But he's dead now," Bridger said.

He didn't know how he felt about his father's death. He labored to haul another mouthful of soup from bowl to mouth, savored and chewed and finally swallowed, all before he responded. "What you're really asking," he said, "is what I think of the institution of slavery. The answer is, I was born into a world where the practice was widely accepted. I knew our cook and housekeeper, Rosebud, had been my wet nurse when I was an infant, and that she had raised my mother, too. She sang songs and told stories and treated me, my sister and our older brother with more affection than either of our parents ever had. I loved her then, and I love her still.

"Then there was Abel, her son. He drove the carriages and acted as a butler when company came, or my mother held a party, which was often. He taught me to ride when I was four years old. How to catch fish, and find the best berry patches in the woods and about a thousand other things. When my father hired a tutor to teach Amalie and me to read, write and cipher, I taught Abel in turn."

"But they were still your slaves, Rosebud and her Abel." Jubie sounded deflated. Her proud shoulders stooped.

"My father owned them, yes," Bridger said quietly. It would do no good to explain that both Rosebud and Abel had been well treated, and even received wages, if small ones.

"And now he's dead. So who owns them?"

Bridger set the bowl aside on the night stand. "Abel was killed in a carriage accident a long time ago," he said, saddened in a way he hadn't been when he'd read Amalie's account of the old man's demise.

"What about Rosebud?" She gave him no opportunity to answer.

He sighed. "I don't know," he said.

"Your brother owns Rosebud."

"No," he answered. "My brother is dead, too." He heaved another sigh. *He* owned Rosebud, and the other slaves still at Fairhaven, although there weren't many left, according to Amalie's letter. A number of them had fled the plantation in search of freedom or been sold by his father to raise badly needed money. Jubie was bound and determined to make him admit the truth. "Rosebud . . . belongs to me."

His whole life, Bridger had never thought of Rosebud or Abel, or any of the other housemaids and field workers and gardeners and stable hands as property.

At last, Jubie turned from the window and faced him. "And you think that's all right?" she asked. There was no sarcasm in her voice, no fury in her bearing, only an

402

ancient resignation. "That some full-growed woman belongs to you, like that little dog down there in the yard belongs to Rachel?"

"No," he said. "I don't think it's right."

"Then why you willing to fight so nothing will change?" Jubie asked, aggrieved.

"I'm fighting," he answered quietly, "to protect my family's land."

She frowned at his response.

"Slavery *is* indefensible," Bridger continued. "I'm not in this war to preserve it. I'm in this war because the South is my home, and it's a home worth fighting for. Furthermore, vast sections of it are as beautiful as the Garden of Eden to me, maybe more so."

He paused. "Win or lose, when this war is over, I plan to free my . . . the slaves at Fairhaven."

Jubie collected the bowl of soup, half-empty now. She was no longer meeting his eyes.

The dog and the child could be heard bounding up the stairs, one in pursuit of the other, it seemed.

Jubie smiled slightly, in spite of herself. "That child," she murmured.

Rachel was laughing again. "Sweet Girl!" she cried. "You come back here right now!"

The dog darted into the room, a small brown-and-white bullet of furry disobedience, and bounded onto the bed, landing square in the middle of Bridger's chest.

The pain flared, ferocious, but he looped his good arm around the wriggling, muscular little form. Next thing he knew the dog was licking his face.

Jubie slipped out, bowl in hand, replaced by Rachel.

Caroline rushed in behind her daughter. "I'm so sorry," she said.

Bridger ruffled the dog's ears, enjoying the animal's eager affection. "Now where did you come from?" he asked Sweet Girl.

"A traveling peddler brought her!" Rachel cried. "Mr. Splott. She's mine now because Captain McBride sent her."

Bridger glanced at Caroline, noting the pinkish glow in her cheeks.

She shook her head, as if in reply to the question he hadn't asked. "Rogan isn't here," she said. "He sent Sweet Girl to us, by way of Mr. Splott, who happened to be heading in this direction." A sigh. "So very thoughtful of him."

There it was again — she'd said "Rogan," not "Captain McBride."

"I don't suppose Rogan sent any message to me?"

Somewhat to his surprise, Caroline reached into an apron pocket and drew out a folded piece of paper. "As a matter of fact, he did," she said, handing a letter to him.

Caroline looked so tired, Bridger wished he could put his arms around her, smooth down her hair, promise her that nothing bad would ever happen again, not to her or Rachel or the little dog.

But he could not allow himself to care for this woman for several reasons, the foremost being his best friend's interest in her. He knew Rogan was the kind of person willing to wait out Caroline's mourning period, to court her slowly, carefully and mostly from a distance, if that was his intent. He had another not insignificant advantage — Rogan and Caroline were on the same side. Both Northerners, both committed to the Union cause.

Bridger, in stark contrast, represented the enemy, and Bridger knew his mere presence bruised the widow's good Yankee conscience. He had nothing to offer her, in his current circumstances, anyway; he knew that what Caroline wanted most would be to have her husband back. The second, he felt sure, was his departure.

"Are you in pain?" she asked.

Bridger hadn't expected that particular question. "I'm all right," he said, although he was hurting badly, but he was a pragmatic man, beneath his somewhat reckless veneer. All things considered, he was far luckier than other wounded men; he was alive, in possession of all his limbs and, presumably, his sanity. He could see and hear, and soon he would be ambulatory again.

"My grandmother left a small supply of laudanum," Caroline ventured, almost shyly. "I could give you some, if you're suffering."

He smiled, shook his head. "Thank you, Caroline," he said. "I'm grateful for the offer, but I don't need it." He paused. "That said, if you happen to have any whiskey on hand, I could make good use of it."

She blushed, much to his delight. "Honestly," she said, almost sighing the word.

And that was the end of the conversation.

A moment later, the door was shut and Bridger was alone.

After a full minute of wishing Caroline had stayed, he picked up the message from Rogan, which consisted of a single sheet of heavy paper, sealed with plain beeswax.

No fancy crest for Captain McBride, Bridger noted. Rogan had simply tilted a candle and pressed his thumb into the spill.

He turned the paper over, noted that it had been addressed to "My friend, in care of Mrs. Jacob Hammond, Hammond Farm,

Gettysburg, Pennsylvania."

Finally, he broke the seal, unfolded the page. Twenty dollars in Federal currency, a fortune, even for a Yankee lawyer, fell onto the blanket.

Bridger ignored it for the moment and read.

I hope you are on the mend. By now, Mrs. Hammond will have given you the uniform and boots you will require, along with a letter, which I found, unopened, on your person, and retained. Except for your sidearm and sword, there were no other belongings in evidence. The sword was left behind, for reasons of expediency, and I gave the pistol into Enoch Flynn's keeping, until such time as you may require its return. I trust you will consider past favors if called upon to make use of it in the future — and that you will remember my deep personal regard for the lady of the house. Until better, happier days, R.

Bridger leaned back against his pillow and closed his eyes.

He was grateful for the funds, since he had none of his own, and for the pistol, too — although that came with the subtly stated proviso that he "consider past favors" before shooting any Yankees he might happen upon.

Alas, the letter was a reminder of Rogan's fond sentiments toward Caroline Hammond. Bridger had gotten that message, no question about it.

Lying there, he was forced to confront the truth: he wanted Caroline, too. Wanted her in all the ways a man wants a woman, but it was far more, this wanting of his . . .

He could imagine sitting across from Caroline at meals, listening as she read aloud to him by lamplight, watching the play of emotions flicker across her face, giving her gifts, from field daisies in fruit-jar vases to diamonds and pearls. And, yes, he imagined giving her pleasure, hearing her soft cries and whispers in the sweet secrecy of the night,

Bridger gave himself up to the vision, was in fact helpless before it. There was only Caroline, a Madonna, *his* Madonna, clothed in calico and light.

21

CAROLINE

In the end, Mr. Splott did not pass the night in Caroline's barn, nor did he stay for supper. After his mules had rested, drunk their fill at the water trough and grazed on thatches of grass somehow overlooked by the army's livestock, he announced that he had a train to meet in Harrisburg two days hence, and mustn't tarry. If he wasn't there to sign for the goods he was expecting, he informed her, heaven only knew where they'd wind up in times like these. And there he would be, a peddler with nothing to peddle, and done out of the advance payment he'd sent his wholesaler.

When Caroline had put together a cold meal, to be eaten at his convenience, he accepted graciously. As he left, she said she

409

appreciated his stopping by to deliver the gift of a dog, and noted that the irony of her words had escaped him.

Two hours later, she sat in her parlor, an unopened packet on her lap, Rachel and Sweet Girl at her feet, asleep in a tangle of little girl and dog, having happily exhausted each other.

Jubie entered on tiptoe, carrying a cup and saucer. "I brought you some warm milk," she whispered. "Reckoned tea might keep you awake."

"Thank you," Caroline said.

Jubie set the cup and saucer down within Caroline's reach, but her eyes were on Rachel and the dog.

"You want me to put that critter out for the night?" she asked. "Maybe shut it in the barn?"

Caroline smiled and shook her head. "We'll let her stay in the house, I think," she said.

Jubie eyed Sweet Girl. "She isn't an inside dog," she remarked. "She's dirty, for one thing. Might give Rachel fleas."

Caroline repressed a shudder, but her mind was made up. Sweet Girl needed a bath, and Rachel probably did, too, but she'd already checked the animal for fleas and ticks and found none. The poor little creature was half-starved, and it cowered when anyone other than Rachel approached, as if expecting a kick or a blow.

Clearly, it had been mistreated, possibly abandoned, too.

There was so much misery in the world, and so little one could do to relieve it. Surely, though, every kindness, however small, counted for something.

Besides, Rachel already adored Sweet Girl. Even if Caroline had wanted to turn the dog away, she wouldn't have had the heart to disappoint her daughter, especially now, when there were so many reasons to grieve.

Realizing that her friend was still waiting for a reply, Caroline said softly, "Don't worry, Jubie. Tomorrow I'll give them both a good scrubbing, and if there are any — messes — I'll do the cleaning up."

Jubie nodded and glanced toward the front window, darkened by night. "Do you think Enoch is going to be back soon?"

Caroline had been listening for the sound of the team and wagon herself. It wasn't like Enoch to miss supper, or delay his evening chores, but she hadn't begun to worry just yet. "I imagine he had plenty to do at my grandmother's house," she said. "He'll be here anytime now."

Jubie didn't look convinced. "Suppose he ran into trouble somewhere?" she fretted.

Caroline thought it was more likely that Enoch had simply been delayed. Besides carrying a wagonload of things into Geneva's house — provisions to replace the food looted from the pantry, medical supplies and Geneva's several trunks and satchels — he might have volunteered to chop firewood, if any could be found, board up broken windows, set overturned furniture to rights. It wasn't inconceivable that, after doing all these projects, he'd had to turn around and do similar chores for a number of the neighbors.

"I'm sure Enoch is safe," Caroline said gently. "And there really isn't anything we can do except wait."

Rachel made a whimpering sound and sat up, blinking. Then, seeing Sweet Girl beside her, also awake, she brightened.

"Sweet Girl needs to go outside," she said. "I don't think she can use the chamber pot."

Caroline smiled. "I'll go with you," she said, about to set aside the packet Mr. Splott had left with her.

"You stay right here and rest," Jubie told her. "I'll tend to Rachel *and* her dog. It'll give me a chance to check and see if Enoch is coming."

Caroline thanked Jubie again, and the trio bustled out of the room, headed for the side door.

Then, having delayed long enough, she unwrapped the parcel. Inside, she found a sealed envelope with her name written across the front in strong script, slanting to the right and firmly underlined. She held the letter for a minute or two, savoring the mere fact of it.

Now that Jacob was dead, such treats would be few and far between, if they came at all.

She heard Jubie and Rachel come back into the house with the dog, and climb the rear stairs. Rachel kept up a steady stream of chatter, telling Jubie that she meant to teach Sweet Girl tricks, and that would be just as good as a circus, wouldn't it?

Caroline smiled, even as tears burned her eyes. How resilient children were, she thought. After losing a parent, cringing at the sounds of a ferocious battle staged only a few miles from her house, confused by the sudden appearance of hospital tents in the yard where she usually played, undoubtedly frightened by the screams and cries of wounded soldiers, a dog was able to distract her and bring her joy.

Caroline set the letter aside and examined

the other contents of the parcel. The first thing she noticed was a thick songbook, full of lively tunes. Inside the bright blue cover, Rogan had written, "Your music soothed the souls of men in sore need of warmth and comfort, mine included. Thank you."

Caroline sighed. She missed Rogan's company, wished he was there with her, in the lamp-lit parlor. Perhaps she would have gone to the harpsichord, opened the songbook and played for him.

The thought inspired a certain degree of guilt; if she was going to miss someone, it ought to be Jacob, not Rogan McBride.

She glanced up at the ceiling. But if Rogan *was* still here, she thought, he would have served as a kind of buffer between her and Captain Winslow, whose presence troubled her for reasons she couldn't explain.

She let the songbook rest on her lap while she looked at a smaller packet, wrapped in a fold of delicate tissue paper, marked with Rachel's name. Inside, she found a rainbow of colorful grosgrain ribbons for the child's hair.

Rogan had forgotten no one. He had also enclosed a pouch of tobacco for Enoch, a lace-trimmed handkerchief for Geneva, and a blanket for Jubie's soon-to-be-born baby.

It was like Christmas, as it had been before the war, she reminisced. But then the familiar sound of a team and wagon coming slowly up the road brought her back to the present. Jubie hurried down the stairs. "Is that Enoch, come home?" she asked, sounding eager and desperate at once.

"I'm sure it's him," Caroline said. She stood, placed the gifts on the seat of her chair and followed Jubie along the corridor and out the door.

Indeed, Enoch was back, driving the rattling wagon, its lanterns swaying on either side.

Jubie ran up alongside the wagon before he'd brought it to a full stop and cried, "Where *were* you?"

Enoch, a hulking shadow, threw back his head and gave a great shout of laughter. "I've been about my business," he said. "What — were you worried about me?"

Oh, my, Caroline thought, with a soft laugh of her own.

She wasn't needed here.

She turned around and went back into the house.

In the parlor, she picked up the letter from Rogan, still sealed, tucked it in her apron pocket and headed for the stairs.

Her room was rimmed in pale moonlight, and Caroline could easily make out her daughter's small form, resting at the very edge of the mattress, one arm dangling toward the dog. She went to the desk, which stood beneath a window, awash in silvery light.

Then she took out the letter and laid it squarely in the center of the desktop.

Before she could read it, she heard a thumping sound somewhere in the near distance, and she turned quickly, thinking Rachel must have tumbled to the floor, in the grip of some dream.

But Rachel was still huddled at the side of the bed, sleeping.

Another thump came.

Frowning, Caroline hurried out into the corridor, found matches and a candle on the hall table, lit the wick.

"Jubie?" she called softly.

No answer. Jubie was probably outside with Enoch or in the kitchen house, fixing his supper.

Caroline waited, listening hard. She *had* heard something.

A hoarse voice, cursing, confirmed this, even before a line of light appeared beneath the door to the room that had been Rachel's.

Caroline set the candle back in its place, then blew out the flame. Reluctantly, she approached Rachel's bedroom door and knocked.

"Captain Winslow?" she called quietly. "Is something wrong?"

"No," came the rather terse reply. "Everything is fine."

Caroline drew a deep breath, releasing it as she grasped the doorknob and turned it, then stepped into the room.

Bridger stood at the window, his good hand braced on the wide sill. He still wore the shirt Enoch had lent him and, incongruously, the military trousers Rogan had left.

He turned his head, looked back at Caroline over his shoulder, scowling. "I told you," he said, carefully enunciating each word, "that I'm fine."

"What in heaven's name are you doing?"

He turned away again, rested his forehead against the window glass. "Caroline," he said evenly, "please just go to bed."

"This is *my* house, Captain Winslow," she said. "And I can do as I please, thank you very much."

"Fair enough," he said, with a sound that was almost a chuckle.

"Let me help you," Caroline said, starting toward him.

"I do not need your help," he informed her, warning her off with his tone and the glare in his eyes.

She stopped. "Then I'll get Enoch."

"*Blast* it," he growled. "*I am all right.* Please, just go away."

Caroline did not move. Instead, she folded her arms and looked around, assessing the situation. He'd lit the lamp Jubie had placed on the bureau when he'd been brought to this room, no mean task for a man with one arm bound up in a sling. He'd managed to get dressed, too, at least partially.

"Good heavens," she said. "You meant to leave, didn't you?"

Bridger Winslow lowered his head, closed his eyes. Said nothing.

"Are you out of your mind?" Caroline overcame all trepidation then, walked over to him, taking hold of his uninjured forearm with one hand and placing the other at the small of his back. Steering him toward the bed.

He muttered something, a curse, a protest, Caroline wasn't sure which, but he leaned against her, allowing her to lead him.

He collapsed heavily onto the mattress, nearly bringing Caroline down with him.

She stumbled back a step, in an effort to remain upright.

Bridger had struck his wounded shoulder when he'd fallen onto the bed, and he was grimacing with pain. Blood began to seep through his bandages and the borrowed shirt.

Caroline bent and tried to uncover the wound, to see what damage had been done, but he caught hold of both her wrists, and his fingers rebuffed hers. His eyes were squeezed shut, his face glistened with sweat.

"Please — leave — me — alone. *Please.*"

"I'm not going anywhere, Captain," Caroline said. A sudden calm had come over her.

She heard footsteps on the rear stairway, and knew, without looking, when Jubie reached the doorway.

"Miss Caroline?" Jubie's voice was tremulous.

"Get Enoch," Caroline said. "Quickly."

Jubie hurried away.

"Damn it." Bridger abruptly released her hands.

Holding her breath, trembling with determination and hesitancy, in equal measure, Caroline, as gently as she could, opened the shirt, and removed the blood-soaked bandage.

Blood pulsed from the wound, and Caroline threw off the bedclothes, bunched a corner of the sheet in one fist, and pressed down hard on the injury.

He groaned and closed his eyes again. His breathing slowed, deeper than before, and Caroline wondered if he'd lost consciousness.

"Captain Winslow," she said, pushing down on the wound with both hands now, putting all her strength into the effort.

"Bridger," he murmured.

"Bridger," Caroline relented. "I only wanted to stop the bleeding — and make sure you hadn't swooned."

He didn't open his eyes, but a muscle twitched at one side of his mouth. "I do not swoon," he said, with considerable effort. His lips were dry, and he moistened them with his tongue. "But in case . . . it matters, that hurts."

Enoch was coming up the stairs now, hurrying.

Sweet Girl began to bark.

Rachel woke and called, "Mama!"

"What's the trouble?" Enoch asked, a little breathless.

He stood at the foot of the bed, and Caroline spared him a single glance. "I'm sorry if I've alarmed you," she told him, still bearing down on the wadded sheet. "Captain

Winslow has reopened his wound, I'm afraid. I thought I would need your assistance, but he's settled down."

"You fixing to push that man right through to the floor?" Enoch asked. He sounded relieved, even slightly amused.

"Please stop her before she kills me," Bridger said. That twitch was there again, beside his mouth. His eyes were still closed.

"Let me have a look at the man's shoulder, Missus," Enoch said calmly.

Carefully, she lifted the sheet and they both peered at the wound. The bleeding hadn't stopped completely, but it had slowed.

"What do you need, Missus?" Enoch asked.

"Would you get some bandages and disinfectant?" The voice was Jubie's.

Glancing back, Caroline, now seated on the side of the bed, saw the young woman standing in the doorway. "Heat up some water, too," Caroline said.

Enoch nodded and went out, Jubie stepping aside to let him pass.

"I'll look after Miss Rachel," Jubie offered. "Once she's asleep, I'll be back to help you."

"I don't want to sleep," Rachel protested. She'd come to stand next to Jubie in the doorway.

"Well," Jubie said, turning away with Rachel's hand in hers, "that little dog of yours does."

Caroline smiled, grateful, and when she looked at Bridger again, saw that his eyes were open, and he was gazing up at her with . . . admiration.

"You are a very difficult man," she said, and felt herself blush at the tenderness in her tone.

"And you are a beautiful woman."

Caroline averted her eyes. "You mustn't say such things."

"Nevertheless, I did. And it's true."

"Please," Caroline said. "Don't. I'm —"

"A widow," he finished for her. "I understand that, Caroline. I know you need time to grieve. And, God help me, I know my best friend is taken with you."

"You'll be leaving soon," Caroline said, overwhelmed.

Bridger raised his good hand, cupped it gently behind her head and pressed until her face was nearly touching his.

She knew she ought to resist, to pull back, but she didn't.

And then he kissed her.

It was tender at first, a mere brush of his lips against hers.

A column of sweet fire seemed to spring

up within her.

Stop, she thought, and was stunned to realize the plea was meant for herself, not for Bridger.

He deepened the kiss, and Caroline felt as though she was in freefall, tumbling head over heels into a chasm so deep it might reach all the way to the center of the earth.

A sound from the doorway broke the spell.

Caroline bolted upright, and Bridger released her, but allowed his hand to drift slowly, lightly, down over her shoulder and along the length of her back.

She trembled.

Bridger smiled.

"I have the bandages here," Enoch said from the doorway, his voice a little too loud. "Some medicine, too."

Caroline could not look at him or, for that matter, at Bridger.

Jubie returned, too. "You ought to get yourself to bed, Caroline. Enoch and I can handle this."

Caroline leaped to her feet. "Thank you, Jubie," she said quickly. "I *am* tired."

With that, she hurried from the room, avoiding Enoch's eyes, and Jubie's.

She went to her own room, moving quietly, and took Rogan's letter from the desktop, where she'd left it earlier.

Suddenly she felt exhausted, body and soul. She paused beside the bed just long enough to see that Rachel was sleeping peacefully, then leaned down, patted Sweet Girl's head.

She went into the hallway again, keeping her steps light as she crept toward the front stairway, down the steps, through the parlor, and along the corridor to the side door.

She let herself out, careful not to make any noise, and closed the door behind her.

Once outside, she drew a slow, deep breath, savoring the heavy freshness of the night air. Clouds covered the moon, but there was still enough light to see by, since the sky was popping with huge, twinkling stars.

For a long time, Caroline didn't move, but simply stood there, in the trampled grass of her yard, breathing, waiting for her heart to calm.

Bridger Winslow had kissed her. *Kissed* her.

And she had not resisted.

Indeed, she'd found herself willingly open to him.

She wanted more.

It was immoral. Scandalous.

What kind of woman behaved in such a brazen way, when her husband, her child's father, had so recently gone to his grave?

Caroline began to weep with confused emotion.

She paced, pressing one hand to her mouth in a fruitless effort to restrain the sound. Walked faster, and then faster still, as if to outrun her terrible shame, the regret that seemed about to consume her.

"Jacob," she sobbed. *"Jacob."*

She was frantic to escape, but there was nowhere to hide. Not from herself.

So she stood still, braced to weather the emotional storm.

She waited, breathed, breathed more slowly. Dried her cheeks with the hem of her apron. Degree by degree, the tempest subsided.

In the immediate aftermath, she removed her apron, clutched it in one hand and, because she had no wish to encounter Enoch or Jubie, proceeded to the kitchen house. She did not want to be comforted or consoled — or judged for a moral lapse.

Just inside the door, she took up the two empty water buckets and walked to the well.

There, she filled one vessel, then the other.

They were heavy, and the water was ice-cold as it splashed over the brims, wetting her skirts and her shoes. The metal handles scored her fingers, calloused though they were. She barely noticed her discomfort, for she was a farm wife, after all, used to carrying buckets and firewood and bushel baskets loaded with grain or potatoes or, in season, fruit from the orchards.

Time after time, Caroline made the journey to and from the well, until she had enough water for her purposes. She filled every pot and kettle she could find, built up the banked fire in the cookstove and placed them there, glad to be busy.

The work was hard, but it was also a welcome distraction, a way of restoring her normal stability and common sense.

But even physical labor is finite. Once she'd taken the largest wash tub from its peg on the back wall and set it behind the table, out of direct view from the doorway but not too near the stove, since the night was heavy with summer heat, she found herself at a loss.

Every morning and every night, Caroline filled a basin with hot water and, using strong soap and a washcloth, scrubbed herself thoroughly, but a real bath was a luxury, usually reserved for Saturday nights, part of her preparations for Sunday services at church.

In the aftermath of the battle, however, she'd had neither the time nor the privacy for a proper bath — and no real opportunity to attend church services.

Tonight, however, cleanliness was not her only objective. She wanted, quite simply, to be kind to herself. To lather her skin and hair with scented soap, to think calmly, and to soak away some of the aches plaguing her every muscle, even her bones.

But soaking away the ache in her heart was more difficult.

And so was the realization that she would have to go back to the house for soap, a towel, her nightgown and wrap, and risk meeting Enoch or Jubie in the process.

Enoch had certainly seen the illicit kiss as he reentered the room and she suspected Jubie might have, as well. She was perceptive, Jubie was, and if she hadn't been a witness, she'd probably guessed the situation right away.

Obviously, Caroline couldn't avoid Enoch and Jubie forever, and did not even want to. It wasn't as if she'd been caught committing a crime. A man who was not her husband had kissed her, and she had allowed it. And . . . enjoyed it.

These were the facts, whether she liked them or not.

Granted, she might have responded differently if she hadn't been caught off guard.

If she could live those moments over again, she would slap Bridger Winslow's handsome, arrogant face and storm from the room.

Or would she?

She remembered the taste of him, the strength in his hand as he brought her mouth to his, the warmth of his lips, the hard barrier of his chest against the soft give of her breasts . . .

Enough. *What's done is done,* she told herself.

Caroline returned to the house, feeling more composed. Her only concession to embarrassment was to use the main stairway, so she wouldn't have to pass Bridger's door. Otherwise, she would *not* feel ashamed.

In truth, she realized as she crept into her room, where Rachel slept on, and quietly gathered the things she needed, she *wasn't* ashamed.

She was *alive,* a healthy, normal woman, strong, if lonely and beleaguered, and if she had taken some pleasure in Bridger's kiss, so be it.

Clutching her towel and nightgown, Caroline paused beside the bed she had shared with Jacob, gazing at the beautiful child they had made there. She thought of the many intimate nights she and Jacob had spent there.

After a while, she turned in silence and left the room.

Now, Bridger's door was shut, and no light showed beneath it.

She rested a hand against her apron pocket once more, reassuring herself that Rogan's letter was still there, and wondered at the sudden confusion that welled up within her.

Then, at last, she went down, thinking of the lovely bath that awaited her in the kitchen house.

Once there, she latched the door, picked up the lantern she'd lit earlier, and set it on the seat of a chair she'd pulled up alongside the wash tub. She carried the steaming kettles across the floor, one by one, and poured their contents into the bath.

She pulled the curtains at each of the three windows, and double-checked the latch, just in case.

It was firmly in place; she would not be interrupted.

Slowly, Caroline removed her apron, taking the letter from the pocket, putting it down beside the lantern. She unbuttoned her dress and let it fall into a pool of calico at her feet, tested the temperature of the water with the dunking of a big toe and found it hot, but not scalding.

After making sure the towel, soap and washcloth were at hand, along with her comb and brush, Caroline took off her pantaloons and then her camisole, and stepped into the tub.

Despite the sultry heat of a Pennsylvania night in mid-July, the sensation of sinking into hot, clean water was exquisite. One day, she thought dreamily, when this war was over, she would buy a *real* bathtub, the stationary kind, perhaps of porcelain, or one cast in brass or copper, with a high, sloping back and long enough to permit her to stretch out her legs.

In the meantime, the wash tub would do just fine.

Caroline relaxed in the hot water, feeling tense muscles begin to ease.

She reached for Rogan's letter, opened the envelope, unfolded the pages inside.

A ten-dollar note fell out and floated for a moment before Caroline snatched it up and set it aside.

Rogan's message, so anticipated, turned out to be all business. He apologized once more for any risk and inconvenience she might suffer in caring for his friend — and in the further imposition of the dog. He

430

explained that he had promised one of his dying men he would recover the animal from unfortunate circumstances and see that it was looked after. He asked for a response, at her convenience, and promised to make full restitution for any expenses she might incur on behalf of his friends, canine and human. He hoped Geneva, Enoch, Jubie and Rachel would be pleased with the small remembrances he'd sent, and that she would enjoy the songbook as much as he and the other men had enjoyed listening to her play.

He'd signed the missive as he might have signed a military order, not with the customary "Yours Truly" or "Your Obedient Servant," followed by his given name, but more formally. "Rogan McBride, Captain, United States Army."

Caroline was at once relieved and faintly disappointed.

What had she been expecting? A declaration of love?

No. That would have been wholly improper, even shocking, given their brief acquaintance. A simple "Sincerely, Rogan" would have been nice, though.

She sighed, refolded the letter and placed it next to the lantern, on top of the sodden ten-dollar bill. Then, because she was truly tired and her bathwater was turning cold, she reached for the soap and washcloth and scoured every part of herself. She took down her hair and washed it, rinsing away the lather as thoroughly as she could.

Tomorrow, she decided, she would repeat the rinsing process, using water from one of the rain barrels.

Alternatively, she reflected wryly, she could dive headfirst into the deepest part of the creek. If she'd thought of this before Bridger's kiss, instead of after, she might have drowned, but she would still be the very respectable Mrs. Jacob Hammond, she of untarnished virtue.

22

BRIDGER

As July lumbered toward August, Bridger had plenty of time to regret giving in to impulse and kissing Caroline the way he had. Since then, she had entered his room only to collect Rachel and the dog, both of whom were regular visitors, leaving every other task to Enoch or Jubie.

He wanted to apologize for that kiss, although he wasn't entirely sorry, but Caroline made sure they were never alone. No doubt, she knew he wouldn't broach the topic in the presence of a child; if she hadn't realized that, she wouldn't have crossed the threshold.

Maybe, he often thought, that was just as well.

He was still the enemy, as far as she was

433

concerned, a part of the army that had killed her husband. Even if she could forgive his allegiance to the wrong side of the conflict — and her response to his kiss indicated that at some point, she might — he was a temporary fixture. Soon, he would be gone, with no excuse to return, except as a member of the Confederate forces, should General Lee decide to make another foray into Union territory.

From what he'd been able to gather, mostly from Enoch, who made regular trips into Gettysburg town and often managed to scrounge up a newspaper — shared with Bridger but only after he and Caroline had read and discussed every word — the Confederacy had taken a beating at Gettysburg. Not that this was unknown to Bridger, but he appreciated any additional detail.

The opinion was widespread that George Meade, head of the Union army, had blundered gravely by not pursuing the Confederates immediately after winning the battle.

Such hesitancy was common among Union generals, in Bridger's experience; they seemed to prefer conducting elaborate reviews, complete with flags and marching bands and admiring spectators, to the admittedly messy business of fighting.

General McClellan, since relieved of his

command, was an outstanding example. Though a gifted strategist, a soldier's soldier, much beloved by his troops as well as the Northern public, the man had carried on as if there wasn't a war to be fought. Evidently, he spent so much time on plans and preparations that he rarely got around to engaging the enemy.

Not so his General Lee. In contrast to his gentlemanly manner and soft-spoken erudition, he was audacious, bold and quick to move. More often than not, he succeeded.

By not giving chase when the Army of Northern Virginia was at its weakest, Meade had provided Lee with what he needed most — time. Even now, Lee had surely regrouped his hungry, ragtag forces, men so loyal they would've followed him through the gates of hell; he would have conferred with Davis and with his accomplished generals, studying maps, planning the next attack.

The North, much to Mr. Lincoln's consternation, seemed to have no one in command who understood the way Lee's mind worked. With the possible exception of this man, Grant, who had wreaked such havoc at Fort Donnellson and Vicksburg . . . Bridger suspected that only Grant might be capable of matching General Lee's dogged persistence, whatever the adversity, or his almost uncanny ability to inspire his troops to keep fighting, long after every resource had been depleted.

Bridger, like General Lee whom he so admired, had been ambivalent about the South's reckless determination to break away from the Union and go its own way. He'd understood, even shared to some extent, the South's reaction to the Federal government's growing tendency to bully individual states into submission, but he hadn't seen secession as the solution, let alone all-out war.

There were times when military action was unavoidable — history proved that — but he still believed the battles ripping the nation and its people apart would have been better fought on the floors of the Senate and the House of Representatives, not in fields and valleys, cities and towns.

Still — and again, like Lee — Bridger had known, for all his misgivings, that he could not stand idly by while the home he loved, flaws included, was invaded. He'd decided, early on, that he couldn't straddle the line; he had to throw in with one side or the other, and there could be no pulling of punches, no inner debates, no "what ifs" or "if onlys."

Since then, he'd fought as ferociously as any soldier in either army. He'd been ruthless in battle, killing other men when he had to and, he feared, more than a few boys, as well. His one consolation was this — he had never raised sword or pistol to any civilian, man, woman or child, never ordered a crop trampled or a house burned.

Sometimes, it was enough to know this. Mostly, it wasn't.

He sighed, that hot morning in early August, and went to the window of the little bedroom in Caroline Hammond's house and looked down.

Caroline was there, hoisting laundered sheets from a basket, raising her arms high to peg them to the clothesline, where the sheets flapped like ship's sails.

She wore a simple calico dress, not widow's weeds, and reaching up displayed the lines of her small well-shaped breasts admirably.

Watching her, Bridger smiled, despite his dark reflections.

It was strange to think that no matter how many women he might dally with in the months and years to come, should he be fortunate enough to survive, he imagined there would be nothing to compare with the single tender kiss he and Caroline had shared.

Rachel came into view, running full-out, arms wheeling in sheer delight with the brilliant sunlight and green grass and the joy of being alive, accompanied, as always, by the little dog.

Bridger smiled at the picture they made, even as he felt a sting of sadness at the rarity of such scenes in his own life. In peacetime, it seemed to him, children had been much more visible. They had always been fragile, prone to sickness and accident and early death, but many thrived. In war, they turned into shadows, curious and watchful still, but silent. Always hovering at the edges. Always poised to flee.

Others disappeared entirely, kept out of sight by fearful mothers.

Bridger did not take the sight of a beloved child playing with her dog for granted. Rachel, and Sweet Girl, too, provided a welcome distraction from watching the woman he could never have.

It was a cruel irony, he thought wryly, that despite all the women who had welcomed his attentions, even gone to scandalous lengths to engage with him, the two he had wanted most — Marietta, his half brother's wife, and Caroline — were forbidden. He had genuinely loved Marietta, had expected to love her all his life — until he met Caroline.

Marietta, in stark contrast to Caroline, had at least returned his doomed affections, and the scandal of their one intimate encounter had, for all practical intents and purposes, destroyed his family.

It had happened the summer just before war broke out in earnest, when Bridger had returned to Fairhaven from a sojourn in Britain, where he'd been sent to study economics, cultivate business associations with mill owners and, in his father's words, "acquire the social polish of a true gentleman."

Instead, he had acquired a penchant for shopgirls and actresses, good English ale and unbridled hedonism. Basically, he had disgraced the Winslow name, on both sides of the Atlantic, and his father, once apprised of his younger son's behavior — the son he'd never liked, never valued — had promptly cut off his income and commanded him to come home.

Bridger, summoned to the office of the Winslows' London solicitor, had been presented with polite British disapproval and second-class passage on a ship bound for Charleston. His normal allowance, which was considerable, he was informed, would no longer be forthcoming.

Secretly relieved, because he'd never wanted to be anywhere but at Fairhaven in the first place, Bridger accepted the ticket and boarded the ship a day later.

He and his older half brother, Tristan, had crossed paths, somewhere on the high seas. Tristan had, not surprisingly, been dispatched to succeed where Bridger had failed.

In fact, nothing about that situation had surprised him. Bridger had been sent to England under a cloud of disapproval, well aware that, in his father's eyes, he couldn't equal his older brother, not in any sense. Three months after his arrival at Fairhaven, Bridger had undertaken to comfort Marietta, lonely and bitterly unhappy in her marriage, and wound up taking her to his bed that one time. Even this indiscretion might not have sparked calamity if Bridger hadn't fathered a child on the first and only night he and Marietta had made love. The baby, a son, was born nine months later, and nearly four months before Tristan's triumphant return.

Damned by simple arithmetic, Marietta was loudly scorned. Tristan openly divorced her and she was sent away from Fairhaven, indeed from the whole state of Georgia. The child went with her, the pair of them exiled to New Orleans, where they'd been taken in by distant and reluctant relatives of Marietta's, since she had no immediate family of her own.

Bridger's attempt to follow them had been thwarted only a few miles from the plantation house, when Tristan, with several of his friends, and the white overseer, Banks, had caught up to him. He'd been roped like a steer and wrenched off his horse, landing hard on the dirt road. They'd dragged him several hundred yards to make their point, and then collectively beaten him near senseless.

With his arms bound to his sides, Bridger hadn't been able to put up much of a fight, though he *had* managed a few well-placed kicks.

He'd awakened in Rosebud's cabin in the slave quarters, where he'd remained for nearly two weeks, recuperating. Rosebud, Abel and Amalie had been his only visitors.

During the days and nights that followed, he'd been sustained by two visions, both of which were insane — killing his half brother with his bare hands, and traveling to New Orleans to claim Marietta and his son.

When he'd finally been strong enough to

leave the cabin and head for the main house, he'd encountered a weeping Amalie on the path. She'd been holding a letter in one hand and shaking her head from side to side, as if to deny what she'd just read.

She'd told him then, between sobs, that both Marietta and the baby had taken a fever only days after their arrival in New Orleans. Marietta had recovered quickly, but the child had perished within a few hours.

At first, Bridger had refused to believe his son was dead.

This was some trick of his brother's.

Amalie, still weeping, had shown him the envelope, addressed to her in an unfamiliar hand, then presented him with the letter Marietta had enclosed for him.

At first, he hadn't understood, but when he unfolded the single-page missive, he knew instantly that Marietta had written it. With heartbreaking brevity, she'd told him about the fever and the baby's death. Somehow, she'd learned that Tristan had taken revenge on him, and she begged him, for her sake as well as his, not to come to her, or even write. She was nearly crushed by guilt and regret as it was, and she could bear no more. They had brought this suffering upon themselves, through their own wantonness and treachery, and the child's death was their punishment.

Bridger hadn't said anything, couldn't have managed a word, although inside, he'd bellowed like a panther caught in the sharp teeth of a trap. He had not shared Marietta's belief that the life of an innocent baby had been the price required by a vengeful fate, but he'd known then, and knew now, that he was responsible, in large part, for what had happened.

After all, if he hadn't bedded his brother's wife, there would have been no child. Marietta would not have been sent away from her husband and home, and, while he and Tristan had never been fond of each other, they might have reached some kind of workable truce.

Instead, Tristan had gone to join one of the militias being formed all over the South.

Bridger had never told his father about the beating he'd taken on the road that day, being in no position to cast blame. The old man must have known some part of the story, but he'd never said anything about it.

Bridger had gotten roundly drunk that first night, and he'd stayed that way until those damned fools in Charleston fired on Fort Sumter, and brought the furies of heaven and hell down upon them all.

Enoch's voice, sounding from the open doorway to Bridger's room, jolted him out of the past with a question pertinent to the present.

"You ready to try the stairs?"

Bridger turned to him, marveling, as he often did, at the size and bulk of this man, the intelligence in his eyes, the kindness of his manner.

"Yes," Bridger said. For days, he had been working to regain his strength, getting out of bed, making his way to the window, where he stood now, moving about the small room, and then along the length of the hallway.

Usually Enoch accompanied him on the more ambitious attempts, watching, always prepared to steady Bridger if he weakened, but not hovering, the way he thought a woman might have done.

Maybe it took another man to understand the extent of masculine pride.

Caroline continued to avoid him.

Jubie still brought Bridger his meals, but it was Enoch who sat with him on those evenings he wanted company. Sometimes, they played a game of checkers, using

Enoch's old, scratched-up board.

"I'd like to learn chess one of these fine days," Enoch had observed one night, after they'd established an awkward rhythm and began to speak of other things besides chamber pots and bandages.

Bridger had looked up from his last remaining piece, trapped in a corner of the board by several of Enoch's, and said, "I believe you would make a formidable opponent, Mr. Flynn." The correlation between his situation and that of the Confederacy had seemed disturbingly clear in that moment, as he recalled.

"Enoch," the other man had corrected him.

"Not as long as you're still addressing me as Captain Winslow," Bridger told him.

Enoch's grin was wide, and bright as a beam from a lighthouse on an ink-dark night. "Bridger, then," he allowed, almost shyly.

"I can show you how to play chess," Bridger had volunteered. "Though I'll probably regret it if I do."

Enoch, while obviously pleased, had shaken his head. "I reckon this board would do, but I don't own the right pieces," he'd said.

Bridger had thought of the magnificent

ivory and onyx chess set in one of the parlors at Fairhaven, where, in long-ago and better days, Tristan had taught him the game. Later, in Massachusetts, he and Rogan had spent hours bent over one of the boards in the library, a pair of callow generals pitting their wooden "men" against each other. Like their horse races and fencing matches, their chess games had been cordial enough, but they'd been battles just the same, fought, not played, with ruthlessness and cold strategy.

Back then, neither of them could have guessed that, within a few short years, they would be facing off in earnest, on a much grander scale, with cannon and rifles taking the place of pawns and kings, and living horses for knights.

Now, Bridger drew in the sight of Caroline and the little girl and her dog before he turned to meet Enoch's gaze.

He and Enoch had never spoken of Caroline, but she was always between them. Enoch had seen the kiss and had no doubt drawn conclusions of his own . . .

"Come on out here into the hallway," he said. "Get yourself some practice walking."

He traversed the length of the hallway several times, leaning heavily on Enoch.

For Bridger, every step was a strain; sweat

broke out on his upper lip, his forehead, between his shoulder blades. He was clad in plain trousers and a thin cotton shirt, better fitting than the garments Enoch had lent him.

They'd belonged to Caroline's husband, he supposed, but that was a probability he preferred not to consider.

"You're doing all right," Enoch told him. "Just keep putting one foot in front of the other."

The stairs were steep and the passage narrow and cool with shadows.

Bridger pressed on, his left shoulder brushing the wall, his eyes fixed on the descent. He nodded in response to Enoch's quiet encouragement and did as he'd been told.

When, at long last, they reached the bottom, Bridger was about to thank Enoch when he heard a door open nearby, followed by Rachel's giggle and the scrabbling of Sweet Girl's paws on the plank floor.

Then there was Caroline's voice. It came as a sweet shock to Bridger, since he hadn't expected to encounter her. "No running inside the house," she told the child. "Captain Winslow is probably sleeping."

No, Bridger thought, grinning in spite of the raging ache in his right shoulder and the all-over exhaustion of making his way down a single stairway, *Captain Winslow is not sleeping.*

The look on Caroline's face was worth the agonizing efforts of the last several minutes; her eyes widened at the sight of him, and her cheeks went that peachy-pink color. She opened her mouth, closed it again.

She might have been less surprised, Bridger thought with delight, if she'd encountered Abraham Lincoln at the foot of her back stairs.

The dog gave a few happy yips.

Rachel clapped her small hands and crowed, "You got out of bed!"

Caroline, holding an empty laundry basket in both arms, simply stared and flushed all the more furiously.

Bridger, having caught her gaze, held it. Taking pleasure in the knowledge that, for whatever reason, she seemed incapable of averting her eyes.

Her lovely eyes.

It was a delightful interlude, but, alas, far too brief.

Caroline tore her gaze from his, and pinned it on Enoch.

The flush subsided, but she obviously found herself unable to say a word.

Rachel, however, was all but jumping up and down. "Do you want to see the chickens?" she asked eagerly. "I could show you our cow."

Enoch silenced the child by clearing his throat. "Miss Rachel," he said, "you're fixing to wear that poor man's ears right off his head. He's in no shape to look at chickens and cows."

Rachel sighed loudly, reminding Bridger of an actress in a melodrama. A very small actress, with a tendency to overplay her role.

She looked up at her mother and said dolefully, "I suppose you want me to go to Jubie's room and talk to her."

"Or," Caroline said to her, "you could go upstairs and play for a while."

"But I want to play *outside*," Rachel pointed out, sounding eminently reasonable now.

"Later, honey, and take Sweet Girl upstairs with you," Caroline said, careful not to let Bridger catch her eye again.

With another dramatic sigh, Rachel took Sweet Girl and stomped up the stairs.

Caroline rallied enough to smile and Bridger saw her steel herself before looking back at him. "Would you like to sit a while in the parlor?" she asked, as though he were an invited caller, rather than an unwanted guest who'd overstayed his welcome.

Bridger was amused, although he took care not to show it. In pain, perspiring and uncomfortably aware that he was wearing her dead husband's clothes, he nodded.

"Thank you," he said. "You're very kind."

Caroline averted her eyes for a moment. "I'm afraid I haven't been," she murmured when she looked at him again. "Especially kind, I mean."

Was this an apology?

Bridger didn't know. Didn't care. She had spoken to him, stopped pretending he was invisible, and it was enough for now.

"I have things to do in the barn," Enoch said, watching Bridger. "Unless you need help getting as far as the parlor —"

"I can manage," Bridger replied, without looking away from Caroline's face. He wondered if she had any idea how beautiful she was, with her fresh, unblemished skin, her perfect features, her wheat-gold hair, thick and shining, always in danger of tumbling from its pins.

Enoch glanced at Caroline, probably expecting her to ask him to stay. When she didn't, he left the house.

They were alone then, he and Caroline, neither one speaking. If Bridger could have stopped time, he would have done it, and remained in that perfect interlude for the rest of his days.

It was Caroline who broke the silence. "The parlor is this way," she said, moving as if to take his arm, then withdrawing her hand.

That made Bridger grin — just for a second or two. He walked slowly in the direction she'd indicated with a motion of her head, and soon found himself standing in the middle of a modestly furnished but spacious room.

Sunlight streamed through spotless windows, so bright, after the cool semidarkness of the corridor, that Bridger was momentarily dazzled. When his vision cleared, he took in a plain horsehair settee, two upholstered armchairs, a fieldstone fireplace, an old harpsichord with a rag rug between its three intricately carved legs.

Faint fragments of music teased his memory, but he couldn't quite grasp when or where he'd heard them.

"Here," Caroline said hastily, gesturing toward one of the chairs. "I can serve tea if you'd like . . ."

Bridger needed to sit down; he'd hesitated while taking in his surroundings, but he realized now that he'd had another reason — he hadn't wanted to blunder into a chair her husband had favored. "I can't sit," he explained, "until you do."

She dismissed his words with a wave of one hand. "You're not well, Mr. — er — Bridger. I think we can dispense with airs and graces, just this once."

Bridger stumped over to the chair, hesitated again, and then lowered himself into the seat.

"There," Caroline said sunnily. "That wasn't so difficult, was it?"

The woman baffled him. She had been ignoring him for days, and even when she'd been forced to enter his room to retrieve her lively daughter, she had been careful not to speak or make eye contact. Now, all of a sudden, she was flouting the simplest rules of etiquette, urging him to sit while she stood. Allowing Enoch to leave them alone together.

He frowned. "I'd really like you to sit down," he said, somewhat stupidly.

"Not yet," Caroline told him. "I have to make the tea first."

"All right," he said, still confused. "That is, if you want tea for yourself. I don't drink the stuff."

"Oh," said Caroline. She seemed unsettled now, as if she didn't know quite how to proceed. Her small white teeth clamped briefly over her lower lip, and although she wasn't exactly wringing her hands, she'd laced her fingers, and her thumbs twiddled restlessly.

Bridger gave in to the prompting of some passing devil. "Whiskey would be good, though," he said.

He was rewarded by a widening of her changeable eyes and splashes of color on her cheeks. She was standing in the center of the room, about where he'd been a few minutes earlier, just out of reach, and that was probably fortunate, because he would have liked nothing better than to take her hand and pull her onto his lap.

He could imagine only one thing he would enjoy more than pulling the pins from her hair, burying his face in its luster, tangling his fingers in it, kissing her at his leisure — and much more thoroughly than he had before.

But now, he simply watched her, and that was a singular pleasure in its own right.

Caroline's eyes narrowed. Ah, yes. He'd riled her, and it was well worth the effort.

For a long moment, she looked as though she might walk over to him and slap his head off his neck.

He was disappointed when she didn't.

"You *delight* in unsettling me," she accused him in a furious whisper. *"Why?"*

Bridger considered the question. "Because, Caroline, you forget, for a little while, that you're a proper lady, bound by customs and responsibilities, and that's when you catch fire." He paused, knowing he was on the proverbial thin ice and not giving a damn. "That's when I see beyond the lady to passion inside."

She was silent for another long moment.

"Caroline," Bridger said gently. "I'll be leaving soon. Most likely, we'll never see each other again."

Unless, of course, she married Rogan, once the required mourning period was over and the war had finally ended. Rogan would expect him to attend the nuptials, to stand up with him during the ceremony. He would be compelled, for the sake of his closest friend, the man he would have chosen for a brother if that had been possible, to join in the celebration, offer hearty congratulations. Pretend to be glad for both of them, on their wedding day and ever after.

The unending expanse of such a future was painful to contemplate.

His only refuge was *now* — this moment, this day, this time of sunlight and sorrow.

"No," Caroline said, on a note of sad resolve. "Never again."

In the next moment, she was in motion. She didn't come to Bridger, not then, but instead walked purposefully to the mantelpiece, picked up a small object in both hands, held it reverently. Studied it, as though trying to memorize the thing.

Then she pressed the item to her breast, as if to absorb it into her inmost self.

The scene felt intimate, nearly sacred, and Bridger felt like an intruder, a snoop, a spy, but he could not take his eyes off Caroline.

After some time, she moved toward him, and he saw that the object was a small cabinet frame, square, with miniscule hinges on one side. He'd seen dozens of these since the beginning of the war; soldiers often carried them.

Wordless, she held it out to Bridger, her lips pressed together.

His left hand trembled as he accepted it.

Somewhat awkwardly, he released the catch, opened the little box, saw the photographic likenesses inside.

There were two, one of Caroline as a bride, standing behind her solemn new husband, who sat rigidly upright in a straight-backed chair. She rested a hand on the bridegroom's right shoulder, held her chin high, but the expression in her eyes betrayed her innocence, her trepidation, her determination to be a proper wife.

In the second image, Caroline was seated, unsmiling, arms around the very young child on her lap. Here was Rachel as an infant, bonneted and clad in an elaborate christening gown, eyes lively with interest, one small fist held to her mouth.

The shock came first, preceding full comprehension by a second or two.

Chancellorsville. Suddenly, he was back there, surrounded by dead and wounded men. The smoke had lingered, burning his eyes and throat, even though the battle had moved on.

He remembered the crouching Yank who'd drawn Bridger's attention immediately. A second Union soldier lay sprawled on the ground, one of hundreds, either dead or rendered entirely helpless by his wounds.

Plundering the pockets and rucksacks of the fallen, whether dead or alive, was common enough; he'd seen Confederate infantrymen take boots, weapons, canteens and food from friends and comrades, as well as enemies, no longer in need of earthly belongings. And, although he abhorred the practice, he understood the ugly necessities of war.

The Army of Northern Virginia, like the rest of the Confederacy, was always on short rations, when there were rations at all. Boots, blankets, guns were scarce to the point of desperation.

For some reason, the sight of this one thief, gleefully rifling through the modest belongings of a member of his own army, enraged Bridger, drove him to intercede.

He'd wanted to run the greedy bastard through, pulled out his sword for the purpose.

Instead, he'd given the order to take the man prisoner.

He'd gathered the scattered treasures, placed the letters and framed likenesses inside the Yankee's coat, set the Bible, rifle and haversack nearby. Realizing the man was alive, he'd given him a sip of water, left his canteen within reach and wished him well.

And that man, he knew now, having seen these photographs, had been Jacob Hammond.

Bridger closed his eyes, drew a deep breath, and opened them again to find that Caroline had retreated a few steps. She was watching him closely, looking bewildered and a little anxious.

"What is it?" she asked very softly, and he sensed that she feared his answer.

Bridger closed the frame, secured the

clasp, and handed it back to her, stalling, searching for the right words.

He didn't find them. Knew he would have to make do with the ones he had.

"I believe I've met your husband," he said.

23

Hammond Farm
August 3, 1863

CAROLINE

I believe I've met your husband.

Caroline did not consider her reply to the stunning statement Bridger Winslow had just made; she simply blurted out, "Were you the one — Did *you* shoot Jacob?"

Bridger's handsome, unshaven face paled, though whether this was in response to her disjointed question or to the physical pain she knew he still suffered, Caroline could not have guessed.

He took his time answering, rising laboriously to his feet, a protracted process that was hard to watch.

His eyes met Caroline's.

"No." He shook his head. "I did not."

"When? When did you see Jacob? And where?"

"In May," Bridger replied evenly. "At Chancellorsville."

Gruesome images reeled through Caroline's mind at the mention of that terrible place; she saw smoke and blood, heard the thunder of cannon and the crack of gunshots. Nausea roiled in her stomach and surged, scalding, to burn the back of her throat.

She swallowed hard. "You said you *met* Jacob. He was alive, then. When you saw him, I mean."

Bridger looked as though he might collapse, but his gaze was unwavering. "I thought he was dead at first," he said, his voice raspy, like the blade of a dull saw scraping at hardwood. "Like so many others, he was badly wounded."

"Why did you approach him at all? He was the enemy, and one of many, as you just said."

Bridger sighed. "There was another soldier — a Union bummer, not a Confederate — going through his haversack, tossing things around. I guess I'd seen that happen once too often, because the next thing I knew, I was off my horse and moving toward them."

Caroline realized she'd been holding her breath, exhaled and drew in more air.

"I put a stop to the thieving," he said, and

he seemed to be looking *through* Caroline now, not really seeing her at all. She knew he was reliving the experience as vividly as if he'd been standing on that battlefield in Virginia, not in her parlor.

She was tempted to put her arms around Bridger, to hold him, for no reason other than that he was a human being and he was suffering.

She didn't move.

"And Jacob? Did he speak to you?"

Bridger returned from that distant battlefield, shook his head. "I'm sorry, Caroline," he said. "I don't think he was able to speak. He was barely alive. There were more Confederate wounded than we could haul away. I gathered your husband's things, put your letters and those photographs inside his coat, gave him water and put the canteen where I hoped he could reach it, if he had the strength. Then I left. I knew there were Union soldiers close by, rescuing their own wounded."

Caroline saw it all so clearly, her hopeful Jacob — with all his dreams of family and babies, his ambitious plans for the farm — lying mute and bloody and utterly helpless on the ground. She swayed, groped her way to the settee and sank onto it, sitting with her hands to her face, her body bent double.

She wanted to howl but couldn't make a sound. Couldn't even cry.

Bridger came toward her. She felt his hand rest on the back of her head, then withdraw.

"I didn't know, Caroline," he said. "Until I saw those pictures just now, I didn't know."

She moaned, despairing.

"I'm sorry," he repeated.

And then he was moving away from her, slowly retreating from the room.

Caroline heard him making his way up the stairs, knew each step was an ordeal for him, but she didn't follow. Her legs would have folded beneath her if she'd tried, and her head swam.

Presently, she was able to sit up straight. The pain in her heart turned to a curious numbness, one she might have welcomed if it hadn't made her feel more like a ghost than a living woman.

In time, she stood. Crossed the room, took the little frame Jacob had carried with him when he went to war and put it back in its place on top of the bureau.

She didn't see Enoch when she left the house. Perhaps he was still working in the barn, or he'd gone to his cabin on the far side of the orchard.

Jubie and Rachel were somewhere nearby; Caroline could hear them laughing and

Sweet Girl barking happily.

Inside the kitchen house, she located the last remaining bottle of Geneva's medicinal whiskey, held it up and saw that it was three-quarters full. She didn't personally approve of the stuff, but she'd seen it calm men's pain and ease their anxiety, so she supposed it had its uses.

She took a clean jelly jar from one of the shelves and, carrying it in one hand and the bottle in the other, retraced her steps.

Bridger was back in his room when she got there, sitting in the chair beside the bed, his eyes shut.

"Bridger," she said, and hesitated. Then she carried the bottle and jar into the room, set them down on the nightstand and returned to the doorway, pausing there, strangely reluctant to go. She was waiting for Bridger to speak her name.

He did.

"Caroline, no one could have saved your husband," he said.

She remembered her first sight of Jacob in that miserable hospital tent. He'd been so weary, so broken by war, a dead man with a heartbeat.

She'd known then that he was lost to her, lost to Rachel and Enoch and everyone else who cared for him, but she hadn't been ready to let him go. If he'd recovered, she would have learned to love him properly, as a mature woman loves a man. She would have opened her heart and soul to Jacob more completely, more thoroughly . . . instead of guarding herself against those intense emotions.

Loving a man, she saw now, was a choice, a decision. It didn't just happen. You had to *choose,* and be steadfast, in good times and in bad and, perhaps most difficult of all, in the ordinary times between.

No one could have saved your husband.

"You were kind to Jacob," she said. "Under the circumstances, you did all you could for him."

Bridger's eyes were full of ghosts as he regarded her, and she knew he was subduing strong emotions, possibly at great cost. "Is that why you brought me whiskey?" he asked. There was no mockery in his tone, no evident desire to bait her. "Because I did what I could for your husband?"

She thought for a moment. Why *had* she brought him strong spirits?

"I suppose I brought the whiskey because you asked for it," she said. Then, cautiously, trying not to sound too hopeful, she asked, "Have you changed your mind? About the whiskey?"

"I have," Bridger said.

"Why?"

He laughed, a short, gruff sound, but turned serious in the next instant. "If I start," he said, "I might never stop."

Caroline returned to collect the bottle. "What will you do after you leave here?" she asked.

"Probably wish I could have stayed," Bridger replied.

"I'm serious," Caroline said.

"So am I. But, to answer your question, I'll take Enoch up on his kind offer of a horse, and ride in a southerly direction until I find General Lee's army." He paused, watching her reaction, seeing it for what it was. "I'm a soldier, Caroline, and there is still a war to be fought."

"How can you do that, after all you've seen, all that's happened? You've already been wounded once — wasn't that enough? Must you keep fighting until you're killed? Is that what you want?"

"None of this is what I want," Bridger replied calmly.

"Then why not simply *go home*?"

"When this is over, I will. Until then, I will fight."

"For secession? For *slavery*?"

Bridger shook his head. "No. For Georgia.

For Fairhaven, where my family has lived for three generations."

Caroline knew she was wasting her breath; she could not make this hardheaded man see reason, and it was futile to argue. Still, she did. "You can't win! Don't you see that, Bridger? *You can't win.* Oh, I know your General Lee has often outmaneuvered our Union forces, but how long will it be until his luck runs out? In the end, though, the rebellion won't succeed because the North has greater numbers. It has railroads and farms and factories. What does the South really have, other than pride?"

"Are you finished, Caroline?" Bridger asked.

"Yes!" He was so damnably unruffled, so detached.

"Good. Then perhaps you would do me the courtesy of leaving me alone with my . . . pride."

She stalked to the door. "By all means, wallow in your stupid *pride* all you want." She wondered why she'd thought she could have a rational conversation with a Rebel. "See how well it serves you."

There was a shrug in Bridger's voice and anger in his eyes. "As long as I have it," he said, "I won't give up."

Caroline stepped across the threshold,

seething, slammed the door behind her and barely resisted a primitive urge to smash that bottle of whiskey to pieces against it.

She paced up and down the hallway until she'd expended most of the frenzied and chaotic energies any exchange with the redoubtable Bridger seemed to create in her. Other than anger, each emotion, being part of a curious tangle of opposites, seemed to countermand another.

Her life with Jacob, though not without its many joys and occasional sorrows, like any life, had consisted mostly of quiet agreement on shared objectives, such as which field ought to lie fallow for a year or two, which were to be sown, and with what crop.

When it became more and more likely that the long-standing fissures between North and South would result in armed conflict, Caroline had dreaded the coming war between the States, as most sensible people would, whatever their loyalties. She continued down the stairs, back to the parlor, but she was still too caught up in uncomfortable thoughts to turn her hand to some useful task.

Instead, she moved to the harpsichord. She was not a dreamer, or given to whimsical distractions; in fact, she rarely played, although she loved music, for the simple reason that there were only twenty-four hours in a day, and when she wasn't sleeping, she was working. Doing productive things.

As any good wife and mother would.

Today, she made an exception. She smoothed her skirts, sat down on the narrow bench and uncovered the ivory keys, which were chipped in places and had faded over time to a yellowish beige. She cleared her throat delicately, and opened the songbook Rogan had sent to "Flow Gently, Sweet Afton," squirmed a little, to settle herself, and began to play.

At first, the notes were tentative and awkward; as familiar as the piece was to Caroline, she was out of practice, and she hadn't attempted it before.

The effort was calming, however, and her frustration began to subside. For a while, Caroline surrendered to the music, allowed it to carry her far away, into a realm where there was no war, no injustice, no regret.

After the first tune, she played from memory — familiar hymns, passages of Mozart and, finally, sentimental ballads. With these last, however, fragments of lyrics came back to her, all of them sad. Lines about lonely maidens vowing never to wed, descriptions of remembered sunsets and the shores of home fading into ghostly mists, noble lovers lost to death and, finally, empty cradles.

What had consoled Caroline in the beginning seemed unbearably maudlin now, but she needed the music and the making of it, so she resorted once again to the songbook.

She chose a camp song with a sprightly tempo and pounded it out with exuberance, purposely ignoring the lyrics, which were probably bawdy.

It was only as the last notes were vibrating toward silence that Caroline made the obvious connection and was ambushed by thoughts of Rogan.

He was certainly handsome, particularly in his uniform. The gifts he'd sent had delighted everyone, though he might not have acted purely out of generosity — after all, he'd practically forced Bridger on her, and then had the audacity to add a dog.

Not that Caroline minded Sweet Girl; she was such a joy to Rachel.

Yes, Caroline decided. She could forgive Rogan for the dog; forgiving him for inflicting Bridger upon her, however, might be more complicated.

He'd awakened something inside her, changed her in ways she couldn't begin to understand, turned her entire conception of who and what she was upside down and inside out. And he had managed it so easily.

To him, their kiss had been a mere dalliance. Once he'd gone, he'd probably never think of her again.

She, on the other hand, would remember him. She would feel his mouth on hers at unexpected moments, when her defenses were down, when she was lonely or discouraged or weary after a day of hard work.

Whether she married again, or lived out the rest of her life as a widow, running the farm and raising her daughter, she would remember that, in the summer of 1863, she had buried her young husband, and had listened, horrified, to the near-constant roar of guns as a great battle raged all around. She had tended grievously wounded men, in her own side yard and in the nearby town, heard their cries, looked on helplessly as they died. She would recall the hasty burials, all over that part of Adams County.

At least she would not be alone in this; countless others would remember those first three days of July, the unspeakable brutality, the incomprehensible price paid by so many. The earth itself, gouged and scorched, stained with the blood of thousands, would bear witness to what had happened in and around the little town of Gettysburg for a very long time.

Sufficient unto the day, the evil thereof, Caroline thought bleakly. She, like her friends and neighbors, would carry the burden of these memories until she went to her own grave, most likely alongside that of her husband.

"Mama?"

Caroline looked up, saw Rachel standing in the parlor doorway, the dog beside her. She rose from the bench in front of the harpsichord, alarmed by the pinched expression on her daughter's face, the pallor of her skin, the very stillness of her small body.

"What is it?" she asked, already moving toward the child. "Are you ill?"

"It's Jubie," Rachel said, her voice trembling. "She said to come find you, and be quick about it, because her baby is coming."

Dear Lord, Caroline thought, panicked. For Rachel's sake, she pretended to be calm. "Everything will be all right, darling. You mustn't fret."

"I'm scared, Mama. Jubie's holding her tummy and rolling all around, and she's making noises like she's sick."

Caroline took her daughter gently by the shoulders. "Where is Jubie?"

Rachel shook her head, and tears welled

471

in her eyes. "We were in the orchard, Jubie and Sweet Girl and me. And then she started feeling bad, and she told me she needs you to help her."

"I will," Caroline said. "What about Enoch? Where is he?"

"I don't know," Rachel replied. "Tell me what I'm supposed to do now, Mama."

"You've already done all you can," Caroline told her. "Now, you and Sweet Girl stay right here in the house. If Enoch comes in, ask him to ride to town and get your great-grandmother, in case we need her."

"All right," Rachel agreed, with a nod. "But I'm still scared."

Caroline bent, kissed the top of the child's head. "I'll hurry back," she said. "I promise."

She heard the rhythmic thump of Bridger descending from the floor above, as he called out, "Caroline? What's wrong?"

Caroline moved to the foot of the stairs and looked up at him. "Jubie's in the orchard, and she's in labor. I've got to get to her right away."

Bridger nodded, making his painful, deliberate way down the stairs.

"What are you doing?" Caroline protested. "Go back to bed immediately. I don't have time to argue with you!"

"No, you don't," Bridger said, and he kept right on coming. "So go. Do what you need to do. I'll stay with Rachel and Sweet Girl in the meantime."

"But —"

"Caroline, *just go.*"

"But . . ." She dared not hesitate long. It was Rachel who ultimately decided the question by marching to Caroline's side, looking up the stairway at the Confederate limping down, and called, "Will you teach me to play checkers, please, Mr. Windlesnow? I should like that very much."

Bridger's smile was meant for the child, but its warmth spilled over onto Caroline. "All right," he replied, with pretended reluctance, "if you promise to let me win once in a while."

"I promise," Rachel said.

Caroline hurried away without another word, through the parlor, along the short corridor, and out the side door. Lifting her skirts to avoid stumbling over the hem of her dress, she ran toward the orchard.

As she drew closer, she heard Jubie's cries and ran faster still.

She might have called out that she was almost there, that everything would be fine, but she couldn't spare the breath.

When Jubie came into view, Enoch was

already there, lifting her gently from the ground. Caroline slowed to a fast walk and approached, gasping, one hand on her chest.

"Enoch," she blurted. "Thank heaven!"

Jubie moaned in Enoch's big arms, limp as one of Rachel's rag dolls. "Don't let nothin' hurt my baby," she pleaded.

"Hush, now," Enoch told her gruffly. "Nobody's going to hurt anybody."

Caroline scrambled toward them, still breathing hard from her exertions. "Will you carry her to the kitchen house?" she asked. "I'll need the stove nearby, so I can heat plenty of water while you go into town to get my grandmother."

Enoch, heading deeper into the orchard, shook his head and kept walking in the opposite direction, his strides lengthening with every step. His back was broad, its muscles defined beneath the coarse, sweat-stained fabric of his shirt. "No time for that, Missus," he said. "This child must have important business in this world, because he's in an almighty hurry to get here."

"But — how — where — ?"

Enoch did not look back or slacken his pace. "My cabin is closer than the kitchen house," he said with finality.

Caroline offered no argument. Holding her skirts, she followed, weaving her way between the trunks of peach and apple and cherry trees, taking care not to stumble over exposed roots or twist an ankle stepping in a hole.

Enoch's sturdy cabin, the original Hammond homestead, stood in a small hidden clearing, surrounded by venerable oaks and maples. The little house had been kept in good repair over its nearly ninety years of existence; the roof line was level and the stone chimney freshly mortared. Glass windows, a more recent addition, gleamed in the sunlight, and there were brightly colored curtains behind them.

Although Caroline had seen the cabin many times, she had never been inside. Under less trying circumstances, she might have been curious, even intrigued, but Jubie was in severe pain by then, writhing in Enoch's arms and calling out for God's mercy.

Caroline shivered at the sound, remembering her own pain when she'd borne Rachel. She hung back a little while Enoch mounted the steps of the narrow porch, shaded by a small roof. He bent to raise the latch with a deft motion of one elbow, holding Jubie securely all the while.

Jubie continued to wail and keen.

Enoch stepped over the threshold, and

Caroline shook off the worst of her fear, forced herself to go forward.

Closing the door and leaning back against it, in need of a few minutes to overcome her cowardice, Caroline allowed herself to look around.

The single room couldn't have measured more than twelve feet square, but it felt strangely spacious, perhaps because there were so few furnishings — a small cookstove, a wooden table with two chairs, a large trunk and an iron bed covered with a faded patchwork quilt.

Enoch stood Jubie on her feet and threw back the quilt, then eased her down onto the sheets. He spoke a few words to her, soothing ones, although Caroline couldn't make them out.

Jubie arched her back and screamed.

Enoch smoothed her hair. "You go right ahead and carry on, Jubie, if you feel the need. In the meantime, Missus Caroline and I, we'll take good care of you, and your baby, too."

The tenderness in Enoch's voice brought tears to Caroline's eyes, but it gave her strength, too. She unbuttoned her cuffs, rolled up her sleeves and took charge.

24

CAROLINE

"Enoch has gone to the spring for water," Caroline said, clasping Jubie's hands in hers and holding them firmly.

"This child's coming fast, Miss Caroline," Jubie fretted, tossing her head from side to side.

"I know," Caroline said quietly. "It will be over soon. Now, if you'll try to lie still, I'll have a look at you."

Jubie bit down hard on her lower lip and nodded.

Caroline examined the girl, and was startled to see the crown of the baby's head already emerging.

Enoch would surely be back any moment now, bringing the water he'd gone to fetch, but, like the stove, it would be cold. He

477

would've had no cause to build a fire on such a hot day, since he took his meals at the kitchen house with the others.

Caroline, the granddaughter of a physician, yearned to wash her hands, but it didn't seem as though she'd have the chance to do even that.

Jubie shouted again, but this time, the sound was part fierce effort, part triumph.

The head was out, although Caroline could not yet see the baby's face.

"Don't push, Jubie," she said. "Take a minute to breathe before you try again."

"Can you see him?" Jubie panted.

"Yes," Caroline replied, fascinated, her earlier fear forgotten. "He — or she — has a great deal of hair."

The cabin door sprang open, but she didn't look away from the task at hand. "I need hot water, Enoch," she said. "I must wash my hands."

Enoch grunted in reply, and she heard a stove lid clank.

Another contraction seized Jubie's small body. "Miss Caroline," she gasped, "I got to push now. I just got to!"

"That's fine, Jubie," Caroline said. "Push for all you're worth."

With a hoarse cry of pain and victory, Jubie pushed.

One tiny shoulder appeared, then another. After that, the baby slipped easily from Jubie's straining body into Caroline's waiting hands.

The child was very small, but clearly alive, tiny fingers flexing, perfect little mouth working, as though hungry for mother's milk.

"Jubie," Caroline said, marveling at the miracle squirming against her palms, "you have a son."

Jubie lifted her head from Enoch's pillow, her face gleaming with perspiration. "Why isn't he crying?"

More out of instinct than actual knowledge, Caroline cleared the baby's mouth with one fingertip, then turned him over long enough to give him a firm pat on the back.

He squalled, furious, and Caroline settled him on Jubie's chest, careful of the umbilical cord, still attached.

Beaming, exhausted, Jubie murmured to the infant, kissing his forehead.

"Not much to him, is there?" Enoch remarked lightly from behind Caroline. "Little bit of a feller. I've seen field mice bigger than he is."

Caroline turned her head, intending to reprimand Enoch for insensitivity, only to find him smiling as fondly as if he'd fathered the child himself.

"This here," Jubie said softly, still gazing into the face of her child, "is no field mouse. This here is Gideon, and he's going to grow up to be a fine, strong man. A *free* man, never a slave."

Caroline did not look at Enoch, and neither of them spoke.

Enoch went back to the stove, opening its door, shoving in kindling and crumpled newspaper, lighting a match. He filled a kettle from one of the buckets, then set it on the stove top to heat, found a basin and soap and put them on the table.

From the trunk Caroline had spotted earlier, he took a towel, worn to near transparency by long and frequent use, and brought it to Jubie.

"Got to tie off and cut that cord," he said.

Caroline, still standing beside the bed, looked up at him in sudden alarm. "I don't know how to do that," she said, in a useless whisper.

"Well," Enoch said, "I do. I've got some twine around here someplace. Soon as that water comes to a boil, I'll pour a little over the blade of my pocket knife, since I don't have scissors. Then that baby ought to be washed and wrapped up in the towel. By then, he'll be howling for his mama's milk."

Caroline did not blush or wince at such frankness. After visiting Jacob in the squalid hospital tents of Washington City, tending sick and wounded soldiers in the aftermath of a three-day battle and now assisting a woman in childbirth, she was no longer prone to squeamishness.

When there was plenty of hot water, she and Enoch took turns filling the basin, washing their hands with strong soap. Enoch made sure his knife was clean and sharp, then he showed Caroline how to tie off the umbilical cord in two places, then cut between them.

The baby fussed and slept, fussed and slept, snuggled warm in his mother's arms. Caroline washed out the basin, filled it with heated water, and waited until it had cooled, then took little Gideon from Jubie's arms. She bathed him and bundled him loosely in Enoch's old towel. Again, she was careful not to disturb the stub of cord at his navel; she knew from experience that it must be left to dry and fall off on its own.

There were other tasks, of course.

Jubie was delivered of the afterbirth, and Enoch took it outside in the basin, to be buried, as was the custom. He sat with mother and baby while Caroline went back to the main house for sheets, since the ones on Enoch's bed were ruined. Suspecting he had owned just that one threadbare towel, now serving as a baby blanket, she took a mental inventory of her own none-too-plentiful stock of linens as she walked. She could surely spare one or two, she thought, full of weary satisfaction.

When she entered the house, she found Bridger and her daughter sitting on the settee in the parlor, the checkerboard between them, Sweet Girl resting against Rachel's feet.

Bridger looked up when she came in, read her face and visibly relaxed. Then, feigning glum resignation, he indicated Rachel with a slight nod and said, "I knew it would be a mistake, teaching this young lady the game. She is absolutely ruthless."

Rachel glanced up from the board, which she'd been pondering solemnly, and brightened. "Is Jubie better now, Mama?"

"Jubie is *much* better," Caroline replied with a smile. "And there's a brand-new baby at Hammond Farm. His name is Gideon, and he is *beautiful.*"

"Boys aren't supposed to be beautiful," Rachel said. She made a face at the mere suggestion, although her eyes sparkled with interest.

"Nevertheless, Gideon is," Caroline said.

"May I go see him?" Rachel asked, sliding off the settee.

"No," Caroline said, "you may not. Little Gideon has just been born, and that's hard work. He is not receiving guests yet, and neither is Jubie."

Rachel's forehead creased. "But we can't leave them in the orchard!" she declared. "What if it rains?"

"Jubie and Gideon are not in the orchard. They're resting very comfortably in Enoch's cabin."

"Yes, but . . . I'm not allowed to go there by myself."

Bridger, gathering the checkers pieces and returning them to their box, smiled but said nothing.

"Tomorrow," Caroline promised. "I need to take a few things back to the cabin now, but I won't be long," she went on. "When I get back, I'll make dinner."

Bridger set the game board aside and slowly got to his feet. "It's not far to the kitchen house," he said. "And the walk will be good for me. Give me a chance to stretch my legs and get some fresh air." He looked down at Rachel. "Suppose you and I go out there and rustle up some grub? That way, when your mama gets back, she won't have to cook. She can just sit down and eat."

Rachel considered the suggestion so solemnly that Caroline nearly laughed. "All right," she finally agreed. "But I would *still* like to see the baby."

"*Tomorrow,* Rachel Hammond. And you won't see Gideon or Jubie then, either, if you don't stop pestering me."

Rachel's little shoulders rose and fell with her disappointment, but in the end, she relented.

Caroline felt some concern over Bridger's condition. Clearly he was getting stronger, but she'd seen the strain on his face when he'd navigated the stairs. The kitchen house was at least two hundred yards away, over uneven ground.

"I'm not sure it would be wise for you to walk that far just yet," she told him.

"While I appreciate your apparent concern for my well-being," he said, the mild tone of his voice very much at odds with his expression, "I understand my capabilities quite well and do not require your counsel."

Essentially he was telling her to mind her own business. She would not make that mistake again.

Smiling her brightest smile, she replied, "Why, *of course* you don't need my advice, however kindly it might have been intended,

Captain Winslow. *Believe me,* I wouldn't *think* of delaying your departure by a single moment."

"Sweet Girl is hungry," Rachel interjected. "And so am I."

Bridger's smile was genuine, and wholly reserved for the little girl and her dog. "Then I guess we had better address the problem directly," he said.

Rachel, delighted by his attention, frolicked across the parlor, Sweet Girl scrabbling after her, headed for the side door.

Bridger hesitated for a moment, gazing at Caroline with consternation, as if he might be about to say something conciliatory.

In the end, he merely shook his head, like a man faced with a puzzle that could not be solved, and turned away. He hobbled for a few steps, then muttered something and grabbed a door frame.

Caroline, who had been watching his progress, cried out.

Bridger looked back at her, glaring. "What?" he snapped.

"Nothing."

The air between them seemed charged.

"It's just that . . . you seem to need help," she finally said.

"There's nothing wrong with my legs," Bridger told her with determined patience.

"I'm a bit slow, that's all."

Although Caroline doubted he could get as far as the kitchen house on his own, she wasn't about to say so. "Fine," she said lightly. And then she made herself turn away, mount the stairs and head for the chest where she stored her linens. She selected two towels and a pair of sheets. The small blanket Rogan had sent was no doubt in the back room and would have to wait.

When she heard Rachel chattering, she hurried to the nearest window, the one in her daughter's room, overlooking the side yard.

She watched as Bridger progressed slowly across the ground, Rachel and Sweet Girl prancing alongside. His strides were deliberate if a bit tentative.

Caroline turned from the window, the folded sheets and towels still in her arms, and noticed that the bed was neatly made up. The nightstand, previously cluttered with the pages of his sister's letter and the note Rogan had sent, in addition to scraps of paper with their penciled diagrams of imaginary chess games, was bare.

Surely Bridger wasn't preparing to leave! He wasn't ready, wasn't nearly strong enough.

And yet the room looked strangely tidy,

with Rachel's things back in their usual places. It was as though Bridger had never been there.

You should be glad he's going away, Caroline told herself.

But she wasn't. Not at all.

She tried to bring Jacob's image to mind, but it wouldn't come. His features, so familiar, eluded her; she hurried to the room she and her husband had shared, dropped the linens on the bed, and studied the small likeness Jacob had sent home a few months after he'd enlisted.

There he was, her Jacob, in uniform, a rifle propped against one soldier.

She examined the lines of his face, the set of his eyes and mouth, the way his hair, light brown and a little too long, showed on both sides of his cap, a kepi, he'd called it. His uniform looked new, and the stock and barrel of his rifle gleamed, as if he'd just polished them.

He had been so young, so determined, so self-assured. He'd had no idea — how could he have? — of the horrors awaiting him. So many battles, so much pain and blood and death . . . How brutally surprised he must have been in that terrible moment when he first realized that war wasn't the glorious adventure he'd probably imagined it to be, made up of parades and grand reviews and cheering crowds. In some part of his mind, Caroline knew, Jacob had been more boy than man, off to play king-of-the-hill, outfitted in a snappy blue uniform and shiny boots.

Why, she wondered, had she never seen how innocent he'd been, how guileless, how vulnerable?

She had grieved for him, brought his body home in a railroad car, seen his coffin lowered into the ground and covered with dirt. She had wept for him.

Now, she mourned the boy who'd gone away to war, with little thought of dying.

When had it come to him, the knowledge that he was mortal? That combat was no schoolyard game, but a deadly kill-or-be-killed enterprise, and that bullets and cannonballs struck without discrimination or mercy.

It was jarring to think of the ramifications of a single death.

The contributions one man might have made, had he survived, were lost, and so were those of the children he might have sired, and of their children's, on and on.

Taking up the sheets and towels she meant to bring to Enoch's cabin, Caroline set out to complete the errand. As she walked, she continued to consider the terrible cost of war, and every other kind of violence. She'd stepped into the clearing surrounding Enoch's cabin, when she saw him sitting on his front steps, smiling to himself as he whittled at a piece of wood.

She watched him until he noticed her and set his knife aside and got to his feet.

"Before you ask," he said, still smiling, "Jubie is fine, and so is the boy."

"Are they resting?"

He nodded. "Sound asleep, both of them."

"I won't disturb them, then," Caroline said, extending the small pile of linens.

Enoch cleared his throat, took them, then remained in place. His smile wavered a little. "I'm obliged, Missus," he said, in his gravelly voice.

Caroline tilted her head to one side. "Enoch, what is it you want to say?"

He looked away from her, then back. "Jubie and I, we mean to marry, jump the broom, so to speak. When she's able, that is."

She nodded. "Jubie told me a little while ago. I'm very happy for you both." Pausing, she asked, "Where does that expression come from?"

"It's a term slaves use, down South," Enoch explained. "They can't get hitched the same way white folks do, with a license and a preacher and all. In the South, that's against the law."

"Oh," Caroline said, oddly flummoxed by Enoch's announcement. "Why?"

Enoch laughed quietly. "Why is it illegal for slaves to marry?" he asked.

"Why are there slaves in the first place?" she countered, not expecting an answer. Wanting to make herself understood, she blundered on. "I know you've been lonely, Enoch, probably for a long time. If you want to take a wife, you should."

He didn't respond, and she continued. "It's just that Jubie's a runaway. We know almost nothing about her. She's been a great help, with Rachel and Br— Captain Winslow — and those poor army men, and I couldn't be more grateful. Slavery is a dreadful thing, and I don't blame Jubie, not one bit, for escaping, but —"

Enoch's expression was kind. "What is it about Jubie that concerns you?"

"She's so *young,* Enoch. Yes, she's a mother, but that doesn't mean she's ready to be a wife. She's been through a lot, including escaping slave catchers. You remember how frightened she was, before the battle, when all those Confederate troops rode by the farmhouse."

"I was pretty scared that day myself," Enoch said mildly. "I guess I got used to living as a free man all these years, with nobody hunting me down, nobody wanting to drag me off to some cage or whipping post. I didn't have to be afraid anymore. I've had a good place to live, and I get paid for an honest day's work — in money I can spend or save as I see fit. But when I saw all those men in gray coats, it came back to me, what it meant to be a slave, and I wanted to crawl into that hole in the floor, the secret room, and bring Jubie with me. Only difference is, I didn't let on how afraid I was."

Caroline said nothing; her throat felt as if it had been tied into a knot.

Enoch went on. "You're right about Jubie being a little too young to be a real wife," he said. "I won't ask that of her. I just want to keep her as safe I can and be a father to that baby boy in there. And then, when she *is* ready . . ."

"What if they're still after her, Enoch? Slave catchers, I mean?"

"If there's trouble, then I'll do what I have to do," Enoch said, averting his eyes now, gazing at something far off in the distance. Caroline knew he was remembering the man he'd killed that day, in the creek.

They were both silent for some time, thinking their own thoughts.

Then came the muffled squall of an infant.

Enoch smiled, lifted the sheets and towels he was holding. "I'll go on inside with these," he said. "I'm thankful to you, Missus Caroline, for these things here and a whole lot more, too."

It was a dismissal, although a very polite one. Enoch, Jubie and little Gideon were already becoming a family and, for now, Caroline had done all she could for them.

She felt strangely alone as she nodded a farewell, turned and started back across the clearing, careful to keep her shoulders straight and her head high.

Reaching the orchard, she paused, looking up at the leaves stirring in a breeze passing high overhead, casting light and shadow onto the soft, sheltered ground in constantly changing patterns.

Caroline loved the orchard most at this time of year; it was cooler there, quiet except for the occasional trill of birdsong and the faint, tumbling chatter of the creek running behind Enoch's cabin.

Here, she found peace, could almost forget there was a war being fought.

When time allowed, Caroline came to this place and stood among the trees, finding solace when she was troubled, quiet companionship when she was lonely, abundance, or the promise of it, when funds ran low.

In every season, the trees were beautiful, lush and fragrant with pink and white blossoms in spring. They wore a hundred shades of glorious green for summer, reminding Caroline of courtesans in rich velvet or elegant matrons gathering for afternoon tea. In autumn, they donned garments of fiery yellow and russet and crimson, soon to be shed, and all the lovelier for it.

Even in winter, when they stood stark against the whiteness of the landscape, like swift, sharp lines drawn in charcoal, they were gravely splendid, traced in glittering frost or dripping snowy lace.

Sudden hunger ended Caroline's reverie, reminded her that Bridger was in the kitchen house, if he'd made it that far, endeavoring to prepare a meal. Rachel was surely with him, probably getting underfoot, eager to help, reaching, perhaps, for a pot of boiling water or a hot skillet. The image set Caroline in motion, walking fast at first, then running, the sides of her skirts bunched in her hands.

She burst, breathless, from the orchard, her heart pounding with alarm.

And there was Rachel, playing happily

with Sweet Girl in front of the kitchen house. The little girl turned and, when she saw Caroline dashing out of the trees, looked frightened.

"Mama!" she cried, hurrying toward her. "Is there a bear after you?"

"No," she managed to say as the child reached her.

She gathered up the child, laughing, kissing her on one cheek. Over Rachel's head, she saw Bridger standing in the doorway of the kitchen house, watching. He gripped the framework on either side, and Caroline saw his grim expression relax into the semblance of a smile.

Sweet Girl ran in circles around mother and child, making plenty of noise.

Caroline tried to tear her gaze from Bridger's face, and could not.

It seemed to her, not for the first time, that something passed between them . . . Slowly, she set Rachel down, straightened the child's bonnet, shushed the dog, all without looking away from Bridger.

"No bear, then?" he asked lightly.

Caroline shook her head, ignoring what might have been mockery.

The reality was that he'd been a threat to her presence of mind from the first, but for more reasons than the obvious ones — that he was a Confederate officer, an avowed enemy of all she believed in, an incriminating, perhaps even treasonous presence in her household. But now she understood that those were the lesser of the dangers Bridger Winslow represented.

He had only to smile, or look at her a certain way — or kiss her — to sway her from the course she had set for herself. That of a strong, principled woman, a widow and a mother, with a war to get through and a farm to run. Even with help from Enoch and her grandmother, none of it would be easy; she would have to pray hard and work harder to get the fields plowed and the crops planted every spring, see them through the growing season, past such perils as drought and hail and rampaging soldiers and finally, harvest the corn and grain and get a decent price for them.

She had to be vigilant, she decided, as Rachel took her hand and half dragged her toward the kitchen house and Bridger.

"Mr. Captain Windlesnow said we couldn't eat *a single bite* till you got back."

Rachel tugged at her hand so hard, Caroline nearly stumbled.

Caroline corrected her briskly. "Captain *Winslow,* Rachel. The man's name is 'Captain Winslow.'"

"That's what I said," Rachel insisted.

Bridger laughed, then turned from the doorway and went inside. His gait, Caroline noticed, had improved in the short time she'd been away.

There were plates on the table, and the knives, forks and spoons lay in their proper order. Bridger had sliced bread and smoked ham, opened a jar of sweet pickles, put out the butter dish. Fresh-picked lettuce from the garden, crisp and damp from washing, filled a small bowl.

When Rachel climbed into her accustomed chair, he filled a jelly jar from the milk jug and set it within her reach.

Then Bridger drew back Caroline's chair and waited politely for her to sit.

She delayed by washing her hands and insisting Rachel do the same, but the process didn't last very long.

When she turned from the basin, towel in hand, Bridger was still standing behind her chair. There wasn't a flicker of impatience in his eyes; in fact he was the personification of social grace and good manners.

Caroline flushed and sat down.

She lowered her head, closed her eyes and folded her hands.

"Mama," Rachel informed Bridger in a loud whisper, "is going to talk to God."

Caroline cleared her throat. Then she offered thanks for the meal before them, the safe delivery of Jubie's baby and all other blessings, known and unknown, remembered and forgotten. Past and future . . .

When she paused to draw breath, Rachel added an exuberant, "Amen!"

Bridger chuckled. "Amen," he confirmed.

Caroline prepared Rachel's plate, cutting a small slice of ham into manageable pieces, quartering and then buttering her bread. She speared a sweet pickle from the jar, added that and passed the food to her daughter.

Rachel waited until everyone had been served before picking up her fork, looking very pleased with her own deportment.

For a while, everyone ate silently, including Rachel who, Caroline noticed, was slipping a morsel of ham to Sweet Girl for every two that went into her mouth.

When the meal was finished, and once she'd washed and dried the dishes, she would put Rachel down for an afternoon nap.

Bridger, Caroline noticed, seemed preoccupied. He ate distractedly, his gaze turned to whatever inner world engaged him.

In a certain way, she felt *relieved* by his

silence now . . .

And yet, undeniably, she recognized the unsettling truth — that she dreaded his going as much as she yearned for it, and for many of the same reasons.

Soon enough, Rachel was nodding in her chair, heavy eyed and full of good food and ready for a nap.

Caroline, who had wept more in recent weeks than in the whole rest of her life, was weary of her own mewling and sniffling and carrying on. Never mind that it had all been justified, she felt another crying fit coming. "Will everything, always and forever, be sad?" she suddenly asked. She had meant only to *think* the question, not give voice to it.

To her utter surprise, Bridger simply rested one of his hands atop one of hers and said quietly, "No. You won't be sad forever, Caroline. You are too smart, too strong and far too beautiful to be unhappy."

She hesitated for a long time before pulling back her hand, and she did it slowly, even then. *Stay, and argue with me, let me sharpen my mind against yours,* she thought. *Stand behind me, when I'm washing dishes or making supper or pressing a shirt or an apron or one of Rachel's little dresses. Put your arms around me, and brush my neck with your lips.*

She moved away from the table, through the door and across the yard to the house. She took her daughter and led her to the house.

Bridger didn't speak, or follow.

Her bedroom was cool and dimly lit; Caroline had pulled the curtains to keep out the heat.

She lifted Rachel, set her on the side of the bed, then crouched to unlace the child's shoes and pull them off.

Sweet Girl sank onto the hooked rug with a contented sigh.

"No covers," Rachel murmured. "It's too hot."

"No covers," Caroline agreed. "Lie down now, and go to sleep. Before you know it, it'll be time to get up again."

"Mmm." Rachel stretched out, closing her eyes.

There were so many things to do. Carrying water for the garden, pulling weeds, washing dishes, planning supper, going over household accounts.

Verbally sparring with Bridger Winslow.

Caroline moved to the other side of the bed and sat down to take off her own shoes. Then, with a yawn, she settled herself across from Rachel, closed her eyes and immediately fell asleep.

25

BRIDGER

Late in the afternoon, Bridger took his few belongings — the letter from Amalie, that damnable blue uniform, the good Yankee currency, backed by Federal gold, that Rogan had sent him, plus a scrap of paper and the stub of a pencil — and moved from the house to the barn. If he'd been asked for an explanation, in that moment of decision, he wouldn't have had one to offer, except to say it was time Rachel had her room back.

Caroline brought him supper, the plate covered by a red-and-white-checked napkin, crisply pressed. "It may be cold," she said, "When you didn't come to the kitchen house, I thought perhaps you weren't feeling well."

He was cleaning a saddle, glad to have

something to occupy his hands. His right shoulder pained him with a mighty vengeance, but that was to be expected; healing, like most blessings of God and nature, didn't come without cost. So he gritted his teeth through the worst of it and kept on brushing the dirt and mud from the worn leather.

"Thank you," he said, keeping his eyes on his task, marveling at the sorry state of the saddle Enoch had given him. He'd seen plenty such gear, covered in trail dust, blood-stained, too, after a battle, but this relic was so filthy it might have been buried in the earth, or found in some rank old tomb, still cinched to the skeleton barrel of a long-dead horse.

He hadn't said anything about its condition to Enoch, of course. Beggars couldn't be choosers.

Caroline approached, set the plate down nearby. Then she stood in a shaft of light, the last of the day, specks of dust moving around her, glittering like tiny stars in some distant galaxy.

With a sidelong glance, Bridger saw that her eyes were wide. He wondered if she recognized the saddle, if it had belonged to her late husband, perhaps, since it seemed to be the object of her attention.

"You can't be very comfortable out here," she finally ventured, "even if you are regaining your strength." Her voice shook slightly. "You're welcome to sleep in the house."

Bridger shook his head and looked up at her, then remembered his manners and stood. He regretted that he hadn't told her he was moving to the barn. He was finding it too hard to lie alone in that narrow bed, knowing she was only a room away.

How could he have told her that it was agony, the desire to hold her, bury his face in her hair, to kiss her, to pleasure her? That, as he grew stronger, the impossibility of doing any or all of those things was harder and harder to bear?

She would have been insulted, scandalized. Maybe even afraid.

"Is something wrong?" he asked. She was still staring at the blasted saddle, almost as if she expected it to come to life.

"That saddle," Caroline said, meeting his gaze at last. "Where did you get it?"

"Enoch gave it to me," Bridger replied. "Along with the horse." He indicated the bay, standing in a nearby stall, with a gesture of his right hand. Winced at the resulting flash of pain, centered in the wounded shoulder but spreading along his arm and down his side. "Said he wanted rid of the critter, and the saddle, too."

"Oh," Caroline said, and she relaxed slightly. Almost smiled.

"I promised I'd send him money as soon as I could," Bridger told her, wanting to keep the conversation going for a while, so she would stay a little longer. "He said he wouldn't take any payment — that I'd be doing him a favor, since he never wanted to lay eyes on the animal again, or the saddle, either."

She nodded, said that made sense.

Against his better judgment, Bridger took a step toward her. Stopped. "Caroline," he began, frowning now, "that horse might not be anything special, but he's sound. Why is Enoch so eager to see the last of him?"

"If you want to know that," she said reasonably, "you'll have to ask Enoch."

Bridger sighed. "That's all you're going to say?"

"About the horse? Yes."

Strange, Bridger thought, but he knew it would be useless to press the matter. "All right," he said. "We won't discuss the horse."

"No," Caroline agreed. "We won't."

"What, then? Because there's something else, isn't there?" *Easy,* he thought. *Don't push.*

Caroline was reluctant but, thank God, she didn't appear to be scared, the way she had at first. "It wasn't anything important," she told him.

"If you have something to say, I want to hear it," he insisted.

"Unless, of course, you don't agree," Caroline said, with that singular directness he so admired. "Should my opinions happen to differ from yours."

"Whatever it is, I won't argue. You have my word."

She thrust out a breath, and he tried not to notice the rise and fall of her calico-covered breasts.

"Very well, then," she relented, though not sweetly. "Clearly, you intend to leave soon, and I was going to say I don't believe you're well enough to take to the road. Not yet."

He had just given her his word, and already, he was about to break it. So much for Southern honor. Caroline was fetching in any mood, but when she was irritated, he couldn't resist her.

"Such concern," he said, exaggerating his drawl. "A man might almost — *almost* — think you enjoyed his company."

His reward was the instant flare of color in her cheeks, the spark of splendid fury in her eyes. Lord, he could have sparred with this woman for hours, days — the rest of his life.

Caroline glared at him for a long, perfectly delicious moment, then lifted her skirts slightly — far *too* slightly for Bridger's liking — drew back a foot, and kicked the plate she'd just delivered, sending his neatly covered supper sailing. Cold chicken, sliced fruit and two biscuits flew in wildly disparate directions, while the checkered napkin wafted gracefully to the hay-scattered floor.

At that point, Bridger did the worst possible thing. He laughed.

"Go hungry, then!" Caroline said. But seconds later, she went still, raised her hands to her face and gave a strangled sob.

He went to her then, knowing it was a mistake, but unable to stop himself.

Drawing on the last of his restraint, he did not embrace her, but took her gently by the shoulders. Before he could apologize, she dropped her hands and he saw true suffering in her face, and bewilderment.

Bridger despised himself in that moment.

"I'm so sorry!" Caroline wailed. "I don't know why I did that, why I *kicked* your plate and ruined your supper!" A few quavering breaths and some sniffling followed. "It was such a childish thing to do."

Bridger cupped her cheeks in his hands.

"Caroline," he said, using his thumbs to smooth away her tears. "Don't. Please. I was baiting you, and that was wrong. I'm the one who ought to be sorry, and I am. Truly."

"I need to blow my nose," she said.

"Yes," he agreed, taking care not to smile. "Unfortunately, I can't offer you a handkerchief."

She stepped back a little, scrubbed at her face with her apron.

"My behavior tonight . . ." she said earnestly, smiling bravely now. "This is not like me, I assure you."

He raised one eyebrow and moved right back onto the thinnest of ice. "Isn't it?"

Caroline laughed, and the sound was beautiful. But then, in the next moment, she stopped laughing, dropped her forehead to his chest, wrapped both arms around his middle, and moaned.

It was very nearly his undoing, but some shred of control remained to him, and he merely held her, this woman who tried his sanity at every turn. He propped his chin on the crown of her head and ached for what he would never have.

She had just lost her husband.

She was a Yankee, through and through.

The war would go on, with no end in sight.

And the best friend he'd ever had, could ever hope to have, loved her.

"Why," she blurted, in muffled tones, "am I acting like someone else, someone I don't even recognize?"

Bridger knew the question did not require an answer. He went on holding her, rocking her gently, and said, "Shh."

She clung to him for a while, a concession in itself, dampening his shirt with her tears, and Bridger thought he could have stood like that, with Caroline in his arms, until the crack of doom.

Presently, though, she drew back, stepped away. "I would ask one thing of you, Bridger Winslow," she said, "and nothing more."

"I'm listening," he said, his voice hoarse.

"If you must go, say goodbye first. Don't just ride away."

He tried to reply, couldn't. So he simply nodded.

The small distance between them seemed infinite to Bridger, uncrossable terrain, as fraught with peril as any battlefield.

Caroline watched him in miserable silence from the other side of the chasm, then, finally, turned and walked away; Bridger did not follow, although everything in him compelled him to do exactly that, despite the risks. He stood where he was, there in the thickening shadows of the barn, and mourned her as deeply as if she'd died.

The next morning, after a sleepless night, he rose from his bed of straw, stepped outside and began to walk, testing his strength. He went all the way to the gate, stood looking out at the road for a long time, and then went back.

He washed up at the pump outside the kitchen house and walked inside, where he found Enoch at the stove, frying eggs and pork and potatoes, all in the same skillet. There was coffee, and Bridger found a cup, splashed some into it.

He thought, with bitter amusement, that the aftermath of an emotional encounter with Caroline Hammond was not unlike that of a three-day drinking binge. He felt hollow, as though his insides had been scraped out with a surgeon's scalpel and summarily discarded. His head throbbed in time with his heartbeat, and he craved solid food even as he doubted it would stay down.

"You want to tell me about that horse, Enoch?" he asked, after a lengthy interval of silence and strong coffee. "Why you won't take anything for him?"

Enoch studied him for so long that Bridger was beginning to think he wasn't going to reply at all, when he said, "I'm not inclined to say. Not just now, anyway. You need a horse, and I gave you one, such as he is, and that's the sum of it."

Bridger drank more coffee, pondering Enoch's answer. He decided not to pursue the matter for the present; instead, he would wait for a loophole to open.

"Where's Caroline?" he asked, not quite casually.

Enoch turned back to his cooking, jabbed at the potatoes with the end of a battered spatula. "Reckon the Missus might be sleeping late this morning. High time, if you ask me. She hasn't lived an easy day since before that man of hers took a notion to answer the call."

"What was he like? Hammond, I mean?"

"Mr. Jacob was a fine man. He was good to me, and so were his folks. Weren't for his pa, I'd still be picking cotton — or dead."

"Was Jacob good to Caroline?" It was an intrusion, that question, but Bridger needed to know, and he had nothing to lose by asking.

"He loved her," Enoch said. "And his little girl, too, of course. He did the best he knew how."

"But?" Bridger prompted carefully, for he'd noticed a hint of reticence in Enoch's

510

answer, an unspoken qualifier.

The man was under no obligation to elaborate, and for a while, he didn't say anything at all. He pushed the skillet off the heat, took two plates from a shelf, heaped one with steaming food and handed it to Bridger, then proceeded to fill his own.

Finally, Enoch said, "Sit down and eat, Mr. Winslow. You're as pale as if you just woke up in a coffin and climbed out of the hole."

"Thanks," Bridger muttered wryly, taking the plate, helping himself to a knife, fork and spoon from a nearby drawer. "For the breakfast, anyway."

They sat across from each other, eating in silence.

Bridger was half-starved, and after the first few bites, the pounding in his head began to subside.

Enoch chewed thoughtfully, swallowed, jabbed the tines of his fork into a wedge of potato, fried crisp.

Bridger ate, too, between swigs of coffee.

He was going to miss real coffee, once he started south. Because of the blockades, the army cooks had long since resorted to innovative substitutes, only slightly more palatable than birds' nests boiled in yesterday's bathwater.

He'd probably do no better at Fairhaven, where he meant to go first. Now that his father was gone, Amalie was alone, except for Rosebud and a few field hands.

He would ask for leave once he saw how things were, go to General Lee himself with his petition, if that proved necessary. Should he refuse permission — a strong possibility, given the current state of affairs — Bridger knew he would do so regretfully, being a compassionate man, capable of such deep empathy that Bridger had seen him all but broken by the ravages of war. The general seemed remote to those who didn't know him well, but there was real suffering behind that dignity and decorum. He grieved for the fallen, wounded or slain, despaired over hungry men and starving horses, and constantly pleaded with President Davis, mostly in vain, for vital supplies, boots and tents and blankets, quinine and laudanum and morphine, flour and cornmeal and beans.

For all that, Lee was a soldier, first, last and always. To him, duty was paramount; he spared himself no sacrifice, and he expected the same of officers, enlisted men and volunteers, right down to the lowliest private or drummer boy.

His own sons and a favorite nephew addressed him as "General," when they happened to cross paths, and received no special treatment.

No, General Lee, family friend though he was, would not hesitate to turn down Bridger's request for a furlough, brief or otherwise, if circumstances dictated.

Wrapped up in his musings, Bridger was startled when Enoch spoke. "From the looks of you, you're thinking some mighty serious thoughts," he said.

"Are there any other kind?" Bridger countered.

"Not these days," Enoch conceded. He'd finished his meal, and he doubtless had plenty to do, but he lingered. The expression on his broad face was solemn. "What's behind those questions you asked before, about Mr. Jacob and his dealings with his Missus? And don't say you were just curious, because I can tell there's more to it."

Bridger didn't know how to answer without lying through his teeth.

He respected Enoch, and owed him a debt, not only for the use of a horse and saddle, but for his help and company when Bridger was confined to bed, and for all those games of checkers. He'd grasped the fundamentals of chess, even without the proper pieces, poring over the diagrams, asking intelligent questions.

513

Now he rested his forearms on the table-top and leaned forward a little. Everything in his face said, "Well?"

Bridger sighed. He trusted Enoch, and if the favor wasn't returned, that wouldn't be surprising, all things considered, and there was absolutely nothing he could do about it.

"If I'd met Caroline at another time, under better circumstances, I would court her," Bridger said.

Enoch smiled, a bit sadly. "But you didn't," he said.

"No," Bridger confirmed, feeling miserable.

"The Missus will have suitors aplenty when this war ends and folks come to their senses again," Enoch observed. "Her time of mourning will be over, and those left standing will be knocking at her door before the echo of the last bugle fades away."

"If you're trying to make me feel worse," Bridger said, "you're succeeding."

Enoch chuckled. "Reckon that friend of yours, Captain McBride, may try to have a ring on her finger before any of the others get a chance to tip their hats and say howdy."

Bridger groaned. "Is this some kind of revenge? Because if it is, I'm only one

Southerner, not the whole of Dixie."

"Lord, no," said Enoch. "I'm a free man. I've got a woman and a child now, earned wages in my pocket, plenty to eat and a good house with my name on the deed, thanks to Mr. Jacob's pa. That's all the revenge I need."

"You and Jubie?"

"Soon as she's better, we're going to marry, Jubie and me."

Bridger grinned. "That's good," he said. "Does Caroline know yet?"

"Yes. Jubie told her a little while ago," he replied with a nod. "The Missus seems happy about it."

"I'm sure she would be."

Enoch nodded once more. "That baby needs a father, and Jubie needs a home, somebody to protect her. Besides we get along. We care for each other. As for me, well, I've been lonely for a lot of years, so if I can go back to that cabin after a long day and hear a voice that isn't my own, that'll be enough."

"You're a good man, Enoch."

Again, they were quiet, thinking their own thoughts, but it was an easy silence, and a comfortable one.

Bridger stood, after a time, took up his empty plate and Enoch's, carried them over to the work table.

"Right now," he said, with his back to Enoch, "I'm not much use to anybody, but I have property and a few connections. If there's ever anything I can do for you, or for Jubie, write me at Fairhaven, outside Savannah."

Enoch's chair scraped the floor as he stood. "You're not going back to the army?"

"I am," Bridger told him. "But I want to go home first, make sure my sister is well. If you write and I'm not there, Amalie will see that your letter gets to me."

"That's kind of you," Enoch said, but he didn't sound convinced. No doubt he didn't put much stock in the promises of a stranger, especially when that stranger was a Confederate cavalry officer, with a plantation and slaves. In his place, Bridger wouldn't have taken the offer at face value, either.

"I meant what I said, Enoch," Bridger said.

Enoch considered that statement for a moment, and when he spoke again, Bridger knew he'd gained the man's trust, at least in part.

"There's a woman who owned Jubie. She put a price on the girl's head after Jubie ran away. Sent some slave catchers after her, and one of them caught up to her, right here on this farm. I dealt with him, had to, and that's how I came by the horse, and the saddle, too. That's all I mean to say about it, but I don't reckon you'll have much trouble putting the pieces together."

"My God, Enoch," Bridger broke out, stunned. "You *do* need help, whether you know it or not."

"Oh, I know it. Jubie's scared, and not without reason. The Missus, too. They both figure this isn't over, and I have a real bad feeling they're right."

"I'll stay," Bridger said.

But Enoch shook his head. "No. The Union men, they'll be back for their dead any day now. They find you here and there'll be no end to your troubles — or Captain McBride's, either."

Or Caroline's.

"This woman," Bridger said. "The one Jubie ran away from. What's her name? Where does she live?"

Enoch slumped a little. "I asked Jubie, but she wouldn't say. She's half again too scared, and she doesn't want me or the Missus tangled up in it."

"There might be something I can do," Bridger reiterated. "But *I need a name,* and whatever other information you can get out of her. If she won't tell you, ask Caroline to try."

"Ask Caroline to try what?" Caroline was standing in the doorway, wearing her customary calico dress and a starched apron with ruffles, presumably not to be employed as a handkerchief. Her thick hair, gleaming from a recent brushing, billowed around her face. It was already threatening to break loose from its pins and combs and spill to her waist in glorious disarray.

Bridger was too besotted to formulate a response, so Enoch explained.

When he'd finished, Caroline turned slightly puffy eyes to Bridger, full of questions, none of which found their way to her tongue.

She did step out of the doorway, though.

Reaching back to tighten her apron strings, she approached the stove, moved the skillet Enoch had used, then selected a pot, poured water into it and added salt.

"How are Jubie and Gideon this morning, Enoch?" she asked, opening the stove and prodding it with a poker before tossing in another chunk of wood.

Bridger and Enoch exchanged puzzled glances.

"They're fine, Missus," Enoch said, after a brief delay. "They were still sleeping when

I left the cabin, but Jubie's bound to wake up soon. I was about to head back and fry her some eggs."

"That's a good idea," Caroline said. Then, pointing at a crockery bowl filled with eggs, she added, "Help yourself."

Enoch took several and hesitated. "I guess I thought you'd offer an opinion, Missus. About getting Jubie to tell us about her . . . owner and all."

Caroline's spine stiffened visibly. "I am through with sharing my opinions," she said coolly. "They invariably get me into trouble."

Bridger suppressed a sigh.

"You'll talk to Jubie?" Enoch asked. "If she won't tell me what we need to know?"

Caroline reached for a canister, set it close at hand. "Yes," she said with a sigh. "In fact, I think you should leave the entire conversation to me. I will pay another call on Jubie after breakfast."

Enoch nodded and rushed out, eggs cradled in one large hand.

Caroline continued to bang things around — stove lids, the canister, a tin of cinnamon.

"What have I done now, Caroline?" Bridger asked. They were alone, but not for long; Rachel and the dog could be heard playing in the yard, drawing nearer.

519

He saw her shoulders droop beneath the weight of her thoughts, prayed she'd turn around and allow him to catch — and hold — her gaze.

She did.

"It isn't what you've done," Caroline said sadly. "Well, *mostly* not, anyway. It's what you are, Bridger. It's *who* you are."

"A Rebel?" he prodded. "A slave holder? An avowed rake?"

She was taken aback, if only for a moment. "You own slaves," she said. She might have meant the phrase as a question, but it was probably meant more as a reminder to herself.

"My father did. I've inherited them, apparently, along with the land." If the old man hadn't already been dead, it likely would have killed him to see the least-loved of his sons take over Fairhaven.

"Will you set them free?"

"I will," Bridger said. "But I can't guarantee they'll actually leave the plantation."

"You honestly believe they would *choose* to stay — and remain in bondage?" The idea clearly affronted her. Caroline was intelligent, but naive in so many ways. Raised in the North, hardworking but relatively sheltered all the same, steeped in the lofty philosophies of Quakers and Presbyterians and Transcendentalists, thoroughly familiar with Mrs. Stowe's novel and others like it, she couldn't be expected to grasp certain realities.

"Some of the slaves will undoubtedly choose to remain at Fairhaven, yes," Bridger said carefully.

"Why would *slaves* refuse freedom?"

"They *won't be* refusing their freedom, Caroline. I assure you, they will have their liberty, whether they go or stay. And some of them *will* stay, because Fairhaven is their home — for many of them, the only one they've ever known. They've borne and reared their children there. Their dead are buried on the plantation."

"Oh," said Caroline, reflecting now.

"Yes," he said. "Oh."

Caroline left the kettle of water to come to a boil on the stove top, took a few steps toward Bridger, stopped. Her throat worked as she struggled with what she wanted to say — or *not* say — next.

"*Are* you —" here, her voice dropped to a near whisper "— as you said before, 'an avowed rake' "?

"I have been," Bridger said, with neither shame nor pride. "Oh, I've been that and more — a lover of drunken brawls, illicit games of chance and low women."

"Why?" Caroline asked, as if baffled. Her tone was almost plaintive.

"I guess I didn't see any reason to be otherwise. Not until I became a soldier, in any case." *And until I met you.* "If there is anything redemptive about war, it may be that seeing so much pain and death, a man begins to take a tally of things he's done or not done. He looks at his past, the present being largely intolerable, and the future — well — the future may not exist at all. Around the next bend in the road, beyond the next blast of cannon fire, the next bullet or bayonet, there might be nothing. With luck, all this reflection yields a few sobering insights."

"What insights?" Caroline wanted to know. She spoke softly, and without sarcasm.

Bridger gave a great sigh. "Nothing profound or elevating," he warned as a preamble. "I simply took note of certain of my personal failings, which, of course, were obvious to everyone else. There was a kind of anger, for one thing. I always felt an inner outrage — my mother died when I still needed her more than I would have admitted, my father was . . . my father. He always favored my older half brother, Tristan. I was a younger son, and therefore doomed to eternal boyhood, dependent on the old man and, after him, my half brother. That made me a kind of financial eunuch, I thought. Poor, unfortunate me."

Rachel peered through the doorway, her small body framed by morning light. "Are we still having mush for breakfast, Mama? I hope not, because I do not favor mush, and Sweet Girl doesn't, either."

With a little smile, Caroline turned her head to address her daughter's concerns. "That is indeed a pity, Rachel," she said. "Because you are having mush, and so am I."

"I want what the men had," Rachel wheedled sweetly. "What did they have?"

"Mush," Bridger lied.

Rachel frowned, kicked at the raised threshold with one miniscule foot, then turned back to the fresh delights of tall grass, blue skies and a faithful dog.

Bridger laughed. "That child is resilient," he said. "A fairly good checkers player, too."

Caroline stood within reach, and it would have been so easy to kiss her.

There was a wagon out on the road; they both tensed at the sound of it.

"Stay out of sight," Caroline said quickly.

Bridger saluted, started for the nearest window.

Caroline grabbed him by the arm. "Wait," she said. "Let *me* see who it is."

A brief deadlock ensued. Bridger had a bad arm, but he was still a man, and not one who hid behind a woman's skirts.

"There's a shotgun in the cellar," Caroline said. "Behind the flour barrel."

With that, she was hurrying to the door and into the yard.

Bridger started after her, came to a halt when he heard the cordial rise and fall of Caroline's voice as she greeted someone — a man, from the timbre of the answering voice. A neighbor? Someone from town?

He went to the window, keeping to one side, deliberating. When he finally risked taking a quick look outside, he saw the road, the gate, part of the yard, then a soldier in a blue uniform.

He quickly went down the cellar stairs, and shut the door behind him.

Bridger found the shotgun where Caroline said it would be, but he took little comfort in its discovery. The barrels were dull with accumulated dust, and cobwebs coated the stock, dangled from the trigger guard.

Bridger softened the tension in his arms and shoulders, laid the shotgun across the lidded barrel. It was probably useless, anyway; if Caroline called for help, he'd use the thing as a club.

He wanted to go outside, make sure she was all right.

But he heard the horse and buggy making a slow retreat to the road, and a moment later, heavy footsteps sounded overhead.

The cellar door creaked open. "That army fellow is gone," Enoch called from the top of the cellar steps.

Bridger reached for the shotgun, thinking it might be salvaged if the firing mechanism hadn't rusted over, and went up.

Caroline was back inside, muttering as she poured cornmeal into the kettle on the stove. "That man went on so long," she complained, "I thought sure this pot would boil dry."

"Is anybody going to tell me what he wanted?" Bridger said.

Enoch took the shotgun from Bridger's hand and examined it, frowning. "He wanted to let Missus know there'll be some men along, in the next day, to gather up those poor dead boys and see about getting them back to the home folks."

"And he took his time doing it," Caroline fussed. She sliced some bread, buttered the pieces and handed two of them to Rachel, who had just come in with her dog. "Here, sweetheart. I bet you're hungry."

"I am," Rachel said. "And Sweet Girl is, too. Can I share my food with her?"

"May I," Caroline corrected fondly. "And yes, you may." A slight frown creased her brow. "Where is your sun bonnet, Rachel Hammond?"

A cloud overtook Rachel's entire countenance. Then she made her confession. "It's under your bed, Mama. Sweet Girl chewed it up, and I thought you'd be mad, so I hid it."

"You have others," Caroline pointed out. "Eat your bread, and then go and get one."

"Shall I get one for you, too, Mama?" she asked.

Bridger bit the inside of his lip to keep from laughing.

Enoch smiled. "I reckon she has you there, Missus," he said.

Pretending she hadn't heard, Caroline shook her head. "Yes," she said, cheeks pink. "Please fetch a bonnet for me as well."

Rachel started for the door.

"Stay in the shade while you're eating," Caroline called after her. "That sun will turn your skin to leather if you don't."

When the child and the dog had gone, she turned, and the pink had faded from her cheeks. She looked directly at Bridger and said, "I guess you wouldn't agree to hide in the cellar again, or under the — inside the house."

"No, Caroline," Bridger answered, sorry he couldn't stay. Sorry for so many things he was unable to put into words. "I'll leave tomorrow, before dawn."

She nodded and looked away.

"This shotgun," Enoch interjected, a little too loudly, "might do more damage to the one who fires it than it will to the target."

With that, he sat down at the far end of the table and began taking the gun apart, piece by piece. He muttered as he worked, got up to fetch oil and soft cloth and a length of heavy wire for a ramrod.

Bridger left the kitchen house, feeling unaccountably low in spirits. Ensuring he wouldn't be seen from the road, he made for the creek, thought he'd follow it a ways, see where it led. He tired sooner than he would have liked, considering the long ride ahead of him. Eventually he found a boulder partially shaded by a copse of trees, and sat down, tossing pebbles into the water and brooding.

He had to let Rogan know where he stood somehow, tell his friend he had strong feelings for Caroline. He didn't know what Rogan's intent was with regard to her but he needed to make his clear. They were used to competing, and that went back to their days at school and summers at Fairhaven. But this was different. The stakes were too high.

He'd always wondered whether Rogan and Amalie had feelings for each other — feelings beyond the playful affection they'd shared in earlier times, when Rogan used to regularly visit Fairhaven. Bridger knew the two of them still occasionally exchanged letters. Did that mean anything, other than the continuation of a friendship? Back in their youthful days, Amalie's company certainly hadn't interfered with the competition between him and Rogan.

Bridger gave a rueful snort at the memories, tossed another stone, watched it splash and sink. Before every contest, every dance — where there'd be pretty girls aplenty — they'd shaken hands and agreed to a sporting challenge, always with the tacit understanding that there were no holds barred.

And now there was Caroline.

He shouldn't have been surprised, really. But everything would have been a hell of a lot easier if he'd never set eyes on this particular woman.

The odds now, of course, were in Rogan's favor. He was a Northerner and, when the time was right, he could court Caroline freely, without the risk of capture. He would write long letters, each one a little more personal than the last, send her gifts, like that songbook she liked so much. Furthermore, Rogan would probably be a better husband, a better provider, too, with his law degree and his fine military record.

Still, Bridger had stirred Caroline to passion; he knew that one kiss had shaken her, just as it had him.

He'd been tempted to use every trick he knew, no denying that, but he hadn't, for exactly the same reasons that might have compelled her to give in — her loneliness, her sorrow, her vulnerability.

He wouldn't have been able to live with himself afterward if he'd taken advantage of Caroline. She was the kind of woman a man married, loved into frenzies on clean sheets, fathered children with — and cherished forever.

He ought to bow out, wish his friend well and move on. Finish this stupid war, and go home to stay, do his utmost to resurrect Fairhaven. Find himself a pretty Southern wife who'd be proud that he'd fought for the Confederacy, win or lose.

If he had any sense at all, he'd do those things.

The problem was, when it came to Caroline, he didn't have a *lick* of sense.

His love for her was a reckless thing, dangerous and unwieldy, but he could not turn away from it.

No, he'd find a way to square things with Rogan, if they *could* be squared. Make his intentions clear. Anything less would be dishonorable.

It was decided, then. He, Bridger Winslow, the most unsuitable of second husbands for a staunch Yankee widow, was willing to make a fool of himself, and chance losing his finest friend in the process, to have Caroline by his side and in his bed. For now and for always.

26

CAROLINE

They met in the side yard at dawn the next morning, where the tents had been, and stood in the dew-dampened grass, beside the dead slave catcher's horse, Bridger handsome and bearded in the crisp blue uniform of his enemies, Caroline in an ordinary dress, a shawl pulled tight around her shoulders against the chill of the last hour before dawn.

Bridger's rucksack contained his few personal possessions, as well as a few civilian clothes, once Jacob's, that Caroline had given him. When he reached the South, he'd change into them; it would hardly do to be seen in Union blue.

Instead of the relief she'd anticipated at his leave taking, Caroline ached with a sorrow so profound she thought the very structure of her heart might collapse, every pillar and beam, like an old house. She had so much to say, and for that reason, she dared not speak.

Bridger's eyes seemed luminous as he looked at her, and it seemed to Caroline that, in those moments, no words would serve.

She would not weep. Her tears were like the mouth of a powerful river, barely contained, ever surging forth, seeking to break free; she might well be swept away on its treacherous current, spun round and round — to drown or wash up on some dreaded shore, her own ghost, useless to everyone who needed her.

Bridger was the first to move, first to speak; he raised one gloved hand, the gelding's reins resting in the other, and laid his palm gently to her cheek. "Caroline," he said, in a tone of bleak wonder. "I think I would rather die than leave you."

"But you must go," Caroline managed, although the words came out sounding tremulous. "You *must* go."

He touched his lips to her forehead, very lightly and very briefly.

"I know," he murmured, his face so close to hers that she felt his breath on her skin, the tickle of his red-gold whiskers against her eyelids.

Caroline drew back, though only a little way, for she could bear to go no farther. No, she wanted the small grace of standing within the warmth of his body, the scent of his skin and his hair. Surely, it wasn't too much to ask.

"Jubie's owner," Caroline whispered, for something good *had* to come of this parting. "Her name is Mrs. T. A. Templeton."

"Ah, yes," Bridger said, his mouth a fraction of an inch from Caroline's face. "Delia Templeton. We're acquainted."

Caroline drew back again, suddenly, jolted by an unbecoming flash of jealousy, a thing she had no earthly right to feel. She had no claim on this man, and it frightened her how much she wished she did.

"Oh," she said.

He made a chortling sound. "Caroline," he said again, and it struck her as a wonder how much he could communicate simply by saying her name — assurance, humor, tenderness, anger, sorrow. A world of feelings.

"Go," Caroline pleaded, because she wanted to clutch and cling, to stand on the toes of his boots, wrap her arms around him and hold on tight. "They'll be here soon.

533

The soldiers."

"Yes," Bridger replied, but he didn't move to turn from her, mount his horse, ride away into the glimmering shadows of night becoming day. "Caroline —"

She lifted her hand, pressed the tips of two fingers to his mouth. "No, Bridger. Please." *Oh, please.*

Go now.

Stay, for always.

Very slowly, he stepped back. Nodding once, turning to swing deftly into the saddle. She saw his throat work, but he did not say the word she had heard too many times.

Goodbye.

He lifted his cap, gazed at her for a long moment, and then he reined the horse toward whatever fate awaited him.

Caroline stood still in the gathering light and watched as Bridger rode to the open gate, then onto the winding dirt road. She watched as the growing distance melded horse and man into a single form.

Watched until there was nothing more to see.

27

Hammond Farm
August 19, 1863

ENOCH

How the Missus had pined, that second week in August, after Captain Winslow started south.

She tried her considerable best, being who she was, to tuck her grief away, out of sight, but Enoch knew her too well to be fooled; young Mr. Jacob had courted her for a long while before he'd finally brought her to the Hammond farm as his bride, and she'd often been there before that. Used to go along with her grandfather, old Doc Prescott, when he made his rounds in that ancient buggy of his, even as a little bit of a girl, and they'd stop in sometimes, the two of them, so the Doc could water his mule and bide a while with the last Missus to make sure her rheumatism wasn't plaguing her too much.

Seemed like Jacob, just a lad himself, took to her right off. He'd follow her about, tug at her pigtails, show her a newborn calf or a litter of kittens out at the barn, pretend he meant to toss her into the creek, ruffled dress, patent leather shoes and all. She'd get indignant and call him ten kinds of rascal, say she wasn't coming back, ever.

The next time Doc rolled in, though, there she'd be, right beside him on the buggy seat.

Enoch tried to stay clear of the house when there was company, but often little Miss Caroline Prescott would find him anyhow. She'd ask if he wanted to borrow the book she'd just finished reading, chatter on about the last one they'd shared. She always had plenty of questions, that one, about the crops and the farm animals and the weather, and she'd confide in him, too. She'd say she couldn't for the life of her reason out what made Jacob Hammond act like such a fool.

"Reckon he's one of those, all right," Enoch recalled telling her once, when she was thirteen or fourteen. He'd been digging potatoes on a muggy Saturday in late September, and she'd stood at the edge of the garden patch, watching him work, having somehow evaded Jacob for half a minute.

"You just wait, though, Miss Prescott. That boy will get more sense as he grows up."

Enoch smiled at the memory, standing at the cabin stove that hot morning, waiting for the coffee grounds to settle in the pot.

Jubie, who was up and around by then, though a week or two short of being ready to marry, took notice and said, "What you smiling about, Mister-man, looking sad and happy both at once?"

He liked her calling him "Mister-man," though he'd never told her so. "I was recalling the Missus when she was a girl, coming to the farm with her grandfather."

"Is that the happy part, or the sad?" Jubie wanted to know. She'd fashioned a kind of sling for the baby so she could carry him around with her as she went about her day. She had an instinct for mothering, knew when to keep the boy close and when to let him lie in the wooden crate that served as his bed. Enoch was building little Gideon a proper cradle, fine as any to be had, but that was a secret, for now; he wanted the gift ready to sleep in before he showed it to her.

"It was the happy part," he replied, reaching for a mug.

"What's the sad one?" Jubie persisted, handing him a potholder when he burned his hand on the handle of the coffee pot and drew back with a hiss, shaking it.

"I oughtn't to say," Enoch said, using the potholder now and pouring brew into his cup. He didn't have much in the way of household goods, not yet anyway. Just one of everything needful, and few enough of such things as that potholder, since he'd always taken his meals down at the kitchen house.

Jubie gave him a hard poke in the ribs, nearly causing him to spill the coffee halfway to his mouth. "If we're going to throw in together," she informed him, "you can't have secrets from me."

Enoch looked at her over the rim of his mug, saw her through a wisp of fragrant steam. "Is that so? Then I guess you know you've got some talking to do yourself." He shook his head. "There's a little too much I don't know about you."

"Didn't I tell Miss Caroline all about Missus Templeton and how she treated me?" Jubie challenged. "Didn't I give out that awful woman's name and everything, knowing it could get me killed?"

Enoch sighed. "I'm not going to let this go, and don't you think I am." He paused, reluctantly set his coffee aside. "You understand me, Jubie-gal?"

She gave a short, grudging nod. Smoothed the baby's tiny head, resting against her bosom as it was. The baby made sweet murmuring sounds as he slept, content in the soft sturdiness of his sling.

"I believe Captain Winslow took a piece of the Missus right along with him when he left from here," Enoch allowed, trying to convey by his lowered brows that he was keeping track of confidences exchanged. "*That's* the sad part."

"That man's a Rebel," Jubie pointed out, though not as saucily as she might have. "When Miss Caroline's ready to marry up again, and that won't be for a long while yet, she'd be better off taking up with Captain McBride. He's a Northerner, and a good-looker, too."

"Why is that better?" Enoch asked, honestly curious. "Captain Winslow isn't ugly, and when this war's over, there won't be Yankees and Confederates anymore. We'll all be Americans, same as before."

The baby stirred, whimpered.

Jubie went to the table, sat down and opened her dress, put the child to her breast.

Enoch looked away, felt his face burning.

For a few moments, there was no sound but the baby's suckling.

"I don't guess one is any better than the

other," Jubie admitted with a sigh. "Truth is, with all those men out there shooting at each other, Miss Caroline isn't likely to lay eyes on *either* of them again, not in this life. She'll marry some other man, but when she does, I bet she's gonna take up with somebody from around here."

"I hate to think that," Enoch grumbled. "Anybody like that will be looking to get himself a good farm, and if he gets a pretty wife into the bargain, all the better. But the other two, Bridger and Captain McBride, they *love* her."

Jubie rocked in her seat, holding the nursing baby so tenderly that the sight made Enoch feel bruised inside. "Sometimes," she said quietly, musing aloud, "I still think *you* love Miss Caroline, too, Mister-man."

"I guess I do," Enoch said at some length, "but not in the marrying way. More like I cared for Jacob and his folks. I told you that before."

Jubie's dark eyes searched his face. "You might care a whole different way, though, if her skin was the same color as yours."

"It isn't," Enoch said, aggrieved at having to state the obvious. Then, sterner still, he added, "There's no point in thinking such thoughts, no point at all. And I tell you now, Jubie, that although I'm not a man for lording it over my woman, I *am* a man. And I will *not* be nagged and pestered over things that *might* have happened, but never did."

Jubie was not cowed, that much was obvious, and Enoch wouldn't have wanted her to be, but he was quite confounded by the glow that came to her eyes, and the soft set of her mouth. "When do you figure I'll be able to lie down with you proper, Misterman?" she asked. "It don't seem right to me, you sleepin' on the floor of a night, and me all alone in that nice bed."

Enoch went rock hard, and he turned away from Jubie, so she wouldn't see. "I don't know," he said, and was out the door in a few strides. "When you're ready. When . . . when you've recovered from having the baby, I guess."

Once he'd cleared the cabin, he walked even faster, considered changing course, heading for the stream to give himself a dunking in that cold, cold water.

He decided against the idea right away, since it would only cause him more vexation, having to go back to the cabin, fetch himself dry clothes, and then go outside again to put them on, so Jubie wouldn't see.

Instead, he prowled the orchard, waiting for his desire to relent.

Such was his wanting, so intense was his

desire, that he might never have had relief if he hadn't heard the sounds, just then, of at least a dozen wagons coming from way down on the road beyond the main house. Horses, too.

That was all it took to turn Enoch's mind, and thus his body, in a whole new direction.

He made for the edge of the orchard, stood behind the broad, gnarled trunk of one of the oldest apple trees in Adams County, squinting into the distance.

Sure enough, the Yankees had come back for their dead. Three riders were at the head of the procession, all wearing blue, and sitting up soldier-straight in their saddles.

One of them dismounted to open the gate, led his horse through and got back on, adjusting his kepi as he settled in again. The other two riders followed, and the wagons streamed in behind them.

Enoch, already running toward the house, counted ten buckboards, each drawn by a team of four gleaming, muscular horses, none of them matched. Most of the wagon beds were empty, though two were loaded with rolls of what looked like tent canvas.

Seeing the Missus come out of the kitchen house, drying her hands on her apron, Enoch wanted to run even faster, but prudence ruled, and he slowed his pace.

The sight of a man charging toward them like a bull might just inspire one or more of those Union soldiers to draw their pistols or reach for their rifles.

They were bound to be skittish, since they were here to dig up the moldering bodies of fallen comrades, wrap them in canvas and haul them for miles, over rutted roads, bedeviled by flies every inch of the way, and gagging on the stench of decomposition.

By the time Enoch reached Caroline's side, all the wagons were in.

"You go inside, Missus," Enoch said, breathing hard. "Look after Miss Rachel."

She looked up at him, blinked, as though startled to see him there. "I was kneading bread dough," she explained.

Enoch studied her, a little shaken. "Yes, ma'am," he said. "You finish now. Is Miss Rachel in there, too? In the kitchen house?"

Just like that, the Missus came back to herself. "Yes, of course," she said. She cast an anxious glance toward the wagons, which had stopped, as the drivers awaited instructions. Some were glum of countenance, others chewed and spat tobacco, while still others leered at her. "Of course."

With that, she hurried back inside the kitchen house and shut the door.

Enoch hoped she'd latched it, too, but he knew it would be unwise to hurry over there to grasp the handle and make sure. These were Union men, yes, but that didn't mean the women and children were safe around them, didn't mean they were all honorable — and such a move would surely draw their attention.

He wanted them to forget about the Missus.

Forget everything about this farm, in fact, except for the corpses buried in the fallow field soon after the battle in early July.

Let them tend to the task they'd come here for and then go.

One of the riders approached, removing his hat as he came nearer. He looked down from his tall horse, a thin, solemn man, probably in his forties, his skin cratered along one cheek, evidence of a childhood case of smallpox or a youth of cystic pustules. His eyes were gray, hard and sharp, like the blade of a hunting knife.

"I assume," he said, "that the lady is not your wife."

Enoch kept his face impassive, not because he was frightened, but because this kind of impertinence and cold contempt, which, luckily, he'd rarely encountered since he'd come to Pennsylvania with the elder Mr.

Hammond years before, made his hackles rise.

He wanted to grip the soldier by his fine coat, drag him down off that tall horse of his and fling him to the ground. Put one foot on his throat and press just hard enough to make his eyes bulge.

He could not afford to do any such thing, of course, but he wasn't going to grovel, either. He was incapable of obsequiousness, even when it might have been smarter than a steady, level gaze and an implacable tone.

"The lady is not my wife," he confirmed, his voice even. "My name is Enoch Flynn, and I am the hired man."

"Flynn?" the soldier repeated. A mocking smile lit his flat eyes. "You're Irish?"

"I'm an American," Enoch replied. "Like you. And," he added, "I'm a Union supporter, too."

The soldier reddened slightly, and set his back teeth. "We have business here," he said briskly. "According to our records, there are Union remains interred on this property."

"Yes, indeed," Enoch said.

He was thinking of Jubie and the baby and the Missus, but the man he'd killed and reburied in the same field as the dead soldiers hovered at the edge of his mind. Once again, he was relieved that he hadn't moved the body a second time; after much deliberation, he'd decided to leave it where it was rather than call attention to newly broken ground.

Whatever happened would happen.

For now, all he could do was take the next step that seemed right to him, and those after it, one by one.

A second rider came up alongside the first, a young soldier with the cream-and-coffee skin of a mulatto. He kept his expressionless dark eyes on Enoch as he took a small packet from the inside pocket of his coat and handed it to the other man.

A map, Enoch figured. Hand drawn, rather than printed, sketched in haste by one of the soldiers who had done the burying. He wondered if they'd taken an accurate count, those reluctant grave diggers, and hoped they'd been in too much of a hurry to bother.

Wondered, too, about the young soldier gazing at him now. He might be a friend, but he might also be a foe. It would have been a consolation to know which.

The steely-eyed rider, having studied the paper thoroughly, refolded it and gave it back to his companion, who put it back inside his coat. All this time, the young soldier never looked away from Enoch's face, never spoke or gave any indication of what he made of all this.

Nothing, maybe. Just another day in the hard, sorry life of a soldier.

Enoch stared back, just to show he wasn't going to flinch.

"Let's get this over with," the first rider said. He raised one hand, the leather of his glove rein worn and stained with old sweat.

When he nudged his horse into motion, the third rider and then the wagons followed, moving slowly. The second soldier remained, controlling his paint pony without perceptible use of his knees or hands.

For several minutes, he and Enoch looked at each other in silence.

Enoch was the first to concede. He could hold out as long as anybody when it came to a stare down, but he needed to keep an eye on the shovel men, see if they'd find the slave hunter's carcass, and what they'd think about it if they did.

"I suppose we ought to lend a hand," Enoch said, with a gesture toward the departing wagons. Soon, they'd be crossing the creek at the shallow place, following the well-worn trail that wound past behind the cabin.

The young soldier finally opened his mouth. "Go and tell the Missus to hide herself till we're gone," he said. Nothing changed in his face, although he gave a slight nod in the direction of the riders and wagons. "Sergeant Baylor up there, who was just talking to you, he's a bitter man. Figures he ought to be a lieutenant, and he's mad as hell that he isn't and that instead he's been given the detail of digging up the dead. If he gets the chance, he's likely to take his anger out on the lady, tell himself he's owed something for his sacrifice. I've seen him do it before."

Enoch nodded, solemn faced.

The young soldier introduced himself as Corporal Morris, then rode on, willing his deft little pony into a trot.

Enoch waited, right where he was, until the last of the wagons rolled out of sight. Then he sprinted to the kitchen house.

Caroline had latched the door, and he had to pound on it, call out to her.

She opened it, her eyes wide, Rachel clinging to her skirts with both hands, while the dog whimpered just behind them.

"You've got to get yourself to that hiding place inside the main house," Enoch said. "You and the child. I want you to stay there, no matter what you hear outside, until I come for you. I'll take the dog, tie her up in the barn."

Caroline was prone to argument, especially when anybody told her what to do and how and when to do it, but this time, she merely nodded.

Enoch quickly led the way across the yard, ever watchful.

Once they were inside the main house, he could breathe better, not so fast and deep as to make his head spin.

Reaching the parlor, he went straight to the harpsichord, pulled the little rug aside and raised the trap door.

Caroline lowered herself into it, and Enoch handed Rachel down after her.

Only then did Caroline, standing down in that hole, her upturned face a white oval in the darkness, ask, "Enoch, what's wrong?"

"No time to explain," Enoch replied. In his mind, he was already on his way to warn Jubie to stay inside the cabin and keep herself and the baby quiet. "I'll be back for you, soon as I can."

"All right, then," she answered.

Enoch lowered the trap door and moved the rug into place.

He left the main house and hurried to the barn, using a rope to secure Sweet Girl to a stall. Then he ran to the cabin at a speed he wouldn't have dreamed he could reach or maintain.

He found Jubie at the stove, stirring something in a kettle.

He told her there were men in the field just yonder, Yankees come to fetch the bodies waiting to be claimed. He said he had reason to believe there were no-accounts among the soldiers just come, and she was to stay put and keep herself and the child quiet. Lower the latch as soon as he went out, too.

"But if they're Union men — ?"

"Just do as I say, Jubie," Enoch broke in. "And if somebody knocks at that door, don't you open it. If you even think soldiers are prowling around in the yard, you get under the bed, you and the baby, and if he fusses, let him suckle."

Enoch strode back to the door, shut it behind him.

Waited until he heard the heavy bar brought down inside.

By the time he got to the field, Baylor's men were digging while he sat his horse in the deep shade of an oak that had probably been as old as the seven deadly sins long before George Washington took command of the Continental Army and commenced to lead the Revolution.

Morris, the soldier he'd spoken with earlier, was off his pony and right there in the midst of the digging.

Some of the bodies had already been unearthed, and they made for a gruesome sight, those dirt-caked cadavers, still in the process of decomposing. The crew worked fast, rolling them up in lengths of filthy canvas, stacking them in the wagons.

The smell was thick and cloying, amplified by the heavy heat, and most of the soldiers had tied their bandanas over their noses and mouths. One of the youngest was bent double, spewing up his rations, while a few of the others taunted him, calling him "Nellie" and urging him to get back to work.

Enoch stayed clear of Morris, lest Baylor see them together and decide they were in cahoots, both of them being "colored" and thus suspect in the mind of a man like that.

"Say," one of the other soldiers said. "This one over here, he ain't wearin' the uniform."

Enoch broke out in a sweat, wiped his brow with his handkerchief, but did it slowly, so he wouldn't look nervous. He watched as the soldier laid aside his shovel and went over to stand at the edge of the hole and examine its contents.

Enoch knew he ought to be doing something instead of standing there like one of the pillars in Samson's temple, but he couldn't move. Couldn't even draw breath.

Morris glanced his way, but only briefly, then turned back to the hole and the boy-soldier who'd dug it.

"Roll him up and put him with the others," he said. "Must've been a roustabout or a scout."

The younger soldier didn't ask any questions, didn't hesitate. "Yes, sir," he said, then called out for a canvas. When it was brought, the two soldiers lifted the corpse out of its resting place and laid it down, wrapped it in its rough shroud, and went on to another grave.

Enoch felt a rush of sweet relief so intense that it nearly buckled his knees. When he figured he could walk properly instead of stumbling, he helped load the wagons.

The work went on for the better part of an hour; it was hot, ugly labor, and the stench was terrible. There were maggots, and foul fluids seeped through the bundles of canvas, dripped to the ground through the cracks between the slats of the wagon beds.

Enoch thought of sowing corn or grain or hay on this ground, and almost did some heaving of his own. If the Missus agreed, he'd leave the field untilled for a year or two, give the weather time to cleanse it of all that death.

When those poor dead soldiers had been rolled up in cloth and stowed, Baylor rode idly out of his shady haven and told Morris, "There should be twenty-seven bodies, according to orders."

The count was twenty-eight, and Enoch held his breath, waited for some earnest soul to call out that they had one too many bodies, but no one did.

These men were tired, sweating in the heat, their palms and the skin on their fingers raw from gripping the handles of shovels. Several looked sick enough to collapse in their boot prints, might have done just that, if it wouldn't have meant riding back to camp on a pile of dead bodies.

"We've got them all, then," Morris told Baylor.

"You took a count?"

"I did." He paused. "And I believe you're right, sir. The unnamed one is probably a scout or such."

"Good enough." Baylor stood in his stirrups, stretching his legs, turning his gaze toward the farmhouse, although it couldn't be seen from that field.

I wouldn't like to kill you, Enoch told him silently, *much as you probably need killing. But I will do it if I must.*

Strangely, Baylor swung his head around,

as if Enoch's unspoken warning had somehow reached him.

He stared.

Enoch stared back.

"We've got a long way to go," Morris said in a level voice that carried nonetheless. "And there's rain coming on."

Everyone looked at the sky then, including Enoch. Sure enough, there were dark clouds hovering over the horizon, at the edge of all that glaring blue, churning like the stomachs of monsters, digesting things consumed.

It was almost as if the young corporal had conjured up those clouds . . .

Baylor gave the order to move out, and men scrambled into the wagon boxes, released brake levers, took the reins in their hands. The soldiers all mounted their horses, and the slow, rattling exodus began.

Enoch looked around him, studying all those oblong ruptures in the earth, thinking they made for a grim parody of the Judgment.

He turned his face upward, closed his eyes and heaved a sigh that seemed to rise from the soles of his feet. When the last day came, when every clock in the world just quit ticking, all at once, forever stilled, when the sky fractured like thin glass and legions of avenging angels busted through and commenced to sorting the wheat from the chaff, he, who'd taken a man's life, would surely be among those cast into the fiery pit.

It was only right, he decided, to look straight into the face of heaven, invisible though it was, and voice his prayer out loud. Any other way might seem disrespectful.

"I did what I had to do, Lord," he said, as the first warm drops of rain splashed his forehead and his cheeks and the hollow of his throat. "And I can't say I repent of it now, so I reckon there's no sense asking Your forgiveness yet." He passed a few minutes in sorrowful regret, but not because he'd done that slave catcher in like he had. No, sir. He'd never be sorry for that.

He'd be plenty sorry, though, not to go to Glory when his earthly life was over. Never to look upon his mama's glowing face, nor those of young Jacob and his good father and mother and Tillie Mae and all the other folks, dark and light, who'd treated him with decency and varying degrees of kindness. He would miss out on the gathering of the saints, all that singing and blowing of horns and shouting of hallelujahs, never lay eyes on the Lamb of God nor drink of the living waters.

It was a high price to pay, that was for

sure, but Jubie was alive and she was as free as she could be, the way things stood. As for the baby boy, well, he might not be the fruit of Enoch's own loins, but the little mite had taken root in his heart.

Gideon would have a place to set down his feet and grow.

For Enoch Flynn, that was enough.

28

Hammond Farm
October 29, 1863

CAROLINE

As promised, Caroline wrote Rogan at the address he'd given her, a law office in the city of New York. She told him Bridger had gone on his way, although it was more than a week before she was able to collect herself enough to put pen to paper. She mentioned Rachel, said the child was well and very fond of Sweet Girl, who was also well, and she related the birth of Jubie's baby, concluding her letter with a brief account of the day the soldiers came to fetch their dead, leaving out the ordeal it cost her.

She signed the missive "Yours very truly, Caroline Hammond," a sort of compromise between the stiff formality of "Regards, Mrs. Jacob Hammond" and the too-familiar, "Warmly, Caroline."

Enoch had taken the slim envelope to town and posted it, and Caroline put Rogan and Bridger out of her mind, although one or the other of them, and sometimes both, crept in now and then, especially on nights she was too tired to sleep, after a day of harvesting and preserving vegetables from her garden and fruit from the orchard. With baby Gideon content in his sling against his mother's bosom, Jubie worked alongside Caroline, while Enoch labored to bring in the crops, with the help of George McPhee and several of the other neighboring farmers.

Many had nothing to harvest, since their own fields had been trampled or stripped clean by hungry armies, and they were happy to lend a hand to their more fortunate neighbors, in return for a share to sell or feed their families and their livestock over the coming winter.

Caroline had once sold eggs, milk, cream and butter to people from town; now, she gave away all but what she needed for Rachel, Grandmother and herself, and for Enoch and Jubie, of course. Others did the same, in the way of neighbors everywhere and, gradually, the people of Gettysburg and the surrounding area began to find their way.

The last weeks prior to this had passed quickly, with visits to town to see Geneva, as well as Ladies' Aid friends. The place had not returned to normal yet; Caroline suspected that might take years. By now, the dead had been buried and in some cases already exhumed to be returned to their families; the wounded had almost all been taken home. But the damage to houses — pockmarked with bullets — remained, a reminder far into the future of what had happened here. That, and the damage to people's hearts and minds . . .

Alas, the land would be a long time recovering; there were still bodies to be disinterred in town and in the nearby fields, identified and sent home to grieving friends and families. Others were laid to quiet rest in the national cemetery, land set aside, by order of President Lincoln and members of his administration, for the purpose.

The Confederate dead were placed in that same hallowed ground, though apart from those who had perished in defense of the Union, on the assumption that, when peace came at last, they, too, would go home.

Few begrudged them this temporary rest; no person of good will could look upon the shattered bodies of earnest men, impetuous youths and, in many cases, mere children, and feel hatred. Each was a sorrow to someone, near or far, or would be, when the dreadful news came.

Mothers and fathers, sisters and brothers, wives and sweethearts, be they Union or Confederate, were alike in their hearts. They all loved their sons, brothers and husbands, all prayed for their safe return, and all wept the same salty tears when every hope was lost except one — that their dear Billy or Johnny, though perished, might be found and sent back to them, to be given a Christian burial in a place near enough to visit. There must be a proper marker, too, so he would be remembered.

One crisp day, in late October, when the harvest was over, Enoch came back from town with a letter.

He found Jubie and Caroline in the main house, seated near the fireplace in companionable silence, Caroline sewing, Jubie nursing her baby. Rachel sat close by on the floor, rolling a ball for Sweet Girl to scramble after and retrieve.

"There's a letter that's come for me," Enoch said, with a note of wonder in his voice. "I've never got any mail before, except from Jacob."

Caroline said nothing, but her hands went still, settling into her lap as if they'd made the decision on their own.

"Who'd be writing to you, Mister-man?" Jubie asked.

"I don't rightly know," Enoch replied. He held a thick envelope in his gloved hands, which were trembling ever so slightly. "It's come from down South, though — got no stamp, just a mark there in that corner."

Caroline's heart, swathed in purposeful indifference all these months, gave a small, painful leap.

"Well, *open* the thing," Jubie said. "Sit down here next to me and read it!"

Enoch dropped onto the chair without even taking off his coat, hat and gloves.

His big hands were awkward as he broke the seal, lifted the heavy flap and brought out a sheaf of paper, folded in thirds. He made a husky sound that might have been a laugh, then unfolded the document and smoothed it against his thigh.

"Lord have mercy," he muttered. "These are your emancipation papers, Jubie. It was Bridger — Captain Winslow who sent them."

Jubie's response was a stunned whisper. "Are they real? This ain't no trick? No slave catchers gonna come for me and Gideon?"

"No more slave catchers will come," Enoch confirmed without looking up from the papers. "You're free, Jubie, and this is the proof." He began flipping rapidly through the pages.

"Nobody be chasing me no more?" Jubie asked with breathless disbelief. "How can that be? Miz Templeton, she's the kind to hunt me till I drop!"

Caroline's heart seemed to wedge itself in her throat, rendering speech impossible.

And that was a good thing. Yes, she was glad for Jubie, for Enoch and the baby, too. So glad. She was staggered by the generosity of what Bridger had done, and she was truly grateful to him.

Now the realization came, sudden and smarting like a slap.

She was jealous. *Jealous* that there'd been no letter for her.

The documents Enoch and Jubie were poring over with such astonished delight were indeed the stuff of miracles. Heaven alone knew how they had gotten through without being lost or confiscated or simply thrown away, or what risks Bridger had taken, not only to secure them in the first place, but to send them from behind Confederate lines.

Certainly, correspondence passed between North and South, much of it probably by courier, under military guard.

Mrs. Lincoln, born in the South, had brothers fighting for the Confederacy and no doubt corresponded with them on a regular basis. Why, she'd even entertained one of her Southern sisters-in-law in the White House, scandalizing a great many loyal Unionists.

Yes, Mrs. Lincoln could send and receive mail with impunity, but then, she *was* Mrs. Lincoln. The wife of the President of the United States of America, which should, to Caroline's mind, have been called the *Dis*-united States, at least for the time being.

"Is there any other letter in there?" Jubie asked. "How you know it was Captain Winslow who sent them, if there's no letter?"

Enoch cleared his throat. "There is no letter," he said diplomatically. "His signature is here, so I believe that's proof enough as to who sent this. And there's a bill of sale that's signed, too."

"A bill of sale?" Jubie cried, waking the baby and causing him to whimper and then squall. "He *bought* me from Miz Templeton? Doesn't that mean *he* owns me now?"

"No," Enoch replied, very gently. "Bridger had these papers drawn up, and then he signed them, before witnesses. I don't know what else the man could have done to get the point across."

Jubie subsided a little, standing now, stroking Gideon's thick head of hair and rocking him from side to side. "Then why'd he put that bill of sale in there?"

"He probably figured we might need it sometime," Enoch said. "Anyhow, Bridger didn't pay in money. He gave that woman a blooded stallion, probably a fine one. What matters here is that you're *free,* and we've got Bridger Winslow to thank for it."

"Are you going to stay here for good, Miss Jubie?" Rachel asked softly, on her tiptoes to admire the baby in Jubie's arms.

Jubie turned her head, looked fondly at the child. Said in a tender voice, "We're gonna stay right here as long as I'm welcome, little one." Then, over Rachel's head, Jubie's eyes met Caroline's, asking a silent question.

"Of course you're always welcome, Jubie!" Caroline said. "This is Enoch's home, and now it's yours and Gideon's, too."

Enoch's eyes glistened in October's early twilight and, like Jubie, he spoke without words. *Thank you.*

Caroline smiled, rose from her chair and set her mending aside. "Where has the time gone?" she asked brightly. "Supper ought to be on the table by now, especially tonight, when we have so much to celebrate. And I haven't even started it."

Enoch stood as well. "You'll need firewood, Missus," he said. "I'll fetch it for you."

"I'll help you with the supper fixin's soon as I'm done nursing Gideon," Jubie offered.

"You will do no such thing," Caroline told her. "You, my friend, are the guest of honor tonight. And tomorrow, you shall have a cake to celebrate."

"With sugar icing?" Rachel asked eagerly, on her tiptoes again.

"With sugar icing," Caroline said. Then she headed to the kitchen house to make their meal.

Sometime later, with supper over and the dishes washed and dried and put back on the shelves, Enoch lit a lantern, draped his coat around Jubie and the baby and led his little family home.

By then, Rachel was dozing in her chair, Sweet Girl at her feet.

Caroline was about to lift the child into her arms, carry her to the house and get her ready for bed when she noticed a small sheet of paper lying on the table. She was sure it hadn't been there before; she'd wiped the surface clean after the plates were cleared.

With a frown, she picked the paper up, recognized it as the bill of sale Bridger had enclosed with Jubie's emancipation papers. Enoch must have forgotten it, she decided, although that seemed unlikely, given its importance. When she turned it over, she saw writing on the back, just a few lines, slanted to the right and somehow hurried, as if they'd been scrawled in haste.

Her name leaped up at her as she bent to retrieve the slip.

She straightened and began to read.

Caroline, Bridger had written, *I know you need to mourn Jacob, and I will respect your wishes in all ways. In due time, you will have suitors; I know of at least one who will most likely ask for your hand at the first decent opportunity. You owe me nothing, but I am not one to stand on ceremony, so will ask what I must. Wait for me, Caroline. I have things to say to you. If, after hearing me out, you send me away, I will go. Bridger.*

Caroline read the note a second time, then a third, before tears obscured the words. Then, she held the page to her breast, pressing it close, as if to physically absorb what it said.

Enoch had not forgotten anything, of course. He had seen that there was a message written on the back of the bill of sale while he was handling the other papers, and made sure Caroline had a chance to read it in relative privacy.

Did Enoch know what the note said? Almost certainly.

He would have taken it in whole before realizing it was meant for someone else. And why not? It had been enclosed with correspondence directed to him.

He'd probably felt a certain chagrin, just the same, as if he'd been prying, but the fact was, Enoch did not read the way most people did.

Once, on a quiet afternoon in deep winter, the two of them sitting on opposite sides of the kitchen house table with a lamp lit to push back the shadows, Caroline composing a letter to Jacob, Enoch bent over a book, she'd noticed how rapidly he turned the pages.

He'd admitted, gruffly modest and after much prodding on Caroline's part, that he didn't read word by word; when he looked at a newspaper article or a page in a book, whole blocks of print jumped out at him, all of a piece. He'd seemed almost embarrassed by this propensity, even unnerved, as though it were magic of uncertain origin. Some kind of hex or spell, perhaps. He didn't know why it happened like that, he'd told

Caroline. Old Missus had begun teaching him his letters when he'd been at Hammond Farm long enough to settle in, and once he could fit them together into words, it was as if they just took over from there.

Caroline had told Enoch he'd been blessed with a rare kind of intelligence, a true and precious gift, and he'd been so flustered by the compliment that he'd closed his book, offered some excuse about needing to chop more firewood and fled the kitchen house.

She'd been sparing in her praise after that because of Enoch's discomfort, but it hadn't been easy. He built wonderful things, such as cabinets and blanket chests and toys for Rachel, and Caroline dared not raise a fuss, no matter how delighted she was. She'd had to be content with "thank you" and "that's fine."

Enoch. Dear, generous, considerate Enoch.

He knew something of her exchanges with their inconvenient guest; of course he did. He'd walked into the sick room that night and seen Bridger kissing her, and her kissing Bridger right back. He must have overheard at least one of their disagreements, maybe even made the inevitable comparison — she and Jacob had never raised their voices to each other, in public or in private.

If she'd thought of it at all, Caroline suspected she'd been secretly prideful about the general lack of discord in her marriage. Any time she and Jacob were at odds, which was not often, she had usually retreated into quiet reflection, while he tended to remove himself to some distant part of the farm and, hours later, when he had expended his frustration through hard work, he returned, drenched in sweat and covered in field dirt, whistling some tuneless ditty and grinning to himself.

Acting as though nothing was amiss.

For him, that was the case. He'd find Caroline, usually in the kitchen house, and stand in the doorway, asking for clean clothes, stating reasonably that he wouldn't mind fetching them for himself, except that would mean tracking up Caroline's clean floors, wouldn't it?

Still quiet, Caroline would leave off kneading bread or peeling potatoes or whatever else she happened to be doing, go into the main house and up the stairs to their bedroom to get Jacob a fresh shirt and a pair of trousers, bring them to him in the yard. He'd accept the neatly folded garments with a smile so ingenuous that Caroline could not sustain her anger.

At least, most of the time she couldn't.

Jacob would head for the stream, strip off his soiled clothing, rinse himself in the water, and lie naked in the tall grass until he was dry enough to get dressed again. He almost invariably came back to Caroline with finger-combed hair and spiky eyelashes, smelling of fresh air, full of mischief, and damnably certain that the little woman had seen the error of her ways and would thereafter remember her place.

It wasn't that he was harsh or brutal, as so many husbands were, nor was he parsimonious. No, Jacob was kind and good-natured, and Caroline had appreciated those qualities, but she would have preferred an all-out shouting match to Jacob's way of dismissing her ideas as passing aberrations, typical of the female mind. Thinking, after all, was a *man's* sphere. No need to tax her poor little brain.

Caroline felt heat climb from her neck to her cheeks, just remembering how she'd acquiesced so readily, only to seethe behind her sweet, wifely smile, thinking of all the things she ought to say to Jacob, but couldn't.

She might have reminded him, for instance, that she was not stupid, that, indeed, she'd been raised by intelligent and fairly progressive grandparents and educated accordingly. She might have pointed out that, while she never plowed or dug postholes as he did, she cleaned the house, tended the garden, milked the cow, fed the chickens and gathered their eggs, hauled water from the well, chopped and carried firewood, cooked three hearty meals every day of her life, did the wash and a host of other things.

She had never turned from him in their marriage bed, even when fatigue and disappointment and heartache had drained away any possibility of ardor. No, she had received her husband, welcomed him with all the grace she could muster, and never uttered a word of complaint.

She had been a good wife to Jacob, and an excellent mother to their child.

No reasonable man — and Jacob *had* been a reasonable man — could have refuted any of these claims. If she'd had the courage to speak up . . .

What had she been afraid of? Jacob wouldn't have struck her, wouldn't have cast her out into a blizzard, like some feckless heroine in a bad play, penniless and dressed in rags. He had *loved* her, in his steady, predictable way. And yes, she'd loved him. But for whatever reason, she hadn't loved him with the kind of respectful maturity that would have allowed her to challenge him.

Oh, the shining clarity of hindsight.

If she *had* challenged him, he would have sulked for a while, yes. When Jacob was angry or worried, and such states were rare due to his inherently even disposition, his thoughts turned inward, and he needed time to brood over things, walk a mental labyrinth until he found the center, and some solution he could carry back to the ordinary world when he emerged. Almost invariably, he came out of these moods restored to his normal affable certainty and blithe confidence in the rightness of his beliefs.

Had Caroline persisted, after any one of these returns, still determined to make her point, Jacob would have been surprised at first, then displeased. Become sullen again. Eventually, though, if she had stood her ground, she knew he would have *listened.*

Where some things were concerned, he would never have agreed, but that didn't matter. She hadn't needed agreement.

She'd needed to be heard, to feel *visible,* seen as a *whole person.*

Instead, she'd sometimes felt like the faint and wavering reflection of the person Jacob believed she ought to be.

With Bridger, she had substance and fire.

She was present, solid, *alive.*

Rogan, too, saw her as a flesh-and-blood woman. And although she didn't know him as well as she did Bridger, she was aware of his good looks, his unfaltering masculinity and his intelligence.

She'd thought, even before Bridger's oblique reference to him in the note, that Rogan McBride might court her in earnest, as soon as propriety allowed. Furthermore, he would make an excellent husband and be a devoted stepfather to Rachel. So she was surprised that he'd been so formal in that first letter he wrote.

Of the two, Rogan seemed the wiser choice. He shared her belief that the Union must be preserved, for one thing, while Bridger had done — and would continue to do — his utmost to aid in the sundering of one nation into two.

Marriage to Rogan would open a new world to Caroline; he'd written of his life in New York City, the one he meant to return to after the war, and although he hadn't boasted, she knew he'd been successful in his law practice. He had aspirations, plans, goals, had seriously considered running for public office after his discharge.

With Rogan, she would meet a wide variety of fascinating people, live in a comfortable home and enjoy a stimulating environment — the bustle of city streets and the clatter of passing trolley cars, vast libraries, museums and theaters and fine restaurants.

Strange, Caroline thought, as she gathered her sleepy child into her arms, there in the kitchen house, and murmured a summons to the dog, that when Jacob was alive, she had resisted his dreams of travel. She had loved the farm, never wanted to leave it, even for a few weeks or months.

It was the best place to be, green and fertile, peaceful and quiet.

Back then, of course, there had been no war, no tents in her side yard with grievously wounded men inside, lying on flimsy cots, weeping, groaning, crying out for relief from their terrible pain and fear. Dying.

Back then, there'd been no dead soldiers buried there, flung into shallow graves and hastily covered, only to be exhumed and carried away in wagons. No slave catcher's carcass to hide, no sad horse returning over and over again, in search of his master, no matter how many times Enoch had turned him loose.

Caroline loved the farm, as before, but she no longer felt bound to it.

She opened the door to the darkness and chill of an autumn night and stepped out, her right arm around Rachel, holding a flickering lantern in her left hand. Sweet Girl walked slightly ahead, sniffing the ground.

The bill of sale, with Bridger's note scribbled on the back, was tucked into her apron pocket, although it might as well have been resting against her bare skin, the way it pulsed in her awareness.

Bridger. He had spoken of suitors in his brief missive, as if there would be dozens of them pounding at her front door as soon as her year of mourning Jacob had come to a respectable conclusion. As she carried her daughter toward the house, she smiled a little, to think he had so much confidence in her womanly appeal.

She reached the house, turned the knob and let Sweet Girl inside before following with Rachel. Thoughts of Bridger and the note stayed with her, tired as she was.

He had asked her to wait for him, and that could only mean one thing. He meant to make some sort of proposal, perhaps marriage, perhaps something else entirely.

Caroline extinguished the lantern and set it down; she knew the house so well, she didn't need light to find her way.

Bridger had said it himself — he was a rake.

What if he planned to make her his mistress, rather than his wife?

A hot little thrill wove itself through her, even as she carried Rachel up the stairs, Sweet Girl at her heels. Although she would never be any man's kept woman, not even Bridger Winslow's, the idea wasn't without a certain daring appeal. In fact, it sparked scandalously delicious images of naked bodies entangled on starched white sheets and of windows open to sultry nights and the scents of magnolia blossoms, of wild, searing passions . . .

Caroline brought herself up short.

For heaven's sake! What was she doing, allowing her mind to wander like this? She was a Pennsylvania farmer's widow, with a daughter to bring up, not a courtesan in some decadent foreign court. And if she ever took a second husband, he wasn't likely to be either Bridger *or* Rogan, but someone she'd known for years, a veteran just home from the war. Another farmer, she thought glumly, a near neighbor, wanting to extend his property lines.

She took Rachel into her tidy little room, undressed her, helped her into her nightclothes. She washed the child's face and hands, over murmured protests, and insisted the little girl brush her teeth and use the chamber pot.

The instant Rachel was tucked up in bed, she fell asleep.

Sweet Girl, bolder now, jumped onto the mattress and nestled at Rachel's feet.

Caroline stood, looking down at her daughter, loving her so much that she almost couldn't bear it. She wanted everything for Rachel — health and happiness, of course, but more, as well. A good education, travels to interesting places near and far, a prosperous life. Eventually, a husband she loved and who loved her in return. Boisterous, sturdy children, thriving from the first breath they drew.

And more still. She wanted Rachel to be a responsible citizen when she became an adult, with all the rights the Constitution currently afforded white men but had clearly promised to *everyone,* regardless of sex or race, of religion or no religion at all.

Yes.

If she lived to see her daughter so blessed, her *country* so blessed, she would be satisfied. Content with her own lot, whether she married again or not.

For now, she would dedicate herself to raising Rachel to be strong and kind, to love wisely, to stand firm in the face of adversity and opposition, unafraid to be her truest and best self.

Later, there would be choices she, Caroline, must make. Perhaps many of them.

And if she did decide to take a husband, who would he be? Bridger or Rogan or another man altogether? A local farmer, as she'd thought a few minutes ago?

Fortunately, she didn't have to decide anything tonight or tomorrow or next week. There was plenty of time; she would wait and work, love her daughter and watch destiny unfold in its own way, without trying to influence the course it took.

She bent to place a light kiss on Rachel's tiny, smooth forehead. "Good night, my dearest love," she whispered. "Sweet dreams."

"Mmm-hmm," Rachel replied, snuggling deeper into the softness of her familiar bed, perhaps already dreaming.

Caroline straightened, stood watch for another minute or so, offering silent, wordless prayers, and then turned to walk softly away, into the corridor and on to her own room.

She shed her daylight worries as she undressed, washed, donned a nightgown and got into bed. Tonight, she decided, she, too, would dream, not of battles and broken bodies, not of thundering cannon and shrieks of pain, but of ordinary pleasures — the scents of spring grass and freshly tilled earth, the chirping of birds on hidden branches festooned with pink and white blossoms, more fragrant than any perfume, the billowing dance of sheets pegged to the clothesline on a windy day, the rhythm of rain upon a sturdy roof, the sheen of sunlight on the rust-red feathers of her laying hens.

Soothed, Caroline closed her eyes and drifted smoothly into her dreams.

29

National Cemetery, Gettysburg
Thursday, November 19, 1863

CAROLINE

The day was finally here.

Caroline and Enoch had been waiting for this — the consecration of the National Cemetery — ever since they'd heard about it in town and read about it in the *Compiler.*

To say that she was excited at the prospect of seeing and hearing the president was — as she told Geneva when they met in town that morning — an understatement. He and a number of other speakers, musicians and honored guests would be there to consecrate the new cemetery, where many of the Union soldiers who'd died at Gettysburg would be interred. And if Caroline revered anyone in this world, it was Abraham Lincoln.

She, Enoch, Jubie and the children began by visiting Geneva's house, where they enjoyed an early lunch, then made their way south along Baltimore Street. President Lincoln had arrived the day before, staying at the home of Mr. David Wills, who'd done so much to ensure the creation of the cemetery.

Caroline and Enoch quietly discussed Cemetery Hill and what had happened there in July; they decided it was fitting that Lincoln would be speaking from a stand on the Hill itself. As they joined the crowd shortly before noon — already numbering in the thousands — they positioned themselves near a sheltering tree. They were all grateful today's weather was mild. Gideon was asleep in Jubie's arms, while Rachel leaned against her mother; the child's unusual silence suggested she recognized at least something of the sacred nature of this event.

The ceremony began with music and a prayer, and was followed by the Honorable Edward Everett's oration. Widely considered one of the most accomplished speakers of the day, he spoke for two hours — never referring to notes, moving freely across the platform. Caroline was impressed by the skill of his speech, although a little wearied by its length. And she was impressed by the respectful quiet of the audience.

Applause. A hymn specially composed and written for the consecration. Then . . .

Abraham Lincoln stepped onto the stand, tall, gaunt, rather pale, formally dressed. He removed a piece of paper from his pocket — and began to read.

"Four score and seven years ago our fathers brought forth on this continent a new nation, conceived in Liberty, and dedicated to the proposition that all men are created equal."

Caroline glanced over at Enoch, taking his turn holding the baby, and at Jubie with her arms around Rachel, and saw tears in their eyes.

"Now we are engaged in a great civil war . . ." Caroline clasped her grandmother's hand, and she knew that, like everyone in the large audience, they were both absorbing every word.

After exactly two minutes, the speech was finished, ending with the words:

". . . that we here highly resolve that these dead shall not have died in vain — that this nation, under God, shall have a new birth of freedom — and that government of the people, by the people, for the people, shall not perish from the earth."

Two minutes she somehow *knew* would have a centuries-long impact, a meaning that would define the future of their country. Once this war was over . . . Once the Union prevailed. And that *would* happen.

There was an astounded silence, a reverent hush, eventually overtaken by applause. Geneva, Jubie, Enoch, Caroline — they all looked at each other, smiling. Caroline planned to make sure Rachel knew she'd been present at such a historic event.

The ceremony concluded with another hymn and a benediction, and people began to leave in an orderly fashion. Enoch insisted on going to Geneva's house to fetch the wagon; when he returned, he brought her home and then they went on to Hammond Farm. No one spoke. Caroline felt that anything she might've said would have broken the mood, the almost holy bond created by Lincoln's words.

Once home, she and Jubie quickly prepared supper — a simple meal of potatoes, corn and fried chicken. They all retired soon after. Despite having slept that day, Rachel fell asleep easily. Sweet Girl, fed much later than usual but now satiated, lay beside her bed.

Caroline sat at the desk in her own room, took up her pen and began to write.

Dear Jacob,
Today I learned what this was all for . . .

30

Maryland
November 30, 1864

BRIDGER

A squat tallow candle burned low on the sill of a narrow and grimy window in the back room of O'Malley's Tavern, a dim beacon on a cool, moonless night.

Bridger sat with his feet up in the empty, abandoned place, a cheroot between his teeth, and waited, thirsty for a shot of whiskey but resigned to an ongoing state of sobriety, since every bottle on the shelves up front had long since been poured down the gullets of no-accounts or used for target practice.

The whole building listed to the left, floors included, and huge cobwebs dangled from the broken ceilings, like bunting at a gathering of dead politicians fixing to orate, and the smell of rats, dust and bird shit was pungent, but he'd known worse.

Far worse.

He sighed, drew on the cheroot and blew out smoke, listened to the creaks and skitterings, the not-quite-audible echoes of times gone by — whores whispering false promises upstairs in their seedy cribs, the tinny clink of the rotting piano near the bar, the whining of sorry drunks bending the bartender's ear with their myriad and sodden sorrows.

God save bartenders everywhere, he thought.

Outside in the darkness, Orion, the last of Fairhaven's fine stallions, nickered, a quiet, curious sound.

Bridger lowered his feet to the dissolving floorboards and stood, dropping the cheroot and grinding it out with the toe of one boot as he took his pistol from the table and moved noiselessly to the door.

There, he heard them, the hoof beats of a lone horse, moving at a brisk canter along the hard-packed dirt of the nearby road.

He smiled, shoved the pistol into his belt, at the small of his back. He wouldn't need it if the rider was the one he expected, but he wanted it within easy reach if some thieving renegade had caught sight of the candle flame and decided to investigate.

Orion tossed his massive head, set his bridle fittings a-jingle.

"Quiet," Bridger commanded. Except for a small splash of white on his left flank, the stallion was blacker than the back of a mouse hole in a root cellar, virtually invisible in the dark, but this horse would raise three kinds of hell if he turned restless.

There was no moon that night — Bridger had chosen the date for that reason, among others — but he recognized his old friend anyhow, by the set of his shoulders and the way he sat his horse, a big gray, graceful as a spirit floating through a graveyard.

Rogan drew back on the reins, dismounted. Like Bridger, he wore plain trousers, a dark shirt and hat pulled low, so the brim cast a shadow over his face.

The two men greeted each other with a handshake.

Rogan turned to assess the leaning hulk of the tavern and gave a low chuckle. Shook his head. "Damn," he said. "Couldn't you have chosen someplace a little harder to find? I must have ridden past this pile of boards half a dozen times before I saw that speck of light."

"I guess I figured a bonfire might start a party I didn't care to attend," Bridger replied, glad to see his friend again, and, at the same time, dreading the conversation to come.

Rogan crossed the reins loosely over the gray's neck and left the animal to graze in the deep grass. He took his hat off, lowered it to his side.

"You went to a lot of trouble arranging this little gathering, Bridger," he said quietly, "and I went to about twice as much trouble getting here. Go ahead and speak your piece."

Bridger sighed. He'd rehearsed this discussion in his head time and again, since he'd left Caroline's farm the previous summer, skulking away before sunrise like a thief, clad in a Yankee uniform and riding a useless horse. But now, facing his best friend, he fell a little short of eloquence.

"I'm in love with Caroline," he said bluntly.

Rogan thrust the splayed fingers of his left hand through his hair, looked away briefly. "I was afraid of that," he said after a silence so long that Bridger had started to brace himself for a haymaker of a punch. Controlled fury blazed in Rogan's eyes when their gazes met again. "How serious is this?"

"On my side? Very. I'm not sure how Caroline feels."

Rogan cursed, visibly collected himself.

"You've seen her? Since you left her farm after Gettysburg, I mean?"

Bridger shook his head. "No, I haven't. I managed to get a short note through to her, with some papers I sent Enoch, but for all I know, Caroline never saw it." He paused. "Listen, Rogan, I —"

Rogan put up his free hand. "Stop. Don't say you didn't mean for this to happen, because if you do, we're going to have a war of our own, right here and now. I *knew* you were taken with her before I left. That's why I told you how *I* felt about Caroline."

"I could really use a drink," Bridger said.

Unbelievably, Rogan laughed, the sound hoarse and short-lived. He turned, went back to his mount, rummaged through his saddlebags and brought out a silver flask, then tossed it to his friend.

Bridger caught it handily, unscrewed the cap and took a long swallow. The stuff scorched all the way down to his belly, where it burst like a shell loaded with rocks and rusty nails. "Good God," he sputtered, once he'd regained his breath. "What is this? Embalming fluid?"

"You expected good Kentucky bourbon?"

Bridger laughed, steadied himself and took a second drink. Gave back the flask. If Rogan wanted to skirt the subject of Caroline for a while, he'd go along with it. "Not really," he said mildly, running the back of one hand across his mouth. "Would have been a pleasant surprise, though."

Rogan sighed. Gulped down some of the whiskey himself before putting the flask away. He walked over to Orion, ran a practiced hand of the stallion's flank and crouched to examine his legs.

"This is a Fairhaven horse," he said.

"Yes. And be careful. Uniform or none, Orion knows a Yankee when he smells one, and he's likely to cave your skull in if you spook him."

Rogan lingered a few more minutes, at his ease with any horse. It had always puzzled Bridger how a man raised on the streets of New York City could acquire such an affinity; most really fine horsemen had been in the saddle before they were old enough to walk. Rogan hadn't learned to ride until he'd started boarding school at fourteen.

"You've been home since we last met," he said, straightening, patting Orion's ebony neck a couple of times before turning back to Bridger. "To Fairhaven, I mean."

"After I left Caroline's place," Bridger affirmed. "I had to see how Amalie was getting along. Handle some business."

"What kind of business?"

"I did a little horse trading, turned loose the slaves who didn't want to stay, spat on my father's grave once or twice. With Amalie provided for, at least temporarily, I went back to my regiment."

"That's how you got Orion, here? Horse trading?"

"No. He was foaled at Fairhaven, the last of a long and illustrious line. I swapped his kid sister, as perfect a filly as I've ever seen, for a certain runaway slave."

"Jubie, I presume?"

Bridger nodded.

"And speaking of kid sisters," Rogan said, "is Amalie well?"

"She's doing fine, considering," Bridger answered, feeling a wrench at the thought of Sherman and his blue-bellies, ravaging Georgia. He'd begged Amalie to leave Fairhaven, take refuge in the North, but she'd refused, said she'd rather burn with the fields and the plantation house than set foot in Yankee territory.

"She was always a beautiful young woman," Rogan said quietly.

"Believe me," Bridger responded. "Amalie is still beautiful." To prove it, he took a small photographic likeness from his kit, handed it over.

Rogan went to stand in front of the window, examined the picture in the dying light of the candle on the other side of the filthy glass. He was silent for a long time, studying Amalie's image. Then, after closing the case, he extended the photograph to Bridger and asked, "So she's still at Fairhaven?"

"Yes," Bridger said grimly. He didn't take the photograph.

"You do realize that Sherman's in Georgia, swearing he'll leave the place in ruins?"

Bridger nodded. The bad whiskey roiled in his gut, seared its way upward to scald the back of his throat. "Keep the picture," he rasped. "I'm in no position to ask for any favors, but if I don't make it home when this is over, will you see that she's safe? You're probably the one Yankee in all of Creation she would trust."

"You're too damn mean to die," Rogan said. "But if it turns out I'm wrong about that, I'll head for Fairhaven, soon as I get word of your untimely and probably swashbuckling death." He paused. "I intend to see Amalie in any case."

Bridger looked away, wondering as he had in the past what, if any, feelings still existed between those two. He suspected they did, particularly on her part. But when he'd tried to talk to his sister about it, she'd been vague. "Thank you."

"Anything for my best friend," Rogan said, with a slight emphasis on the last two words.

Bridger decided he'd had that gibe coming and ignored it. There were more important things to talk about. "What happens now?" he asked. "Besides both of us doing our best to survive this war?"

Rogan took his time answering, rubbed the back of his neck, studied the sky, speckled with stars. Sighed. "We're back to Caroline," he said.

"Yes," Bridger agreed.

Another silence followed.

Rogan was the one to break it. "This isn't a horserace or a chess match, Bridger, and we aren't kids anymore, playing king-of-the-hill on the school grounds."

"So I've noticed," Bridger said. "I've never had a better friend than you, Rogan. If we were talking about any woman besides Caroline, I swear to you, I would step aside. This is different."

Rogan smiled ruefully. "I know."

For the first time, Bridger consciously acknowledged a bitter truth. No matter how things turned out with Caroline, the loss of this friendship would leave him with a wound that might never heal, and wounds to the mind and spirit festered and spread their secret poison as surely as the physical kind rotted flesh.

The end result was the same. Death of the body, or death of every good thing a man cherished in himself — courage, integrity, reason and, worst of all, the ability to love truly, without reservation.

He closed his eyes at the thought of what he could become. Some version of his father, perhaps, or his half brother.

Mercifully, although he probably hadn't intended it, Rogan jolted him out of his black thoughts. "Maybe we had the right idea when we were kids, both of us going for whatever — or whomever — we wanted, after a handshake. From then on, it was full steam ahead, no holds barred, devil take the hindmost. Remember?"

Bridger's voice was hoarse, and his eyes smarted. "I remember," he replied. It had been the handshake that mattered most, the tacit agreement that, win or lose, the friendship would stand.

Without another word, Rogan put out his hand and Bridger clasped it.

Both men tightened their grip, held on, silently sealing the bargain, then letting go.

Rogan turned away, headed for his horse, mounted. "Don't catch any cannon balls," he said in parting. With a wry salute, he wheeled the gray around and rode off in the direction from which he'd come.

Bridger did not watch his friend out of sight. Though he'd never subscribed to superstition, he'd been immersed in it from an early age; his mother and all the house slaves had worried over small signs and portents — the dangers of placing a hat on a bed, of spilling salt, of opening an umbrella inside the house, of gazing after someone leaving until you couldn't see that person anymore.

He had deliberately flouted such rules, walking under ladders, courting the company of black cats, refusing to knock on wood at the mention of some dire possibility.

Tonight, however, he was taking no chances.

He stepped inside the wreck of O'Malley's Tavern, snuffed out the candle and said goodbye to the ghosts. He left the door agape, in case any of those forlorn spirits longed to roam, swung up into Orion's saddle and started back to his regiment, back to the blood and the hunger and the proud refusal to admit defeat.

Even though it seemed inevitable.

31

Appomattox, Virginia,
April 9, 1865

ROGAN

General Robert E. Lee, clad in his splendid gray uniform with its dashing scarlet sash, cut a majestic figure as he rode up to the home of one Wilmer McLean, mounted on his great dapple-gray warhorse, Traveller. To look at him, no one would suspect there'd been a fierce battle that very morning at the Appomattox Court House, a Union victory, though there was still intermittent cannon fire as the fighting dwindled.

Rogan watched the great enemy from the porch of the McLean House, a tangle of emotions in his throat — admiration, sympathy, relief, sorrow. As the general stepped down from the saddle, the ceremonial sword at his side glittered in the afternoon sunlight. He had to be the most dignified, self-contained man Rogan had ever seen, this legend, this Titan of strategic warfare; he was beaten, he had to know that, yet he stood tall. Handed off the reins to a young Federal soldier, who stood waiting in tremulous awe.

It was still speculation, of course, that General Lee intended to surrender himself and his beloved Army of Northern Virginia to the highest Union authority save Lincoln himself, General Ulysses S. Grant.

Rogan had been promoted to the rank of major during the endless siege of Petersburg and, by a fluke, he'd been assigned to Grant's staff several months back, when the general had seen him lay out a cavalry lieutenant for whipping his horse.

To Rogan's utter surprise and, at first, alarm, Grant had approached him, stood at his side, a cigar clamped between his teeth, his eyes keen on the lieutenant sprawled at their feet. As usual, he had looked nothing like a general, a man of small stature and quiet intelligence, standing there in his mud-spattered boots and the garb of a lowly private.

"I'm obliged, Major," he'd said amiably. "You've saved me the trouble of taking a bullwhip to that fellow. Can't abide cruelty to a dumb beast. It's a sign of deviant character."

"Yes, sir," Rogan had answered, somewhat bewildered. Until that day, he'd seen the general only from a distance, but he'd heard plenty about him, good and bad.

He was purported to be a hopeless drunk, for one thing. Rogan had doubted that, even before his reassignment, when he'd come to know Grant as a man whose worst failings were probably his tendency to trust too readily and a simple but extreme case of homesickness. He sensed that Grant missed his wife and children sorely, and brooded over them in the rare quiet hours the war allotted him.

His gifts, being more obvious, were his fierce determination to finish the war and restore the Union, his extraordinary horsemanship and, in stark contrast to his predecessors, the capacity to dog Lee's army relentlessly, like a hungry hound in pursuit of a rabbit. He seemed to understand, as McClellan and Hooker and even Meade had not, that Lee and his wily cohort, notably Jeb Stuart and the late Stonewall Jackson, elusive as they were, had to be chased until they were caught, even if it meant following them right down into their holes. To Grant, they were not superhuman, as Northerners feared, but mortal men, tired and hungry and beleaguered on all sides.

They could be brought to heel; it was a matter of wearing them down, cutting off their supply and telegraph lines, destroying their bridges and railroads and, finally, cornering them, once and for all, as he'd done at Petersburg in Virginia. That siege had lasted the better part of a year — 292 days to be exact. By the end, a little more than two weeks ago, it had cost about 70,000 deaths.

Yet Grant's objective was not one of vengeance, but of resolution and, eventually, reconciliation. In order to reach those objectives, however, he granted no quarter. He would settle for nothing less than complete victory; hence his nickname: Unconditional Surrender Grant.

Now, Rogan thought, here it was, within his grasp.

He had to know that Lee was at the McLean place, ready to discuss terms.

So where the hell was he?

Lee was approaching the front steps, and his solemn gaze met Rogan's. He gave an almost imperceptible nod of greeting or acknowledgment, but his expression was bleak.

Rogan removed his campaign hat, nodded

in return. He respected this man, even admired him, though he had fought to the full extent of his abilities to see him vanquished, would have done so all over again, and stuck with the enterprise until victory was assured, regardless of the terrible cost.

Once General Lee had gone inside the McLean House, escorted by several Union officers but not under formal guard, Rogan replaced his hat and scanned the small crowd gathered in the dooryard.

All were Federals of varying ranks, standing in small groups, talking among themselves, quietly and earnestly. Rogan knew, without listening to their words, that they were speculating, wondering what, if anything, Lee's visit might mean. Some would be convinced that the worst of the war, if not the war itself, was finally over.

Wishful thinking probably played a part in their reasoning; battle weary and yearning to put soldiering behind them for good, they wanted to go home.

Others, however, were almost certainly arguing that a man like Lee would never surrender, and their position had its merits, given the general's many successful campaigns.

Mentally, Rogan reviewed the situation, trying to think objectively. Although Lee himself had proposed this meeting with Grant, after losing more than half his broken, footsore and starving army in the course of a single week, and with events culminating that same morning in a decisive Union victory right there at the village of Appomattox Court House, the head of the Confederate forces hadn't actually agreed to surrender.

He and his army were caught, like so many Sunday-supper chickens wrestled into burlap sacks, destined for the chopping block. Rogan knew that there would be no escape; Lee's one hope, that of joining forces with General Joe Johnston, currently in North Carolina, regrouping and then carrying bravely on, was finished.

If Lee had not believed this, he wouldn't be here.

The proud South had, at long last, been brought to its knees, but Rogan took no satisfaction in that. To him, the South was more than the setting for books like *Uncle Tom's Cabin,* more than cruel overseers, spoiled aristocrats, cotton fields and slaves. It was Bridger's home, and Amalie's.

He had seen his share of derelict towns, shabbiness and poverty, both in the South and the North.

The South had shacks and sharecroppers,

yes, but it had no corner on poverty. He himself knew that firsthand, orphan that he was. Besides, there were small farms as well as hardscrabble patches of rocky dirt, Southern farms worth the time and grit it would take to make them productive again. There were factories and shops, cities and towns, churches and schools and cemeteries.

And there were grand — or once grand — houses, such as Fairhaven. It had changed him, that mansion, from the moment he'd stepped down from the carriage that first long-ago summer, right behind Bridger. There were larger homes on Park Avenue, where he'd once shared an airless attic room with his mother before she decided to be quit of him, but none of them equaled Fairhaven, with its vast grounds, its flourishing gardens and many shade trees, its barns and paddocks and pastures of sweet grass.

For all Rogan knew, Sherman had reduced that glorious, sweltering Eden to timbers and ash.

If so, what had become of Amalie since that letter he'd received two years ago? She'd grown into a beauty, he knew that from the likeness of her Bridger had given him the last time they met; he carried the photograph with him everywhere he went, looked at it often.

Amalie had been a bright, pretty tomboy those memorable summers, with her black hair in pigtails. She'd follow Bridger and Rogan wherever they went, constantly up to mischief — stealing their breeches from the banks of the pond when they went swimming, hiding herself under their beds or inside their wardrobes and giving her presence away with giggles.

He remembered that last morning of the third summer they'd been there, just before he and Bridger were to return to school. She'd caught hold of Rogan's hand, and tugged until he'd leaned down. "When I grow up, I'm going to marry you, Rogan McBride," she'd whispered in his ear.

He'd smiled, straightened his back, pulled lightly at one of her pigtails. "Well, Snippet," he'd told her gently. "I'm flattered. Suppose we talk about this again when you're older."

Not to be placated, Amalie had glared up at him and accused, "You think I'm just a little girl, and that I don't know *one thing* about choosing a husband!"

"Snippet," he'd said reasonably, trying valiantly not to laugh, "you *are* a little girl. And it's going to be a long, long time before you even consider getting married. When the time comes, you'll have your pick of beaus."

She'd set her small fists on her narrow hips and jutted out her chin in a way that had reminded him of her older brother. Her wide amber eyes had flashed with conviction and temper. "I don't *want* any beaus," she'd declared. "I want to marry *you*, and if you don't come back to Fairhaven and court me properly, you'll be sorry, because I'm going to be the most beautiful woman in the *entire* state of Georgia!"

He smiled at the memory, touched the breast of his tunic, felt the outline of the small case that held the photograph. *Sure enough, Snippet*, he thought sadly, *you grew up to be a beauty, just as you said you would.*

That last thought was troubling, but it was better than going over the contents of Caroline's letter, which had reached him a little over a week before. Like a fool, he'd written her, a month back, said he planned to visit her at the farm as soon as he could get leave.

Caroline's reply had been polite, but prescient. She'd be glad to have him visit as long as he understood that she was doing fine on her own and was not interested in a relationship on a romantic level.

She had explained that should she marry again, it would be for love and, yes, passion.

At first, Rogan had been wild to defy her wishes and go to her, convince her, somehow, that *he* could offer her passion, that he loved her enough for both of them, until she came to love him in return.

In the end, though, he had realized that *because* he loved Caroline, he had to honor her decision.

He'd written her once more, to tell her he appreciated her forthrightness and that he understood. He wished her good health and every happiness, whether she chose to remarry or not, and expressed the hope that she would always consider him a dear and faithful friend, as she was to him. And if he could manage it, he would visit on his way back north when the war was over.

Since Caroline's letter, he'd concentrated on fighting. The enemy had cooperated, leaving him, along with the rest of the Union army, little time to think of anything beyond staying alive.

The Rebs had fought so fiercely that it was hard to believe these dusty, bedraggled foot soldiers he was looking at now, drifting in from all directions to stand silently in the near distance, were the same men.

Those who still had weapons held them by the barrel, with the stock to the ground. It was tacitly understood that they hadn't come to fight, these Johnnies, but simply to stand witness to whatever might come next. To show, if only by their presence, their deep regard for their general.

They were gaunt, almost skeletal, with feverish, haunted eyes and shadowed hollows beneath cheekbones that stood out like ledges on a steep hillside. Most were little more than schoolboys, armed with squirrel guns, and many carried no weapon at all. They gave off a collective stench of sweat, stale urine, latrines, putrid wounds and rotting teeth, and yet, for all that, there could be no doubting their dignity; they had fought bravely, even valiantly, and they knew it.

Pitiful, cadaverous and starved as they were, they had been the instruments of many a brilliant campaign, plaguing Federal troops time and again, appearing out of nowhere, streaming over hillsides and around bends in the road, hundreds or even thousands of them, piercing the air with that eerie demon's shriek, the Rebel Yell. The sound, especially in chorus, could fracture the shaft of a man's bones and freeze the marrow.

Rogan spoke to a red-headed lad with more freckles than white skin. "You need water, John?" he asked. "Something to eat?"

The Reb looked wary at first, but then he gave a clipped nod, his eyes met Rogan's, and he said, "Yes, Bill. We need just about everything you could name, right about now."

"I'll send for supplies," Rogan told him. "In the meantime, there's a hand pump behind the house. You can fill your canteens there."

"Obliged," the Reb said. He spared a glance for the Yankees clustered in the dooryard. "They gonna shoot us?"

"No," Rogan said. "I'll walk beside you. If they fire, they'll hit me."

"You can't walk alongside all of us," the boy pointed out.

"I'm the highest-ranking officer here at the moment," Rogan answered. "There won't be any shooting, though I suppose some of them wouldn't mind blowing off a chunk of my head. They'd have to account to General Grant, though, and he would not be pleased, particularly with General Lee on the premises."

"We'll go then," the boy decided, after some thought. "But we'll do it in relays, a few at a time."

Rogan nodded. "All right."

They set out for the pump then, Rogan,

the boy and about half a dozen thirsty Rebels.

No one fired at them.

"You Federals better treat the general right," the red-headed boy said as they walked. "You don't do that, well, us lads won't be so peaceable as now."

Rogan smiled to himself. Wondered if Bridger had been in this latest fight. If he'd survived it. "Understood," he said gravely. "Fact is, most of us think quite highly of your General Lee. General Grant will drive a hard bargain, it's true, but he'll be a gentleman about it."

The boy made a huffing sound. "Useless S. Grant," he muttered. "He ain't fit to spit shine General Lee's boots."

Rogan said nothing. If the lad needed to give off a little steam, let him.

By the time the last canteens had been filled and the supplies sent for, General Grant was riding up, accompanied by a small party. His uniform was as muddy and disreputable as ever, the customary cigar jutted from between his teeth, and he returned the salutes of his men in a distracted way.

He dismounted, climbed the porch steps and strode purposefully into the McLean House, flanked by a few of his most trusted associates.

The meeting went on for some time.

The supply wagon arrived, and Rogan oversaw the dispersal of hardtack, dried fruit and jerked beef. The Confederates devoured everything they were given.

Rogan was so absorbed in the process that he forgot about the two men inside the house, working out the fate of armies, and didn't notice Bridger until he was off that stallion of his and standing right next to him.

"Well," Rogan managed to say, startled and vastly relieved, "I guess I won't have to ride down to Savannah and call in at Fairhaven after all."

Bridger was thinner than before, and in sore need of a bath and a shave, but otherwise unscathed. "No," he replied. "You can head straight for Pennsylvania."

Rogan drew his friend aside. "I'm not going to Caroline," he said. "Turns out, she's not interested in marriage — not to me, at least. Thinks it might ruin our friendship."

Bridger smiled slightly, but his eyes were sad, probably for a great many reasons. "I'm sorry, Rogan."

"Don't be. She might turn you down, too."

Bridger nodded. "There's a good chance

she'll do just that," he said. "But I've got to try."

"I know," Rogan said. He felt glum and, at the same time, strangely hopeful on Bridger's behalf.

Bridger's gaze shifted to the house, and the sadness spread from his eyes to his entire face. "If this *is* over," he said, when he was looking at Rogan again, "what will you do? Go back to New York City, take up your law practice again?"

"I'm not sure. Maybe I'll go out West. Start over. You?"

Bridger gave a raw chuckle. "My enlistment was up six months ago. All I want to do is marry Caroline, if she'll have me, and go back to Fairhaven. There's a lot of work to be done."

"Sherman didn't raze the place?"

"He did some damage, but the house and barn are right where I left them. A little the worse for wear, of course, but still standing."

Pleased, Rogan slapped Bridger lightly on the shoulder. "And Amalie? Is she all right?"

Bridger grinned. "My little sister is furious with every Yankee from Lincoln on down, but she's in one piece. She's made up her mind to be a spinster, since, as she put it, the only marriageable men she's likely to meet, once this war ends, are either over eighty or under fourteen."

Rogan smiled, remembering the girl who had planned to marry him when she grew up, comparing her to the photograph in his shirt pocket. "Maybe I'll make my way to Savannah before I head west. I wouldn't mind seeing Fairhaven again."

"It isn't the place you remember, Rogan," Bridger said, wistful now. "But you're welcome there anytime. I wouldn't show up in that blue uniform, though. Amalie is a fair hand with a shotgun."

Rogan laughed. "I might risk a visit anyhow."

"I would consider that a favor," Bridger told him. He looked and sounded serious.

Seeing Rogan's expression, he went on.

"Life has been hard for Amalie for a long time now. She puts on a brave face, but she's tired, Rogan. Frankly, I'm worried about her. A visit from you would break the monotony, to say the least."

"Even if she greets me with a shotgun?"

"*Especially* if she greets you with a shotgun," Bridger answered. "No need to worry. Amalie won't shoot to kill, as long as you don't present yourself in that uniform. Even then, she might let you live, if only because she's been in love with you since those summers you spent at Fairhaven."

"As a matter of fact," Rogan replied, "she proposed the day we left after one of our visits. Said she'd grow up to be the most beautiful woman in all of Georgia, and I'd regret it if I didn't come back."

Bridger laughed again. The sound was weariness itself, but it was genuine, too. "Well, then, I guess you'd better do the honorable thing and go back. I doubt she'll want to marry you, but she was accurate about one thing, my little sister. She is definitely beautiful."

Rogan didn't speak. He wanted to see Amalie again, and Fairhaven, as well.

And then he would go west.

If Bridger succeeded, and brought Caroline home to Fairhaven as his wife, Rogan wasn't going to be there when they arrived.

32

Hammond Farm
May 10, 1865

BRIDGER

Caroline was in the yard when he and the stallion rounded the last bend in the road. Her arms were raised, pegging laundry to the clothesline. Her black frock, in stark contrast to the snow-white sheet flapping behind her, made her stand out in sharp relief, even with her back to him.

Bridger, nervous, tired to the bone, full of anticipation and sweet dread, felt his heart stumble as he registered Caroline's mode of dress.

He nudged Orion from a trot to a gallop with a motion of his heels, and she must have heard the stallion's hoof beats pounding the hard ground. She slowly lowered her arms, turned her head.

The farm gate was shut, but by then

Orion had hit his stride and, with a burst of speed, he soared over the fence that ran alongside, like a raven taking wing.

Caroline, still as a post until that moment, raised a hand to her mouth, let it drop and, bunching the somber fabric of her skirts in both fists and lifting them to her ankles, began to run.

Bridger reined in the stallion, swung a leg over the saddle horn and landed at a sprint.

They met — or more accurately, collided — midway between the road and the clothesline, Caroline wrapping her arms around Bridger's neck, Bridger lifting her off her feet and swinging her around in circles until they were both dizzy.

Her face, burrowed into his shoulder, was wet with tears, and she clung to him, like a shipwreck survivor to a sinking mast. "Bridger," she whispered. "Bridger."

He set her on her feet, steadied her. Planted his feet to steady himself until the green countryside stopped spinning around them.

At the edge of his vision, Orion nickered and sidestepped, reins dangling.

"Caroline," Bridger said gently. "Look at me."

She drew her head back, but her eyes were lowered, and he curved one finger under her wobbling chin and raised it so he could see her face.

"I didn't think — I wasn't sure I'd ever see you again," she murmured, making an effort to recover her composure.

He smiled, brushed his lips against the center of her forehead. "I told you I'd be back," he reminded her.

A shudder moved through her, and she bit her lower lip, looked up at him with red-rimmed eyes. Nodded.

He took her by the shoulders, afraid her knees might buckle. "Who died, Caroline?" he asked gruffly, terrified of the answer. *Please God, not the child. Not Rachel.*

Caroline blinked, sniffling, and he saw bafflement in her expression, although it soon changed to realization.

She looked down at her mourning garb, then back up again. "The dress," she murmured, as if in reply to some question she had asked of herself, and not of him. "The *dress.*"

"Not Enoch," Bridger said. "Or . . ."

"Oh, no," Caroline said quickly. "Everyone here is well. Some of the local women, members of my church and the Ladies' Aid Society, have agreed to wear mourning garb in memory of poor Mr. Lincoln. Just until the fourteenth, when he'll have been dead a month." She glanced down. "A number of us went to Harrisburg when the funeral train stopped there. We . . . attended the viewing in the evening."

"That must have been hard," he said, thinking of the pain and sorrow she must have felt, and the memories it would have brought back.

She nodded.

Bridger moved his hands from her shoulders to cup her face, careful not to chafe her skin with his calloused palms. For a long while, he simply looked at her, not sure what to say.

Lincoln's assassination, occurring a mere five days after Appomattox, had overshadowed the surrender; Northern headlines, crowing victory and the restoration of the Union, immediately turned to grim eulogies, accounts of the tragic events at Ford's Theatre, the death vigil, the simultaneous attacks on others that same night, most notably those targeting Secretary Seward and his son, both of whom had sustained near-fatal wounds.

Federal troops had tracked the actor, John Wilkes Booth, who had put a bullet into the back of the President's head and broken a leg in a dramatic leap from the balcony to the stage, for days. They'd found him hiding out in a farmer's barn, in the Virginia countryside, along with an accomplice. A standoff had ensued, according to the newspapers, and — here, the story took two different directions — one side claiming that Booth had set the fire that consumed the barn, and him with it, in a maniacal display of defiance, the other equally convinced that his pursuers had ignited the blaze in an effort to smoke out their prey. Or kill him.

Bridger started to speak, but Caroline kept him from it by pressing two fingers lightly to his mouth.

"Not now, Bridger," she said softly. "There's been too much sorrow, too much death. Let us talk of happy things. The war is over, and you're here, before me, safe and sound. For now, that is enough."

Bridger kissed the fingers that had silenced him moments before. "I love you, Caroline," he said.

She blushed, averted her eyes shyly, but when she looked back at his face, she smiled. "Truly? I will not be your mistress, Bridger Winslow."

He grinned. "No," he agreed. "It's a wife I want." He paused, delighting in her warmth, the scent of her hair, the fetching glow in her cheeks. "Though I wouldn't mind if you acted like a mistress now and then."

Caroline's color brightened from pale pink to apricot. For a second or two, he thought she would pull free, slap him hard across the face.

But then she spoke. "There are a great many reasons I should refuse your proposal, sir," she said, not withdrawing, but nestling closer. "If that's what you meant."

He bent his head, kissed her, very briefly, on the mouth. "It is precisely what I meant," he said. "And, given the opportunity, I believe I can . . . convince you to accept my proposal, rather than refuse."

Caroline gave a soft, contented sigh that left Bridger hard with wanting her, and the way she'd settled against him, she had to be aware of that.

"We ought to go inside," she said, so quietly that he barely heard her. "We're behaving scandalously, standing out here, embracing like this."

Bridger cleared his throat. "Caroline," he whispered. "I have declared myself. Now, do you love me or not?"

She tilted her head back, her eyes bright with mischief and something more. "Yes, Bridger," she replied. "I love you."

"And?"

"And I will marry you, heaven help me."

He laughed, lifted her off the ground again, this time by her waist, and spun her around, in celebration. Orion, startled, whinnied loudly.

Caroline laughed, too, putting her hands to Bridger's face, rising on tiptoe to kiss him. "We have much to talk about, Mr. Winslow," she said, stepping back. With that, she took his hand, pulling him up the low, grassy slope toward the house.

Orion followed, docile as a circus pony.

Bridger freed his hand from Caroline's and gathered the stallion's reins, frowning now. "Where is everyone?" he asked. "Enoch? Rachel?"

"They've gone to town for the day," Caroline replied. "Enoch, Jubie, little Gideon and Rachel. Enoch is making repairs at my grandmother's house."

"Oh," Bridger said.

Once again, Caroline laughed. "Settle your horse in the barn, Mr. Winslow," she instructed. "While I change out of this dress."

"And then?"

"Then," Caroline teased, "who knows what will happen?"

What happened, as it turned out, was this. Bridger led Orion to a stall, relieved the animal of saddle, blanket and bridle, brushed him down, made sure he had plenty of hay and ample water.

Caroline, meanwhile, went into the house, where she remained for so long that Bridger had time to bathe in the icy waters of the creek, dry off with his shirt, and put on the relatively clean garments he'd taken from his saddle bags, along with a sliver of soap and a folding razor.

When he got back from the stream, still shivering a little and covered in goose bumps, he heard Caroline bustling about in the kitchen house. She was singing, and her voice floated out through the open doorway into the yard, where Bridger stood, praying he wasn't dreaming, sprawled on a bedroll in some army camp.

Rachel's dog appeared in the doorway, watching him curiously.

Caroline materialized alongside the dog, smiling. Her hair was down, wheat-gold waves tumbling to her waist, and she was wearing a pretty summer dress, fashioned of thin cotton, tiny pink roses splashed against a pale green background.

Bridger, who had endured immersion in cold water for reasons that went beyond personal cleanliness, hardened again, instantly and, this time, painfully.

He groaned aloud.

Delighted, Caroline smiled. "Are you hungry?" she asked.

"God, yes," Bridger ground out. He was, in fact, ravenous. But not just for food.

Again, she laughed. She knew exactly what she was doing to him, reveled in it. "Come inside, then," she said. "I'll have a meal ready for you in a few moments."

"Caroline —"

She pretended puzzlement. "Is something wrong?"

"Come out here," he said. "Please."

"But I've just made sandwiches."

"The sandwiches will keep. You're driving me crazy, Caroline, with your hair down, wearing that dress and . . . where the devil are your shoes?" Bridger paused, exasperated. "You're doing this on purpose, damn it. Wasn't it punishment enough, losing the war?"

Caroline came to him then, stood close. Soft all over. Delicious.

"You *said* you wanted me to behave like a mistress," she reminded him sweetly. "How am I doing?"

Bridger leaned in until his nose was nearly touching Caroline's. "You're doing *just fine.* If you're trying to kill me, that is!"

"I'm not trying to kill you, you bull-headed fool. I'm trying to *seduce* you."

"Caroline," he warned. "We aren't married yet."

She actually batted her eyelashes at him. "We will be," she said. "Won't we?"

"Yes, if you don't send me to the lunatic asylum first!"

Her smile was downright saucy. "We might both go insane," she said, "if you don't make love to me. Very soon."

That was it.

He swept her into his arms. Carried her toward the house. Stopped.

Another man's house. Another man's bed.

But *his* woman.

Caroline rested one hand against his cheek, traced the contours of his lips with the pad of her thumb, and settled his dilemma with a single word.

"Hurry."

33

CAROLINE

Caroline stood in the spacious, airy bedroom of her childhood, clad in a simple frock of dusky rose, fashioned from one of her grandmother's evening gowns, before the cheval mirror, turning slowly to one side, then the other. Her hair was up, pinned into a loose chignon, and in lieu of a bridal veil, she wore a crown of spring wildflowers.

Rachel and Jubie were seated side by side on the four-poster bed, Sweet Girl nestled comfortably behind them, on the pillows, watching them.

Gideon, walking now, squirmed on Jubie's knee, one tiny hand resting on his mother's protruding belly. In a few months, Jubie would give birth to a second child, hers and

Enoch's, and she fairly glowed with happiness.

"Down," the little boy fretted. "Giddy, *down.*"

"So's you can go right over to Miss Caroline and grab onto her pretty dress?" Jubie responded, bouncing her handsome son and holding him fast. "That isn't going to happen."

Rachel, in ivory lace, patted Gideon's plump baby thigh and said, "You be good, Gideon, or you won't get any wedding cake."

"Rachel," Caroline warned, distracted. "Stop it."

"Will you quit your fretting, Caroline?" Jubie teased good-naturedly. Lush with pregnancy and the private joys of her marriage to Enoch, she was lovely in her best Sunday get-up, an emerald green dress she'd sewn herself. "You look right beautiful. You're gonna set all them snooty Southern belles right back on the heels of their dancing slippers when they get themselves an eyeful of Mrs. Bridger Winslow."

Caroline forgot the image in the mirror and stood facing her small audience, wringing her hands a little. If it hadn't been for Rachel's presence, she might have burst into tears on the spot. How was it possible for one person to be so happy, and scared half to the death at the same time?

Jubie put Gideon down, stood, and walked over to Caroline. Took her hands in her own.

"That man down there in the parlor, waiting with Enoch and the preacher and your grandmother? He *loves* you, Caroline. Except for my own husband, I've never seen a man look at a woman the way he looks at you. You know Enoch and me, we'll take care of the farm, so you just go on ahead and let yourself be happy, stop looking for things you can worry about, you hear me?"

"I'm going to have a big room, big as this one, in our new house," Rachel piped up, moving quickly to steer Gideon away from her mother's skirts. She doted on the little boy, and Caroline wondered if she realized how much she'd miss him once they set out for Fairhaven, Bridger's plantation outside Savannah, Georgia. Not yet six years old, the child probably had no conception of the distance. "I'll have a pony, too. And we'll come back to visit, soon as the railroads are fixed. My step-daddy promised."

Caroline and Jubie were smiling damp and misty smiles, still holding each other's hands.

"It's *six hundred miles* to Savannah," Rachel chattered on. "We're going in the wagon my stepdaddy bought, and some nights, when there aren't any inns to stay in, we get to *sleep* in it."

A light knock sounded at the bedroom door, and Geneva peeked in, then entered.

"My, my," she said, admiring her granddaughter. "You are the *loveliest* bride, Caroline."

"Am I lovely, too?" Rachel wanted to know.

Geneva smiled. "Yes, darling, you most certainly are."

Jubie stepped back, squeezing Caroline's hands once before she dropped them, corralled Gideon and hoisted him onto one hip, reaching out to Rachel.

"Let's head down them fancy stairs to the parlor and get ourselves situated just right, so we can throw ourselves a weddin'."

Rachel took Jubie's hand, willing to be led, but cast a sideways glance at Caroline. "Are you and him going to jump over a broom handle, Mama, the way Jubie and Mr. Enoch did, when they got married?"

"No, sweetheart," Caroline said, with a laugh. Jubie and Enoch were married at Hammond Farm the previous year, in a ceremony that included both a minister *and* the broom tradition.

Rachel looked disappointed. "Well," she

said, as Jubie tugged her toward the door, "when *I* grow up and get married, I'm gonna jump the broom."

"Lord have mercy," Jubie laughed. "That's a sight I hope I live to see. And I reckon you'll have your way, too. Now, you come on, 'cause your stepdaddy, he's down there waitin', about to bust right out of his hide, he's so eager to make your mama his wife and you his own little girl."

The dog jumped down and followed them out of the room, and Jubie closed the door softly behind them.

Rachel's voice drifted in from the hallway. "My new papa isn't *really* going to bust out of his hide, is he?"

Jubie chuckled, and the sound was rich and resonant. "No, child," she answered. "That's just a way of saying Mr. Bridger, he's ready to get on with things."

Caroline accepted the handkerchief Geneva offered, dabbed at her eyes. "You're sure you won't come to Georgia with us, Grandmother?"

Geneva smiled and shook her head. "I'm too old to travel so far and, besides, there's still plenty right here that needs doing."

Caroline nodded. "I'll miss you so much."

"And I shall miss you. But we'll write, and keep each other in our prayers, and we'll be just fine, all of us."

"I never thought I'd leave the farm," Caroline confessed.

"I know you didn't," Geneva agreed. "It's a grand thing you're doing, though, for Enoch and Jubie, and for Rachel, too. Enoch and Jubie will have a good place to raise their children, a fair share of whatever the crops bring in when they're sold, and a clear deed to twenty acres of their own. When Rachel comes of age, Hammond Farm will make a very nice legacy, whether she chooses to live here or not."

"I hope I'm doing what's right, that's all," Caroline fretted.

"Do you love that man you're about to marry?" Geneva asked.

"Yes," Caroline answered. "Very much."

"Then you're doing the right thing. It's not easy to leave the people and places we know, Caroline, but sometimes life requires us to do it anyway, just hauls us off to someplace new, and we can sink or we can swim. If we make up our minds to be happy, though, we will be. No matter what."

"Was it that way for you? When you married Grandfather?"

"It was," Geneva said. "And I'm so glad I did. If I'd stayed put, afraid to take a chance on a handsome young doctor, poor as a churchmouse and positively crackling with love and ambition and a whole lot of other interesting qualities, I would have missed out on so much."

Caroline sighed, smiled. "I'm not sure I'd have the courage," she said.

"Nonsense," Geneva replied. "You have it now. You had it when you were a child, and you lost your family. You had it when you searched a strange city for Jacob, and when you brought his body home. When you took Jubie in, and mothered your child and, most of all, when the war found our quiet little farming community and brought its many evils to our doorstep. And now you love a man you may believe you shouldn't, a former enemy who will take you to live in a place that's strange to you, among people who rebelled against your most cherished values."

"Are you trying to talk me out of marrying Bridger?" Caroline asked, with a tremulous smile.

"Could I?" Geneva asked.

"No," Caroline replied without hesitation.

"Then stop trying to talk *yourself* out of it. Go downstairs, take your place beside Bridger Winslow, and *marry* him, for heaven's sake."

A little thrill moved through Caroline, a

sweet shudder. She linked her arm to Geneva's. "Forward, then," she said. "Into the storm."

34

BRIDGER

She was a marvel, his bride. She glowed, a goddess in calico and a bonnet, even as she bade Enoch and Jubie and young Gideon a tearful farewell in the grassy yard beside the stone house.

Enoch stood, weeping without shame as Caroline took his big hands in hers and rose on tiptoe to kiss his cheek.

Having said his goodbyes, Bridger stood apart, beside the loaded wagon.

Orion, tied behind, would follow.

Rachel, like Bridger, had completed the formalities, and she'd shown remarkable equanimity for such a small child. Eager to begin the grand adventure, she was already in the wagon with Sweet Girl, gripping the locked tailgate and bouncing on her knees.

631

She was framed by the arch of crisp new canvas that would shelter them and the few things Caroline had decided to bring.

"Why doesn't Mama *hurry*?" Rachel asked fitfully.

"Some things are too important to be hurried," Bridger replied with a smile. "Be patient, Sugarplum. This is going to be a long trip, so right now is a probably a good time to practice."

Caroline and Jubie were embracing, two babies between them, one yet to be born, the other wriggling and reaching for Enoch.

With a deep chortle, Enoch took the boy from his mother, grinning proudly as his son put a fat little palm to his wet face, trying to smear away the big man's tears.

After the wedding, when Caroline had told Enoch she wanted him and Jubie to move into the main house so they'd have room for their growing family, he'd refused at first. Shaken his head and said, "No, Missus. It's too much and, anyhow, the cabin is fine."

To Bridger's amusement, Jubie had elbowed her husband and informed him that if he was fool enough to live in one room when he could have that nice big place instead, with a kitchen house and a sturdy barn, he'd better get used to his own company again, because *she* wanted a real bedroom and a parlor and a place where she could cook without holding in her elbows. Furthermore, she didn't intend to hike through the orchard to milk the cow, weed the garden and hang her wash on a clothesline, then haul her weary self back up that hill after working all day.

Wisely, Enoch had conceded the point.

"Gideon will be a big boy when I see him again," Rachel announced. "That's what Mama says."

Bridger leaned against the tailgate, his arms folded. "He'll be bigger than he is now, all right. You'll see him sooner than you think, though."

The goodbyes were almost over now; Caroline was beginning to tear herself away, promising to write often, reminding Jubie and Enoch that she expected replies. She wanted to know all about the new baby and Gideon, she told them for about the hundredth time. Oh, and if they couldn't find this or that, they ought to ask her grandmother.

Bridger smiled again. There was a list, of course.

Caroline had seen to that.

She was coming toward him now, looking back, dashing away tears with the back of one hand.

Bridger held her with his eyes.

God, he loved her. He'd never dreamed it was possible to care for a woman the way he cared for Caroline Hammond Winslow. His wife, a lady by day, a wildcat by night, and so damn beautiful he could get lost just looking at her.

Smart, too, with a mind that kept unfolding into new territories of thought, a mind that explored his own in return, and opened door after door, letting in the light, stirring the dust, raising windows.

The whole exchange was fascinating.

She reached him, looked up at him. "This is hard," she said.

"I know," Bridger replied, kissing her forehead.

"Me and Sweet Girl are going to ride all the way to Georgia in this very wagon," Rachel said.

Caroline laughed softly. " 'Sweet Girl and I,' " she corrected. "And, yes, you're going to ride all the way to Georgia in this wagon. It's much too far to walk."

Bridger rested his hands on either side of Caroline's narrow waist. "Ready?" he asked.

She beamed at him. "Oh, yes," she said. "I am definitely ready, Mr. Winslow."

"Well, then, *Mrs.* Winslow, we'll be setting

off." He took Caroline by the hand, led her around the wagon, helped her onto the high seat.

Enoch, Jubie and Gideon stood, smiling and waving and weeping.

Bridger performed an easy salute, made sure the tailgate was securely fastened and Orion's long lead rope would hold. He patted the stallion's neck, then rounded the wagon, climbed up beside Caroline and released the brake lever with one foot.

She had produced a handkerchief from some hidden place, inside a sleeve or tucked between the buttons of her bodice, and she was dabbing at her eyes.

"I'm so glad we've already said goodbye to Geneva," she said.

Bridger took up the reins. The team was four horses strong, and the harnesses were stiff with newness. "If you want to see her again, we'll stop in town."

Caroline shook her head. "No. I'd only start blubbering, and then Grandmother would lecture me about taking hold of life with both hands and shaking every conceivable blessing out of it."

He brought down the reins, and the team was in motion, heading for the open gate and the road beyond. "Sounds like a good philosophy to me."

Caroline leaned into his side and lingered there. Then a thought must have struck her, because she sat up straight and frowned, turned to look into the wagon bed, past the quilts and the harpsichord and the trunks of clothing.

"Is Rachel safe back there?"

He put an arm around her shoulders, squeezed once, ignoring the twinge of pain from the sword wound. "She's safe, Caroline."

Apparently reassured, Caroline faced forward again.

"And so are you," Bridger added, very gently.

They turned onto the road, and he glanced back, saw Jubie still standing in the yard, holding Gideon, and Enoch striding resolutely down the dirt track to shut the gate.

Caroline let her head rest against his shoulder again. "Tell me about Amalie, and about Fairhaven, and don't you dare say you've already told me. I want to hear your voice, that's all, and you can talk about anything except the war and the women you knew before we met."

He kissed the top of her head, felt the fabric of her bonnet against his lips, and then he began.

"Once upon a time, in the kingdom called Dixie . . ."

35

Fairhaven
June 15, 1865

AMALIE

She'd been sweeping and dusting and polishing all morning — and Amalie Winslow was just getting started. There were still beds to be made, and rugs to be beaten and sheets to be pulled from the furniture in the best rooms, especially the parlor and the dining room.

The dining room.

Lord have mercy. She hadn't given a single thought to food, and Bridger and his Yankee bride were bound to be hungry when they arrived, and the little girl, too.

They'd be worn out after weeks spent rattling along rutted roads in that most unsuitable conveyance. A covered wagon. Not a trim little surrey, a gracious vehicle that would be of some use in the future.

Amalie had her suspicions. Although Bridger had reassured her repeatedly about Caroline's kindness and her intelligence, her new sister-in-law might be one of those domineering sorts, forever speaking her mind and making demands. Women were like that in the North, she'd heard, strident, marching in the streets, carrying signs and banners. They lacked social graces and wore drab, ugly clothing and some of them even smoked and drank whiskey. Probably played cards, too.

And now that Mr. Lincoln's army had laid waste to the South, leaving Georgia in ruins — other than the city of Savannah itself — they'd be even more insufferable than before, looking down their ax-blade noses with their beady little eyes at everything and everybody who tried to live in a civilized fashion, clucking their wicked tongues.

Granted, Caroline had sent her a lovely letter — but Amalie had to ask herself how genuine it was . . .

The front door, twice kicked in by rude Yankees, crashed open just then, slamming hard against the inside wall and probably denting the mahogany wainscoting in the process.

Amalie tried to remember where she'd put the shotgun. She liked to keep it close at hand, and that was a good thing, too, because Fairhaven would be nothing but charred beams and broken marble if she hadn't. But now that General Sherman's army wasn't prowling the countryside, she hadn't been as vigilant.

She would simply have to make do with the broom.

"Miz Amalie! Miz Amalie, you to home?"

Amalie sighed. Released her hold on the handle of the broom.

The voice belonged to Bella and Joseph's seven-year-old spitfire, Molly Sue.

"Miz Ammmmmmmmalie!"

Amalie reached the grand foyer, saw the child standing barefoot and big-eyed under the chandelier that had once graced some European palace.

"Molly Sue Ryan," Amalie scolded. "Why are you carrying on so? And you'd better hope you haven't scratched the wainscoting —"

"Miz Amalie," the little girl whispered, and every tiny braid on her tiny head looked about to take off in a different direction. "They's a *Yankee* coming, sure as I'm borned! He's dressed all in blue and he's ridin' a horse I ain't seen the like of since Mr. Bridger took Orion away!"

In her mind's eye, Amalie saw the shotgun.

She'd left it in Papa's study.

"Molly Sue," she said, already heading for the tall double doors opposite the best parlor, "you go on and tell your daddy what you just told me, fast as you can. And don't you let this Yankee see you, either!"

Molly Sue nodded, setting her braids to bobbing again.

"Go!" Amalie ordered, shoving open the doors to the study. "Use the back way and remember what I said — you've got to stay out of sight. No matter what."

Molly Sue's lower lip wobbled, but she nodded again and ran toward the back of the house, her small feet slap-slapping the floor as she went.

Amalie lifted the shotgun down from the rack behind Papa's desk, cocked it, saw that it was loaded.

Good.

She could hear the horse now, clomping along the cobblestones out front.

She straightened her spine, marched back into the foyer and planted herself squarely on the threshold, shotgun at the ready and fighting mad.

She'd had all the harassment she was going to put up with from those devils in blue, and that, by God, was that.

He sat tall in the saddle, this Yankee, and

his uniform was so new, it probably hadn't had time to start smelling of sweat. Brass buttons gleamed like baby suns on the front of his tunic, and his black brimmed hat was spotless, banded with gold braid. His legs were long and muscular, and his boots shone like onyx.

He took her in, from head to foot, with a sweep of his eyes. Registered the shotgun, too, unless he was blind, which didn't seem likely.

Bold as could be, the Northerner rode right up to the hitching post, dismounted and tethered the horse loosely, so it could drink from the metal trough while he paid his call, and never mind that he hadn't been invited.

He walked over, all easy like, and there was something vaguely familiar in the way he moved, but Amalie didn't think about it.

She aimed the shotgun. "You can stop right there, Yankee," she said. "One more move, and I'll send you off to your Maker in pieces."

The Yankee paused at the base of the three steps leading onto the verandah, but he didn't look one bit scared.

"Mind if I take off my hat?"

That voice. She'd heard it before, but where?

"Go ahead," Amalie said, gun still sighted on his midsection. "Just don't get the impression I'm going to invite you in, because I am not."

He reached up, removed his hat, and Amalie nearly swooned when she saw his glossy black hair, his indigo eyes and that white flash of a smile.

"Well, Snippet," said Rogan McBride, "I heard you were handy with a shotgun."

ACKNOWLEDGMENTS

My heartfelt gratitude goes out to:

Grady "Skip" Lael, my late father, and Hazel Bleecker Lael, my mother. Dad taught me dogged persistence, and Mom gave me my great love of reading.

My siblings, Jerry Lael, Sally Lael Lang and Pamela Lael, who have been pillars of strength.

Irene Goodman, my agent of thirty-five years, and Alex Kamaroff, her husband and business partner. Irene and Alex have believed in me, and in this project, from its earliest conception.

My daughter, Wendy Miller, who inspires me just by existing, and her partner, Jeremy Hargis, one of the finest men I know. I love you both.

Jennifer Readman Gebhardt, my niece/ assistant, who has traveled with me on many occasions, driven rental cars, checked baggage, booked hotel rooms, and run errands in unfamiliar cities.

Kathy Sagan, my editor at Mira, who guided me wisely and patiently through the process of drafting this story.

Paula Eykelhof, my long-time editor at HQN, and a very dear friend. Special thanks, Paula, for working your magic, and for our many long conversations about the Civil War and our various and much beloved pets.

Debbie Macomber, world-class writer and truly amazing plotting partner. Thank you for the adventures we've shared, the times we've laughed and the times we've cried.

Sandra Penesse and Janet Wahl, my "Gettysburg" friends, who have made me feel so welcome on every visit, shared their knowledge, and spoiled me shamelessly. I cherish both of you.

Cynthia Miller Taylor, who read my manuscript and offered invaluable reassurances.

My deepest appreciation to the experts:

Gary Roche, Licensed Battlefield Guide, Gettysburg National Military Park. Gary's knowledge of the American Civil War in general, and the Battle of Gettysburg in particular, is truly mind-boggling. His presentation on his ancestor, Patrick DeLacy, of the 143rd PA Volunteers Regiment, who was awarded the Medal of

Honor, is an education in itself.

Gary was tireless in his efforts to show me the sights and explain what happened, where, and when. His lovely wife, Marsha, brought warm smiles and cool bottles of water just when we needed them most.

Wayne E. Motts, Licensed Battlefield Guide (Gettysburg), shared his tremendous expertise, and gave our little group an extensive tour of the American Civil War Museum in Harrisburg, Pennsylvania, as well as arranging a visit to the Spangler Farm, near Gettysburg.

Debra Novotny, also a Licensed Battlefield Guide at Gettysburg National Military Park, showed us around the National Military Cemetery and the Evergreen Cemetery, for civilians, and shared many fascinating stories. My favorite involved a loyal dog, a brave soldier in his own right.

Colonel John Fitzpatrick, Esq., Licensed Battlefield Guide, Gettysburg National Military Park, filled in a rainy day with a comprehensive talk on Lincoln and the legendary Irish Brigade.

Finally, my thanks to Nancie W. Gudmestad, who generously gave us a detailed tour of the Shriver House Museum, in Gettysburg.

Many, many others have contributed to

my research; it would be impossible to include all of you.

Any errors to be found in THE YANKEE WIDOW are entirely my own.

ABOUT THE AUTHOR

The daughter of a town marshal, **Linda Lael Miller** is the author of more than 100 historical and contemporary novels. Now living in Spokane, Washington, the "First Lady of the West" hit a career high when all three of her 2011 Creed Cowboy books debuted at #1 on the *New York Times* list. In 2007, the Romance Writers of America presented her their Lifetime Achievement Award. She personally funds her Linda Lael Miller Scholarships for Women. Visit her at www.lindalaelmiller.com.